Borderline Normality

LAUREN LLOYD

First published 2024

Copyright © 2024 Lauren Lloyd

The moral right of the author is asserted

Set in 12/14pt Garamond MT
Typeset by Bernie

All rights reserved, including the right to reproduce this book, or portions thereof in any form. No part of this text may be reproduced, transmitted, downloaded, decompiled, reverse engineered, or stored, in any form or introduced into any information storage and retrieval system, in any form or by any means, whether electronic or mechanical without the express written permission of the author.

This is a work of fiction. Names and characters are the product of the author's imagination and any resemblance to actual persons, living or dead, is entirely coincidental.

This book is sold subject to the condition that it shall not, by way of trade or otherwise, be lent, re-sold, hired out, or otherwise circulated without the author's prior consent.

ISBN: 9798322582236

Dedication

Borderline Normality is dedicated to my Ayrshire and Glasgow Book Group Friends. May you all see a little of yourselves, your colleagues, your ex's, your lovers in these chapters.

Let the discourse be as glorious as the Alton Inn cocktails we sup alongside our tales.
And of course, to my incredible children, who inspire me to tell the stories that matter.

Epigraph

Gritty? Passionate? Brave? Extraordinarily delicious?

My writing has been called all those things. Sometimes I write about things I'm familiar with: hospitals; life; death; the interplay between physical and mental health. Sometimes I write about faeries, selkies, magic and Scottish folklore. Sometimes I write about relationships, power and the patriarchal hegemony. Mostly I write what I want to write. Often what I write resonates. Sometimes my writing makes people feel stuff.

We need to play more with writing. Play radically. Communicate creatively. For that is how we influence change. When women push at the margins, we influence change.

I once said if I was going to be a super-hero, I'd be the wonderful anti-hero Harley Quinn. Harley Quinn (the inimitable Margot Robbie in The Suicide Squad) completely rejects conventional patriarchal superhero tropes. She's colourful, renegade, eccentric, brutal, messy, deliciously horny and utterly delightful.

PLAY is the way to change the world, from the inside-out. We all need to make time to do it, and do it radically, creatively, joyously.

Lots of us have 'Borderline' traits: Fear of abandonment; rage; sorrow; shame; terror. Intense, unstable emotion and angst. To send 400 messages to a partner, firing one after the other, fearing rejection over something tiny. 75% of those diagnosed with

Borderline 'Personality Disorder' are women. I welcome the debate on the reasons for that and a compassionate, trauma-informed understanding for those who live with the crippling distress.

Likewise, we all have the propensity for narcissistic behaviour: taking advantage of others; a lack of empathy or responsibility; entitlement rooted in an all-consuming, soul-destroying fear of being discovered for who we really are. A pathological fear of vulnerability.

Like Icarus to the sun, the one is attracted to the other.

Trauma is written into our DNA and we play it out time and time again until it reaches resolution.

I asked a learned friend and psychotherapist whether the profiles in Borderline were authentic.

"Absolutely," he said, "Rachel's an air-head. Adam's a complete….. (insert blunt Glasgow-ism here) and I hope Amy finds peace."

I love them and understand them all. Every breath. They lived on my shoulder for several years. They are part of me.

I will end with a wonderful review of Borderline Normality from an equally wonderful beta reader and friend:

"If the eyes are the window to the soul, then the mind is surely the portal to madness. Borderline Normality by Lauren Lloyd is testimony to human emotions. Beautifully written, powerful, thought provoking and terrifying. How far can an individual go in the

pursuit of self-gratification? I know these people, I live amongst them, I share some of their characteristics and am equally bewitched by them and afraid of being them. Another must read from Lauren Lloyd."

I hope you enjoy the book and can't put it down until it speeds to its final descent. To everyone who picks up my book, thank you for giving my words a chance.

Connect with me on ***www.lauren-lloyd.com***

Table of Contents

Title Page i
Copyright ii
Dedication iii
Epigraph v
Acknowledgements xiii
1 AMY: Borderline Normality **1**
2 RACHEL: Borderline Normality Too **9**
3 ADAM: Borderline Trouble **20**
4 DR JIM WALKER: Borderline Psychiatry **29**
5 RACHEL: Forgiveness Cake and the Kindness of Strangers **41**
6 ADAM: Can You Dance the Polka, My Dear? **54**
7 AMY: The Riptide That Pulls You Back **67**
8 DR JIM WALKER: The Shame of Being Ordinary **79**
9 SARAH EMMERSON: An American in Manchester **90**
10 AMY: Intoxicating Omnipotence **104**
11 RACHEL: A Normal Kinda Guy **118**
12 ADAM: Who's Sorry Now? **127**

13 DR JIM WALKER: Just Another No Show **136**

14 SARAH EMMERSON: Packing Dinosaurs for Valette **143**

15 AMY: He That Falls In Love With Himself Has No Rivals **154**

16 ADAM: Dance with Me? **164**

17 SARAH EMMERSON: Blessed with a Front Row Seat **177**

18 AMY: Buckets with Holes that leak Apple Pie **180**

19 RACHEL: Walking with a Map **193**

20 ADAM: The Biggest Risk is Not Taking the Risk **202**

21 AMY: Fall Seven Times, Stand Up Eight ...**211**

22 ADAM: I'm Not Ill, My Pancreas is Just Lazy **221**

23 RACHEL: An Apple a Day Keeps the Fairies at Bay **236**

24 AMY: The Biggest Gamble in the World **246**

25 ADAM: You Only Regret the Roads You Didn't Take **257**

26 DR JIM WALKER: An Inspector Calls **275**

27 ADAM: Reverie is the Groundwork of the Creative **291**

28 AMY: Assisting with Inquiries **302**

29 RACHEL: Where is She?......................*322*
30 CAL WATERS: Brothers Don't Walk the Dark Alone........................*334*
31 ADAM: The Last Dance *350*
32 RACHEL: Call for Help............................*371*
33 AMY: Rescue *377*
34 Epilogue RACHEL: New Beginnings *388*
About the author *396*
Also by Lauren Lloyd *399*

Acknowledgements

I have so many people to thank for breathing life into these pages.

To Bernie for the technical wizardry and know-how to turn Borderline into a bona-fide book that people can read. For the friendship, light, cake-inspiration and the endless supply of Revels.

To Paul B for walking the journey, believing in me and being excited about the end result.

To my gaggle of girls and besties, Eve, Margaret and Susan who know the music which underscores the writing and all about the chapters which weren't written.

To my Diplomacy gang… turns out there's more to life and Diplomacy than ordering F Lon – NTH. Roll on Tour of Britain in Manchester, Isle of Man and Glasgow.

And to my Glasgow and Ayrshire Book Groups, along with cat-herder extraordinaire Ali. I give you a smorgasbord of Borderline Cocktails to celebrate the launch.

To stories - the timeless architects of humanity.

1 AMY: Borderline Normality

After it happens, I know I'm a fuckwit. I can smear the shame over my body. Coat myself in it several inches thick, then crumple myself into the tiniest atom of loathsome awfulness. I'm undoubtedly the worst human being who ever lived.

He's gone. Slunk out, taking his MacBook with him. I know why. He's worried I'll take a hammer to it. His life in his MacBook, typed from this spare-room. I can obliterate all his work in a split second of uncontrolled fury. More likely, I'll throw it against the wall like I've just done with the glasses and tumblers. Amy Hawes, demented glass thrower and killer of ex-boyfriends.

Oh God, the wall. There are fucking bits of glass embedded in it. Like deeply embedded. An Adam-shaped crime silhouette in shards around where he's been sitting on the bed.

I remember coming into the room. I remember asking him something. What was it I said….? I planned it so carefully. I tried three different outfits trying to get the impression right: pretty; casual; sane. Hair down, no hair up. I briefly considered naked, but last time I tried that it terrified him.

It's been a year since he moved out of our

bedroom and into the spare-room - stroke office - stroke prison - stroke safe haven. Five years since we've had sex. I remember it. We made love the morning after we flew back from Japan. Since then, he can't seem to get it up around me. Because I'm fat? Because I'm a loathsome human being? I hate him for making me feel like that. Then I hate myself even more. Add it to the bottomless bucket of self-loathing.

I crave the comfort of his warm body. I crave him wrapping himself around me. Being held like he used to hold me. I ache for it so much I cry. I can't face a future without it. I can't think about being alone. It gives me panic attacks. I hyperventilate and feel like I'm dying. Without him, I will. I'd give anything to make it right again.

What was it the therapist said?

"You're an empath, Amy. You feel deeply. You love deeply. You need to reclaim power over emotional overload. Maintain boundaries."

I remember knocking on the door, the lightest rat-tat, stuck my head around, tried to smile with my eyes. Every fibre ready to explode in joyous optimism, passionate, wild, reconciliative, me-on-top sex. Just like it was in the beginning. He said he'd fallen in love with my 'colour' and my 'energy.' I was sunshine yellow with more than a hint of untamed abandonment. The sex had been awesome. Even he admitted that.

I can make it right again. Light, Amy, keep it light and happy.

"Hey." Small voice. See, I can do light-hearted, no drama.

He's sitting upright in bed, working on his MacBook.
He looks up. I feel a surge of love. Is it happiness? Yes. I can sort this.

"Hi." He shuts his MacBook and looks up. Oh God, he looks worried. Nerves make his face twitch.

"I don't know how to start this Adam. I want to be a proper couple again. Neither of us is perfect. I'm a witch sometimes. I know I am. I fly off the handle. I drive you mad with obsessive house re-arranging. I'm working on it. All of it. I can be better."

No response. Is that fear?

"But you're not perfect either, you know. You do what you want to do, when you want to do it. We never spend time together. You prefer your mates over me. You brush over how I'm feeling. I feel… Dismissed. Emotionally Invalidated… Everything is always my fault. You make me feel like I'm going crazy."

I'm getting faster. I'm building. Losing control. My voice goes up an octave. I'm at least half-way up the hill.

"Ten years is a long time. We've got something, haven't we? I've… I've been thinking…. You're always telling me I overthink but I don't think I am

this time. You think we could…? Can we maybe…..
give couple counselling another go?"

I am faltering and finishing weakly.

"I love you."

I limp it home. Wait and study his face for the response I need. My face is crumpling. I am literally holding my breath trying to stop myself from crying.
And still I wait. Is he chewing a wasp? His mouth is contorting, but nothing's coming out. As if he's agonising over the words.
When he starts, it's slow, quiet, deliberate. Jeez, autism? He certainly lacks the empathy and emotional intelligence. Eventually.

"Amy, we've been here. I can't. I don't want it anymore. I thought we agreed. A break. You can stay here. I'm not throwing you out. As long as you need. But I can't. I'm sorry….." His turn to tail off.

It's like a switch flicks in my brain. I'm not even part of my body.
Someone who looks like me, but a monster. A loathsome wounded creature. A howling, screaming, morphing banshee from a horror movie is hurling glasses from a table at his head.
Adam has a habit of sneaking glasses of lemon squash up to the room and never bringing them down again. There are about 15 of the buggers. One after the other I fill them with venom and hurl them with super-human force. Each one shatters into a maelstrom of glittering agony. Glass three….

four…… seven….. nine. Boof, boof, boof. I must be a terrible shot. Not one hits him. I don't even know if the fragments cut him. It must have been crazy Armageddon. I don't remember. There's a red-wall of blank-fury between asking him the question and being back in my room.

When I rip my clothes off hoping to rip the shame off alongside, I find fragments of glass in my bra.

He slinks out at some point. Still naked, I set about rearranging the furniture in the house. Cleaning and getting things into a new order. I start with the bookcase. The books are out of size order. The small books look better over there. The big books here. The interesting books have to go at eye level, where people can see them. Hide the trashy ones on the bottom shelf. Intersperse them. See how our lives intertwine. We can't separate. One book of Adam's, one book of mine. Order is control. Scrub away at the shame until it's raw, sore and I've paid the price.

Ordering and cleaning always makes me feel better. So does Social Media and feigning middle-class contentment. In between ordering, I post some happy comments on other people's pictures.

'Whit-Whoooooo. Lookin' amazing girl, you sassy stunner.' A friend's new profile pic. It gets a 'love' immediately.

'Happy Birthday, Lovely-Lady. When you coming round so we can open that Prosecco?'

Just for good measure, I post a load of comments on Adams' friends pages.

'Gorgeous doll of a baby. Can't wait to meet her in person. Congrats Proud Daddy-Bear.' 'Loving it. Looks amazin'! Remember our invite to the house warming.'

Normality is returning. I'll make it up to him. I'll cook something special for dinner for us. Maybe lamb Rogan Josh. Made from scratch with all the spices ground in the pestle and mortar. No cheating jars here! It's his favourite meal and one of the first I ever made for him. Raita, mango chutney, home-made flatbread, the works. Don't mention the Glass-War and all that. I'll have a drive on being extra, extra nice.

Hope is a drug I embrace without question. I'll sort the wall out too. I begin flicking through expensive Edwardian wallpapers that might suit the room. What the heck, I stick 3 rolls in the basket. He'll probably quite like those.

It's about three weeks after the War of The Glasses, that it happens.

I get a message via Social Media. Sent to me from someone I don't know. A girl. Woman. Whatever. I scrutinise the pages, her posts. Mostly it's private. I don't glean a lot. I get fixated on whether she's fatter than me or vice versa and bizarrely whether she has nice teeth. I read the message over and over trying to make sense of it. Losing him, losing this, here, now. It's a suffocating blanket extinguishing life.

The utter, absolute bastard. I hate him. I love him. I hate him. Terror and anger make it difficult to breathe. Already I'm dying.

Hi Amy
I apologise for the unsolicited message and

hope it doesn't come as too much of a shock.

I've been seeing the guy you're living with, Adam for almost a year. He's lovely, smart, funny, charming. I've fallen hard. I really like him.

He describes things at home as 'complicated.' I still don't know what that means.

He told me when we met that he was single. Yet entertaining me at his home has been off limits for almost a year. So are most of his friends. He says you're living there temporarily as a friend until you find somewhere new to live. After a year, something doesn't feel quite right.

I was brought up to respect the sisterhood and wouldn't stand on another woman's toes.

I'm checking in to see what the situation is. If you guys are still together, then I will respectfully bow out.
Yours
Rachel

Without warning I'm up, over and hurtling off the cliff of Emotional Dysregulation. Before I can think about counting. Let alone practice the mind focus, mindfulness or breathing exercises.

I don't remember emptying the medicine cabinet and laying the contents over the bed. Venlafaxine, Diazepam (the heavy duty 10mg bad boys and the weeny baby 2mg ones), Quetiapine, Paracetamol. The Piriton? I'm not sure what I think that's going to do. Maybe stop me coming out in hives to the other cocktail of drugs. Finally, Lansoprazole and Cerazette just to make sure I don't get heartburn, or a baby along the way.

The last thing I remember as the ambulance arrives is Adam holding my hand and crying. I don't even know when he came back or into my room. His voice is faint. It feels a long way away.

"Hold on Amy, just hold on. I'm here. I'm not leaving you. I'm not going anywhere."

The barely beating pulse of hope and love. Hope is being able to see there is light despite all of the darkness.

2 RACHEL: Borderline Normality Too

End to end, the journey is just over three years long.

A journey is full of magic things patiently waiting for our senses to grow sharper. Sometimes you have to close your eyes to see them.

For us, me and Adam, the journey starts in the most unlikely of places, an online war-game called Diplomacy.

There is a phrase in Latin, "omne trium perfectum", or everything that comes in threes is perfect. Our journey is three years long. Our first game lasts three months. It starts like any other game, but sometimes magic is quiet, it sneaks up on you.

Adam draws France, I draw Turkey. I always want to win. I'm ranked number three on the site. I win, it's what I do!

To win, I need not to be attacked. The first message in any game has the aim of catching an eye. Being noticed. Sometimes I hit a bullseye, sometimes I miss altogether.

I send him a video of the beautiful Zooey Deschanel with my favourite Catcher in the Rye Quote, "You don't always have to get sexy to get to know a girl."

My second message is a photoshopped picnic

basket on a rug with some golden apples and the message "Darn it Sappho (the girl speaks to herself). You were meant to pack the Apples of Immortality, not some cheeky Apples of Immorality. Careless! Would you like one anyway, Paris?" Ha! Yes, I underline it too.

Reference to Greek Mythology has a tendency go over players' heads. Poetic introductions often go down like lead balloons amongst geeky gamers.

Not here. Bullseye Plus. Keeeeeerching. In the beginning (several hours a day for three months), words and magic are one and the same. Turns out, despite the initial bullseye I am the lumbering novice at words and romance.

The first time we speak on the phone - like real people and not Greek Gods - it moves up a gear.

I am being bullied on the site by some asshole. Usual sexist nonsense from a Neanderthal.

"I feel this pain when someone hurts you. I actually can't bear it. Let's talk. Please. Let me phone you. I want to hear your voice. I need to know you're ok."

Within two phone calls, he formulates a cast-iron case for the site mods. The guy is banned from the site.

It's like having this warm blanket of love and safety wrapped around me. I've never experienced that before. I don't think I want it, until it happens. We speak pretty much daily from that point on. We phone randomly for a snatched five-minutes, just to hear each other's voice. Hours pass in a moment. Magic.

We talk about everything. I learn that his dad had been in and out of psychiatric care. That he was cited in his parent's acrimonious divorce, aged 4. I learn that he couldn't bring himself to visit his mother when she was dying. I also learn that a previous girlfriend had died tragically young around the same time as both his parents.

An inevitable hop and a skip takes us to our first date in an old abbey converted into an intimate pub with nooks and fairy lights. His choice of venue is perfect. Midway through the evening he puts his hand on my hand and tells me something is happening to him that's never happened before.

Our first date is also our first night together. I all but stop playing Diplomacy online. I think it's sweet that Adam gets jealous. I don't send my epic introductory messages, or have sustained game-long alliances with other players. I'm not playing enough games to maintain my top three ranking. I don't care. Then comes a bombshell.

"I've thrown Amy out the house. Told her I need a break and she can't stay here. I'm managing her out permanently. She's gone to friends in Sussex. I'm selling the house, Rachel. I want to move. I want to be with you. Can you come down for the weekend?"

Wow! That's unexpected. Amy, the lodger, ex and madwoman who bullies him. I didn't expect her to go without a fight.

I didn't expect him to offer the house up for sale either. He has a beautiful house, bought with multiple inheritances. He lost his gran, his mum and his dad over the space of a few years and bought a 5-

bedroom townhouse just around the corner from his mum's old house.

"Only if we can go to your dodgy Nepalese restaurant and you spoon feed me lentil dahl (teasing ya). Of course I'll come down. I'll see if I can take the Friday/Monday off too. We can have a long weekend."

Amy is out the house for five glorious months. I don't know how Adam does it. Mostly, he manages to ignore the six-thousand daily texts and phone calls from her. During that time, she dyes her hair blue and gets herself referred to mental health services (who also try to contact Adam). She continually pesters his brother and all his mates to get Adam to contact her. I'm either holed up in an Adam love-bubble or doing silly miles up and down the M6. I'm going into work on no sleep, having driven through the night. I'm leaving work, changing in a service station and driving straight to his. We live on sex, oatcakes, brie and a weird shared love of pickled herring, washed down with Prosecco in bed.

To this day, I don't think any of his friends, or his brother know of my existence. I'm never introduced to any of them. He knows that bothers me. It's not right. In contrast, I am bursting with Adam-ness. He pours out of every cell of my being. I am a self-confessed Adam-bore. I guess love affects people differently.

He says he has a list of jobs to do to get the house ready for market. I can't see what else needs doing. It looks perfect. I imagine it will sell quickly.

We look at houses near me. Perfect tiny executive

conversions as well as interesting 'project' properties. Both our eyes light up as we wander round a 'project' with 4 acres of ground and a pile of outbuildings.

"Airbnb pods" he whispers as he squeezes my hand. "We'll square the house off with a two-storey extension. I'll buy you chickens."

He looks so happy. He grabs me in the muddy field, behind an outbuilding, swings me round and kisses me.

"You'll always be a part of me. You know that, don't you. I will never love anyone as much as I love you. You are a bewitcher, Rachel Donaldson. You are the last and only chapter of my life worth writing about."

It's a Monday in April when Adam phones me. April 15th. I remember.

"I've just booked a train up to you for tomorrow. I get in at one o'clock. Meet me at the station?"

Well, that's kinda cool. The Hoojamama's are playing at the jazz club tomorrow night. There's also a Korean film on at the Film House. Adam adores Korean cinema.

He keeps the reason for his visit from me until after we make love that night. In fact, it's after 1am when he breaks the news. He breaks it to me at the same time as wrapping himself around me in a post-coital embrace.

"I've got something I need to tell you."

I know by his tone it's something serious. I stiffen in his arms, bracing myself.

"Shhh... it's going to be ok. Don't go mad. Please. Just listen to me. Amy is moving back in again. Temporarily. Just for a few weeks until she finds somewhere to stay. All her stuff's at mine. She's got nowhere else to go. I'm sorry" he finishes by winding his muscular leg around my body and squeezing me hard into him. "I've been so worried about telling you."

"We've gone all day Adam, all night. We've just made love. Why didn't you tell me earlier?"

"We were having such a good time. I didn't want to ruin things." He looks like a boy about to cry.

"Does she know about me?" I feel sick. I know the answer to that one already. He shakes his head,

"I'll tell her. I promise."

"When?" We both know I'm asking about when she moves.

I know he'll never tell her about me. Maybe he knows that I know.

"Wednesday. I need to go back tomorrow."

He says he'll phone me on Wednesday night, once

she's 'settled back in.' He doesn't. Says they'd watched a bit of TV and he'd fallen asleep. In fact, speaking to me on the phone from the house seems to be a problem now. He only ever phones when he's out and walking somewhere. I call them my 'pavement calls.' As if he's worried she'll walk in or overhear him. Weeks become months. The house is definitely going on the market in June. Then September. Then December. Then he says that maybe the market isn't buoyant and perhaps it isn't the best time to sell.

He cuts the phone off without answering on Christmas Day. One ring and cut.

Still, he sends me photographs of bookcases that she's supposedly cleared as evidence of her commitment to moving.

"If you've changed your mind, Adam – just tell me. It's fine. I'd rather know."

Or:

"Things feel different, Adam. This isn't how it used to be."

Is always met with a:

"You're being ridiculous," "it's in your head", "nothing's changed, I love you more than ever Rachel" and my favourite… "fairy tales don't happen if you don't believe, Rachel."

Adam tells me he's going on holiday with his brother. A cycling tour of the North Coast 500 with a bunch of his brothers' mates. He's taking a rented campervan. Following on as the support vehicle.

"Fantastic Adam! I LOVE the North West Highlands. It's my favourite place in the world. Wild camping, fairy pool swims, sunsets on beaches. Can I come?"

"It's not really that kind of holiday, Rach. It's a lad's thing. Boy's adventure. I'd rather go back when it's just the two of us. How about I stop off on my way back and we spend some time together?"

The sick knot of disappointment in my tummy is becoming a regular feature. I swallow it down.

"Perfect." I say cheerily. "Shall I book somewhere special for us? Something to look forward to after your week of roughing it? That van's going to smell like something died in it!"

"Now that…. is an awesome idea. Yes. Can't wait to see you."

I spend ages finding a little pub-inn on the beach. Live music, real ale and our own beach sunsets. I book two nights as agreed.
Adam parties hard. I barely hear from him. On the last night, the lads have an absolute skinful. We'd arranged to meet at 2pm. He's late in leaving Inverness and crushingly hungover. He misfuels the van. Fills the tank with petrol instead of diesel, then breaks down in the middle of nowhere.

"Rescue services can't pick the van up until Monday," he tells me over the phone. "I'm so sorry. Cancel the hotel. I'll pay you the money."

Not the point, but I know he won't. It occurs to me that I've paid all the hotels, meals, drinks and outings over the course of our three-year journey.

"Shall I try and move the booking? Maybe we can just move it forward a couple of days and get the van fixed."

There's a pause.

"I'm sorry, Rach. I can't. I told Amy I'd be back on Tuesday. She's expecting me."

Ah, the lodger expects him back. Once again, Adam 'forgets' to phone me to let me know he's safely home. His phone rings out when I try. No answer. No answer either the next two nights when I call at the time we'd agreed to talk. He's in the pub with mates.

Adam isn't one person, he's a hundred people. An empty shell that reflects back what you want most.
- The gentle poet, a romantic who makes you feel like the only woman in the world
- The lover who wraps himself around you and contains you in an exclusive bubble of bliss
- The gallant hero and protector
- The best friend who is wonderful, helpful, caring, smart and funny – when he remembers you exist

- The creator of epic fairy-tales and 'happily-ever-afters' that he never intends to action
- Someone who looks into your eyes and says you'll always be part of him one day, then conveniently forgets you the next
- A 4-year-old boy, perpetuating a pre-wired code of dysfunction and unhappiness

I don't know what's lies, truth or whether it's all bullshit. Was it ever love? I am confused and bewildered.

The truth is hard to reconcile but unavoidable. The only person at the centre of Adam's world is Adam.

With a sigh, I pick up my laptop and open up Social Media.

Amy Hawes, I'd looked at the profile a hundred times and wondered about her. I know the answer to what I'm writing already. How can a heart feel desperately sad, filled with grief and liberated simultaneously?

Hi Amy

I apologise for the unsolicited message and hope it doesn't come as too much of a shock.

I've been seeing the guy you're living with, Adam for almost a year. He's lovely, smart, funny, charming. I've fallen hard. I really like him.

He describes things at home as 'complicated.' I still don't know what that means.

He told me when we met that he was single. Yet entertaining me at his home has been off limits for almost a year. So are most of his friends. He says you're living there temporarily as a friend until you find somewhere new to live. After a year, something doesn't feel quite right.

I was brought up to respect the sisterhood and wouldn't stand on another woman's toes.

I'm checking in to see what the situation is. If you guys are still together, then I will respectfully bow out.

Yours
Rachel

3.... 2.... 1.... I detonate the send button and watch the nuclear bomb fly out the window.

I flick screens on to our gaming site. Our Faraway land, the place beyond imagination where it all started. I open up my profile.

Under 'profile signature,' I begin to type:

"She wanted…. Secrets whispered at midnight, Road Trips without a map."

Whatever adventures the future holds, they don't involve Adam. I want someone real or no-one at all.

Nothing appears to be left but the pain of a ghost who once meant everything – Sappho's Eulogy:

> *"You may forget but*
> *Let me tell you this,*
> *Someone in some future time*
> *Will think of us"*
>
> *Sappho*

The bigger the scar, the better the story. Let the healing begin.

3 ADAM: Borderline Trouble

Six months of my life disappeared when Jo died. I don't remember it. I barely left my room. Three people died within three years. Mum, dad, then Jo. I lay on the floor. I slept a lot. I wanked.

I fantasised about women I knew, vaguely knew or had known. If I was wanking, I wasn't thinking about horrible stuff. If a horrible thought pounced like an evil 'Stephen King Clown' jack-in-the-box, wanking made it go away. I'd sleep without dreams. If I woke and the bastard was there, ejaculating saw it off. Horrible thoughts were replaced by nothing. It worked.

After six months, I didn't need to wank so much. Jo was the one that got away, quite literally. I met Jo at Bristol. We were friends. Didn't start dating until after we graduated. Didn't see the point of dating one woman at University. At one point I had four, spaced out on designated days of the week. There was the virgin. Sociology. Red hair. Shit, what was her name again? To be fair, she didn't tell me she was a virgin. The way her eyes stared at me still freaks me out. Kerri was married. She wasn't a student, just in a bad marriage, older and fabulously liberated in bed. My flatmates thought I was an absolute legend. Maybe I still am.

It was Kerri I was texting when Jo threw me out of our flat on Christmas Day. I'm not even sure why I hooked up with Kerri again after all those years. It meant nothing, really it didn't. I was just curious. The text was apparently the straw that broke the camel's back.

I was single (after Jo kicked me out) when mum died. She had dementia. Deteriorated rapidly in the end. My brother Cal and his wife, Paula converted their downstairs. Paula did all the nursing. She likes being the martyr. They said mum enjoyed being around the buzz of the grandkids.

My mum loved Jo. Adored her. So did Cal and Paula. They were gutted when we broke up. I struggled with it all. Cal, mum, death and happy families. Blame my dad for that one. Selfish, womanizing twat. Wrote endless books of poetry but barely knew we existed. He died in the psychiatric unit of a care home not much later.

Cal phoned me exactly at the point I was stepping onto a train to go to a party.

"They reckon mum's got less than a day. You should come."

My foot was already on the train. It was a split-second decision. I couldn't face her. The thought made my stomach lurch. She had Cal, she didn't need me. Cal had the wife, the family. Now him and Paula had the inheritance too. Cal had always been the favourite one. I phoned Jo from the train. Despite her best efforts, I carried on to the party, got hammered and didn't see my mother again.

About a year after that I met Amy. Rather, I sort

of crashed into the chaos that is Amy. She was working in a local Government office where I landed an IT contract.

Amy got into strife at work. Amy-Strife was not unusual. When she was good, the world loved her. When she was bad, she'd start a fight in an empty room. She had an opinion on everything. I sorted it. I always sorted it. She hugged me for sorting it. She ground her hips in. I got a hard-on and well, the rest is history. The Amy thing was never meant to be long-term. I actually thought Jo and I would get back together. That's what I wanted. Then Jo died.

I think I'd blown my nose into the sink or something. I was bunged up. Amy went Amy-Ballistic. Called me a disgusting cretin, threw a casserole dish at my head, then threw me out the house Amy-style.

I tried to phone Jo from the pub. It rang out. I tried three times. It rang out because Jo had been dead in her flat for three days.

It wasn't suicide. She wanted to live. I know she wanted to live. They found letters from a fertility clinic in her flat. She wanted a baby. People who want babies want to live. She'd been drinking quite a bit. Got herself hospitalised with pneumonia. The post-mortem said scarring on her lungs due to chronic pneumonia. Recurring chest infections. Heart failure is a common complication.

The family didn't want me at the funeral. Amy left me to wank and to sleep. Probably wise. Beyond wanking, I didn't feel anything.

In my kinder moments, I think of myself as a free spirit: "Don't be a wage slave;" "Climb that mountain (virtually from your bedroom);" "Do what makes you happy;" "Admire me from the ground or fly with me." I'm also a procrastinator. I've not had a contract in a while, years. Not my fault. It's a young man's game.

I need to decide what to do with the rest of my life. Networking on Connect2Me, where people think I'm Steve Jobs, doesn't really pull the money in. I'm what they call asset rich – I have a big house in a nice area – but cash poor.

"How much are you drinking, Adam?"

I look at my GP quizzically.

"How many units of alcohol do you drink in a typical week?"

"20? – ish?" As long as you say something under 21, they don't hassle you.

"How often are you having 8 or more units in a single sitting?" He was consulting a chart as he was speaking to me. "You're borderline diabetic."

Shit. Nerve problems, blindness, amputation, heart attacks, strokes, erectile dysfunction. It's a funky list. I'm having palpitations walking home already.

I turn my MacBook on and flick onto the Diplomacy site. Message.

I open it and a gif of some attractive female winks at me.

"You don't always have to get sexy to get to know a girl." Cute! Catcher In The Rye.

Rachel has a bit of a following on Play Diplomacy. The mysterious female player that everyone wants to play. No 3 player. A catch. She's flirting with me. Of course she is. Cal and I used to compare notes on getting women into bed. Cal says it's a numbers game. Chance your arm with fifty women, one's bound to say yes. I say I can get any girl into bed by the end of an album. Three things. Right words, right moves, right time. I call it the dance.

I take Rachel to the 'The Monk and Minstrel' for a first date, although we'd been chatting for months. It's really nice. She's nice. Reminds me of Jo. Easy company. Fun. Smart. The dance is perfect.

Bosh! Turns out I'm not suffering diabetic impotence. Turns out I'm still rather good despite the lengthy sexual lag. I'd been worried. Performance anxiety droop. This could go somewhere. I think she's feeling it too. I let the emotion wash over me. She has amazing eyes. I love the way she talks to everyone. Marry her? I probably could, you know. She's got a great job. Decent salary. Probably building an awesome pension. Would impress my mates.

Amy? I feel a bit bad about that. Amy's away for the week with her sister, mum and a few hangers on. They always go to some spa place for her sister's birthday. It's the opportunity to create a bit of distance. I send her a text and within five-minutes I get the phone call back.

"I just need some space Amy. A break for a while. No, it's not the end. Just some time to myself. No, you can't come back. Not just now. A break. Then we'll talk. No, there's no-one else, I promise."

Sheesht. Then I get the sister on the phone, pleading. Then the bloody mother phones me, hysterical, telling me that all Amy's stuff is there. She has a right to come back and they're going to get a lawyer. It goes on for hours. I hate drama. It gives me sick knots in my stomach. I feel four years old. I want to hide in my room and lie on the floor under the bed. Anyway, it's done. I turn my phone off.

Not joking, those five months are the happiest of my life. Sadly it comes to an end over a giant cake. Amy drives up from Sussex, leaves a huge cake on the doorstep and drives away again. A note says:

"Cake forgives anything. I'm sorry for being a pain. I'm working on it."

By the end of the day, she wheedles an agreement out of me to move back in. All her stuff is here. I can't keep her out forever. I'm exhausted from trying. I lie on the floor, I wank, I sleep. I don't know what I'm going to say to Rachel.

Jo once called me weak. Said I always drifted, taking the path of least resistance. I think I'm pushed along the path by whoever shoves hardest. Amy was an expert shover. You had no choice but to go along with the plan, or have glassware and casserole dishes flung at your head. Sometimes I agree to things without even realising I've agreed to them, just to get peace. Sometimes I agree to things by saying nothing. Sometimes I don't even hear what I've agreed to.

I'm doing the best I can. I don't know if Rachel believes that, but I am. Rachel's conversations go from magical and happy to anxiety provoking. I get the sicky knots. She calls them pavement calls. Asks when I'm going to tell Amy? When's the house going on the market? When can she come down?

Sometimes I go to the pub to get away from both of them. Often I ignore the phone. Frequently I want to lie on the floor in my room and wank.

Amy gets more and more obsessive about organising and re-organising the house. The space I occupy gets less and less. All that's left is my body-space on the floor in the spare room.

I'm out at Sainsbury's buying beer when Rachel sends her message and Amy does what she does. I don't understand why the fuck Rachel did it. It makes no sense. I thought she was better than that. She's not. I'll cut her off for a few months. No contact. Punishment.

I'm sitting in the foyer of a hospital ward. Amy's in a room somewhere. They won't let me see her. I have uber-knotty-sickness. I think I'm going to barf. I'm furious. Beyond furious. I could wring Rachel's neck. Throw her against a wall. She knows I despise drama. Fuck's sake, where's the loyalty. Single most important thing in a relationship – loyalty. Everyone knows that.

Amy won't even have taken the tablets. It's her usual Oscar winning performance for sympathy. Attention seeking. She does it to manipulate me. Once again everyone will love her, hate me. It will be all 'poor Amy, unfeeling Adam.' My friends will blame me. She does it all the time. That's why she doesn't want me in the room. Doesn't want me to know it's a scam. Bet they're not even pumping her stomach. Amy's sister appears. I didn't even know she was here.

"Go home Adam. She doesn't want to see you. She doesn't want to go back to the house again. Ever. She's adamant. It's over."

"What?" Has someone taken Amy and replaced her with someone else? Doesn't want to go back to the house? Sorry, brain does not compute.

"Can I just see her for five minutes?"

I've got it all worked out. I'm telling her Rachel was just some random online gaming interaction. I've spoken to her, like twice max, in a game. No intention of speaking to her again. Mad woman Rachel. Crazy. Stalker-Girl. Internet's full of weirdos. I'm the victim here. Bish-Bash-Bosh. Sorted.

"You've done enough damage. Go home, Adam. I'll be in touch about picking her stuff up. GO. She doesn't want you here."

Amy's sister turns on her heels and leaves me. I'm alone. It must be late, the place is empty. The sick feeling won't leave. Emptiness and desolation begin to settle. Fuck. Fuck. Fuck. I've got palpitations. My heart is fluttering, irregular, stopping. Fucking diabetes.

Rachel, I need to speak to Rachel. With the decision to do something. To speak to someone who can comfort, who can understand. I feel calmer. She'll know what to do. I pick my phone up, find the number and hit the button. It rings out. It rings out another twice.

Three calls, Omne Trium Perfectum.

"Where are you Rach? I need to speak to you urgently. Please, I need help."

The message isn't delivered. Actually, I can't see her profile picture. The penny drops. I stare at the phone. Rachel has blocked me. I try her on Diplomacy. Our place. She's blocked me there too. I have no-one. I have nothing.

It wraps round me like a suffocating blanket. I can't breathe. I feel my heart pulsing in my head. It still sounds irregular. Like a pause, then a mega-beat. I'm having a heart attack.

A life without love is a prison. Emptiness overwhelms me. I'm sinking into myself. What I need is beer. Then a wank. Then sleep. Maybe I need all of Amy's tablets. The one's she didn't take. An overdose. More than anything, I need nothing. Feeling is fucking horrible.

4 DR JIM WALKER: Borderline Psychiatry

"Tell me about your childhood, Adam. Your parents. Growing up. What were things like?" Standard question for a first appointment.

He's a bit dishevelled. Crumpled, like a crisp bag. I can hear him crinkle. Not tall, 5ft 9 maybe? He's slumped, so he might be taller. Portly - from beer and good living. Definite beer belly. He still has the remnants of boyish good looks. Now a heel's hanging off battered shoes and he looks like he needs a shower and a shave. The guy is a curious mix of defeated and arrogant, overlaid with a smog of depressed and stale air. He'd shuffled in, the way that most depressed folks who came to see me do. Wearing the weight of his life on his shoulders.

Another middle-aged bloke carrying too many rocks in his rucksack? My clinic is full of them. A modern-day epidemic. My day consists of emptying the rocks out, examining them, choosing what one or two need to go back, discarding the rest.

He turns his car key over and over in his hand. I have the unpleasant thought of wondering how long it's been since he changed his underwear.

It's unusual for someone to get to the age of….. how old? I glance at the date of birth on the referral, do the mental maths and write 52 on the clinical notepaper. I draw a doodle-circle around it. Unusual to see someone present to psychiatry for the first time at 52.

The GP had pegged it as a reactive depression. Situational following the breakdown of a relationship. Query excessive alcohol consumption and borderline diabetes. Alcohol as a means of blunting emotion? Diabetic distress also linked to anxiety, depression and suicidality?

That's not the whole story though. It rarely is. Unresolved grief? Is that why he's drinking rather than feeling? After a longer than normal pause (slowed cognition? – I note it down), I am eventually launched back into the consult with his response to my question about his childhood.

"Pretty average, I guess." Adam shrugged. "To be honest, I don't think my childhood comes into it. My girlfriend had a breakdown, took an overdose and her sister persuaded her it was all my fault. I thought I could help her through it. Darling sis had other ideas and it all went a bit Pete Tong."

I look at him and nod ruefully.

"I know. I'm going to come back to recent events in a bit. Sometimes hearing about your childhood helps me understand how you cope with things. Starting at the back and working forward if you like. If it makes you uncomfortable, we don't have to…"

The pause is practised and well-timed.
"It's ok. My parents divorced when I was 4."

Adam breaks off. A light touch gets it going again.

"You remember it?" I ask.

"I remember my mum couldn't stop me from crying. She cited me in the divorce. 'Emotional damage to the 4-year-old' it said. For years I wondered what came first, my crying or their fighting."

"You were an only child?"

I note 'parents divorced age 4.' I circle 4, a key developmental milestone. I scribble 'Trauma, query disruption/fragmentation of object constancy.' Object constancy, the ability to have a healthy difference of opinion and still value someone, or the ability to continue to love someone when they aren't physically in your presence.

"My brother Cal is two years older than me. He seemed to take it better."

I nod and pause, waiting for it to unfurl.

"We wandered for a bit, Isle of Man, Runcorn, settling in Manchester. My mum remarried. He drank a lot. Had a son and a daughter." With notable sarcasm, he adds, "One big happy family."

"Not particularly happy then?"

"It was a big, empty house. I got on with things. Sometimes she was there. Sometimes she wasn't. He was mostly drunk. She looked after him. Cal and I took over the attic rooms. We were sneaking into clubs when I was 15. Legend and Sandpiper. Knew a bunch of blokes who would knee-cap anyone for £7.50. We all pretended to be a bit hard and in with them."

"And your father?" I note down 'inconsistent maternal attachment.'

Adam laughed sardonically. "Cloud cuckoo land. He never owned a phone. Not even in the house. My mum would pack us in a bus to visit him. We never knew if he'd be there or not. Long straw – dad would meet us from the bus. Short straw – he'd forget we were coming, no sign and we'd sit on the pavement in the rain for hours. Different times back then. The house was full of shit. Piles and piles of newspapers, magazines, thousands of books, bits of bicycles, old window frames, rolls of carpet. He slept in a chair. He couldn't get to the bedroom."

"He hoarded things?"

"He was a 'creative,' a poet, a womanizer. Well, until the women couldn't get into the flat because of all the shit at least. Had a couple of breakdowns."

"He had a history of mental illness?"

"No idea. Never talked about. I guess so? Don't

know. I guess we could have gone and tried to find old notes or something. It never seemed that important. Depression maybe? Really, I've no idea. Is it important?"

"I don't know Adam. Maybe. At the moment, I'm trying to gather as many bits of the jigsaw as I can. It doesn't sound like there was a lot of love or constancy in your childhood?"

When I say that, it triggers something in him.

"Hang on, I have a picture."

Adam stands up to get something out his back pocket and I get a whiff of stale air. It's his wallet. He pulls out a crumpled photo and hands it to me. It's a recent picture of him at a waterfall. There's a small red waterwheel in the foreground. The picture is of his back as he looks across the flow of water. He looks as though he's on his own, but someone must have taken the photo of him from behind, so he can't have been.

"Groudle Glen, on the Isle of Man. We lived there for a bit. "Mum used to always make us toss coppers into the waterfall. Said we had to pay the Manx fairy folk for safe passage. Then we all had to dance across or they'd take us to the fairy world."

There he is. Boy Adam. The picture is of a portly, middle-aged man. The feelings are one of a small boy. Boys and mums. It's always boys and mums.

"Looks like a recent photo" I say.

"It is. Reminds me of my mum. More than anywhere else. The fairies of Groudle Glen. I think she speaks to me when I go there. I hear her."

"Tell me about her death, Adam." I keep a deadpan face as he recounts his mother's death, the phone call, Jo and the party.

"Anyone would have done it. It was a split-second decision. She was out of it by then. Cal was there. For the best. She wouldn't have wanted me to see her like that. If she were compos mentis, she'd have told me to go. They both knew Cal would get the inheritance."

Oooft. Almost callous. The inheritance? It was at odds with the 4-year-old fairy boy from a moment ago. I wrote 'empathy' with a downward arrow. I also went back and drew two arrows out of object constancy with 'mother' above one and 'Jo' above the other. Relationships are out of sight, out of mind. Being able to still have feelings for someone when they're not there. Unless they're with the fairies, it seems.

Asperger's? Narcissism? Sociopathy? None of those bodes well for a good prognosis from therapy. Let's hope the GP's right and he's depressed. That's at least something I can do something with.

Not Asperger's. He could be a charmer. Charm the knickers off any woman by the sounds of it. Just apparently didn't have much time or respect for them once he had them. He likes the chase, the big catch but not the intimacy.

A fortress of defence that masks a deep insecurity. Scared of letting anyone know who he is? Frightened they'll discover he's as rotten deep down he believes himself to be?
Childhood trauma and an incomplete sense of self? Almost certainly.

"Thanks Adam. All interesting stuff. Changing track slightly for a second, if I might? What do you do for a living?" I flick down the referral letter. I don't think I know.

He draws himself up. There's pride here. That's something to work with.

"I've got a couple of companies. Business partners I work with. Mainly product design, IT, e-learning, some training. I've had contract work in the past. Lucrative, but I don't like being chained to a desk. Nine to five gives me itchy feet. Kills my soul. I like to think I'm more of a free spirit. Never looked for work. It falls on my lap. Headhunted, contract-wise. I guess I'm pretty good at what I do."

"Sounds impressive." i.e. if I'm not sceptical and don't think he's over-egging it by a tonne.

"My brother and I developed the UK's first multi-modality Equality and Diversity Training. Just when the Government was making Equality and Diversity mandatory across businesses. I developed a ten module, online, e-learning course. It was damned awesome! I was the brains, Cal was the beauty and the marketing. Sold the company and the training at its peak. Made a tidy packet at the time."

"You don't have to worry about money, then?" Adam half laughed, half groaned.

"I don't know I'd go that far. I'm not great with money and I've not had a contract for a while. Contracts are a young man's game. Frankly I've got to a point where I can't be arsed. But with Amy gone now, I've got all the bills. I need to find some source of income, and quick. Either that or sell the house and release some equity."

"Is money an issue Adam? That can be a big stress too."

"Not really. I've taken out a loan against the house. Just need to get my arse in gear. Stop procrastinating. Maybe a 5-bedroom house is too big for a single guy. Downsize. I've got some ideas. Corporate conferences. Product design, scaling-up, user-experience, iterative design. Newest corporate hot potato-type stuff. Creating a buzz is straightforward."

"Sounds fascinating."

"It really is. Lots of money to be made. Corporate training budgets are huge."

I glance surreptitiously at my watch. Ten minutes of the scheduled consultation left. I need to move it on. I need to get to the questions about his mood.

"Sounds like you've had a lot on your plate, Adam. Your GP thinks you're low in mood. Would you say you've been down?"

"Down? I don't know what that means really. I feel empty. Like I'm floating from room to room. Like I'm not even in my body most of the time. My girlfriend of ten-years has just left me. Would be strange if I didn't have a wobble. I'm ok though. I'm not crying. I'm not thinking of ending my life. She wasn't even the right girl for me. She was bonkers. I certainly didn't want to marry her, or have kids."

"Sleeping, how's that?"

"Fuck. Sorry. S'cuse the language. I could sleep for Britain. Anytime, anywhere. I'm knackered. Struggling to get up until late afternoon."

"Can you still get into a book, a TV programme, enjoy things you used to?"

"TV's a noise. I used to be social animal. Fuck. I'd be out every night. Sometimes I wouldn't come back. I'd be down the pub, people back at the house. Jo used to call places like Sandpiper my 'gangsta-club.' Nowadays people seem to have kids and pregnant wives cramping their style. They're decorating their hallway, going to Ikea and having an early night. Not quite the alcohol and coke haze of the 90's eh?"

"How about the alcohol?"

"14- maybe 15 units?"

I reckon I can probably triple that as a more reliable estimate. Easily.

"Concentration and memory?"

"I'm 52. Not as agile as I used to be. Been a while since I've done the Times crossword. A bit foggy." Adam tapped his head and grinned ruefully. "Making money or finding women seems harder than it was."

"Indeed." I grinned back. He was a chancer, a fly-by-night, but he did have an irrepressible charm. You just couldn't keep up with him in the pub and wouldn't want your daughter (or any women you knew) coming across him. "We've only got a few moments left, Adam? If there was a bit of your life you could change, what would it be?"

It's difficult to be certain after an initial appointment. Normally I'd want two or three before reaching any kind of diagnosis. But it's a good working hypothesis. He wouldn't be the first charmer who reached his 50's and hit some sort of narcissistic collapse. No happy family, no marriage, friends dropping off, lack of career breaks and the latest opportunity eluding him yet again.

Therapeutically, you patch them up. Sort the low mood, help them identify some tenuous previous achievements which allows them out of the danger zone of small boy vulnerability and collapse. Defences re-established, they move on to their next victim.

"Not sure why my GP thought I should come.

You've listened to a lot of my crap."

"Under the circumstances and given everything you've gone through, sounds as though you're doing ok. Maybe you should give yourself a bit of credit?"

He looks pleased with that. A stroke. Golden rule of psychiatry. Always send the patient away feeling better than he was when he came in. Concentrate on getting him back again. I continue on. Next appointment will be waiting. I'm over time.

"I think you're a bit down. You look down. Unsurprising given everything you've been through. I could prescribe an anti-depressant. It won't make you super-happy. What it will do is help you see the wood for the trees, help with decision-making, maybe the sleep, concentration, memory and the procrastination?" I print out a prescription for 50mgs sertraline. "When that kicks in maybe I can help you sift through some of the other stuff. I'm not promising anything, but a clear head and the opportunity to talk things through sometimes helps." It occurs to me that I haven't asked one of my standard questions. I'm slipping. "Meant to ask, Adam. Have you ever felt like this before? I mean low in mood, down, depressed. Anything ever crashed in on you before?"

"I had a bit of crash when Jo, my last ex died."

I nod. We've covered all that. The relationship spider's web. The multiple deaths. The ex whose funeral no-wanted him at.

"Did you get any professional help at that time, Adam?"

"Nah. Just got over it myself."

I nod and note it down. "I'd like to see you again in a fortnight Adam. Is that ok? Check all's well with the prescription." I hand him the prescription. "Slight nausea. Maybe a bit headachy for a day or two. Persevere. Some patients report a spot of temporary erectile dysfunction, so don't worry if it goes a bit funny. I look at him pointedly. "Finally… and seriously Adam. Cut down on the alcohol. Not every night. Not to cope. It's another depressant, it works against the sertraline and you're a borderline diabetic. It's a bad combo. We'll chat more next time, yes?"
A lot of psychiatrists won't dream of treating the depression whilst he's drinking so much. I'm a fan of multi-modal therapy. You got to start somewhere. "See you in fortnight?"

Adam nods and grins from a foppish fringe. The sole of his shoe wobbles comically from the foot balancing on his knee.
I know already it's unlikely he'll ever take any of the tablets I've just prescribed. Nor will he come back and see me again. These guys rarely do. Nor will he cut down on the drinking.
You patch them up when their world collapses and they find a new shiny reflection to chase in the water. You can never change them.

5 RACHEL: Forgiveness Cake and the Kindness of Strangers

Never again did I think I'd be doing the old journey down the M6. It's surprisingly painful. An ache for something that's gone. Like a mirage I can never touch. It makes my stomach lurch.

All the familiar motorway landmarks. Once they signified everything. The anticipation of a joyous reunion. The tummy thrills. The toothpaste and eyeliner in the glove compartment. A garden centre. Gretna Services. Signposts for the Lakes.

Now they're grumbling roadside gremlins that lie in wait.

This time it's not Adam I'm going to meet. It's Amy. In a coffee shop of her choice on the outskirts of Manchester. How weird is that? I've spent so long hating the woman and she's just like me. The only difference? Hers has been a 10-year-long scam, rather than a 3-year one. Do I regret the Social Media message? That's a hard one. It was four months ago now. I regret that it caused Amy to do what she did. That's awful. I didn't realise at the time. She only told me about it recently. No-one ever wants to be the reason another human being doesn't want to live.

Adam though. If I hadn't, he'd still be stringing me

along. Stringing us both along. He talks his way out of anything. Makes everything seem legitimate. I'm always the crazy one for having doubts.

I can still hear him: 'Don't be ridiculous, Rachel, who do you think I am?' 'You'll always be a part of me;' 'Fairy tales don't happen unless you believe, Rachel;' 'You're the last chapter of my book, the only one worth writing.' I still struggle with the fact that not one word of it was real. Three years of gaslighting gives you a helluva demon. Goodness knows what damage he's done to Amy.

Meeting up with Amy is a chance for me to say sorry. The chance to explain, compare notes. Sister to sister. Maybe I can help her. Heal each other even. I throw the radio on to try and distract myself from him. Happy music? I don't think so. I tune in to a radio debate about feminism, schools and cultures of harassment. Let's see if I can hate the bastard even more by the time I get to Manchester.

The café is called the Fig and Sparrow. I have an address for the sat nav. Amy says there's parking outside. Hurrah for sat nav's.

I'm almost an hour early. It's fine, a leg-stretch will be good anyway and it's dry. I pop some money into the ticket machine, reckoning 4 hours will be way more than I need. I'm not sure how things are going to go but it's always a bit of a faux-pas to excuse yourself to move the car.

I buy Amy a candle and some hand-made chocolates. Tasteful cardboard bag in hand, I walk into the Fig and Sparrow. It's an independent coffee shop. Artisan, but low key. Mismatched chairs and a wooden floor. A coffee grinder makes a noisy assault on the space whilst the smell engulfs you.

I spot Amy straight away. Stowed away in a quiet corner. Although to be fair, there are only a couple of young mums and a pair of toddlers playing crash with bears in pushchairs at the other end of the shop. She waves.

God, she looks exactly like she does in her Social Media profile. Blonde hair pulled back into a pony tail, a fringe falling over her eyes. She looks girl-next-door. Cute. Black jeans, boots, a pale pink shirt. I don't know what I'm expecting, grief-stricken widow, monster, madwoman, weeping hysteric? She's normal.

"Hi. Rachel?" Amy jumps up and holds out a hand. "Let me get you a coffee. Least I can do. What can I get you?"

I smile. She's at least as nervous as me. I think this is going to be ok. "I'm on my feet. I'll go and have a look." I peer into the mug in front of her. "You look like you could use a refill too." I stick my jacket over the chair next to us. "What do you want? You can get the next one."

She sits down again. I watch the nerves make her exhale. She's been pulling at her eyebrow hairs. There are barely any left. Her body's trembling.

"White Americano, no sugar."

"Perfect. Oh and I was early. Got you these. Somewhat of a peace offering. Hopefully you'll let me say sorry to you." I dumped the cardboard bag on the table in front of her. "Coffee," I motion to the counter. "Back in a tick."

It gives both of us the chance to breathe. I carry the two mugs of coffee back to the table. Amy has her nose buried in the candle.

"I love candles," she said, "this one smells divine."

"I thought you might. And what girl doesn't like chocolate." Phew. I did wonder if gifts were a little over the top given the circumstances. Amy kicks off.

"You know, you look just like your Social Media profile. I've looked at that picture so many times," She giggles nervously, sips her coffee and burns her lip. "Hot." She blows on her coffee.

"That's funny, that's exactly the same thought I had about you when I walked in. You are your Social Media profile. That, and how pretty you are!" I lean back in the chair and take a deep breath. "This is the weirdest situation. I can't believe we're sitting having coffee. How much would Adam hate this."

"He'd have a fit. I'm glad. It feels good to put a face to the mystery." Amy rubs a finger back and forward over her lips. She looks like one of those pop-up, sucker toys that you stick down and wait on exploding in your face. You know it's coming. You just don't know when.

"I'm sorry, Amy. I am genuinely sorry. For everything. I didn't know. He told me it was over between both of you. Said he was single. Said you were just staying in the house for a few weeks until you found somewhere new to live. I believed it all. He was so damned plausible. I'm so sorry."

Amy shrugs. "It's ok. Plausible is what he does. Hardest part is learning to be on my own again. Have you heard from him?"

"Adam?" I shake my head. "No. Thank God. I cut-off. Blocked him everywhere. He could turn up at the door I suppose. He won't though. Not got it in him. He'll be too busy telling himself that I wasn't all that and he's got a lucky escape."

Amy nods. "I know," she takes a deep breath. "Sometimes you get the little boy. Crying. Says things like 'everyone hates me,' 'I'm really struggling,' 'it's not just you that has problems.' But he says it to win you back. Like he doesn't mean it but he knows you can't resist falling for it. Before you know it. You're suckered."

"Has he been in touch with you?" It suddenly occurs to me that maybe that's what he's doing. Hoovering Amy again. Reeling her back in.

She shakes her head. "Absolutely nothing. Not a peep." She studies the table as she speaks. "I know it's wrong. I know he's bad for me, but not hearing anything is hard. Ten years and nothing. Not an 'are you ok?' 'I'm thinking about you.' I know it's wrong, but I got obsessed. Checking my phone every thirty seconds. What I wanted to see, desperate for was an 'I'm sorry. I've made a terrible mistake. You mean everything to me. I love you.'"

Amy's voice is wobbling. Her eyes fill and she dashes tears angrily off her face.

"Stupid, huh? I've not told anyone that. That I miss him so much it hurts. I feel like there's a bit of me missing. Like I'll never be happy again. I know he's bad for me, but not having him is almost as bad."

I know exactly what Amy is talking about. I look for the 'I'm sorry. I've made a mistake. I love you' text. I obsess too.

"He's fucked up, Amy. That's the bottom line. Him. Not us. He's incredibly fucked up. To the point where no-one will ever be able to fix him. He's not capable of texts like that. In his head, everything that's happened is our fault. My fault, probably."

Amy shakes her head. "Mine too. My fault, I mean. I'm not easy to live with. I've got a terrible temper. I shout. I scream when he winds me up. I throw things at him. I live with so much shame for the way I am. I keep thinking, if I could just have been normal… maybe we'd be married kids…. dinner parties… normal together."

I hadn't lived with him. I'd see him for weekends. Holidays and dates and days away. Mini-break bliss. Amy had ten years of gaslighting and abuse. Ten years of being made to feel she's crazy and everything's her fault. I remember how he described her: mad Amy; bonkers; a nut-job; histrionic; how he feared for his safety around her; how she bullied him; manipulated him; 'damaged goods;' how he never wanted to be with her from the beginning. I feel ashamed that I believed him and that I didn't stand up for her. I wanted him for myself. I wanted her to be a witch. Ten years of abuse leaves deep scars. Karma that it's probably me being talked about like that now.

Amy's picking skin from her lips nervously. They're red and raw. She's a wreck. I want to wrap my arms around her and make it better again.

Something pops into my head. "I was there, Amy. When he opened the book."

She looks quizzically at me. "Book?"

"The book you made him for his 50th. I was there when he unwrapped it."

It's a forgotten memory. I was at his house for his 50th birthday. It was during those months when he'd chucked Amy out and I'd more or less moved in. Looking back now, I still can't believe he made all that seem like a normal relationship.

Amy had left him birthday presents. She'd sent him a text to say there were a pile of presents, wrapped and hidden in the eves of the attic room for his 50th. He was to go and open them. We were in bed. He'd taken my hand. We were naked when we went up there. So wrong.

Sure enough there was a beautifully wrapped pile of presents hiding in the eves. He'd opened them one by one. He had a look of disgust on his face as he opened each one and complained about it.

There was a print she'd had professionally framed

for him. It was beautiful. A classy, muted shadow-grey wood that complimented the surrealist print. But to him, it was all wrong. Mostly it was wrong because she'd dared to have it framed. It was a print he'd bought in Spain when he was a student. Years ago. His complaint had been along the lines of 'how dare she meddle with his stuff' and 'that print is from a time long before her, now she's all over that bit of my life too,' 'she doesn't belong there.' Probably the print is linked with some other woman.

At the bottom of the pile of presents there was an oversized, leather-bound book, with ribbon. His name and date of birth were gold embossed on the front. She'd made him a book of his life.

She must have gone to relatives and friends. Found rare photos from his childhood, of his parents, his aunt, his brother. Student days, graduation, holiday snaps from all over the world, in chronological order as it took him through his life. There were photos from an awards ceremony when the company he and his brother owned won some Equality and Diversity award.

The last section was entitled. Adam and Amy, Soulmates. It was a sweet selection of photos from their life together. That was the section he had most issue with, was most sneering about.

"One fucking grainy picture of Jo, and six million of Amy."

He'd literally hurled the book into the opposite corner of the room. Some massive, heavy-duty, rose-coloured blinkers I must have been wearing to not be offended and horrified. Thinking about it disgusts me.

So much love and care and time had gone into creating something meant to be cherished. I am the fuckwit.

"You saw the book?" Amy jolts me back. "Did he like it? It took me almost a year to pull it all together. I had to write to people all over the world to get some of those photographs."

"It was incredible Amy. One of the most beautiful things I've even seen. I only hope one day someone loves me as much as you loved him. He was a bastard. The only person at the centre of Adam's world is Adam. You deserve so much better."

I had to give myself a shake. I'd been complicit in the whole thing. He'd strung me along. We'd both strung Amy along. I need to move. I am beginning to disgust myself. I'm a bitch. A bitch or an airhead. Probably both.

"Coffee," I say, grabbing her mug.

"But it's my turn," I hear her protest as I start to walk from the table.

I grin at her. "This time, I need a massive slice of cake too. When we have our night out on the town, and you show me round the bright lights of Manchester, you can get the first round in. Deal?"

The time the coffee is brewing is time to recentre. Just breathe, Rachel, breathe. Hold it together. Perspective is a funny thing. All this time I've been a lego figure that Adam moves around himself on the periphery of his life. Amy is another lego figure in a separate part. Goodness knows how many he has. He's directing actors in his theatre.

I come back to the table with two more coffees, a giant raspberry and white chocolate muffin and a huge slab of lemon drizzle cake. 'Cake forgives anything.' The giant doorway cake and Amy moving back in. Marking the beginning of the end for him and I with cake. Hold it together, Rachel.

"What's he doing with himself now?" I change the subject. "Where's the money coming from? I can't imagine it's cheap keeping a big, old house going."

I halve the muffin and the lemon drizzle and stick two halves on a plate for her. There is something vulnerable about Amy. The feistiness masks a fragility. She looks as though she's lost a load of weight. She deserves some peace.

"You know Adam. He's always ducking and diving. You never know where his money is coming from."

Me, I thought to myself. I funded a good chunk of it for the last three years. A new MacBook, several car bills, not to mention all the hotels, holidays, meals and beer. Me with a hefty mortgage on a new two-bedroom flat in Glasgow, him with his paid-off Edwardian mansion.

"I think he's met someone online. I mean.... aside from you," she blushes and takes a mouthful of cake.

"He's addicted to Connect2Me. You know, the online network for business contacts."

Oh yes, I know Connect2Me. Adam spends whole days on Connect2Me, waving at people, making cheesy comments and 'building up his networks.' Frequently he'd forget to return any of my messages, whilst spending days 'working' on building his business.

"I think she's American. Hang on, I'll see if I can find her. All white teeth, long hair and designer business suit. He says she's going to invest in his new venture, Corporate Conferences or something."

Amy picks up her phone, clicks onto Connect2Me and scrolls through profiles. "Here she is. Sarah Emmerson. Based in New York. Head of Product Design and Product Management at INSpire."

Amy hands her phone over. Sarah Emmerson certainly does have very white teeth. Long blonde hair. It's a corporate photograph. She's wearing a sexy, fitted tweed suit. She looks tall. Taller than him. American. Smooth. Plastic. I click on the profile.

"Entrepreneur. Former corporate banker. Wife and mum to two junior-school-sized Rugrats. New York-based although given to travel. Twenty years' experience in industry. International reputation in DesignOps, ResearchOps, PeopleOps.
Designer? Product Manager? Marketing

Specialist? Engineer? Business or Customer Stakeholder? Connect with me!"

"Wife and mum?" I look at Amy.

She shrugs. "She's got money. He thinks she'll invest. She's a catch. He can't help himself."

I dissect the muffin and scoop some raspberry and white chocolate goop up with my finger. Bastard. Of course, there was never just me and Amy. I look at Amy and grin. This girl doesn't need more maudlin.

"Right. We've ascertained he's a bastard. We've ascertained we want nothing more to do with him. We've ascertained we both got a lucky escape, girl. What's next on the horizon for you, Amy Hawes? Onwards and upwards."

Amy sighs. "I need to get a job. Adam persuaded me to give up HR when we met. Said working for someone else was wage-slavery, especially big business. Said I should aspire to something better. My own business. Working from home. Teaching and training. Organisational development. Online courses. That's fine when you own a house and don't rely on a regular, guaranteed salary. I need to get the job to get the house. Mortgage companies don't like sporadic income. Can't stay with my sister forever."

I recognise the patter. He played the same line with me. Repeatedly. Wage slavery. Nine to five hell. Work for yourself. What I didn't appreciate until Amy said it, was that unless you have the assets, it just makes you dependent on him, and his house. Paid employment is not wage slavery, it's borrowing power and financial independence.

"Then we have a plan! Job. House. Friends. Happiness. And you'll come to Glasgow?"
She smiles. It's nice. It lights her face up.

"Of course."

"Stay well Amy. And stay away from Adam. He'll kill you."

I don't mean literally of course. But she knows that. I have a long drive ahead of me and am rueing the decision not to book in somewhere overnight. But over-riding the tiredness is the need to get away from Manchester and all its associations and trauma.
I give Amy a hug as we part company.

"I'm glad we did this," I say to her as we walk to my car. "Stay safe. And stay in touch."

"Thanks for the candle. The chocolate. And the cake."

Cake forgives anything. My mini-convertible was back on the road. With each mile, the weight begins to lift. Good riddance Adam. You fuckwit of fuckwits.

6 ADAM: Can You Dance the Polka, My Dear?

Neeyah... bleurgh. My mouth is so dry and tacky. The corners of my mouth are crusty and stuck. I open one eye and squint into the sun streaming through the window of the spare room-office-living quarters. Fuck. Defending against the light, my arm sweeps a half-empty bag of salt n vinegar twirl crumbs all over the floor. I need to get some curtains. Who ordered sun? It's got no right to intrude.

What time is it anyway? There are the dregs of a bottle of beer by the bed. Flat and warm but it slakes the immediate thirst. Mouth feels like a badger's arse.

12.30. I feel shit in the mornings. I get the urge to roll away from the sun and pull the duvet over my head again. My head's throbbing. I'm allergic to sunlight. I drag myself out of bed and over to my laptop on the desk. I switch it on and check my phone whilst it fires up.

Four missed calls from Steve. Steve, my manic business partner. Persistent bugger. Should phone him back. The longer you leave Steve, the more wired to the moon he gets. Heading him off at the pass is usually the best strategy. He'll be sitting at around nine-hundred miles per manic-hour as it is. Do I have any paracetamol? Probably not.

Meeting with Sarah Emmerson, the American investor, 4pm my time, 11am hers. Build in showertime, a shirt iron, a tidy and some staging so the house doesn't look like a Kansas tornado hit and there's a dead witch under my fridge.

Oh fuck off, six emails from Steve, wanting me to check some stuff about the Conference for the company website. Why send one email when you can rattle out six? I bet that's what he's phoning about.

Oh, and awesome. Four tickets for the conference sold on the 'buy three, get one free deal.' A cool £3K in the bank. Need to get an actual Conference for them to go to. Maybe some speakers, workshops and a programme? But hey-ho, 99.9% of Conference success is creating the buzz. The illusion that everyone who's anyone is going, and that you're missing out if you're not. Then everyone who's anyone does go. Actually... the venue. Need to get the bloody venue sorted or there will be no Conference.

I activate the Connect2Me Connector. It's a cool little app that automatically generates connections. You just set it to go and leave it. It uses an algorithm to match likely connections based on keywords. Then it reaches out to people connected to people connected to you, asking if they'd like to connect. It even sends out a cool, personal message with their name and details from their profile. Then another friendly message when they reply. As if I'm sitting doing the legwork myself. I don't have to do anything. I don't even need to be in. Totally against the rules of Connect2Me. What the Connect2Me Mafia don't know won't hurt them. I have to make sure I don't fall asleep and leave it running for like 12-hours. Short bursts are key to not getting caught. No more than four hours in a sitting. Having my Connect2Me account suspended would be a disaster. Everything dies. My life in a business app. I check connections. I'm up at 42,764. 42,764 peeps from all over the world have connected to my Conference Network. It's true. I'm a legend. Money is easy. It's all about the buzz, man.

Oooft. My head. Pee. Then Coffee. I'll make coffee. Then I'll phone Steve. No milk. Damn Amy. There's always milk in the house when Amy's here. Clean mugs too. Where are all the sodding mugs? The kitchen's like a war zone.

"Steve. Hi. It's Adam. Sorry, had a few things to do this morning and missed your calls. Yup. Another 4 tickets. Told you it was worth the 'buy three get one free' deal. 3K. Yes. The super-early bird runs for another 4-weeks. Super early is 50% off full price. Early bird for the 8-weeks after. Early is 25% off full price. Then we whack it up. Same for group discounts. Listen, mate. We need to confirm the venue. We're going with the Hilton, yes? People are asking about the programme too. Shall I put another call out for speakers?"

It's genius this Corporate Conference malarkey. People think we are industry experts. Big cheeses. Turns out experts love other experts inviting them to speak at conferences. You don't even need to pay them. Especially if you give them free rein and let them talk about what they want to talk about. Win-win. We get interesting speakers. They get to sell their wares and a three-day jolly getting hammered on Conference wine. We theme it as best we can, put the speakers into broad topics that make it look as if we're asking important industry questions. Companies think they're missing out if they don't send at least someone to the party. I mean, how else will they find out about their competitors and product designs of the future.

Corporate training budgets are epic. Nobody bats an eyelid at £1500 plus for a three-day ticket. Bargain if they bag it early and get 50% off. Steve tells me he's netted another 6 speakers. Google, Airbnb, HSBC, BT. Amazon, that's a catch. Magic Lab too. Four women. That's good. Someone always gripes if it's an all-male line-up. He's emailed speaker profiles for the website. Excellent. We'll 'star attraction' it and see if we can't sell another throng of tickets. Good work, Steve. We need photos of speakers, some idea of speaker content, some quotes. He needs to work on the colour palettes and branding. Oh, and the bloody venue.

I don't tell him that I set up a new Trust yesterday. The 'Werner Trust.' A suitably dull and generic name. An old contact uses this law firm in the Cayman Islands. The Werner Trust is essentially a shell company set up by them. A trust on paper, but with no employees or active business operations. Offshore. Somewhere I can stash money. Nobody looks at it, money disappears and can't be traced back. It's all legitimate. Everyone does it. Respectable folk. David Cameron, Vince Cable, Gary Barlow. Everyone. Legitimate tax dodge. Money makes money. The lawyer tells me there's increasing international regulation on offshore companies. Company owners have to register. Trusts are totally different. Unregulated. My money's as hidden as if it didn't exist. Coz it doesn't. Can never be traced back to me. Still, the fewer people that know the better. My contact's not exactly known for his legitimate business. Not all offshore banking is dodgy, but I do still know some bad boys.

"You got the sponsorship packages sorted?" Steve brings me back to earth.

The sponsorship packages are my brain-child. Basically, we offer limited companies the opportunity to sponsor us. Depending on the level of sponsorship they buy, they get free branding and product advertising, some free tickets. Higher level packages get air-time at Conference, they get to host workshops, fringe events, conference dinners and entertainment. Basic sponsorship starts at £107K, rising to £982K for a Platinum Package. Steve has some notion about odd numbers being more attractive to sponsors. He says it looks like we work out the costings in detail rather than pluck them from the air. Makes us look precise, professional, value-for-money.

"Yup. Got a meeting with Sarah Emmerson scheduled for 4pm. INSpire are talking about a Platinum Deal. I'm hoping to clinch it this afternoon. Cool customer. Cool company."

"Employing the Dick-On-A-Stick-Charm?" I can hear Steve taking the piss. I think he thinks I'm some sort of Casanova character.

"For £982K, I'll happily take my pants off. I've got my work cut out. Uber-professional, doesn't crack a smile, sharp as a box of tacks. Smooth. takes no nonsense. Sucks lemons as a hobby. Wife and mother. The worst. Dick-On-A-Sticking it to her won't be easy. I hope you appreciate the lengths I go to for you. Professional on every level."

"I'm just impressed you think your cock's worth £982K. Whatever works for you, man. Just close the deal before she gets cold feet. Or realises you've a limp maggot in your pants and not a King Cobra Head. Seriously Adam. No shit. No flirting. Just close the deal. Get a signature today. Don't let her away with coming back to us. We can't afford to let her change her mind. You want me to join the 4pm meet?"

Jesus. I most certainly do not want that. Manic Steve is a loose cannon. I do not want him going off on tangents about maggots and King Cobras.

"I'm good Steve. I've more chance of closing the deal on my own. Me and the American got a good thang goin' on. If you catch my drift." I mimic her New York accent badly.

"Just don't do the accent. Keep me posted, man."

"Will do, Steve. Don't fret. You know I don't do well when you fret."

As we're talking another 6 tickets sell (two times '3

plus 1 free' deals). Another 6K worth of ticket sales. Piss easy money. I leave the Connect2Me Connector working its magic. Working from home is the biz. No-one breathing down your neck. Your life is your own. Time for a wank and a snooze before I get organised for Sarah. Clear the head. Best lay off the beer until after the meeting.

If Sarah Emmerson bites on platinum membership, I'll let the Cayman law firm handle the finances. Put the money in the Werner Trust. Looks more professional. Adds distance and anonymity. I'll sell her the fact that he's my lawyer and an old University mate. It keeps it out of Steve's mitts. I strip down to my boxers and jump into bed. Doesn't hurt to think about conquering Sarah Emmerson in more ways than one.

SHIT. 3.30pm. FUCK! How did that happen? I'd slept the afternoon away. 30-minutes to lift off. Shower. Shave. Iron shirt. Gel hair. Tidy kitchen. Stage backdrop. I'll set the webcam up in the kitchen. Pointing out towards the patio doors and into the garden. Quintessentially English. Makes the house look huge. Also, hides the beer bottles, dirty pants and general skank of bachelor living. Garden still looks great. Amy is obsessed with weeding and tidying. Unlike the house, the garden hasn't had a chance to over-run yet.

3.58pm. I'm logging on. She's waiting.

"Adam. Good to see you."

She's so full of herself. Super-American confident. She looks hot. In that effortless, New York, corporate way. Looks like a modern, open-plan, New York apartment. Wonder what she's worth?

"That garden. Your house. So...... English." She laughed. It tinkled. I've got a hard-on. Fuck. Shouldn't have wanked over her earlier. Keep it together. At least I managed to iron my shirt. Although, blast. Is that a shaving cut? Blood. It was all so quick. I suck my finger surreptitiously and daub it off.

"Sarah. You look beautiful, as always. Yes, welcome to my English Country Garden. I look forward to a time when you can visit me in person here. Smell my delphiniums, so to speak."

"All in good time Adam. Let's not get ahead of ourselves. How are the Conference preparations going?"

"Couldn't be better, Sarah. High profile speakers are queuing up. Everyone who's anyone wants a slot. Amazon, HSBC, Google, Magic Lab all confirmed this morning. Seems like our Conference is the place to be. You know this is our third year. We're the preeminent global conference for professionals leading and scaling research, design, development and innovation operations in the digital product-service continuum." I reel it off. I'd been practising that.

Fuck. I can see the round, firm darkness of her nipples through her cream silk shirt. Deliberate tease. The minx. She wants me. I see nipples standing to attention and wonder what sound she'd make if I bit on them. I dash the sweat from my brow and carry on.

"We only have one platinum sponsorship slot, Sarah. There's a lot of interest. I'm holding it for you. You're our preferred sponsor. But I'm under pressure. A lot of pressure."

"Remind me what I'm getting for my money. It's tough times for everyone, Adam. I'm under scrutiny to justify value. There are four levels of sponsorship, yes. Who else is in the picture? Who's my competition?"

"Entry level is bronze. Then we scale up to silver, gold and the ultimate, platinum sponsorship. Twenty free tickets. A keynote slot on each of the three days. Exclusive branding on all backdrops, presentation, staging and conference materials. Open access to delegates during the Conference. An exclusive workshop on Day 3, opportunity to host the main conference dinner, market stall for the three-day duration, access to delegate details post Conference. It's a pretty good deal. We've got two Cabinet Ministers and the Mayor of Manchester signed up."

"You guarantee INSpire would be the only platinum sponsor?"

"You drive a hard bargain, Sarah." Adam grinned and pushed his hair back. He winked. Was that cheesy or sexy? "But yes, for you. An ongoing collaboration with INSpire means a lot. We are prepared to give you preferential treatment and offer you exclusivity for platinum. Provided you can sign the deal today.

We have other keen investors."

"Your accent is charming, Adam. It makes me think of Colin Firth, It's almost lunchtime here. Let me fetch my tea. I think better with tea."

Colin Firth? Tea? She's flirting with me. Sarah gets up from the video call. I see bare, tanned legs. Silk shirt-dress and bare legs. Talk about using feminine wiles to drive a bargain? The minx. I like it. Two can play at that game. She returns to screen with a china cup and sits down again.

"I find I concentrate better with tea. I was born to be English."

She takes a slow sip from the cup and closes her eyes as if concentrating. She's toying with me. Never has closing a deal hinged so much on being cool. I am desperate for one of the beers in the fridge. She thinks better with tea. I think better with beer.

"I know where all the best tea is in Manchester. I hope you'll let me indulge you. Here's to a continued collaboration." I pretend to take a swig and rub my own fingers over my lips. "Have we sealed the deal?"

Who's toying with who? It's delightful. I'm still hard for her. She's powerful. Powerful, classy and rich. She leans into the camera. I got a close-up of eyes and lips. We're all about the lips, eyes and webcam. Intensio.

"We can't drink tea and not bring it to a close. I

think we have a deal, my English friend."

I let out a sigh of relief. Get it signed, Adam.

"It's a big enough deal to use my lawyers, Sarah. I like to keep it all above board and squeaky clean. I use a law firm based in the Caymans. Guy I was at University with. Salt of the earth. Good friend of mine. He's the best. Man of integrity. I'll get him to arrange the transfer of funds."

I'll put the money into the Offshore Trust Account for now. Decide what to tell Steve later. Whether to fess up to scooping the jackpot.

"Co-incidentally, I'm going to be in Manchester next month. I have some business in London and thought I'd pop up. Eyeball the Conference space and facilities. Check things are on track. See if there are mutually beneficial opportunities to evolve the relationship. Block your diary from the 18th to the 21st? Can you entertain?

She's forward! Can I entertain?

"Of course. I'd be delighted. I can book the Hilton. That's the preferred Conference venue. Or you can stay at the house if you'd rather." I motioned around me. "Quintessentially Mancunian." Shit. Once I get an army of cleaners in to fumigate that is.

"The Hilton's probably easier."

Was that a rebuff? Or is she toying? There's time

to work on her. Sign the deal Adam, sign the deal. In the bag.

"Let's get the funds transferred and the sponsorship secured in the next day or two. I'll get my lawyer on the case. Then we can concentrate on the social side of things and make your visit one you won't forget."

"I'll feel happier once I've seen things in person, met you in person, eyeballed the space, got a better picture. You'll send a list of speakers, a programme and a list of delegates through? I'd like to know who've you've contracted the visuals and audio to. We'll host the conference dinner, obviously. Lots to do. I'd like to do an elite dinner too, maybe pre-Conference. Get some of the keynotes there early. Including your politicians." She looked at her notes, "Amazon, Google, Magic Lab, HSBC, two Government ministers and a Mayor. Impressive haul. I'll type some action notes from our meeting and send them over. I like to be organised." She pours herself more tea from a pot.

"Here's to a long, fruitful and professional alliance, Adam. I like long-term collaborators I can trust. Englishmen always seem so trustworthy. It's the accent. And the tea. Proper gentlemen. Respectful. Everything above board. I'm looking forward to working with you."

"A long and fruitful alliance." I raise my mug.

I study her face. Minimal make up. Bet she looks great in the morning. High-fliers with money and power often like you to take control. I'd like to take control. Don't get distracted. It's going well. She fancies me. I think I'm keeping it professional. Not overdoing the flirting. She's coming over too. 18th to 21st was it? I'm to 'entertain.'

The least said to Steve, the better. This deal is all mine. I'm feeling very INSpire-d. All Sarah-d up. The key to business is knowing when to keep the ace up your sleeve and the cobra in your pants. I think I've earned that beer.

7 AMY: The Riptide That Pulls You Back

I'm not sleeping well.
3am….
3.30am….
4am….
4.30am….

I watch the seconds. I'm paralysed with fear. Scared to move. Scared not to move. I stay rock still. Trapped in my body. My pillow is soaked with silent tears. There is a catharsis that comes with wailing. When I wail, scream, howl, shout, kick, fight back - I know I'm going to be ok. Silent crying means all hope has gone. I'm ingesting myself. All that's left when morning comes is the saturated pillow I've melted into.

Life with Adam wasn't perfect. I don't need people telling me that. I really don't. I'm done hearing it. Woop-de-doo. It doesn't help. It just makes you better than me. You're all better than me. I've won the race to the bottom.

Life without Adam is Hell. No-one wants to hear that. So I don't tell anyone. I bleed it silently into a pillow every night.

I've been staying with my sister, her husband, my teenage nephew, Elmo the Border Terrier and four bald, ex-battery hens for five months now. They're on 24-hour suicide watch. But shhh…. don't tell Amy, she might…. err… what?... kill herself? There's not a single knife in the cutlery drawer, no chemical cleaning products, nothing but plasters in the medicine cabinet. I'm not allowed belts, ties or the cord from my dressing gown. They've replaced all the door handles with 'ligature-safe' ones.

They think I don't know. People keep asking how I am. I don't know what to say. What I want to say is that I'm a big, fat bottle of flat-coke. Black water that someone has shaken vigorously for an hour, six times a day, for the past five months. Not even the tiniest of fizz remains. Not one miniscule, transparent bubble.

I'm nothing. I need to get out of here. Hello tear-drenched 3am. I see we're back here again. Helpless and hopeless. Consume me. Then it happens. After five months of nothing. It happens. Two letters at 3.07am

"Hi"

Shit. It's Adam. Shit. Shit. Shit. No way. I sit bolt upright. My heart is pounding. Do I say something? What do I say? Can anyone see me? I run my hand through my hair. Scrub my wet face. Rub my eyes red. I'm in a Disney Film, songbirds flutter around my sleeves, squirrels sing, my fairy Godmother peeks through a crack in the putrid walls.

Someone has injected a soda-stream cannister of fizz into veins. I'm all fizzy. It's exploding round my body. I fizz-drop the phone. Shhh…. Someone will hear my energy. The change in direction. I'm alive.

My fizz-fingers don't work. Work, damn you. Even my fingers are fat. Do I text back? What happens now?

Are you kidding....? OF COURSE I TEXT BACK.

AMY: 3.09: Hi

ADAM: 3.10: I wasn't sure you'd want to hear from me.

AMY: 3.16: I'm crying Adam. You are the only person I want to hear from.

ADAM: 3:20: Did you know that Hadrian's Wall never marked the boundary between Scotland and England? Those Kingdoms never existed when the wall was built.

ADAM: 3:21: Don't cry Amy. I miss you.

AMY: 3.22: I miss you too. Are you watching a documentary about Hadrian's Wall?

ADAM: 3.26: Ha! You know me too well.

ADAM: 3.27: Don't worry Amy. Everything will be ok.

AMY: 3.28: I want to believe you.

ADAM: 3.35: Believe me.

ADAM: 3.37: Maybe best not to tell anyone that we're talking?

AMY: 3.38: Ok.

AMY: 3.52: I love you xx

ADAM: 4.42: Get some sleep x

Nooooooooo. Adam, don't go. Don't leave me. The night-time walls turn dark and putrid again. I wake up at 9am in the same position, upright in the bed, knees up to chin. I haven't moved. I'm curled around my phone. This morning smells different. The sky seems more blue, the sun a little brighter.

"Toast?" My sister places a plate of buttered toast in front of me at the table. They are trying to feed me up. Keep me alive with toast. Kieran, the monosyllabic teen has already left for school.

"You look brighter" she says, clucking round me like one of her baldie hens. "Sleep better last night?"

I nod. "I thought I might get the bus into town today," I say. "Grab a coffee. Read the papers. Watch the world go by for a bit. Can't mope about forever."

"Want me to come? Girl's day out?"

I shake my head. Emerging from a cocoon is a solitary business. "I'm good, sis. I feel good.

Honestly. Don't worry. I'm going to start looking at jobs. Today's a good day."

"Call me if you need me." She gives me a hug from behind before handing me a mug of coffee.

Two hours later, I'm showered, scrubbed and looking half decent. I've lost a load of weight. Everything is hanging off me. My black jeans are baggy round the bum and loose at the waist. Even with a belt. I try a summer dress on. Better. I'll have a look around the shops in Manchester. Maybe I'll buy something new.
I spend the bus journey to Piccadilly Gardens reading and re-reading last night's texts.

AMY: 11.32: Heading to central Manchester. Coffee and shops. Will be on my own most of the afternoon if you want to give me a call.

He's probably busy. I drop Rachel a text to pass the time.

AMY: 11.46: Hi Rachel. Out and about in central Manchester for the first time in ages. Shopping! Decided it was about time I treated myself to some clothes that fit. New jeans are practical. Heart says the girl should buy a dress.

My phone buzzes a text alert. I jump and drop it under the seat. Adam always says it. I am SO clumsy. Fat fingers that trip over their own feet.

RACHEL: 11.48: THIS girl says you should double-treat. Dress AND jeans. Plus shoes and pretty undies. Shop 'til you drop. You deserve it. I want photos! Onwards and upwards. If there's a choice to be made, phone me. Wish I was there!

Another text comes through straight after. It's a link to a Monsoon dress in the sale. "Elegance of a 50's swing dress. Beautiful floral print with shades of orange, green, white on turquoise background." Followed by:

RACHEL 12.01: This would look STUNNING on you. If only I had your legs. Pretty dress for a pretty girl. Perfect with your blonde gorgeousness. Happy shopping!

I get off a crowded bus onto an even more crowded street. My confidence in crowds is non-existent. Shame and terror swamp me. I'm burning up. Sweat is trickling down my back. I gulp for air. It's so busy. The world around me is moving in super-fast motion. I'm slowing down. Blinking in slow motion takes hours. Everyone is staring. I'm grinding to a stop. I can't breathe. I'm a fireball. Spontaneous combustion. I'm not even in my body. I force my legs through treacle-air and into a shop, desperate for a quiet space to calm down. I'm terrified of panic attacks. I find a spot of my own behind a clothes rail and hold on. That's why I've got the diazepam. Only for emergencies. I pop a tablet, close my eyes and grip the clothes rail. Focus on the breathing and the counting.

5 things I can see around me: Fat man; hooded sweatshirt; empty crisp bag; 2-pence coin; someone's knickers under gym leggings.

4 things I can touch: Clothes rail; sweater; ground under my feet; my hair.

3 things I can hear: Baby crying; someone on the phone; carrier bag rustling.

2 things I can smell: washing powder from someone's clothes; bus fumes.

1 thing I can taste: Between my teeth, mint toothpaste from this morning.

It's passing. I'm cooling down again. Things are moving at a more normal speed. There's a Monsoon in Market Street, I'm sure. I'll start there. It's not far. I think I can make it. Hug the wall so I can hold on. Prop myself up. One foot after another.

I could have kissed Rachel. It's good to have a purpose. If not for her Monsoon link, I fear I may have been stuck to a clothes rail in a cheap sports shop for the rest of the day. Returned home with some running tights. Yes! Monsoon. I see it glowing and happy. Sale still on. I feel triumphant when, against the odds, I see the real-life dress from Rachel's picture. They've still got it. She's right. It's pretty. I grab my size, run to the till, turn down the offer to try it on. Take my card, take my card, take my card. Why won't they take my bank card? Hurry up. My face begins to burn. Yes, yes, receipt in bag. Yes, sale items are non-returnable. Just give me the bag.

Mission accomplished. I want out of there. I clutch my purchase to me, safely folded in tissue paper in its 10p paper bag. Shame burns my face. They must think I'm a lunatic. I am. Fruit loopy. Adam's phrase. I feel like I climbed a mountain. I head for the comfort and reward of Starbucks, where the lunchtime rush is receding. There's a downstairs. It's quiet, dark and anonymous. The barista offers to carry my coffee downstairs whilst I collapse in a seat. I must look like a fruit loop. I pull some of the fabric out of the bag on the table, take a photo on my phone and send it to Rachel.

AMY: 2.04: Bagged!

RACHEL: 2.09: OMG, YOU FOUND IT! Today is a happy shopping day. You deserve coffee AND cake. BEAUTY-BEAUTIFUL!

Still nothing from Adam. Still busy. I send my sister a text, knowing it will reassure her.

AMY: 2:20: All good. Pretty Monsoon dress bagged in the sale. Chilling over coffee. Life is good.

She'll be happy with that. I lean back, sip coffee and feel happy.

ADAM: 2:51: Hi

He likes his 2-letter texts.

AMY: 2:52: Hi. Been shopping. Just chilling with a coffee. On my own. Phone me?

I stare at the phone for the next 47-minutes. It rings at the point when I think I should give up and get the bus back to my sister's. I stare at it for the first four rings. Eventually I pick up.

"Hi," the familiar voice.

My chest hurts. It's a struggle to keep my voice level. "Hi Adam. How are you?"

"Yeah. Ok. Surviving. Busy with conference things. It's all beginning to take off. How are you?"

"I'm ok, Adam. Surprisingly ok. I managed Manchester city centre. Did some shopping. Relaxing with coffee. I'm ok. Getting there, I think."

"I miss you, Amy. I can't believe things got so mad."

"I miss you too Adam. It's been hard. But maybe we're not so good together."

"You really believe that Amy? You don't think we're good together?"

I don't know what to say, he always gets me so confused. He sounds really hurt. I hate that. Boy Adam tears me apart. It makes me want to protect him, love him. He jumps in again whilst I'm battling brain-fugue.

"Don't you love me?"

"Of course, I love you Adam. You know I love you. I always have."

"You love me. I love you. Nothing else matters."

He's right, he's right, he's right. I know he's right. But what will Rachel say? My sister?

"My sister….. ?" I falter.

"Your sister knows nothing about us. This is our lives, not hers. Don't listen to other people. Trust yourself. Trust me. Trust in us." He sounds angry.

He pauses. For emphasis? To let it sink in? It's easy to get carried along. I want to get carried along. Carry me along, Adam.

"C'mon Amy, we've had good times, haven't we? We have fun? We need to get things back to the way they were. Before Rachel spoiled things. You were always my girl. She had no right. She never understood what we had." He scares me when he's angry.

"You make me feel like I'm going crazy, Adam. You want me. Then you don't want me. Then you want me again. I thought you didn't want to be a proper couple. I wanted to go back to counselling. You refused. I threw glasses."

"Can't live with, can't live without, eh. We're passionate, Amy. That's a good thing, no? Do you still wear that pink blouse I love?"

"What?"

"You never realise how beautiful you are. The pink silk blouse?"

"Sometimes."

"It's not the same without you Amy. The house feels soul-less without your music, your life. I dream about you all the time. I've been writing poetry. About when we met."

"I dream about you too, Adam."

"Dinner, Amy. That's all I ask. Dinner at the house. I'll cook. We can talk. Start over. One night. And if you still think it's over, that's fine. We can part as friends. We owe each other that much, don't we?"

"I don't know, Adam."

"One night, Amy. That's all. No pressure. Just food, wine and chat. Ball's always in your court. One last time. Ten years is worth that at least. I'm worried about you."

I use the napkin to wipe the perspiration off my forehead. My brain is completely fogged.

"Ok, Adam. One dinner at yours. We'll see how it goes. But no more lies."

"I've never lied to you, Amy. You mean too much to me."

I'm sure that's not right. Is it? Is Rachel not one big lie? 3-years of a lie. What about Sarah Emmerson? I'm sure there are others, aren't there? I thought he didn't want a proper relationship. Maybe I am mad. Fruit loopy. I can be better. I want marriage, babies, love.

"Ok. Just don't tell my sister. She'll go mad."

"Yes, you're right, we shouldn't tell. Absolutely. Just between us. Can you get away from your sisters on Friday? Maybe make an excuse about going to see a friend in Stockport or something? Plead an overnight away? No pressure. I don't want you driving or worrying about getting back. I always worry about you."

I was always going to go, wasn't I? How could I not? I'm weak. He deserves better. Someone like Rachel. Or Sarah Emmerson. I have a new dress and everything.

"I've just bought a new dress."

"Then how can you turn me down?"

No going back now. I've just signed myself up to a date on Friday night and lying to my sister. Excitement, trepidation and shame rolled into one.

"Ok, Adam. I'll come for dinner on Friday night."

"Perfect. We can both be better, Amy. See you around 5pm? I love you."

8 DR JIM WALKER: The Shame of Being Ordinary

"Your next appointment is here, Dr Walker," Shona's voice crackles through the intercom. It's code for 'gosh, he's turned up.'

Shona's great. It takes a special kind of person to be a psychiatrist's secretary. Unending patience, a warm smile and a wicked sense of humour. She's been mine for twenty years. The NHS keep trying to move her. I kick up a fuss. Good secretaries are worth their weight in gold. You don't give them up without a fight. She diagnoses patients in the waiting room before they get to my room. She's rarely wrong. I trust her with my life. She keeps threatening to retire. I tell her she'd miss me too much. What would she do with her time? We're both old-school NHS. You don't go home until the job's done.

She knows I'm anticipating a no-show and has the kettle boiled for coffee. I'm banking on a spare hour to catch up on admin and case notes. I didn't think I'd see Adam again. These guys get cold feet about disclosure. They run from all forms of intimacy – especially therapy. Therapy requires empathy and feelings. Processing a feeling is painful. Easier to solicit adoration and tell a joke.

"Excellent, Shona." Codebreaker 'no coffee for me, then.' "Tell him to come straight through."

A few moments later the door opens. Adam shuffles through. I don't think it's possible. He looks more dishevelled than at our last meeting. He's lost his defiance. Vulnerability bubbles over a trepid surface. Our narcissist has well and truly collapsed.

"Have a seat, Adam. Good to see you."

He sits down. Crosses a leg over a knee. The soul of his shoe is even more detached from the body. The balanced leg tremors and bounces. I can't take my eyes off his wobbling soul. It's hanging right off the shoe. He's wringing his hands too. He looks tired and restless. He can't sit still. A notable decline in a fortnight. Interesting. I'd expected him to bounce in, all cheeky-chappy, smart-arse. My superficial Good-Time-Gordon. Perennial Peter Pan. Wonder what's happened?

"How you doing, Adam?"

"Ok, I guess."

"Really?" I raise my eyebrows. Cut to the chase. "You look tense."

"I've a lot on my mind. I'll be fine."

His legs are trembling in double-time now. He's

toe tapping. Psychomotor agitation. He's going to start pacing and getting cranky in a minute. Not the first time an agitated patient has gone for me. I'm glad Shona's outside. He's got alcohol withdrawal or an agitated depression. Amphetamines maybe? Go gently, Jim.

"Sometimes just voicing it helps. You're here. I'm listening. Try me."

Adam's eyes dart around the room. He's fidgeting with the wobbly soul. He's going to have it off. I notice his socks don't match.

"Anything I say is confidential, right."

Paranoia? Nope, not expecting that. No indication of that last time. Was hoping he'd bounce in after a fortnight on antidepressants. Where's my cheeky fly-by-night? Schizotypal episode? Fascinating.

"Well, yes. Mostly. Unless you're about to tell me you've murdered someone or you're a risk to yourself or someone else. Like priests, even doctor-patient confidentiality has a limit. NHS Code of Practice. We can't condone anything illegal. Try me, you've obviously got something on your mind."

He looks at me suspiciously. Ok, try another direction. It's something illegal.

"Can't help noticing that your legs are jumping about all over the place. Restless. Fidgety. Jumpy leg syndrome. We call it psychomotor agitation. Have you noticed that before?"

"Yes, they seem to be doing it a lot at the moment."

"Uh-huh. When did it start?"

"Things got a bit crazy at work last week. I guess it started then. I put some money in an offshore trust. It's legit," he added quickly. "It's not dodgy. Just to keep it safe. My lawyer sorted it."

"If it's legit, why's it worrying you?"

"I haven't told my business partner. I closed the deal. I got the money. My lawyer. My Trust Fund. I don't trust him."

"You have reason not to trust him?" I ask, wondering where this is going. My knowledge of offshore banking and Trust Funds are limited, aside from once reading a John Grisham novel.

"I've reason not to trust lots of people. There are some that would be quite happy if I disappeared. I'm having difficulty sleeping too. It's not like me. I've always been able to sleep for Britain. I'm knackered."

"You're not sleeping because you're worried about money you've put into an offshore account and not told your business partner about?"

"Yes. There's something else. I don't know how to say it."

"Try me."

"I'm hearing voices. At night."

"Ok… well… it's quite common to have auditory hallucinations when you're stressed. Nothing I haven't seen before. Is it anyone you know? Do you recognise the voices?" Adam looks uncomfortable.

"It's my mother. This must sound like an episode of Psycho. It's not like that."

"I never said anything. Lots of people get auditory hallucinations. Lots of reasons. Lots of causes. Is it just at night? Do you get them at any other time?"

"Just at night."

"Have you been drinking when you hear her?"

"Sometimes"

"Are you seeing or smelling anything usual? Headaches? Other sounds? Weird tastes?"

Adam looks puzzled and shakes his head. "Just her. Am I going mad?"

"What kind of things is she saying, Adam? Are they unpleasant?"

"I'm bad, rotten, wicked. I'm just like my father. I'll die like my father. I'll get found out. Amy or Steve and others are no good for me. That I shouldn't keep them around. That I need money. I'll end up poor and on the streets. It's what I deserve. I'm a useless cunt. Blah Blah."

I look at my notes. I started him on sertraline a fortnight ago. Never seen it tip anyone into a psychotic episode. Rare, but I've read it can happen. More often it risks hypomania than paranoia.

"I prescribed sertraline a fortnight ago, Adam. You been taking it?"

He looks sheepish. "No. I never picked it up. Sorry."

Ah. Not the sertraline then. That rules that out. "How much are you drinking, Adam. Be honest with me. I'm trying to help. More than usual? People do when they're stressed."

"Probably."

"Beer or spirits?"

"Beer. Maybe 5 or 6 bottles."

"Every night?"

"Most."

"Drugs?"

"No."

"Do the voices ever tell you to hurt yourself? Or anyone else?"

"Sometimes. I wouldn't do it though. My girlfriend has taken overdoses. Tried to kill herself. I've seen what it does. I'm a scaredy. Too much to live for."

"Has it crossed your mind?"

"Not really."

"Do you know how you would do it, if you did?"

"No. It's just the voice. Then it passes. I'm dreaming about her too. My mum. It's weird. From nowhere. I dream of Groudle Glen. The waterwheel. The waterfall. Falling down the precipice. The same dream. Freefalling from a cliff. Maybe that's how I'd go. The ground rushing to meet me. I think it's just the stress of everything."

"I think you're right."

"I've had to increase the loan on the house. To cover the outlay for the Conferences. We have to pay the venue and hospitality costs up-front."

"What about the offshore money? Was that not to cover the Conference costs?" I grin at him. Light relief. "You can tell I don't know about these things. Psychiatrists don't earn enough."

"Yes. There's just a time-lag. Spend to accumulate and all that. The money worries are temporary. I have money coming to me. It'll all get sorted."

"Was there a reason you didn't pick up the prescription?"

"Not really, I didn't get round to it. When I remembered, the pharmacy was closed. I dunno. Maybe I didn't think tablets would help."

"I think they'll help more than the beer."

"Probably."

I look at him. I scoot my chair over to him and reach out to take his pulse. It's racing. His leg is still bouncing. He looks tired. He's developing the classic look of a drinker. He's sweating. Sweating buckets actually. It's beaded on his forehead. Damp patches under his arm and around his neck. His skin's grey. I think we need liver and kidney function tests. Full blood work up. Diabetic status. Thyroid. ECG. He doesn't look well. He's not a risk. Says he's not suicidal. I believe him. I don't think I can justify admitting him. He wouldn't go willingly anyway. He wouldn't come close to meeting the criteria for sectioning.

"Why do you think I'm dreaming about my mother, doctor? Hearing her after all this time. She's been dead, like 12 years or more. It didn't even hit me that hard. She was old. She died. That's life. I got over it. Why's she haunting me now? Why Groudle Glen? Why's it horrible things, not the nice things a mother should be saying. It's not like she abused me or anything. It's not like I hated her."

"It sounds like an acute stress reaction, Adam. That's all. When we're under a lot of stress, the brain copes with it in ways that don't always make sense. Sometimes things we think we've dealt with come back to haunt us. The good news is that stress is transient. It resolves itself. The brain usually works it all out. We just need to give it the space, time, peace and forgiveness to do it. Taking it easy. Staying safe. Being kind to yourself."

I'd made a load of random notes. Random key words. I'll need to go back later and fill the gaps. Acute stress reaction. Psychotic features. Auditory hallucinations. Negative content. Depressed presentation. Alcohol – 6 beers daily. Not actively suicidal. Low risk to self and others. Unresolved, complicated grief (mother). Money worries/risk to house. Groudle Glen. Where was Groudle Glen again? Isle of Man? I flicked back his notes. He was 5 or 6 when he lived there? The dreams, the precipice, the falling. Metaphors for something.

"Sometimes we need to grieve a death again. Especially a parent. We don't process it fully at the time and end up having to revisit it years later to complete the process. Often happens when a relationship was ambivalent or complicated or when there are multiple losses. I think yours were quite complicated."

It's a pity he didn't pick the sertraline up a fortnight ago. That would have helped. It would have maybe moved him forward a bit, helped him cope, rather than sliding him into an agitated abyss. I need to be more directive. He needs concrete instruction. We can't do another fortnight of 'I couldn't be arsed picking the prescription up.'

"I have a plan, Adam. I'm going to write it down."

I got a piece of paper and started to handwrite instructions for him.

1. PICK UP PRESCRIPTION TODAY. TAKE ONE TABLET TODAY, THEN ONE TABLET DAILY

I look up at him.

"One tablet today. One tablet daily thereafter. I'll see you again in two weeks. Two weeks of daily tablets. All going well, I may look to increase the dose, or I may add something in if the voices are still bothering you. Ok? I'll give you a new prescription. The chemist should still be open when you leave here."

2. MAKE A GP APPOINTMENT FOR BLOODS

"Make a GP appointment today. I'll email the request through this afternoon. We need to get a full blood work-up and rule out anything physical that could be bringing you down. Liver and kidney function, blood sugar, full blood count, thyroid. Let's just get you checked over." I hand Adam a new prescription. "Any questions?"

He shakes his head.

"We have a plan then. I'll see you back here in two weeks. Good food. Exercise. Fresh air. Get out every day. Walks. Sleep hygiene – don't turn night into day. Get to bed at a decent time. Calm routines. Lay off the booze. Finally, just a thought, is it worth getting some independent advice on your finances? Citizen's Advice, Money Welfare Services. Maybe they can help manage your debts, even if they are only temporary until you sort your cash flow out."

I sneak a glance at my watch. Over-time again. Adam looks as if he's had enough. I motion to his handwritten paper instructions and prescription.

"We have a plan."

He nods. "We have a plan," he repeats, child-like.

"Good. Make an appointment with Shona for two weeks-time. I need to see you again in a fortnight. Yes?"

Adam folds his handwritten note and his prescription and puts it in a pocket.

"Don't forget to pick those up," I point to his pocket as he's heading out the door, "and make an appointment with Shona."

I wonder what he's not telling me as he shuffles out the door. His dodgy shenanigans are stressing him out. I don't want to pry too much. I might discover something I have to pass on to the police. Wouldn't be the first time my notes have been lifted as part of a police investigation. If I'm going to help him, it's better not to know the details. I hope it's not too unsavoury. I can't be doing with patients losing their fingers or their houses. I'm too old for gangster nonsense. I'll get Shona to email his GP about a physical exam and blood tests. Unless I can create some time this afternoon, there won't be any case notes for the police to impound anyway. Problem solved. Just my registration at stake.

9 SARAH EMMERSON: An American in Manchester

"Ok, we leave the cooker on after burning the pizza. I let both boys divebomb into the bath from the basin. They play 'stab dad' with sharp knives, before 'how far can you lean out an apartment window without falling.' Yes?" Will laughs. "Sarah! Stop fretting! I know I'm male. But at 42, I reckon I can just about manage to not kill myself, or anyone else, in the space of a week." Will pokes the small boy hanging from his neck on either side of his ribs. "Pancakes and ice cream EVERY morning for breakfast when mom's away. Right?" He turns back to me, with a boy still dangling. "Besides there's NO WAY your mom's gonna leave us to our own devices for a week. We'll get no peace for poker, beer or wild women, will we tiger?"

"Grrrrrrr......." Oli growls back. He erupts into peals of laughter, then promptly bites his dad's ear. "Grrrr…. tiger bite."

"You'll pay for that." Will rotates the boy-tiger in his arms and holds him upside down by his ankles, threatening to drop him on his head. Oli squeals in delight.

I look at my darling husband. I never thought I could revel in such domestic bliss. I feel a surge of love. He's perfect. Life is pretty damn perfect. International financier to work-at-home mom. Breastfeeding used to be the excuse. Now I think I'm losing the killer career instinct. I'm happy being momsy. Yoga pants, sneakers, boys, toilet routines and cheerios. Is it wrong to dread putting a power suit and heels on again? I plop a kiss on Will's neck and run a hand upwards under his open-necked linen shirt, across his perfect, warm chest. Bury my nose in his man-chest smell before pouring myself an orange juice from the fridge.

"Mom's getting frisky, Ols." Will teases the boy and swivels round. "So what's this in honour of, m'lady? What you after? Aside from my body."

"The perfect man, the perfect husband, the perfect family? Lucky Charms and bed-time stories." I sigh. "Will, do I really want to travel to the UK? I'm not sure I can be bothered."

Will puts Oli down and turns his attention to me, scooping me into his arms, falling backwards into the chair so I'm sitting on his lap. He buries his nose in my hair.

"Hey, hey, hey. What's all this? Cold feet?" He pulls me into him. "Where's my front cover, Ms 'One to Watch Under 30' New York, 2011. Flights are booked. It's a week. One week. Seven days. One hundred and sixty-eight hours. We will manage without you, you know. What International businesswoman grounds herself in New York? You love your job!"

"I know, I know. Five years since I travelled out of New York. What if something happens to me? To you? Kids need parents. What if there's some sort of terrorist attack, a plague of locusts?" I cut to the chase. "Will, what if I can't cut deals like I used to? What if I'm an imposter?"

Will squeezes me again. "Is this the same woman who complains that looking after two small boys turns her brain to smoosh-mush?" He laughs. "You are Queen of the Pitch. You can persuade anyone to do anything. About time you got yourself back on that corporate gravy train. How else we gettin' our new apartment?"

I nose butt him. "That's why I married a top New York lawyer."

"Uh-huh, uh-huh, uh-huh. You mean a struggling judicial law clerk-hick from Oregon who takes the cases no-one else wants. You married me for my heart, remember. The cups of tea I make you. Not my wallet size. Oh, and my fabulous body." His turn to run his hand up the inside of my shirt and hover there, "whereas I marry a woman who can keep me in the lifestyle I have yet to become accustomed to."

"Mmm…. Like the peanut butter and jelly sandwiches, corn dogs and nuggets you once said would never pass your lips. That was until the day you had two fussy babies that wouldn't eat smoked salmon and capers."

"You can bring me back…. erm…," he pauses to think "I know, some beans on toast, how about that?" English muffins. Proper English breakfast tea. Yorkshire pudding. Toad in the Hole. I'm on a roll now. Broaden my hick-horizons, you international mom of delicacy and finery. You'll enjoy it. It will be good for the boys. We'll do boy's stuff when you're away. Football. We'll talk women. They'll have a strong, aspirational, feminist, role model who cuts top deals and takes no shit from weak, fat, English men."

"It's just a week," I say, more for my benefit that for Will's.

"Who are these guys anyway? I'm assuming none are handsome, charming aristocrats. Jane Austen, Heathcliff types? I'm assuming they're all fat, old, bad teeth, bad diets and bad breath? English heart attacks waiting to happen. I'm assuming I'm not losing my gorgeous wife to some cad in a country house?"

"I think you rightly assume they are portly, middle-aged, unattractive types," I swivel around to straddle him, face to face. "Why would I want that when I have perfection right here? Two meetings in London, then a train north to Manchester, before flying back." I kiss him. "Heathcliff was Emily Bronte, by the way."

"Eh? Who's Emily Bronte?"

"Heathcliff was Emily Bronte. Wuthering Heights. Jane Austin was Pride and Prejudice. Colin Firth. Sense and Sensibility. You need to brush up on your English romantic literature."

"Hick from Oregon," he grins, "But still not as bumbling and awkward as Colin Firth."

The Manchester connection is a new one. Two guys, new on the scene. They've run a couple of design conferences. People are talking about them. A risk, maybe. Not the usual American suspects. They do seem to know what they are doing though. They're exciting. Edgy. It's good to spot new talent, a new investment. It makes me feel alive.

I like Adam. I know he's a chancer. Too much patter. Full of himself. But he gets me excited about innovation. He's fearless. Thinks big. Digital creation and opportunity. Experimentation. Scaling up. Actually, I'm looking forward to getting out and about in the field again. Feeling the buzz and channelling it. Maybe I like the attention he gives me too.

I've sold it to the Directors. They want to invest overseas. I was damn persuasive. The UK will be where it's at in a few years' time. They say your brain shrinks during childbirth and takes a good five years to recover. I think I'm ready to hit the road again. This time, I've got everything to come back to.

I turn to Will. "What you got on today, darling?" I know he's got a couple of cases he's working on.

"Two families about to be turfed out the same apartment block. Albany. Landlord is subject to rent control based on Maximum Base Rent - MBR. We're challenging. He's a shark. Bad man. Mega-breached maximum allowable rent. Mega-breached. Thankfully our tenants have rights. They just don't know it yet. I'm working on what they're due based on a reasonable, and for reasonable, read *legal*, formula. I think we can save them. See, you married a poor but principled super-hero. I am making sure children are not homeless and can eat tonight. You?"

"Two video calls and a transfer of funds to sort out. New York transferring funds from INSpire to Manchester via Cayman. Then New York calling Manchester to confirm the transfer and organise my visit. Make sure I'm not stood-up drinking Mai Tai's on my lonesome on the Manchester Hilton rooftop."

"Will you be ok? The papers on the rent cases are all at the office. I gotta go in." Will pulls an apologetic face.

I nod. "Sure." Home working suits me well today. "I got tea. I got chocolate. Me and the boys got waffles, syrup and bacon for lunch. We are sorted. You be missing out, legal Superman."

"Always. I miss out whenever we're apart." He kisses me and lowers me off his lap.

The two boys come squealing through the door. Will Junior in pursuit of his younger brother Oli. Oli runs as fast as his dumpy, sausage, small legs will take him with the lego brick Will Junior needs.

"Lego, lego, lego, lego….. my lego," squeals Oli, running past me. "My lego." MINE. Noooooooooooo." He trips over the corner leg of the coffee table and catapults himself across the floor, screaming. Will Junior launches himself on top of his brother.

Oli howls. "Get off him Will"

"MOOOOOOOM. He's got my lego. It's the bit I need. He's been chewing it. It doesn't fit on the other bits now. It's chewed. Squished. Not square. It's got *teeth on it*." Will is plaintive. "MOOOOOOOOOM. TEEEEEEEEEETH."

Oli promptly sticks the plastic brick in his mouth and grinds his teeth on it. Big Will picks a boy up under each arm and carries them out the room, towards their bedroom, squealing. Will Junior is still grumbling about lego and teeth.

"Give your mom some peace, you horrors. Settle down. Clothes. Now."

I chuckle. I've no doubt the place will run like clockwork whilst I'm away. I'm sure I'll miss them much more than they'll miss me.

Time for a run before Will has to leave for the office. Clear my head and get organised for the day. My mom's coming round to take the boys to the park and organise lunch. As good at spinning plates as I have become, I can't take video meetings and manage the boys. I need to shut myself in a room, concentrate. Assume the corporate 'I am an in-control business-woman,' head free from lego squeals and boys flooding the bathroom.

Meet with the Directors at 10am. Legal at 11.30am. NY Team meeting 12.15. London One at 1pm. London Two at 2pm. Manchester at 3pm. Today's priority - make sure we secure the exclusive sponsorship deal with Manchester. Get that signed off. Get the money transferred to secure it. INSpire can't lose the opportunity now the Directors are on board. I'll look like an ass if that happens. Persuasion needs rapid follow through. Once that's in the bag, I can concentrate on the UK itinerary. Maybe then, the anxiousness will go and I can enjoy the planning. I'm always happier when I'm organised and there's no uncertainty. Business first.

Ok, run. I love New York, but Will's right. Now I'm over the mom-guilt, I'm looking forward to escaping and getting my head firmly back in the game. Re-size the brain. What is business if not international. I grab my sneakers. God, getting on a plane. Airport control. Security and baggage scans. It seems like a forgotten world. Business class travel. Always business class.

"Quick run, Wills. Back in thirty? That ok?"

"Perfect darling," the disembodied voice over the childish squabbles coming from the bedroom.

We've got this parenting thing licked. Between us we fit together like jigsaw pieces. It just works. We can do business and parenting. Everyone in New

York does.

I'm back, sweaty and just jumping in the shower as he's heading out, suited up for the office. He promises to pick up dinner on his way home. Twenty minutes later and my mom arrives, much to the glee of the boys who know how to wind their grandma round their little fingers. Why is it that all the rules and chaste living you impose on your own kids goes out the window when you have grandchildren? From too much TV to an open biscuit barrel. They adore her. I adore her too. Most of all I love that her presence gives me peace and quiet to get on with work. She's brought lunch. Biscuits and a new board game too. She spoils us all.

The day speeds by. It always does. With multiple cups of tea. The Directors are happy. I have the go ahead to transfer funds today. I've authorised the Cayman Island law firm as instructed by Adam. All good. Seems above board. Transactions go smoothly. Done. Boxes ticked. My diary is filling up for my week away. Three days in London. Three days in Manchester. Three days for Manchester seems quite a long time, but it's a city I've never been to. I've done London loads. Edinburgh, Dublin, Bristol too. Don't tell anyone but I'm a little bit obsessed with Adolphe Valette and L.S. Lowry. Manchester art. Valette especially. In my head that's what Manchester looks like. A world of impressionist, urban street scenes from the 1900's. Romantic lilac, blues and greys, morphing into Lowry's iconic matchstick factory people. Adam seems impressed that I know who Valette is. Of course I know who he is. History of Art Degree. Dissertation on the influence of Parisian impressionism. Not only Lowry's tutor and mentor, but acclaimed French impressionist in his own right. Bringer of a Parisian Impressionist mecca to an industrial Northern English city. Were it not for Valette's Victorian rooftops and street scenes, there would be no Lowrian matchstick people. I tell Adam so.

"So, I want to squeeze in Manchester Art Gallery AND The Lowry. Yes?" I tell Adam excitedly on our video call. "I mean, work. Yes. That's the priority. I need to see the venue, sort out the hospitality, menu and dinners. Work out the branding. Confirm the programme. I need delegate lists, organisations and contact details. Fringe events. Workshops." I tick things off mentally in my head. Can't let the Directors down. "We can squeeze in a couple of art galleries, can't we? I mean it is the main reason INSpire is coming to Manchester." I grin at him, like a child. "Aside from the business opportunities and financial future our companies will share." Fake Russian accent, "for we *will* conquer the world of design ops and digital innovation, Adam-Manchester."

"Sarah, Adam-Manchester could not live with himself if he didn't schedule in plenty of time to do both Manchester Art Gallery and The Lowry! I can't buy you the real thing, but maybe we can find space in your suitcase for a couple of Valette prints. A moment of Victorian Manchester for your swish New York apartment. Remind you of the romance of northern grime. I'm amazed you know who Valette is. Lowry, I can understand. Valette never really gets the attention he deserves. Believe it or not, I have a Valette print hanging in my hallway. He's a favourite of mine too."

"Student days. I majored in History of Art. The French Impressionists. Valette was French," I say by way of explanation.

"You're telling a Mancunian that Valette was French?" Adam winks at me. I like this side of him. "Your next piece of Mancunian homework, by the way, is to watch the Mike Leigh film 'Peterloo' before you come over. I think it was released 2018 or 19. Peterloo Massacre. 1819. Peaceful pro-democracy protest of 100,000 unarmed people that went wrong. Seed of reform and birth of national journalism. Explosive. You'll love it. We can visit St Peter's Field too. Do the galleries and St Peter's Field in a day."

"As long as we get the work done," I wink back at him. "You determined to educate me?"

"Educate you? I'll make you want to relocate here by the time I'm done. You'll not want to leave." Adam paused for a second. "Funds all transferred? My legal guys sorted everything? £982K done and dusted?"

"Indeed," I reply, nodding. "£982K transferred today. New York to Manchester, via Cayman. Here's to a long and fruitful alliance." I raise my tea mug to him.

We cover all the nuts and bolts of the sponsorship, investment and funding. It really is mainly business. Will would approve. Adam is like a squat English

Bulldog next to my sleek American Greyhound.

"Actually Sarah. Talking of making the most of your visit. In all seriousness, it would be an honour to show you around. Combine work and pleasure. Manchester is great. I'll certainly show you the city." He pauses. Adam hesitant? That's a first. Hesitant or shifty? Whatever it is, it's gone. He carries on. "This is left field. Very left field. But will you let me take you for a day trip to the Isle of Man. Before we land in Manchester proper. We can work on the boat. One day, Isle of Man. Two days Manchester. I swear it's like no-where you've ever been. You're so close. Seems a missed opportunity not to show you my homelands."

I've never even heard of the Isle of Man. I'm googling as he speaks. 'The Isle of Man, a self-governing British Crown dependency in the Irish Sea between England and Ireland. It's known for its rugged coastline, medieval castles and rural landscape, rising to a mountainous centre, with Celtic and Viking heritage.' Then randomly, 'The Isle of Man TT is a major annual cross country motorcycle race around the island.'

"Celts, Vikings, castles and the Isle of Man TT," I laugh. "Less than ideal as a conference venue." If I thought the Isle of Man TT was a random contribution, Adam makes it more random.

"And the Isle of Man Fairy people. Don't forget them. The Fae is what makes the island truly magical. You have to pay passage in coppers and you can't stop dancing as you cross. Or the fairy folk take you to the Underworld."

And suddenly I'm hooked. An escape from Barney the Dinosaur, brain smoosh and corporate finance. A whiff of adventure. I laugh at the nonsense.

"Work Adam, we need to get the work done. It has to be about the work."

"Trust me, we will. We can do all the prep on the boat. Have a Fae adventure, feed our souls, then hit Manchester running. All work and no play…. It will be fun and productive. You'll see. Just trust me. It's called Northern hospitality.

"This is purely a business trip, Adam-Manchester. Figures, finance, business opportunities, networks, design ops, digital innovation. I'm a happily married woman. Cards on the table. Professional. No funny business."

Adam feigns a hurt face. It makes me smile.

"Sarah, I'm shocked that you would think anything else of me. Hurt, even. Trust me. Some sea-wind in our lungs, fae magic in our soul and the business becomes even more viable. It's settled. Take the train from London to the ferry at Heysham. Pack light. We'll do London to Manchester via Groudle Glen. I'll get you safely back to the Manchester Hilton by evening. Me and the fairy people never come to blows. You're in safe hands. No funny business. Merely being the perfect, honourable International

Conference Host."

Is it ok to build some sight-seeing into a business trip? Of course it is. All work and no sight-seeing, makes Sarah the dullest mom of International delicacy and finery. Manx Kippers, google says. That's what the Isle of Man is famous for. Not sure I can get them through customs for Will. Not sure he'd appreciate some smelly fish sweated out in a suitcase. But maybe I'll take everyone back there in the summer. We'll all go and dance for the fairies. The boys will love it. Tie it in with the TT. What small boy (or big boy) doesn't like a high-speed motorcycle race round a Fairy Island. Manx cats. Cats without tails. Magical. I can't wait for my UK travels.

He's a gentleman. It's all about being the perfect host. Mostly business, 95% business with a tiny bit of sight-seeing. Life's all about the 5%.

"Sarah…" Adam jolts me back from tail-less cats and motorcycles. "Keep it a secret from the family. The world is full of magic things. Keep the photos and adventures for your return. The greatest secrets are always hidden in the most unlikely of places. The boys will love it all the more. Trust me."

I do. I trust him. I will keep it quiet. Shhhh…..

10 AMY: Intoxicating Omnipotence

Bottles and bottles on the shelf. Hundreds of bottles. 4 levels of them, ground to overhead. Why are there so many? Do they taste that different?

I want to buy champagne. Decent champagne. Not cheap stuff. They're all blurring into the same giant bottle, with eyes, teeth and menace. I feel myself hyperventilating. I'm absolutely roasting. I don't want my sister to see I'm dressed up. I've got an oversized, stripey-fluffy jumper and a jacket over my dress. I'm melting. The sweat's running down my back. I can feel a trickle down the side of my face. I'll leave them in the car when I get to Adam's. I'm scared someone sees me. I can disappear in layers. Blend into the shadows.

Definitely not Tesco's champagne. Even the premium Tesco's one doesn't say forgiveness or love. Tesco's champagne makes me think of fish and chips out of newspaper. Moët & Chandon, Taittinger, Bollinger. I've at least heard of them. Bollinger costs most. I'll take that. It's on the top shelf. That's where they put the best ones.

I want tonight to be special. Hedge bets with beer. Where is the beer? FROGS! Why is not in the same aisle? Why do they split the booze up and put nuts and crisps in-between? Next aisle. Breathe, Amy. Craft beer. Six different bottles. Chance says I'm bound to hit on at least a couple he'll like. One with an angry ferret on the label. One with an evil goblin. Obviously, beer labels are aimed at male shoppers.

Finally, cake. It worked before. Nothing says forgiveness quite like cake. Wish I'd picked up a trolley rather than a hand basket. Carrot and walnut with frosted icing.

I park two streets away. Just in case my sister drives past, although I'm not sure why she would. Adam will approve of the secrecy. I've got one of those heavy-duty, 'bag for life' shopping bags. I clink noisily up the street. Every step clinks all 7 bottles in unison. The whole neighbourhood can hear. Bottle cacophony. So much for discretion.

I'm standing outside his door, feeling naked but cooler without the jumper and jacket. He said 5pm. I sat in the car for forty-five minutes. I didn't want to be early. My phone says it's exactly five o'clock. Shit. I stuck a toothbrush, some knickers, a deodorant and my make-up bag in the Tesco bag. He said overnight, didn't he? I'm not being presumptuous. I'm so nervous. It's like a first date all over again. Trepidation, uncertainty, hope, with a major dose of terror. New underwear. I jump, even though it's me that presses the doorbell. I jump again when I see the shadow approaching the door through the frosted glass. I should have taken a prophylactic diazepam. I was worried it would floor me. I've not eaten anything since yesterday morning. I want my tummy flat. I dry my palms on my new Monsoon dress. He speaks first.

"Hi"

Do I hug him, kiss him, shake his hand? Probably not on the doorstep. He'd hate that. Why is this so awkward? I thought he wanted me here.

"Champagne and beer," I lift up my bag. My doofus moment. Like Jennifer Gray when she berates herself for the 'I carried a watermelon' comment in Dirty Dancing.

"Come in."

We're not embracing on the doorstep. Ok. That answers that. I dump the bag in the hall, with an extra-loud clink. Jeez, why do I take up so much space.

"Hi," I'm standing in front of him.

"I'm glad you're here," he says. Well, that's a good start. "I like your dress."

Ok, go in for the embrace now. That's the cue. I put my arms around him. "Thanks for inviting me." I've made it hard for him not to kiss me. And there it is. Not the passionate, falling into each other, ripping each other's clothes off, tongues and lips I was fantasising about. Dry and slightly maiden aunt. I try pressing into him and running my hands over his back. I can escalate into passion. I want to. He kisses me back and pulls away, still holding my waist, looking at me.

"Amy, I am so sorry. I have a meeting that I have to take first. I am really sorry. It was the only time we could manage. I won't be long. I didn't think you'd mind. It's really important. A big financial investment. If I don't meet with the investor to confirm the detail, I'll lose it. You don't mind, do you?"

I don't know what to think. I feel crushed. I was hoping we'd be in bed by now, leaving a trail of clothes up the stairs. That's the fantasy reunion.

"Is it the American investor? Sarah What's-her-face? From New York?"

"Yes. I'm sorry. I would absolutely have cancelled or done it another time, but it was the only slot we had. Time difference is a pain in the arse. I'm so close to clinching a massive deal. I don't want to lose it. You really don't mind, do you? It's just work. It's not like me and you. Me and you, well we're really important. After this meeting, I'm all yours. All night. I promise. It'll be special. It's just……" he looked at me and shrugged, "well this is money. We need money. I want to be able to look after you."

He kisses me again. A peck. Dry lips. No lingering. I once read that a proper kiss needs to last seven seconds to trigger the oxytocin rush. That's ok though. I'm not sure I can muster lingering and tongues.

"It's fine Adam. I'll be fine. Maybe I can do a naked dance in the background or something. Where she can't see me. Entertain you."

I tease him, try to make light of the situation. Swallow the disappointment. The sick feeling. I am being unreasonable. Selfish. He can't help it. It's work. He needs money and I'm not really earning any. It's reasonable. He looks absolutely horrified though. I want to laugh. I have a vision of an old 80's TV programme. A naked lady dancing seductively in a flame as the backdrop to his meeting.

"I was thinking you could make yourself comfy in the living room. TV, music, wine. Whatever you want. I don't do well with distractions, Amy. I need to concentrate. It's just a work meeting."

"I'm teasing Adam. I'll be fine. Go meet. Like you say, we've got all night and this is work. Can't be helped. I can entertain myself for an hour or two. Don't worry about me."

"You're a star, Amy." He pecks me on the lips again. "Love you, baby. You're the best. There's wine in the fridge. Nuts, crisps, chocolate and stuff. Make yourself comfy. I'll be as quick as I can." He starts up the stairs and turns back "I love you." I believe him.

"I love you too Adam. Go sock it to them. You're brilliant. If I had the money, I'd invest in you."

This is weird. I pace the room, unable to settle. I feel bad for being annoyed. The weight of shame again. A bad person. It's work. He can't help it. I'm more important than any of it. He said so. And he loves me. He's tidied the house. I always do the tidying. I was expecting it to be a heap. He's run a hoover round and taken the plates and glasses through. That's touching. He cares. I don't feel like wine. I don't like drinking as a solitary activity. Years of therapy drummed it into me that alcohol is a depressant. I put the kettle on for coffee. There's a massive pile of Adam's dirty washing in the utility room. May as well stick that on. I'm not doing anything else. I sort the coloureds and the whites and put a load on. I wash the dishes, plump the cushions, fold the blankets. It's my house, but not my house. Familiar but cold. I feel like a ghost. 6pm. That's an hour in. Surely, he must be close to finishing. Should I? Probably not. He'll kill me. Will I? Yes. Creep upstairs and have a listen. Only to see if it's close to ending. He'll never know. Stealth mode. In the shadows. I've already taken my shoes off.

He's in the 'office-spareroom-bedroom' room. I can hear laughing. I can hear a woman's voice. American. They're both laughing. A smidge closer. I can hear words now. Groudle Glen. I heard Groudle Glen. Molly Quirk. Bibaloe Walk. Douglas. Isle of Man. They're talking about the Isle of Man. Not investment or sponsors. He's telling her the polar bear story. Visitors to Groudle Glen would stand on the iron bridge and look down on two chained up polar bears. Sea Lion Rocks. A narrow-gauge railway ran through the headland so visitors could look down on the animals. During the second world war the animals were 'released' into the wild Irish Sea to haunt the Isle of Man. Adam and I have walked that glen many times. Stood on the bridge. Listened to waves crashing on rocks. Felt the surf in our faces.

It's his place. They're talking about the Heysham Ferry. About the Manchester Hilton. I feel sick. I've not heard the conference mentioned once.

Rachel pops into my head. 'She was just some random woman I spoke to a few times on the internet.' Adam has a habit of bending truth round corners, upside-down and back again until your head explodes. The one who's mad.

My mother always said no good comes of listening at doors. The only person you hurt is yourself. I creep back downstairs. I'm sick in the downstairs toilet. I really need something to eat. I pour some nuts into a bowl and turn the television on. Anything to drown out the laughter and voices. Sometimes it's better not to know. Does he speak about Groudle Glen to everyone? I send a text:

AMY: 18:28: Hi Rachel, how are you? Forgive my randomness. Indulge me. What do you know about Groudle Glen?

RACHEL: 18:35: Well! That's a place I haven't heard about for a while. Groudle Glen, polar bears and sealions. Not to mention fairies, dancing, Little Isabella and the murder of Molly Quirk. Some of Adam's favourite pillow talk. You're not with him, are you?

So, he did talk about it with everyone. It wasn't just me. It wasn't our place after all. Reused material. Either we're all special, or none of us are. Pillow talk. Interesting turn of phrase. She's right. It always felt intimate. Special. Lovers.

AMY: 18:42: No. Don't worry. Just watching something on TV. It sparked a memory. I'm fine.

RACHEL: 18:46: You ok, Amy? Want to talk?

AMY: 18:48: No. Honestly, I'm fine. Just chilling out with some TV

RACHEL: 18:52: As long as you're ok. You know where I am if you need me. Don't hesitate xx

I can hear Adam moving about upstairs. It sounds like he's jumping into the shower. Call must have ended. I'll open the wine. Recline. Make it look like I've been lying on the sofa the whole time.

"Hi," Adam appears, damp and tousled, through the living room door. I'm projecting the ultimate in laid back cool. Reclining, wine in hand. Uncomfortable push-up bra. I do my best to smile.

"Hey," I reply. "Successful meeting?"

"Very. All good. With any luck, we'll get a windfall from these conferences. Not have to stress about money." He comes over, pecks a kiss on my lips. "I'm so sorry about all that." He looks at his watch. "7pm. Longer than I meant to be."

"It's fine." I smile again. "I've been relaxing." I lift my wine up. "Plus, I'm a glass up on you."

"Come to the kitchen and speak to me whilst I cook. I bought steaks."

Wow! Adam's cooking. I can count on one hand the number of times Adam has cooked a meal for me. He pours himself a wine and gets pans out. I perch on a stool at the kitchen table. It's all so familiar.

"I don't think I've ever seen you cook steak," I say. "Want me to do it? I don't mind."

"Nope. You sit there. Everything's in order. You are my guest. You don't lift a finger." He really was trying. "Sit there, look beautiful, feel happy. I'm so glad you came. What did you tell your sister in the end?"

"Just what you said, staying with Carolyn in Stockport. I'm not expected back until tomorrow."

"More wine then," he runs his fingers softly over the back of my neck as he tops me up.

No food, apart from a handful of nuts. I can feel it going to my head. I know better than to mention the upstairs conversation. Forget it. Nothing good ever comes from earwigging.

I have to commend him. He does a great job with the steaks. Perfectly cooked. Butter soft. Steak chips, salad and a yoghurt and peppercorn sauce. I'm starving.

"Bollinger," I announce. "Doesn't the occasion

call for Bertie Bollinger?"

"You bought champagne?" He puts his hand on mine. I feel goosebumps. A warm glow. I did good.

"Bertie Bollinger. Not just any champagne." I'm already tipsy. "You do the honours." I hand him the bottle. "Pop it, Bollinger-Boy." I know where the champagne flutes are. I don't think he's got a clue. I dance back to him and wiggle in front of him with the glasses. A clumsy attempt at seduction. "When did you suddenly learn to cook?"

"I'm full of surprises. I got pudding too." He gets up and goes to the fridge. "Lemon mousse. Ready-made, but still. Thought's there. "And hey," he holds the pots aloft, "it's pudding." He plops down a pot and tops up my glass again.

We scrape slurpily to the bottom of the sweet pots before carrying the remainder of the champagne to the living room. This is the version of Adam I love. I could wrap myself around him. I switch on the fairy lights that sit above our prints. Adolphe Valette. He turns on the music. We huddle under the same fleecy blanket. I lie between his legs. I decide I like champagne. Not as much as pink wine. But Bollinger is definitely ok. He pours me a pink wine and opens a beer for himself. Angry ferret beer.

"Did I choose ok?"

"Perfectly. You chose perfectly." He squeezes me with his thighs. Adam's muscular thighs were always my favourite bit of him. He's taken his jeans off to get comfy. We watch a film before Adam suggests going to bed. I'm acutely aware we've not shared a bed for a long time.

"Shall we just hold each other?" he says, following me upstairs. "I've had too much to drink to do anything. I'm not sure I can…" he hesitates "perform?" He looks at me sheepishly. "Sorry. Shoulda drunk less. Doofus."

"I'd like that."

It takes the pressure and expectation off everything. Holding is good. Naked to naked is good. I brush my teeth, sneak off my clothes quickly and dive under the duvet. First Adam wraps his leg around me, then his arm. I fit perfectly into his chest. I stroke his chest hairs. He smells boozy. So do I, probably. He feels peaceful. I feel his breathing deepen first. He's falling asleep. Snoring gently. Little snuffles. I'm not far behind.

If I'm honest, I'd hoped for sex. Sex signifies ownership. It's symbolic. Seals the deal. But this is fine. I sleep better than I have for months. Years even. I don't even move. Blissful sleep. Safe. The constant terror of abandonment is quieted. A potently addictive drug. Effective in the short term. Feeding the now is all that matters.

I escape the early morning wakening that's been plaguing me for months. The constant black cloud that consumes me when I wake has gone. It's short-lived. Adam is not in the bed. I'm on my own. The space beside me is empty. I look at the clock. Just after nine. Late for me. I pull on one of Adam's t-shirts and my knickers from beside the bed, pad off through the house. Unravel the mystery of the missing lover. Not so much of a mystery. He's in the spareroom-office-bedroom. I creep in, barefoot. Tiniest of barely there tip-toes. I don't know why. When Adam is asleep, a marching band can't wake him. He's sleeping in the bed. He must have got up in the middle of the night to do some work. There are a couple of beer bottles by the bed. His MacBook has slipped off his body. It lies, still open beside him. It's not the most attractive sight. Just to reinforce it, he gives a snort and several snores, rolls over. He's all caught up in the power cable. I wonder if anyone has ever strangled themselves in bed with a laptop cable.

I know better than to wake him. Or try to. I know better than to touch his MacBook, even on the premise of safety. He'll assume I'm prying into all his secrets. I creep back out again. What do I do? I told my sister I'd be back at lunchtime. It's only just after 9am. I run a bath to pass the time. The good thing about the house is the space. You can co-exist and barely see each other. We've been doing it for years. He's left the heating on. Small mercies and all that. I could weep at being alone again. There's a poignancy about putting yesterday's dress on. The morning after walk of shame. Without the actual sex either. Wish I'd brought fresh clothes. He's still sleeping. Even though I'm banging about. I sigh. See, this is what got me into all the glass-throwing bother last time. He can be a bit selfish, I guess. Mornings were never really his thing. He's been working hard. He needs the money. Maybe we're both a bit selfish. Confusion reigns. I make coffee. Hang the load of washing out that I did last night. Do last night's dishes. Take the garbage out. Send my sister a text:

AMY: 11.14: Leaving Stockport shortly. Had a great night. Don't worry. Home soon.

Guilt is knowing you've done something bad. Shame is knowing you are bad. Then to Rachel:

AMY: 11.21: He really was a selfish prick, wasn't he? Do you ever truly get over loving someone who hurt you?

RACHEL: 11.26: He IS a selfish prick and always will be. And YES, you'll get over him and find someone worthy of your love. He is not. P.S. Guess what? I have a DATE tonight. A proper date. #life-after-pricks. When you coming to Glasgow? Xx

Well, I know it's not Rachel he was messaging during the night. Sarah Emmerson? Someone else? Everyone else?

AMY: 11.30: Soon, I promise. #life-after-pricks, lol. Good luck for tonight.

I creep upstairs and stick my head into the spare-room-office. Sleeping and snoring. I silently gather the beer bottles and take them downstairs. Gather my stuff together, not that there's much. A toothbrush and some underwear. I leave the cake we didn't eat. Put the empty champagne and beer bottles into the recycling. I quietly let myself out, closing the door gently behind so as not to wake him. I remember that I parked two streets away. Shame is a two-street walk that tells me, even with champagne and a Monsoon party dress, I'll never be good enough.

11 RACHEL: A Normal Kinda Guy

I know, I know. I'm wicked. It makes me chuckle. Stick that knife in Adam's chest and wiggle it round a bit. Partly because I have an impish streak. Partly because I'm nosey (and let's face it, he is a fascinating case study). But also, partly because it's hard to completely wipe someone you once loved out of your life in one go.

What do I do? I send a connection request to Sarah Emmerson on the business app, Connect2Me. There's a button that says 'connect' and it sends a friend request - a bit like Facebook. Generally, I can't be arsed with Connect2Me. Maybe because Adam introduced me to a side of it that seems seedy. People connecting to sell things, 'create a buzz' or use other people to make money. It's shallow.

The Corporate Conferences malarky is an internet scam. Adam's a modern-day snake oil merchant. Hooking people up to sell fresh air and rhetoric. Or as he says, 'A free spirit, Rachel.' 'At least I'm not a public sector *one-bar-heater,* like you.'

Call it 'innovation' or 'design,' don't pay your speakers ('they're be proud to be part of the brand, Rachel') and charge your guests £2K a pop. Then you don't need a proper job. You can drink beer, sleep all day and spend your spare time waving at strangers on social media waiting for the next great thing, or the next trophy girlfriend to fall into your lap.

Sarah Emmerson looks very glamorous. Much more of an ego trip for him than Amy or I. International businesswoman, looks like a model. A conquest truly worthy of his brilliance. Until someone better comes along that is. I get the standard reply back.

'Hi there. Thanks for connecting. Do we know each other?'

'Distant mutual connection, I think. Adam Waters.'

'Yes! Adam. He's great. Quite the livewire. You work in design too? Adam and I are meeting up in Manchester next week. Business Venture. Corporate Design Networks.'

'No. I'm just a doctor, lol. These things are beyond me. I'm a techno-luddite. Enjoy Manchester. It's a great city.'

Leave it there Rachel. Anything further just gets stalker-like. I don't want to know. The wound is sutured shut. Healed over. No point in picking a scab. I don't feel anything at least. She's welcome to him. Better he stays away from Amy too. I worry about Amy. Recent texts are strange. The Groudle Glen text. What's that about? She's fragile. Adam's a bastard. If there's still gain to be made from sucking more out of her, I'm sure he'll try. Funny enough, I got an email from him a few days ago. I block him everywhere except email. If there's a way to block emails, I don't know how. He can't phone, text or get me through gaming routes. Short of turning up at my door or emailing me, his options are limited. What is it they call it, 'narcissistic supply?' These guys keep coming back as long as there is a possibility you'll bite and they can pull you back in again. It's a one-liner.

'Hi Rach. Just wanted you to know I still think about you.'

Bleurgh. Yes, because I'm far too good for you, you asshole. I don't say it. I know better. Don't engage. That way lies insanity. I recognise the strategy. Gotta love a trier. Don't reply. Delete the email. Doesn't mean his name in my in-box doesn't cause a sharp stab to the heart. Even after all this time. How long? Nine months since Amy's overdose? Enough time and distance to realise how screwed up the whole thing is. Some people never get over the personality fractures caused by childhood trauma. If I'm ever lucky enough to have kids, being there for them transcends everything. Turning them into happy, compassionate human beings. What's the famous quote, 'they fuck you up your mum and dad, they may not mean to, but they do.' The splendid bugger, Philip Larkin. Maybe Guy's the guy. Ha! Yes. The new date is called Guy. I laugh about it with folks at work. Jokes too numerous to mention. Wonder what this Guy's like. Date with a Guy. Better than all the other Guys. It goes on. I enjoy being ribbed. Who knows? Maybe this Guy will be the one. Ever hopeful. Finally, Rachel's Guy.

I lay out three different outfits on the bed. Basically, it comes down to smart jeans or a dress. First date tonight. An actual date. Proper old fashioned one. Meal out. Nice restaurant. University Lecturer from Edinburgh. Dr Guy, the Biochemist. We've been chatting online for a month. Work is mad. It's takes a couple of weeks to find a day we're both free. I'm late finishing work, he offers to come through to Glasgow. Easier than Manchester at least. A forty-five-minute train journey this time. It's slow. Normal. Chatting about all sorts. Work. Family. Walking. Holidays. Books. Films. Why my day was shit. Why his was dull. The patient that brought me a home-made cheesecake full of dog hairs. The day he had a breakthrough with epigenomes. That kind of thing. It's not gone at the breakneck rollercoaster speed that me and Adam went at. A month in and no declarations of love. Nowhere close. We'll not end up in bed on date one. He has to get the last train back. The jeans have it. And a crossover top, with just a subtle hint of ample boobage. Café Gandolphi's in the Merchant city. Old medical student haunt and one of my all-time favourite Glasgow eatery-drinkery's.

When you're a doctor, people think it's easy to find dates. It's not. It's impossible. People assume that you're unavailable or scary. You work weird hours, you invariably get caught working late. You can't down tools, switch your computer off and go home. The only people you meet are a steady stream of patients in various states of health. Dates think you spend your days looking at bodies. Trust me, when a doctor looks at a body, they see….. yup, skin, organs, weird swellings and smelly infections - a body. A set of systems, structures and functions. Why it's working, why it's not. When I look at a date's body, the last thing I compare it to are the other thirty elderly, malfunctioning ones I see most days. It's why doctors date other doctors. I somehow manage to miss the boat, date some duffers, focus on my career, and all the good ones get taken.

Now I stand at Glasgow Queen Street Train Station, and wait on my date guy, Guy showing up. I feel nervous all over again. Train shows up. Date guy, Guy shows up. We hit Waxy O'Connor's for a drink first off to break the ice. Waxy's is a Glasgow institution. The first pub we fall into on exiting the train station. Unlike most train pubs, it manages to be cool and full of nooks and crannies. The entrance is lit up with these huge flaming torches. A massive fairy tale tree is carved through the centre of its two floors. It reminds me of a Harry Potter set.

"Welcome to Glasgow," I raise my glass to him and grin.

"The dark side," he grins back, "my mother told me to watch out for the wild women of Glasgow."

"My mother told me Edinburgh men speak posh, but always make you get the round in."

He laughs. "Touché, Dr Donaldson. I see I've met my match."

This is fun. He's fun. We have a couple drinks before strolling to Gandolphi's for an 8pm reservation. Got his own place in the West End of

Edinburgh, near the city centre. Fountainbridge. Been single for a year. Two previous long-term relationships. So far so, good. Normal. I like normal.

"You ask lots of questions," he says taking my hand as we walk, "must be the doctor in you. My turn. Last relationship?"

"Nine months ago. Three years."

"Reason for break-up?"

Oooft. Right to the point. "Some people are too broken to be fixed, even by love."

"Good answer. Over him?"

"Oh yes. Very. My self-worth is still intact."

"Dating or settling down type of girl?"

"This is like quick-fire, twenty questions. I'm on dating Mastermind." I laugh. "When's it my turn again? How about if I say, want to travel a bit, not too long, then settle down. One last adventure."

The waiter takes our coats in Gandolphi's and shows us to a booth at the back.

"Nice," he nods approvingly, looking round.

"One of my favourite places. The fish chowder is the best you'll ever taste. Makes it on to all the 'top places to eat in Glasgow' lists."

We order some wine and some food. The topic gets back to travel again. I've been formulating a plan around travel for a while. My feet are itchy for an adventure.

"I've been thinking about locuming. Short term contracts. Basically, work for 6-months and then travel for 6-months. South America maybe. I've always wanted to go, but not just a couple of weeks. Longer. Live the real experience. Do it justice. Six-months of travelling. Backpack, hiking boots, passport, toothbrush and knickers. Machu Pichu, Sacred Valley, Bolivia, Bogota, Buenos Aires. Semi-planned it."

It's true. I stick things into a folder most days. Along with a spreadsheet of flights. Do I want a companion? Do I want to travel solo? I haven't decided. He reads my face.

"I could take a sabbatical, if you fancy a companion. Think we'd survive six-months? If I bore you, or smell too bad from the humidity, just abandon me in a South American country of your choosing. Might be cool to be dumped in Rio de Janeiro. Seriously, it's one of the few perks of university life. Unpaid leave for adventure. My flat is rentable."

That takes it from fantasy to reality. Maybe. I mean, what's the worst thing that could happen. You can break up in Glasgow, Edinburgh, Manchester or Rio. I point my soup spoon at him.

"That, date Guy, is definitely worth some thought."

Turns out he's been to Argentina. Who knew biochemists get to go to fancy conferences in Argentina. Argh.. swoon. He's been to Iguazu. I have waterfall envy. He says you can get close to them, get soaked by the spray, deafened by roar on the Argentina side. Although the Brazil side boasts the best views. A boat takes you across. One waterfall, two countries. I want to go. This is what happens when you date someone with a proper job. You make proper plans. The night passes so quickly. We run back to Queen Street so he can catch his last train. No expectation or suggestion of an overnight. I'm glad.

I have a friend who insists on the six-date-rule. Six proper dates before you even contemplate an overnight. Although, to be fair, the rule hasn't worked that well. She is still single. We kiss at the station. It's all very civilised. It's also quick, his train is about to leave.

"Text me when you're back," I call after him.

"Yup," he calls "thanks for a lovely night. I had fun."

Me too, I think to myself. I jump on the underground back to my flat. I text Guy first.

RACHEL: 23:42: Thanks for a lovely night. I had fun. I have Iguazu envy!

GUY: 23:46: Turns out my mother was wrong. Glasgow girls are fun. Hope to see you again soon. Maybe one day I'll show you my favourite waterfall for real.

What the heck. I send Amy a text.

RACHEL: 23:54: I had such a nice night, Amy. An old-fashioned date. Turns out there is life after pricks. Hang on in there. #life-after-pricks

12 ADAM: Who's Sorry Now?

I poke my fingers down my ears. So hard they sink into the squidginess of my brain. Then harder, and harder still. Like ten-tonne drills. Twisting and boring. Only people with brains are scared. My eardrums explode. My two fingers meet in the middle of my head. Mummy and daddy are screaming so loud everyone in the world can hear them. The angels, the fairies, God, the Devil and the Queen. They will kill each other. Daddy bashes a hole in the wall that I can climb into. Right through the plaster so the wolves in the walls can get out. Mummy is shrieking. I hear 'Bastard, Selfish and Go 'F' Yourself'. It's so high pitched, it melts my brain. She's crying, howling, yelling and throwing things, all at the same time. She sounds like a wild animal, not a person. I imagine she's a wild, shape-shifting octopus with a hundred whirling arms. Hurling torpedoes at daddy. Daddy's voice is deep, angry. Like a monster. Please don't hit her. Please. Please. Please. Ten lots of pleases, ten times. Don't hit her. I promise, if you don't hit her, I'll be good forever. Don't put a jaggy hole like the wall-hole in mummy's head. Daddy puts holes in anything when he's got temper. I squeeze my eyes shut and burrow my fingers deeper. If I hum and twist my fingers round in my ears, I can't hear it so bad. I'll hum one of mummy's songs. Something smashes. I jump and whimper. I'm so scared, I'm frozen. If I don't move, lie like a stone, the carpet swallows me. Like Dracula in his coffin, I become a bat and fly out the window. It's my fault. They're arguing because of me.

Last week I wet the bed. I don't mean to. I try to hide it. I get up early, put the sheets in the washing machine. I turn it on and get water and slippy soap powder all over the floor. Mummy cries. I cry too. She says that's it, she's had enough. She can't go on. Life's not worth it. She sits on the floor, in the soap puddles. She's wet. I crawl under the table and watch her. I want her to stop crying.

"I'm sorry mummy. I won't do it again. I promise."

She cries again and says she's sorry. She takes me and Cal for ice cream. They've been arguing for hours. Something about me. Daddy is roaring. He's swearing. 'Stupid cow.' 'Bloody pregnant.' 'Useless.' The 'f-word.' That's me. If I wasn't here, they'd be happy. I crawl under the bed. It's dark. No-one can see me. If you hold your breath for long enough, you die. I try to hold my breath forever. Until I die. Or burst. It's no good, I always end up breathing. The blood pulses in my head. Like monster footsteps behind you ready to pounce. Thump. Thump. Thump. My hair's all wet from sweat. I'm too hot. I count the beats. I know my numbers all the way to ten. Start at one again. I can start at one, ten times. I can make the counting voice loud. Louder than daddy. If I manage to hold my breath for three lots of ten, he can't hit her. That's the rule. I worked it out. Like magic. A spell. I can do it if I take an extra big breath and stay still. I count quickly, I'm run out of breath. Does it still count? Mummy screams about another lady daddy knows. It makes him angry. Hold my breath. Count to ten. Got to make it four times to ten now. Or mummy dies. I must fall asleep under the bed. I think mummy lifts me out. Tucks the blanket round me. Kisses me. It's quiet. No, no, no NO. NOOOOOO. I sob. Please no.

I fall asleep. It's wet. I've done it again. I hide the sheets in my wardrobe. I am useless. Smelly and bad. Like an apple that's gone black and squishy. I'm covered in flies. Rotting.

Mummy and daddy have gone. Auntie Bea is looking after us now because I've been bad. Auntie Bea says it's just for a day or two. Whilst mummy and daddy sort things out. I don't believe her. I cry for two days. Two days after mummy and daddy leave, I put my hand on the ring of the electric cooker. Auntie Bea is making soup for lunch. I move the pan and put the palm of my hand flat on the ring. I thought I could hold it there and count to ten. I got to two. Is that me screaming? Or is it Auntie Bea? It smells like bacon. I didn't know hands could sizzle. Smells bad. Hurts a lot. Putting my hand on the cooker feels better than being alone. Sore hand feelings fill my body up. Less scary than mummy being gone. Mummy comes back that night. Next day we leave for the Isle of Man. Just me, mummy and Cal. We take our suitcases on the boat. The Isle of Man. It smells of fish, wind and sea. Where the fairies live.

"Keep dancing, Adam. The fairies take small boys for their own. Don't stop dancing."

I don't want to be zapped to the Underworld. The fairy queen takes boys for slaves. She replaces them with changelings. Fairy boys that look like real boys, but aren't. That's what mummy says. I'm drawing a picture. In our new house. Black crayon. A lady. I need yellow. She has long yellow hair. Blue eyes. A pink top. It's gone all black and scribbly. Fierce, thick scratches that use all the crayon up. Now it's all red. All over her. It's Amy. Amy is all red. Thick red crayon. All over her face and body. Groudle Glen. Groudle Glen. Groudle Glen. Groudle Glen. You can't see Amy. Just thick red, spurting, oozing scribbles.

I'm standing on the cliff at Groudle Glen. Adult Adam. 52 years old. The knife in my hand is one of our kitchen knives from Manchester. A long, thin, sharp carving knife with a black handle. I think it's a Jamie Oliver set Amy's sister bought us. It came with a sharpening block. It slices through skin like butter. If I hold it one way, I can see Amy in the blade. Her blonde hair blowing in the wind. If I hold it another, I can see the crashing waves below us. What's more beautiful? Amy's soft, pale, perfect skin. Or the glint of the steel, shiny and powerful. The way it commands me. I decide the knife has it for sheer beauty. Amy's in front of me, standing on the cliff with her back to me. Feeling the wind in her face. Breathing sea air into her lungs. Her lungs. I can see the outline of her back under her blouse. Her bra under the semi-sheer fabric. The contour of muscles, her ribs. The spaces in-between where you need to slip the blade. Like one of those anatomy books for doctors where all the muscles and tendons have names. The soft downy hair on her body a sharp contrast to the beautiful, unforgiving, cold steel. The deep red slice that opens her insides to the world, shockingly red against pale flesh. My heart speeds up. I can taste sulphurous adrenaline. She's singing. Facing into the wind and singing. What is it? I recognise it. I recognise it from somewhere. I have to lean in to listen. She sings louder. As if she wants me to hear her. The wanton bitch. The fairies sing to reel you in. They hypnotise you. Wipe your memory.

Who's sad and blue?

What is that? It's an old song. I can hear it crackly. Like a gramophone.

I cried over you.

WHO'S SORRY NOW!! That's what it is. Connie Francis. My mum's song. It pleases me to remember the title. She used to sing it to me, Who's Sorry Now. That's my mum's voice. Is she talking to me or Amy? She's wearing a dress like Connie Francis. Glamorous. Is it 1950's?

You had your way, now you must pay.

I plunge the knife in swift, hard. I envision an upward arc from back up to head. As if the blade is creating the space in her body. A ventriloquist's dummy. The channel for my arm to fit in and mime the singing. A version of Amy that's already dead and lifeless. The blade penetrates to the right of her spine, through a gap I can see between her ribs. Her skin parts. I can see inside. Am I aiming for lungs?

Who's Sorry Now? Who's Sorry Now?

I throw my weight into the thrust. They say when you kill a chicken, it should be with as much force as you can muster. So it doesn't suffer. The force shunts her body forward like a doll. Almost off the cliff. I want it to be quick. Painless. I don't want to see her face. I've kissed a face. Made love to it. That's a different face. Not this one. A different time. A different universe. This Amy is a fairy changeling. Swapped at birth. She stopped dancing. A demon picture of red and black scribbles. My mother knew this Amy wasn't worthy. She spent weeks telling me. Her small, slim body is surprisingly resistant. She looks like soft, warm butter. But she's like hardened leather. The blade grates against bone and sinew. I didn't know it would be noisy. Like a butchers. It smells like sweat. Is that me or her? I taste sulphur again. Acrid. Bacterial. Bad eggs. Which one of us is infected? Amy, surely. Her ribs keep the blade straight. Like sliding death between two volumes of encyclopaedia. On the top, L for Lungs. I for Intestines below. Her body takes on a life of its own. It jerks and twists around the metal. Now the changeling dances. Too late. Pulling the knife out feels even more effortful than plunging it in. It makes a sucking sound. Imagine air rushing into a vacuum-packed bag sliced open. She's making funny gurgling sounds. I can still hear the singing.

Who's Sorry Now?

Who's singing? Why won't it stop? The iron smell of blood mixed with sulphur and sweat makes me gag. My senses are filled with bloody body excretions. She staggers and turns around in my arms. No. NO. NO. I don't want to see her. Absolutely not. The movement causes panic. I stab her front. Where is her heart? Left side, yes? I plunge the knife in. And out. Again. Again. And again. Is there any space I haven't stabbed? She's all knife, insides and blood. Why doesn't she scream? No-one would hear. Screaming would be release for us both. Vent some sulphurous fumes to the wind. That would be healthy. She gurgles. Pathetic. It's wrong that she's just accepting it. Blood starts pouring from her mouth. She looks at me. Oh God, those eyes. She has beautiful eyes. She looks confused. Shocked. I think she still loves me. Blood starts pouring from her. Every orifice. Her face is distorting. Don't look at me. Don't. Her eyes are bleeding. Who's Sorry Now plays gently in the background. Her face has dislocated. Her jaws have come away from her face. A grotesque chimera. Her body is seven feet tall. Seven feet wide. A Gaping demon of death. She can absorb and digest you the way a giant snake can dissolve a whole cow or a human. Gasping, grunting black and red scribbles that surround and swallow. I smell pear drops. She's liquifying. I'm being swept away in red and black, warm, sticky, sweet, putrid death. A living, toxic effluent. I feel what's left of Amy (Parallel Amy, Amy-Changeling, Liquid-Amy) flood my groin. A warm, wet, sticky wave. Seeping outwards, inwards, over, under, around. Rotting and destroying. Foul and fetid. My mother's voice.

"See what she is Adam? She won't dance for you. You deserve so much more."

FUCK! I sit bolt upright in the bed. WHERE AM I? The spare room-office-bedroom. HOLY JESUS. WHAT THE FUCK JUST HAPPENED? I'm soaked. My head, my hair is plastered. My back drips. The sheets are stuck to me. Cold and wet. Clammy, saturated, horrid. I can still taste sulphur. I'm drenched in sweat. I'm gulping air. Shit, the bed's wet. Realisation dawns. I wet the bed. Pee myself. My boxers are saturated. It's everywhere. Warm, but rapidly cooling and unpleasant. Fuck's sake. I have a nightmare. Wet myself. I can smell pear drops. Why does my pee smell of pear drops? It does. I'm not dreaming. Maybe I'm still not properly awake. My heart is pounding. Breathe. Maybe it's a heart attack. Lack of oxygen. Shhhh… Breathe. Just a dream. They've been getting worse, but that was the best yet. By a mile. I lie there, hyperventilating, trying to get some control. Trying to work out what the hell is happening. I wait as consciousness and reason come back, piece by tiny piece. I need to get cleaned up. I need to get my shit together. I am truly losing the plot. My breathing is slowing down. The sweat is evaporating. It's cold. Shit, I'm soaked. I need to clean up. It stinks. I need to strip the bed. There must be disinfectant downstairs. Lemon spray.

I look at my phone for the time. I've only got an hour before my meeting with Steve. I need to tell him that Sarah Emmerson and INSpire have backed out of the conference sponsorship deal, so we're almost a million down on the funds we thought we had. We need to find another sponsor and double down on ticket sales if we're to cover the costs. Adam-Charm-Offensive fail. The American Investor changed her mind. Times are tough. Game-head, I need my game head. Everything hinges on being convincing. These conversations are never easy. Steve's a manic fruit loop. It is what it is, Steve. Plan B. There's always a Plan B That song's still playing in my head. Damn Connie Francis. Who's Sorry Now?

13 DR JIM WALKER: Just Another No Show

"Next appointment, Shona?" I buzz through, looking at my watch. Ten minutes late. They should be here.
I look at my list, Adam Waters.

I rack my brain, Adam Waters? Who's he? Pick up his notes. Ah yes, gangster businessman having a breakdown.

"No show yet, Dr Walker. Shall I put the kettle on?"

I sigh. You think the 'no shows' give you breathing space to catch-up. Temporarily you think, oh yes, that's good. But actually, they create more leg-work. It's not clinically prudent to let them disappear into the ether without at least trying to put some safety nets in place. I haven't lost a patient to suicide this year. I don't want Adam Waters being my first. Having to organise and write-up an adverse event review after a suicide is tortuous.

"Give him 5-minutes. He's maybe held-up. Can you find the GP's number? I'll give them a phone and let them know."

Ten minutes later Shona opens the door, balancing a small plate on a mug of coffee. Bless her. A steaming mug of coffee and a plate with two Jaffa cakes and a Viennese whirl.

"You're too good to me," I grin at her. I believe she is.

"You work too hard," she grins back. "Got that phone number." She has a piece of paper between her fingers, balanced between everything else. "Warrender Park Surgery. You were sure he was going to be a no-show last time. He looked terrible."

"He did. Was worried about him. Hoped I'd engaged him enough that he'd come back. I'll phone the GP now, and try phoning Adam later. In fact, let's just get a letter out with an appointment for next week. See where you can squeeze him in."

"You're pretty busy next week," Shona raises her eyebrows at me. Like all the best secretaries, she protects my time and my sanity.

"Squeeze him in where you can. I don't want to leave him any longer." I pick up my Dictaphone and press record. "Dear Adam….. I was expecting to see you for your appointment today…… brackets, date, close brackets……. Maybe there was some confusion about the time…. New paragraph….. I'm keen to catch up and see how things are. I could see you at…… date and time….. early as you can squeeze him in, next week. If this date or time doesn't suit, or if things have gotten worse, please give my secretary a ring and we can arrange an emergency appointment.... New paragraph.... Hope things are ok and look forward to catching up soon. Yours sincerely….. blah blah."

I click open the machine and hand her the tape. I'm old school. I use my Dictaphone for everything. I'm glad that's the way Shona likes it too. They gave us voice recognition software. It's meant to type what you say directly. Dictaphones are obsolete, they said. The new software types gobbledygook and nonsense. Everyone went back to Dictaphones. You can't go wrong with a cassette.

"Get it out first class today if you can, Shona."

She nods and scurries out the room. I know Shona too well. She'll have it typed up and in the outgoing mail before I finish my Jaffa cake. It's good to work with people who still care about other people. I know colleagues who hold the view that no-shows are just voting with their feet and making a choice about not wanting to engage in therapy. That we should just let them walk away. Leaving people in pain never sits comfortably. I read back through the case notes, jotting a few points down for the phone call I have to make.

- Referred back to GP for physical exam. LFT's, kidney function, full blood count, thyroid, blood sugar, blood pressure.
- 52, borderline diabetic

- Dishevelled appearance, self-neglect.
- Depression.
- Agitation (psychological and motor).
- Psychotic symptoms – auditory hallucinations with negative content. Deprecating. Self-worth. Possible risk to self and others.
- Poor sleep, bad dreams.
- Denies suicidal ideation or intent.
- Excessive alcohol consumption, daily > 8 units.
- Recent relationship break-up
- Lives alone
- Money worries

Lots of risk factors. It's quite a list. If I can get him on the phone, maybe I can talk him into a home visit tomorrow night. See if one of the nurses is free to come with me. Just to reassure myself. I add 'Groudle Glen' to the bottom of the list. I'm not entirely sure why. It keeps popping up in the case notes. I doodle around the words as I call Warrender Park Surgery. I get through to a receptionist.

"Good morning. Jim Walker, Consultant Psychiatrist from Wythenshawe. I'm phoning about one of your patients. Is it possible to speak directly to Dr Robertson?"

"Dr Robertson is in clinic at the moment, can I ask what it's in relation to?"

Oh, for goodness sake. Honestly, gone are the days when you pick up the phone medic to medic and sort something out.

"I'd rather discuss it with one of the doctors directly. It's a delicate matter." I still believe most patients would rather not have their mental health discussed openly with the receptionist. "Perhaps one of the other partners is available?" Did he attend for his physical exam? I suspect not, given he didn't pick up his anti-depressant medication.

"All the doctors are busy."

I had a mental image of a young, over-made-up, young woman, twiddling the phone cable and looking bored as she inspected her purple nails. Never was I more grateful for Shona. Sometimes I despair at the way our health service has gone and what it means for patient-centred care.

"Name?"

"Sorry?" she shocks me into confusion with her abruptness. "Jim Walker. Dr Jim Walker, Consultant Psychiatrist."

"Patient's name?"

I can feel the eye-roll. She thinks I dad-dance, tell corny jokes, reminisce about Walkmans and cassette tapes. Was a time when Psychiatrists commanded at least a little respect. Now everyone thinks they do our job. Twenty years of training, but the receptionist knows more than I do.

"Sorry," I sound flustered. I should have left this

to Shona. "Adam Waters."

"Date of Birth?"
Back to boredom and nail-inspection.

"Ok, I'll see if I can get one of the doctors to phone you back when they're available. We're very busy."

She was gone before I could say thank you, or suggest there was a degree of urgency about returning the call. I think they send all GP receptionists to the same School of Charm. I remember, a few years back, they were talking about an initiative to train GP receptionists up in mental health. Basic suicide risk assessment, counselling, listening and signposting to self-help resources. Lord help us. They'd need to teach them to look interested and not cut people off. Do I have a number for Adam? Please tell me I don't have to phone Warrender Park Surgery back for his phone number. Yes, I have a number. I dial it, but it cuts to voicemail. Gangster Adam.

"Sorry, can't take your call just now. But if you leave your name and number, I'll get back to you as soon as I can."

"Hi Adam, it's Jim Walker. Was expecting to see you this morning. Hope all is well. Maybe you'd be good enough to give me a ring and we can schedule a new time to meet. The number here is" I reel out the number. "If I'm with someone, my secretary will be happy to help." I wait on people returning my calls. It's all I can do.

14 SARAH EMMERSON: Packing Dinosaurs for Valette

I snuggle down in bed with Will Junior and Oli. We're in Oli's tiny boy bed, all three of us wrapped in a fleecy dinosaur bedcover. I have a boy cuddled under each arm. There's a big dinosaur book propped open in front of us. It's called 'Dinosaurs Don't Have Bedtimes.' Ironically, a bedtime favourite. 'Dinosaurs don't have to brush their teeth, SO WHY SHOULD I – we all roar together.

A whole week before I see these snuggle-bugs again. Before I get to read Dinosaurs Don't Have Bedtimes. Will gets that pleasure, all on his lonesome, for a whole week. I'm almost jealous. More than a little scared. I need them more than they need me.

"C'mon, mum," I hadn't realised I'd stopped reading. "Dinosaurs don't have to eat all their dinner, SO WHY SHOULD I," we scream even louder.

"Will they have dinosaurs in England, mommy?" It was Oli. My flight out of New York, is preying on everyone's mind.

"I think they'll have very English dinosaurs in England," I tell him in a serious voice. "Ones that drink tea with their little fingers in the air, like this," I cock my little finger and poke Oli's ear. "They'll eat muffins with marmalade and play croquet on the lawn with their funny little T-Rex hands," I wiggle little arms around.

"Like Paddington Bear," says Will to his little brother, "Paddington Bear eats marmalade sandwiches, wears a hat and goes to London. Mommy's like Paddington Bear."

"Let's hope I don't get into as much trouble as Paddington Bear," I laugh. "Or as greedy. My marmalade sandwich has to keep me going for a whole week."

"I wish you didn't have to go, mommy." Oli's face crumples.

Will gets angry with him. "OLI. I said… I told you. DON'T SAY THAT TO MOMMY. It's selfish. She has to go. It's work," he says with the seriousness and wisdom of his gran.

I squeeze them both into me. "Hey, hey, hey. No fighting on my last night. I wish I didn't have to go either sweetheart. It's just a week. 7-nights. You and daddy are gonna have so much fun. It will fly by. I'll be back before you know it. Plus, daddy does much better bed time stories than me."

"That's not true, mommy. Your stories are best."

Oli's face is still crumpled.

"Well, how about the first night I'm back, I tell you the extra special story about the English dinosaur I meet in London. The dinosaur that comes to London, first to meet the Queen. Then the Prime Minister. Then to meet his ancestors in the British Museum. You know they've got an actual Tyrannosaurus Rex there. An Iguanodon, Triceratops and Scolosaurus too. People say they come alive at night."

The boy's eyes open wide. "You've seen Night at the Museum, right? These dinosaurs rampage through the streets of London when everyone's asleep."

"I wanna go. Mommy, I WANNA GO." Oli is tired and plaintive.

"We will Oli, darling. We'll all go and do all these things. We'll go back when I don't have to do boring work things. With daddy. Spend all our time doing good stuff. Like dinosaur hunting. Harry Potter and Hogwarts. Right? But now, you two need to get some sleep."

"NOOOOOOOOOOO, mommy! MORE!"

"Dinosaurs don't have to go to bed…" I say, knowing the response it will get.

"SO WHY SHOULD WE?" they both scream. I pounce on them both, like a big dinosaur, growling and wrapping them up in the blankets so they can't move. I pretend-bite them all over, turning them into kisses and cuddles.

"Right, you two. Sleep time if you want to come to the airport with daddy tomorrow to wave me off. Early start. You still wanna come? Or will I get gran to come over?"

"We wanna go," they cry. Of course they do. I want them to go too. I need to fill my senses with them, inhale them and keep them in my heart for a week. Last thing I do. England will be hard enough without my boys. One last fix. I tuck them in to their own beds and kiss them both again.

"Shhh…. sleep time, darling boys. Or none of us will be able to get up tomorrow. I love you."

"Love you too mommy."

I turn off the main lights, leaving their little dinosaur night lights glowing. It'll be a sad day when my cherubs decide they're too old for dinosaurs and we have to change all the décor. From wallpaper, to bedcovers, to nightlights, to posters, not to mention thousands of plastic dinosaurs of every variety. They can name every one. You know you have grown-up boys when they progress from dinosaurs to NY Yankees. From there to computer games and girl-boyfriends. Yikes! I leave the door ajar and find Will Senior in the kitchen finishing off two plates of Lobster salad.

"Special treat," he says waving the plates about in

the air. He pours a glass of white wine and hands it to me. "Gotta make sure you come back to me somehow."

"You don't get rid of me that easily, Mr Emmerson." I drink the wine quickly and hold out my glass for another.

"Steady Tiger, you got an early flight tomorrow."

"One more with my man, before I hit the lonely road to London."

Will tops up my glass and looks at me. "I'm proud of you, *Moya Ganoush*."

"You've not called me that for a long time." It was sweet. A nickname from our early days. Our first date when he tried to convince me he was a Russian spy. Sent to recruit beautiful American Double Agents. A honeytrap recruited to the cause.

"I was winning you over with my intellect. I knew I was going to marry you."

"You were trying to get me into bed. You told me you were Alexander Ovechin's cousin. I only slept with you because I was such a massive hockey fan."

"I have a confession, *Moya Ganoush*," he looks at me seriously, "after all this time. I should come clean. I'm not actually Ovechin's cousin. Big lie. Wicked husband. Forgive me?" he sticks his face in my face. So close I can't actually see anything. Giant nose in my face. He makes me laugh.

"Well, that's a long time you've been stringing me along, boy. Good timing by the way. For the confession. At this moment, I'd forgive you anything. Wish you were coming with me."

"No you don't. I'll cramp your style. Your job to charm these stuffy English suits without the poor Yankee lawyer in tow. Sock it to them. Leave them speechless and in love with you. Signed on the line in triplicate. Just like you did to me." He pauses for a mouthful of salad. "This is actually really rather good. I believe you will miss my cooking after all."

There is nothing like NYC Seafood Market Lobster. I close my eyes and savour the taste. "I want this. This lobster on my return. Promise me you'll have lobster salad sitting waiting for me when I get back."

"I promise you I'll have fresh lobster waiting for when you get back. You promise not to fret about us, enjoy yourself and stay safe."

"Ugh, I still need to pack," I declare finishing the last forkful of food. "I'm going minimal. Flat shoes and three outfits max. I'll break my neck if I try heels in London after living in yoga pants and sneakers for years."

"The boys already packed something for you." Will grins. I look at him quizzically. "Nope, not meant to say." He shakes his head.

"What?" I poke him. "What you sneaked in there?"

"Nope, you can't wrestle it out of me. I am….." he paused and winked, "I am sworn to secrecy. Boy thang. If you catch my drift."

I straddle him on the dining chair, lift his shirt and bite a nipple.

"Ouch. You fiend."

"Yup, tell me what you snuck into my bag, so I know what I have to defend at UK Customs, you demon-husband."

Will laughs. "Ok, ok, you win. The boys made me sneak a T-Rex into the side pocket of your bag. They call it Marc. With a little help from me, obviously. Marc with a 'c' He's going on his holidays."

"Marc with a c? What on earth?" Honestly, my family are mad.

"Oh, c'mon Muffin!" Marc with a c? T-Rex? England? Marc Bolan of course. Do we not have the coolest children? What other 3-year-old can bust killer moves to I Want to Boogie."

I laugh. "You prompted that, you and your retro glam rock, lawyer thing. Ok, Marc shall visit England. He'll be photographed at all the sights, and stay in touch with everyone. Marc and Mom on their travels."

"Marc and mom on their travels," Will nods, pleased with himself for coming up with the nefarious plan to help small boys engage with their mom's journey. "Now take wine, and go finish packing. I plan to ravish my beautiful wife on our last night together before she leaves me for some fat English dude with bad breath." I linger over a kiss.

"Give me half an hour, then come ravish me."

Hoping I look enigmatic and sexy, I flounce out the room. I'm just taking the small leather weekend bag. It's easier to carry and less cumbersome than the suitcase on wheels. I find Marc, the T-Rex, skilfully stashed down a side pocket. I imagine the conspiratorial giggles when they plotted the stowaway between them. He's an awesome dad. It's like a boy's gang of giggles and fun. Will makes parenting a joy. Wear my sneakers for travelling, pack my flats. Two sets of semi-smart clothes for meetings. One casual. Toilet and make-up bag. Laptop bag and papers for three meetings. Two London-based. One Manchester. And of course, my illicit Island hop.

I pop a new book into my laptop bag for the journey. I'd ordered it especially. 'Valette and Lowry.' On the back it boasts 'an unprecedented insight into the relationship between the painter L. S. Lowry and his teacher the French impressionist Adolphe Valette.' I'm not sure what I'm most excited about, Manchester Art Gallery or my illicit Island day trip to see Victorian Polar Bear ghosts emerge from the wild surf of the Irish Sea.

I make sure, for the tenth time, that my travel companion is safely stowed in a bag. I'll make an album up with the boys when I get back, 'Travels with a T-Rex Who Likes to Boogie.'

"All done?" Will pops his head round the door.

"All done," I confirm and flop on the bed. "But... I've got the only toothpaste, you'll need to buy one tomorrow. Yes?"

"Or let my teeth go black and rotten in time for you coming back," Wills throws himself on top of me and starts pretend biting, like I'm one of the boys.
Biting turns to desire. He has a habit of managing that! Making love is gentle, sweet, prolonged. A mutual sense that we're making up for the week we're not going to see each other. I don't think it's possible to love anyone more than I love Will. Then he does things that make me fall even more deeply than I knew I could. Before I know it, he's gently waking me with coffee and a kiss.

"C'mon Muffin. You got a flight to catch."

Argh! It's 6.30am. Torture. Two excited small boys roll out to the car with jumpers and joggers pulled over their pyjamas. Hair tousled. Excited about a trip to the airport and planes.

"We stuck a friend in your bag, mommy." Oli giggles uncontrollably.

Will Junior nudges him fiercely. "Shhhhh... OLI!"

Both boys erupt into fits of uncontrollable giggles.

"Well, I hope whoever it is has a passport and a ticket. And I hope they don't snore at night." I pretend to look stern. I'm gonna miss my boys so much. All three of them.

"Passport?" says Will

"Check."

"Tickets?"

"Check"

"Currency?" he asks as his final checklist item.

"Check," I confirm. "Plus laptop and meeting papers. Check. Good to go."

We park up at the short stay carpark. The boys want to come to the departure gate and watch the planes through the window. Don't cry. Don't cry. Don't cry. Damn it. I'm crying. Those last hugs are torture.

"I'm gonna miss you guys so much. You be good for daddy."

Oli looks at me seriously. "I'm always good, mommy."

It makes us all laugh.

"Love you darling. Don't worry about us. Just come back safely." Will holds me long enough to let me know he's struggling too. "Lobster salad awaits your return. And look after our friend." He winks at the boys. They erupt into giggles again.

It's time. No sense in prolonging. One last hug. One last kiss. My heart is so full of love. I'm holding the plastic T-Rex in my hand as I board the plane. I balance him on the window looking out before take-off and take a photo for the boys. The adventure begins. I have a temporarily empty seat next to me. My fellow traveller, whoever they are, has not arrived yet. Perhaps they're saying their own goodbyes. I sit Marc in the seat, fasten the seatbelt around him and take another photo. Safety at all times. Get it on. Bang a gong. Get it on. Marc Bolan. I stick my book, my water and the bag of snacks Will made for me in in the pocket in front. England here we come.

15 AMY: He That Falls In Love With Himself Has No Rivals

"So where are you now?"

Adam's phone calls are a semi-regular thing. Well, I mean he's phoned me three times since I stayed over.

"In the park, sitting on a bench." I can't risk talking to him from my sister's house. I can't bear the disapproval or the scrutiny. She thinks she's doing what's right, but she doesn't understand.

"I'm sorry, your sister's made things so tough, Amy. It won't be like this forever, I promise."

A friendly yellow lab bounds up to the bench to say hello. I give the big, goofy head a rub. He lolls his tongue out the side of his mouth and licks my hand. A breathless owner comes up, lead in her hand mouthing 'sorry' to me, and drags the reluctant hound off. He's hopeful of food, I think. I smile, shrug, shake my head and mouth 'it's fine.' Actually, I love dogs. Unconditional love and honesty.

"Can we get a dog, Adam?"

"What? A dog?" He laughs. "Where did that come from, crazy-girl? We can barely look after ourselves."

Ouch. "I'm not crazy."

"I mean crazy-lovely, not crazy-mad. You know me, Amy. I don't do mornings. I don't do past thinking what I'm doing tonight. Or what I want for dinner. I like doing what I like, when I like to do it. Dogs are a commitment."

"They've got happy, waggy tails, goofy faces and are always pleased to see you. They love you when nobody else does. I want to come home to something, to love something. I want something I can love and that loves me back. I want to care for something that needs me."

It all comes tumbling out. A deep-seated yearning for something to love. Something to complete me. Some purpose to live. Something to fill the gap.

"I was thinking we could get a campervan, Ames. How amazing would that be. Open roads. No ties. No rules."

A campervan? In what way is a campervan like a dog?

"A campervan? Wow! You've never mentioned it before. Aren't they like, really expensive?"

I thought Adam was short on cash. Is he planning on cashing in on the house?

"They're an investment. Not like cars. Campervans don't lose value. Some business came good, at long last. About time. Been brewing for a while. Nice to buy something for us. Imagine. Sunsets on the beach. Travelling forever. Just the two of us. The three of us. Heck. We can get a dog if you want. Yes. Anything you want. You, me, a dog. No-one else. Campervan heaven."

"Is it the American investment? Is that what's come good? Sarah What's-her-face from New York?" I can't help the stab of jealousy.

Adam's grand schemes have a habit of not coming off. I'd rather get us straight, with money in the bank, than invest in expensive campervans with conference income that never seems to materialise.

"Noooooo. Sarah What's-her-face ditched us. Pulled out. Turns out she and her company were just stringing us along. Dropped us like a hot potato. Happens all the time in business. They were never serious. Steve's raging. We're having to find another sponsor."

It all sounded so cosy and conspiratorial when I overheard them at Adam's. He's right, clearly I know nothing about business. It's tough.

"Actually, I wanted to talk to you about that. It's

why I was phoning. Two things."

I pull my jacket around me. A wind has got up and is whipping round the park bench. Roll on the day when I don't have to speak to Adam furtively from street corners and parks, out of earshot. He carries on.

"Firstly, I wonder if you'd come to my Aunt Bea's for dinner tomorrow night. Like, as a couple," he added coyly. "She's been asking after you. She wants to cook for us. Has been asking me to ask you for ages. I've wanted to ask you for ages." Then even more coyly, "stay over at mine, afterwards?"

My stomach flutters. A warm, flush spreads over me. I know I'm grinning. I'll need to try and find another excuse for my sister. She knows I'm getting better. Everyone seems a bit more chilled about my comings and goings. I'm sure it will be fine.

"Of course, Adam. I'd love to. Do you want me to come over to the house and we can leave from there?"

"NO"

Oops. That was emphatic. Did I say something wrong? Maybe too keen. Need to calm it.

"No," that was more gentle. "That was the second thing I wanted to ask you. Steve's being an arse. With the American investor pulling out and the conference costs being tight. He's on the rampage. I'm keeping a low profile and avoiding him. For my own sanity."

Well, I know how that feels. He rolls on.

"You know how manic and mad he gets when he goes off on one. Sometimes I have to make some space away from him for a while. I've told him you and I are spending the day together tomorrow. In Leeds. Doing couple stuff. Going to Ikea, lunch out and shit."

"You want to go to Leeds and Ikea tomorrow? As well as Aunt Bea's for dinner?" This is getting weird and confusing.

"No, crazy-girl. I'm just making up an excuse to keep him out the way. I'm meeting another potential investor. Exploratory meeting. Probably come to nothing, so I don't want to wind him up for no gain. You know what he's like. Better he doesn't know at this stage and thinks we're just spending the day together. Is that ok? Will you cover for me? Anyone asks, we were in Leeds looking at drawers and kitchens?"

"Sure." Sounds a bit weird, but Steve is full-on. Makes sense Adam needs some space. It's nice being able to help him out. No harm in white lies if they make life less stressful. "Happy to cover if it helps. We were in Leeds looking at drawers and kitchens. Got it. Drawers and kitchens."

"You're a star Amy. A star. I wouldn't ask if he wasn't driving me insane. Don't say anything to anyone about the other investor. That's really important. It will most likely come to nothing."

Adam can ask me to do anything for him. He knows I'll do it. Everyone tells white lies for people they love. Especially if it gets them out of bother. No harm.

"I'll pick you up at 6pm from Chorlton Metrolink. Yes?"

"Chorlton?"

"Aunt Bea's tomorrow night. I'll meet you at Chorlton Metro at 6pm. We can walk round."

My head is in Ikea Leeds. "Yes. Chorlton. 6pm. Yes. That's fine. I can do that."

"And you'll come back to mine after?"

"Yes, that'll be nice. Do you want me to bring anything? Wine, flowers, chocolate?"

"That's so nice. You're so nice. It's you she wants to see. Me too. I want to see you too. It'll be fun. We can talk campervans and dogs. What kind would you get, anyway?"

"I don't know anything about campervans."

"Not campervans, you doughnut. I've already picked out the campervan I want. Retro. With a bedspace in the roof. Dogs. I mean dogs. What kind of dog would you get?"

"Labrador," I said straight away. "Unconditional love and loyalty. Dogs you can't help loving. Dogs that can't help loving and looking after you."

"Now there's your perfect campervan dog there. Know what, Amy? I got a feeling things are going to get good for us. We can stop worrying about money, or other people and just be happy. Peace. It's all I want for you. Let's start mapping out places we want to go to. Anglesey. Let's make our first road trip Anglesey. I've always wanted to take a campervan there and live on the beach. Or a tour of Europe. Just get in the van and go."

All I want is Adam. All I've ever wanted is Adam. I don't need money. Or things. Just love. And being the centre of his world. I don't care if we have a posh campervan or a big house, or if we eat beans and live in a bedsit.

"Are you still seeing the psychiatrist?"

I felt him roll his eyes and knew by the dismissive sigh that he wasn't.

"These things don't help. You have to sort your own shit out in your own way. Overpaid, overeducated quacks that talk a lot of hot air."

I've always had a lot of faith in my therapists over the years. Maybe too much. I've never missed an appointment. They've been my lifeline at times when things have been at their bleakest. I panic if my tablets run down to less than a fortnight's supply. I always have at least a month in reserve. Adam knows best. Maybe he's right. He sounds more optimistic than I've heard him for a long time. Maybe making some decisions about things helps. He needs the big house, campervan and lifestyle more than I do. I've always believed we can heal each other. I know he believes it too.

Dinner at Bea's is a big deal. His only family left, besides his brother. Dinner is significant. So is being asked to help him out with a white lie to protect his mental health. Adam always struggles with being vulnerable. Finally, I'm being let in. Maybe I'll persuade him to go to Ikea for real.

I can fly with the campervan fantasy, although in reality, it terrifies the pants off me. No toilets. No showers. No clean bed. Wet shoes and jackets. Mouldy smells. Not knowing where I'm going and what facilities there are. Digging a hole to go to the toilet. Ugh! I shudder. Stuff of nightmares. No order, control or cleanliness. Everything higgledy piggledy. I hate camping with a passion. He knows that. Why bother when I can have a hotel room, comfy bed, clean sheets, hot water and an on-site restaurant. Where do I wash my hair, shave my legs, get changed? Europe in a campervan? I can't imagine anything worse. It'll be fine. He wants me as part of his adventures. It's all that matters.

"So, you'll meet me at 6pm tomorrow. Chorlton Metro. Definitely. Tell me now if there might be a problem. I'll be hard to reach tomorrow. Might turn my phone off. No distractions. Helps me concentrate.

Tell me now if you think you might not make it."

"It's fine. I'll make it." I will. I'll always make it for him. No matter how many hoops.

"And Leeds. Ikea. Lunch. Day together. Should anyone ask. It's important. I can't have Steve hassling me. My brain won't cope."

"You can trust me. Drawers and kitchens. All day."

We sign off, agreeing to meet at 6pm tomorrow. I hug myself. I'm all warm and glowy. Campervans, Ikea, Leeds, Aunt Bea's, staying over and covering for each other. It's all so couple-like. Proper forever couples. All those things say commitment, don't they? At some point I'm going to have to tell people. I'm really hoping my sister doesn't ever bump into Stockport Carolyn. The girly mate who's been entertaining me overnight and promoting my recovery. She'll find out I've not been in touch with her for almost a year. Oopsie. My Adam excuse.

This time it feels different. He's buying a campervan for us. I'll learn to like roughing it with outdoor toilets. It's romantic. Do I dare to dream marriage and babies? I'm not getting any younger. Neither is he. Fertility drops like a stone after 40. He's always been dead set against children. Maybe he's softening. Blokes feel differently when it happens, don't they? I don't blame him. I was dead against it too.

Well sort of. But not really. I'm scared. Terrified I'll be an awful mum. Ruin it big time. Bring a baby up all wrong and scar it for life. Being scared is not the same as not wanting one. In fact, lately I've been dreaming about babies. Really weird. I haven't told anyone. Worried they'll think it's part of my madness. Historically hysteria was thought to be related to being a woman. In fact, anxiety, insomnia, depression irritability, even fevers and kleptomania. All thought to be attributable to having female organs. Marriage, sex and babies are the cure.

One of my therapists was into the myth of mental illness and feminism. She lent me a book. It was heavy duty. She also hated Adam. People can change though. He's different today. Am I his girlfriend again? It's all a bit ambiguous. Dinner at Aunt Bea's is a massive statement. A campervan and a Labrador are definitely a positive start. I realise I'm stroking my belly protectively.

16 ADAM: Dance with Me?

I'm in a science fiction movie. It's a strange feeling. I make coffee as I begin packing a bag for the Isle of Man ferry trip. I'm playing some sort of Keanu Reeves character. The Matrix meets Sliding Doors. Today is a Schrödinger's Cat day. Sarah Emmerson is dead in the box, and not dead in the box simultaneously. My own version of a metaphysical thought experiment. It's intellectually fascinating. A paradox of quantum superposition linked to a random subatomic event that may or may not happen. Until I slide the knife in, if I do, she's both dead and alive. Is the knife random and subatomic? Is it my decision to act? Or is it the physical process of puncturing flesh and organs that defines it? Metaphysics. Fascinating. I wrap the long, sharp carving knife in a towel and place it carefully in my rucksack. I changed the plans yesterday.

"Let's go from Liverpool rather than Heysham. It's a high-speed ferry and Liverpool is so much easier to get to from London. Two hours. There's a direct train from Euston first-thing. We can make an early start. Make the most of the day." I tell her.

It also has no ID checks and no baggage checks. Buy a ticket. Walk on. Walk off. Perfect anonymity. We make plans based on train timetables and ferry crossings. I need to be on the 3pm return ferry if I'm to make my date with Amy at Chorlton at 6pm.

I'll make a real effort with Amy tonight. Romance her. Not drink too much. Sleep with her when we get back. All part of the show. Metaphysics is wonderful. Today I am in Ikea Leeds and Groudle Glen simultaneously. By tomorrow I'll have been in Leeds all day.

Sarah says she's travelling light. She has all her bags with her, having packed up from her London meetings. I just need to get rid of everything. Piece of cake when there is an inaccessible and desolate coastline, a plunging drop and a raging Irish sea. I feel like I should have a sense of foreboding or occasion or something. I don't. I feel quite serene. Happy even. Everything is planned to perfection. We're aiming for the 9am ferry from Liverpool. We'll be in Groudle Glen by mid-day. I'll be on the ferry back to Liverpool by 3pm. Thank goodness for the summer timetable and frequent crossings. It's perfect.

I'm travelling similarly light. Laptop and conference papers for show. Some snacks and drinks for the ferry. Change of clothes. I have no idea how messy these things are, but best to be prepared. I can tie rocks round the old set and hurl them into the impenetrable surf. One knife concealed in a towel. I check things off as if I'm going on holiday. Will it happen? I honestly don't know. Schrödinger's Investor. Only the fairies know. And perhaps my mother. Whether Sarah paid the toll and whether she can keep dancing.

One universe sees me coming home with a new international business partner and investor. Someone I can grow the business with and expand internationally. No need for Steve and his tantrums. I've then got two days of Manchester art galleries, hospitality and the Hilton Hotel. A parallel universe sees me coming home an instant millionaire, with no money worries, no need to invest money I don't have and hours upon hours of legwork in a faltering business. No need to carry the can for a tempestuous business partner. Road trips, sunsets, beer, fun and doing my own thing. Forever. Adam's idyl.

No-one else could have pulled this choice off so effortlessly. I am genius. I should write a book. My phone buzzes. Text from Sarah. She's on the train to Liverpool and excited to meet me. Hoping I won't stand her up. There's no chance of that. That's not a parallel universe option. I need to make sure her phone goes as a priority. It must be completely destroyed and the sim removed. The sea can receive the shattered fragments. Text from Steve asking me to phone him when I get up.

ADAM: 07:16: Sorry mate. Meeting Amy early. Off to Leeds for the day. Promised her an Ikea trip to look at furniture and lunch out. Dinner at my Aunt Bea's tonight. Busy day keeping the women happy! Catch up tomorrow? I have some new ideas about sponsors. We'll work it out.

I'll not be back at the house again until Amy and I come back late tonight. There needs to be nothing relating to where I'm going. Quick tidy and check. All looks good. Ok, half an hour before I need to leave. I've got spare shoes in. It makes the bag a bit bulky. Do I really need spare shoes? Probably yes. I've been in the room when Amy's watched back-to-back episodes of 'Silent Witness.' Forensics always get them on shoes. Blood or Groudle Glen mud or unique treads on the sole. Something like that. Rocks tied to shoes and in the surf. No risks. This has to be the perfect end. Shame though, I like these shoes. Nothing chucked to the sea gods at Groudle Glen could ever be discovered. They'll be lost forever. Even if you knew where to look, divers could never get down and vessels could never get in. Poseidon's treasures for eternity. Watched over by fairies. I'm organised.

I feel a bit tense. First time. Hope she doesn't pick up. Wonder if I should take one of Amy's diazepam. There's still a packet in the bathroom cabinet. No, that's daft. I need to be alert. C'mon Adam. You've planned this to perfection. You're smart, talented. By tonight you'll be a millionaire. Almost a million in an untraceable offshore account. Just thinking that gives me a thrill. She's a businesswoman who embezzles company funds and disappears. It happens all the time. Occupational hazard when you're a corporate director. People are inherently untrustworthy. Without a body, there's nothing.

The journey to Liverpool is remarkably uneventful. Calm before a raging Irish sea storm. I wait on her coming off the London train when it pulls into the station. Laptop and papers in one bag. Rucksack slung over my back. I spot her instantly. Why wouldn't I, she looks just like her persona on videoconference. Tall, leggy, fit. Self-assured and confident in that American way. Pretty. Long blonde hair tied up in a work-like pony tail. She's wearing expensive looking camel slacks and a cream sweater. Flat loafers. She's carrying a small leather holdall and a laptop bag.

"Adam!" She spies me too and comes in for the hug. I get a warm embrace and a kiss on the cheek. "How lovely to finally meet you in person."

I take her hand and look her warmly in the eyes. "I can't believe you're finally here. We are going to have so much fun today. All I ask is that you put yourself in my hands. Here let me." I take her holdall and sling it over my shoulder.

"I can carry…." she begins to protest.

I shake my head. "You're my guest. I get to look after you today. Did you have a good journey?"

"Lovely. The countryside is so…. English. Quite different from New York brash. Like a Regency drama."

"Wait until you see the Isle of Man. Countryside, coastline, magic and fairies. I promised you everything. I aim to deliver. C'mon," I take her arm, "we have a ferry to catch. I already bought tickets. Just need to board."

It's a typically grey day. Not raining. Just dull and grey.

"I'm only sorry, I couldn't bring the sun out for you." I guide her on to the waiting ferry. "Outside or inside, you choose."

"Let's start outside. Fresh air and surf and rain. The whole English experience. I need some photographs. Wait there," she pulls a small plastic dinosaur out of her pocket. "Hold this up with the sea as a backdrop. Like that." She puts her hand over mine and moves it. "That's it, so I can't see your hand. As if he's standing up and holidaying on his own."

I hold the plastic T-Rex up to the sky and she snaps away. I look quizzically.

"My sons sneaked a dinosaur into my bag. I've to send photos of his travels."

"Are you sending now?" I feel a moment of panic. This could be bad.

She shakes her head. "No. I'll check through the best ones tonight. I've been looking out the best ones, making a story and sending them at night from my hotel. Travels with a dino. None from today so far."

I breathe a sigh of relief. Gotta get rid of that phone. Cute with the dinosaur. I forgot she had kids. I don't want to think about that. She jumps when the ship's horn sounds. I instinctively put a hand across her back to steady her. The flesh is warm through her sweater. My hand brushes her ribs. Flesh and ribs. Intrusive memories of the dream of Amy on the cliff top. Her ribs. The horror of her metamorphosis. Sliding the knife through the layers of ribs. Slicing the skin. The gaping, swallowing disintegration. The putrid smell. I taste sulphur again. Derails me momentarily.

"You ok, Adam?"

I shake myself out of it. Damned dream. "She's not good enough for you, Adam. You're talented. You deserve this." I know, mum.

"I'm fine," I smile at Sarah. The first jolt of movement. Always turns my stomach. Takes a moment or two to find my sea legs."

"You live on a tiny island," she pokes me good naturedly and grins, "I thought you Brits were all born with sea-faring legs. Evolution's meant to weed out the non-naval types."

"I'm a rotten swimmer too. You'll need to save me if I go man overboard."

"Not a problem. Regional swim champ," she flexes a non-existent bicep, "more years ago than I care to remember. You know this is so nice."

"Hmm…?" I'm not sure what she means.

"Being here. Being Sarah again. Just for one day, not being Businesswoman Sarah, Mom Sarah, Wife Sarah, all things to all people. The last few days have been great. Very serious. London is always serious.

High pressure diplomacy. But good to be away from New York and Mom-Duty. Exercise my brain. Do what I do, what I love. But this….." she motions to the sea and scape around her. "Here, I mean. Here, I feel like I'm reconnecting with the me I lost somewhere. The adventurer. The me that has fun, travels, meets people, can be silly, impulsive, loves life. I haven't thought about me in a long time."

"Hmm….?" I can't help it, my mind has wandered. I'm not listening.

Sarah is standing with her hands on the rail, looking out to sea. I'm studying her figure. She's taller than me. A lot taller than Amy. Fit and toned, but slight. How do I get a knife out my bag without her seeing? I need to create a moment like this, when she has her back to me, looking out over the cliff. She's strong. I need to be swift and decisive. I study her back. Visualising the ribs and muscles under her sweater. Use force, slide in between, hit an organ for a rapid end. Lung or heart. Get rid of the body over the cliff. Straight into the tumult of angry sea. Rocks in the bag. Clothes tied to rocks. Everything swallowed by Poseidon's wrath and forgotten.

"Adam?"

I jump.

"You're a million miles away. I guess being here makes us both reflective about what's important. Penny for them?"

"Hmm….? Jeez. I seem to be only able to converse in monosyllables. Hardly the charmer.

"Penny for them. Your thoughts. What you thinking about?"

"My mother actually. Travelling to the Isle of Man always makes me think of my mother. This ferry ride was the first trip we made after my parents separated. I remember, I was wearing a patterned, knitted bobble hat. Fair Isle. My brother and I both were. I'd never experienced wind like it. The way it whipped round your head. She said, just remember Adam, any man can lose his hat in a fairy wind. I used to be terrified the fairies would come for me, take me with them to their world, whilst at the same time thinking how wonderful it would be to escape the dull, grey world we actually lived in."

"It's certainly a magical place, says Sarah wistfully looking out to sea. "Do you think we should retire inside and do some work?"

"Are you in the mood for corporate conferences?" I raise my eyebrows at her and she laughs.

"Not really!"

"Well, we have three whole days to discuss every detail of our partnership. I'm lucky to have found someone I feel such a connection to. If I help you to rediscover yourself in some tiny way, then that will be as important as anything else. Let's just savour the adventure."

She looks pleased with that.

"I am going to go and get us some takeaway coffees to wrap our hands around. I don't promise you great coffee on the Isle of Man ferry. Some things the fairies haven't quite mastered yet. But it's hot. You'll be ok? Back in two ticks." She nods.

The walk to the café bar gives me some time. I'm not sure I can be bothered going through the pretence of conference accounts and sponsorship agreements. I did prepare them, just in case, but my head's not really in the conference game. I've also turned my phone off. I can't be bothered fielding irate calls from Steve. Not today. Not when I'm going round Ikea with Amy. Seriously Steve, you know what she's like. I'll tell him that when we do finally catch up. Maybe I'll actually take Amy to Ikea tomorrow and buy something. Give the whole story a bit more substance. It did occur to me that I was lucky that Amy was so obliging and would do anything for me. She'll stand by the alibi no matter what.

Damn. Forgot to ask Sarah what kind of coffee she wanted. Argh. Black. White. Americano. Latte. Cappuccino.

"Two Americano's please."

Can't go wrong with that, can you? I fill my pockets with sugar, milk pots and stirrers. If it was the wrong thing, she has the good grace not to say and gratefully wraps her hands around it.

"Wish I brought gloves. Your English climate.

Brrrr." She remarks, holding the cardboard cup to her face.

"Here. I've got a pair." I pull a pair of black gloves from my jacket pocket and give them to her. I'm not thinking, am I? They're the gloves for doing the deed. Stupid. I thought gloves would be easier. Cleaner. Make it stronger, quicker. Now she either dies with my gloves on. Or I have to find some way of asking for them back again. Idiot. She has very slender, pretty hands. Soft. Manicured. Perfect nails. Perfect skin. I can imagine them stroking my back whilst I'm screwing her. Long fingers. Explorative. By contrast, mine are short, fat and sausage. Roughened. Rubbing her back and taking the soft, perfect skin off, like sandpaper. Which sort wields a knife better? Mine probably. Yin and yang. She is soft and yielding. I am power and direction.

Yin-Yang actually translates from Chinese as bright-black. Seemingly contrary forces that are actually complementary, interconnected and interdependent. The universe creating itself out of primary chaos organised into positive-negative. Today Sarah and I are Yin and Yang. An inevitability about what has to happen for life to continue. Life-Death. Fuck's sake. I have a hard-on thinking about all this stuff and looking at her. Fucking weird. Well, we'll be staying out here for a bit, whilst I stand to the rail to cover my modesty. Subside, man. Down. Stop being weird.

"Thanks for today, Adam."

I've still got a hard-on.

"I've reconnected with something I thought I lost. Me. Life. Time and space."

"Land," I say simply, pointing ahead.

The beginning of the end. I'm almost sad. I would like our journey to be longer. I begin wiggling my hips and moving my arms. Sarah looks at me as if I've gone mad. It must look like that.

"Adam…. What on earth are you doing?" She looks around to see if anyone else is watching my insanity. "Stop it," she laughs. "You're mad."

"Dance," I instruct her. "C'mon, dance." I take her hands and begin moving them, like a puppet.

"What are you talking about."

I start moving around.

"The Groudle Glen fairies. If we dance, we get safe passage. We don't get stolen away to the underworld. Our bodies replaced by lookey-likey fairy folk. My mum always made us dance as the ferry drew into port. We were terrified not to."

It works, she starts swaying and moving around on the spot. People look at us. We laugh. A carefree moment. The beginning of the end.

"Adam. You are mad. Lovely, wonderful, eccentric. Definitely mad."

We sashay our way off the ferry, holding hands and laughing. It's hard to dance well with a holdall, a rucksack and a laptop bag.

"We'll work on your dancing," I say as we dance to a stop on dry land. I wink at her. She slaps me on the arm in feigned indignance. "My mum would love you," I say. It's true. I think she would have. "But time will tell whether the fae grant you safe passage."

Sarah has colour. Colour and spirit. I never once managed to get Amy to dance for the fairies.

17 SARAH EMMERSON: Blessed with a Front Row Seat

What came first? The breath-taking, all-consuming sharpness of my body being sliced in two? The mixture of incredulity, confusion, betrayal? My brain does not compute. No sense. None.

I think shock registers first. Searing pain takes longer to reach the brain. Maybe the neural pathways are severed by whatever penetrated my body with superhuman force. Has something skewered my back? A projectile? A gun? An arrow? ADAM. I NEED YOU. SAVE ME. I weep. Blind panic. My instinct to turn and face the assault. I can't. Something has skewered me right through my middle. I can't breathe. I can't move. My face is dissolving. Silent tears of terror. I don't realise my body needs to be whole for sound to emanate. My lung is pierced, my brain doesn't work.

I open my mouth, nothing comes out. Like a goldfish out the bowl flapping pointlessly. Involuntary spasms on the road to death. NO. This can't be where it ends. My boys. I've failed them. I've failed everybody. I won't let it. A millisecond of defiance. The plastic dinosaur is first to plunge to his death. He was clutched in my hand. With the pain, I let go. I'm sorry. I failed you all. I was leaning over the cliff, looking. The sea rages. Now the dinosaur hurtles towards it. A craggy, unforgiving end. A small, plastic dinosaur. A sheer 200ft plus drop. A raging, deafening, crashing sea. The little blighter has no hope. He's gone forever. I mouth: "I'm sorry." Or at least I think I do. It's all in my head. Everything. Confused and bloody.

The pain is unbearable. All-consuming. Yes, horrific. I can't breathe. The pain has no escape. System shutdown. Will is here, smiling. Where did he come from? *Moya Ganush.*

"I'm sorry. I'm so sorry. I've let you all down." I weep.

"Shhhhh…… my darling. My beautiful, sweet darling. You've let no-one down."

He's so tender. My constant. My soulmate. He wraps himself around me. Pulls me into his chest and wraps himself protectively round the intolerable pain and grief and regret. I relax.

"You are loved darling girl. You were always loved. You will always be loved. It's ok. I've got you. I always did."

Will Junior and Oli wrap themselves tightly around me. "I love you mommy. You're the best mommy. We'll look after you." They cry in unison.

My darling boys. My heart is bursting. I smile. I

feel joyous. Elated. They came. I am complete. It's time. Will holds me tight and kisses me, tenderly, lovingly, eternally.

"Let go of the pain, Sarah. It's going to be ok. We've got you."

We're falling through the air, as one, Will, Will Junior, me and Oli. No, not falling, we're flying. I hear singing. Through the fog, I hear singing. A gospel choir? It's beautiful.

'I tried to warn you somehow.'

'Who's sorry now?'

It ends when I bounce the surf like a broken, bloodied rag doll.

18 AMY: Buckets with Holes that leak Apple Pie

Twenty past six. He's late. I look at my phone for the six-hundredth time. C'mon Adam, where are you?

I'm standing outside Chorlton Metrolink, scanning the street in both directions, looking for his build, gait and the familiar brown leather jacket. Chorlton is one of my favourite bits of Manchester, combining history with a cool vibe. Far enough away from the city centre to be fierce about its culture and history. Expensive enough to keep the students out. Not as full of itself as Didsbury.

Chorlton is apparently an ancient English word for farmstead. Chorlton is also famous for rural rebellion. The lord of the manor was imprisoned for loyalty to the pope in 1567, the local priest was executed in 1641, and future generations were executed during the Jacobite rising of 1715. The big tourist board by the metro is a cheery read. I've read it several times now. Chorlton-cum-Hardy (I don't know why, but the full name makes me giggle) a leafy suburb of Greater Manchester 3 miles southwest of the city centre, boasts a population of fifteen thousand and a plethora of independent boutiques and trendy wine bars.

ADAM!!! I see him trundling down the street. I recognise his cheeky loll. He holds his arms open as he sees me from 200 yards away and cocks his head with exaggerated affection. Who's crazy, me or him? Nutter! You're late Adam Waters. Don't charm your way out of it.

"Hey, gorgeous girl," he embraces AND kisses me. On the lips too. He should be late more often. I like it. I squeeze him back.

"Your shirt's on inside-out," I say, noticing the seams that should be on the inside. I turn him round, yup, "label on the outside," loon! "Have you spent all day with your shirt on inside-out?"

"Hmmm......??" He looks confused, and looks down at his buttons, which are on the inside, next to his skin. "Must've. Definitely inside-out. Buttons on inside," he pulls at the placket to make it more obvious. "I'm a doughnut. Got dressed in the dark."

"You are," I laugh. "How do you put a shirt on inside-out. Don't you notice that you can't do the buttons up? Or do you pull it over your head already buttoned up?"

"It goes into the wash buttoned up. In fact, I don't think I ever undo the buttons." He grins. "See how much I miss you, now you're not living with me. It all just turns to chaos. I can't even dress myself. Surely you must see I need you back in my life, Amy Hawes." He kisses me again. I like this Adam.

"Hang on he says," and puts his hands round my waist to move me to the side and squeeze past, "the public gents," he points to the Metro toilets. "Quick turnaround. Back in a sec. The right way round."

He returns moments later with his shirt on the right way.

"Respectable?"

"Definitely more respectable," I confirm.

"Ready for Aunt Bea?" he links my arm.

"Defo."

Adam has a habit of not walking with you, but walking several steps ahead of you. I can't remember him ever linking arms and walking with me. At least not for a very long time. What's got into him.

"You seem happy," I tell him. "It's nice. Good day at the office?"

"An excellent day at the office, actually. Everything going according to the Masterplan. Don't want to say too much in-case I jinx it. Drawers and kitchens and a lovely dinner at Bea's with a beautiful girl. It doesn't get any better."

I get those flutters and feel warm and tingly. We walk round to Bea's house, a white bungalow in a quiet residential area with a wrought iron fence and a garden with lawn and roses. She's lived here forever, certainly as long as I've known Adam. Bea sent me some old pictures when I was pulling Adam's life story book together for his 50th. Old pictures of Adam and Cal as boys. Bea looking youthful and glamorous, like an old movie star. Unmistakable 70's fashion. Pictures of them all with their mother on the Isle of Man.

Bea's had a few mini-strokes this past year. She's in her 80's, but fiercely independent. I sometimes think her presence in this world is what keeps Adam present. Her little elderly Ford Fiesta sits in the driveway. Elderly, grey, reliable, a constant. A living replica of its owner. When the car's there, all is well with the world. She says herself she'd be lost if they took her driving license away from her. I wonder sometimes, with the strokes and things, whether she should be driving. No-one has dared suggest otherwise. Adam rings the doorbell and takes my hand.

"Come in, come in," we hear Bea bustling about, calling from behind the door. "Door's open."

Adam pushes the handle of the door down and sticks his head in. Bea comes dashing up. Or as dashing as you can be when you're 83, have had a series of strokes and your hips don't function too well anymore.

"Welcome, my darlings. Welcome. You made it. It's good to see you both. Amy, it's been far too long." She puts a hand on each of my arms as if to steady herself and stands back to look at me. "Tsk.

You girls. You're all so thin. You don't eat enough. Tonight, you will eat. I have a big spread on. Roast beef, Yorkshire puddings, roasts, the works. Apple pie for pudding. I hope you're hungry." She turns to Adam. "I think you've put on the weight that Amy's lost. You look like you need a good sleep and some looking after. You don't look well."

She busies around us. There's also a glorious smell of roast beef and Yorkshire puddings wafting round the house.

"Amy, you'll take a sherry with me before dinner, yes? I won't hear no. Adam, there's beer in the fridge. You go help yourself. Amy and I will find the sherry."

I don't like to tell her I hate sherry. She ushers me into the living room and pours two small glasses to the brim. I'm ok if I don't smell it. I have to hold my breath whilst I take small gulps. She hands me the glass. I hold my breath and gulp.

"I'm glad you and Adam are sorting your differences out. I worry about him, Amy. I always have. He's more fragile than people know. He needs a good, steady woman to keep him on the straight and narrow. He was such a sensitive child. Took things to heart. Especially when his parents split up. I thought he'd never get over it."

"I think we're good for each other, Bea," I tell her, holding my breath and sipping.

"Ach, I was heartbroken when he told me you'd moved out. He doesn't cope in that big house on his own. I'm surprised he's not burned it down or flooded it. He's all over the place."

Adam walks in with an open bottle of beer in his hand.

"You two talking about me?"

"Of course," Aunt Bea has a twinkle in her eye.

"Did I get the right beer?" Aunt Bea motions to the bottle in his hand. "There's so many to choose from. It's quite bewildering."

"It's perfect, Auntie. Thank you. "I'm trying to cut down though. Got to get rid of this beer belly." Adam pats his stomach. "Doctor says I'm carrying too much. No surprises there. Less beer, more exercise."

"You're looking more and more like your dad, Adam. Every time I see you, I think that. You're the spit. I'd almost think it was him standing there."

"Thank goodness he's not, eh? Or we'd all be on edge and hiding the carving knives. That roast beef smells so good Auntie. Can we do anything?"

"You could take it out the oven for me, Adam. Put it on the cooling rack. We'll give it half an hour to rest, then you can carve. I always like to see the man of the house with a carving knife."

Adam trots off to the kitchen to do as asked, taking his beer with him.

"Is he alright, Amy? Adam, I mean. Is he alright? He doesn't look well. His dad had his struggles too. He was a weak man underneath all the show. Sometimes Adam reminds me of him in more than just his looks."

"I think he's well, Bea. He went through a rough patch. We both did. He's been much more upbeat recently. Great mood today. Positively buoyant. Work seems to be going really well. A new business opportunity. Even talking about buying a campervan for holidays. I think he's doing good. If he's good, I'm good."

"Just keep an eye on him, and look after yourselves." Bea tops up my sherry again as she talks. "I do like a sherry before dinner. Whets the appetite, don't you think."

"Lovely," I say, holding my nose and glugging again.

"More sherry Auntie Bea?" Adam walks back into the room, "you'll get Amy tipsy. She's developing a real fondness for sherry, you know. Always sneaking a bottle into the trolley." He winks at me, the swine. He knows I hate sherry. If we were sitting at the table, I'd be kicking him under it. "Amy and I have been through in Leeds today. Ikea. Furniture. Drawers and kitchens."

"Lovely," says Bea, "I like an Ikea trip myself. You must take me next time. Did you buy?"

"Just looking," Adam looks at me, smiling. Conspiracy! "I think we're going back tomorrow though. Have another look and pick some stuff up. We have a new campervan to furnish."

He puts his hand on mine. After the third sherry, I'm feeling a little tipsy. Bea fills our glasses up again. I don't know where she puts it.

"The secret to living well into your 80's," she says as she pours, "and beyond." She clinks my glass with hers. "Cheers, beautiful Amy. May you and Adam have many delightful years together."

I'm sure I'm blushing. I need some food to soak up my thimbles of what tastes like pure ethanol. Still, hold nose and glug.

"Adam!" Bea makes a grand statement and gets up with a flourish. "I think you should bring the food through and carve, don't you?"

Dinner is lovely. It reminds me of old family roast dinners at home with my parents and my sister. Before my dad got dementia, I got crazy and started trying to kill myself, and things generally got difficult. Adam always seems to charm my mum. My dad says he can see right through him. He's a difficult man. Maybe they both are. Maybe that's what attracts me to Adam in the first place. Adam wields a carving knife like a pro, slicing through the flesh and carving beautiful, regular slices. Bea claps her hands at each slice.

"Your dad could carve a roast perfectly too," she says as she claps.

She opens a bottle of red wine now. I don't think I should drink any more. It's all going to my head. Adam fetches himself another beer from the fridge. It's so homely.

"So, tell me about this campervan, Adam. You know your mum always wanted a campervan. She was a hippy at heart. A romantic. Always wanting to swim in waterfalls and sleep on the beach. I'm sure that's what drew her to the Isle of Man. All those cliffs and beaches."

Adam pulls out his phone and brings up pictures of campervans. He starts talking about concertina roofs, pop-tops and upper floor bedrooms. Vanlife shower systems and tankless water heaters. I love seeing him excited. He's really into this. Even Bea's getting swept along.

"We'll take you back to the Isle of Man, Auntie. A campervan adventure. There are downstairs beds too. The sofa converts into another double bed."

Bea sighs a little sadly. "I think I'm too old for camping adventures now, my boy. Would have been a time when I'd have chewed your arm off for a campfire and a beach. The bones not as willing as they used to be. Memory not so great nowadays either," she taps her head.

"Are you keeping well, Bea?" I wonder if she's trying to tell us something. I worry for Adam. He'll not cope with losing her.

"Bless you, Amy. As well as can be expected for an old codger. No marathons or hurdles anymore." She starts clearing plates.

"We'll do that," I say.

She waves her hands dismissively. "Tomorrow," she says. "What else have I got to do. Dishes are not important. You and my darling boy, Adam are." She turns to him. "I only wish your mother could have been here to see your campervan. She'd have been so proud. I'll need to be proud enough for the two of us. Now. Who's got room for my apple pie?"

I am so full. But it seems churlish to refuse the apple pie she's made for us. She's made a second for us to take home. Apples from the garden need used up, she says.
It's getting late. I'm mindful of not tiring Bea out. I nudge Adam under the table. He nods.

"We should be making tracks, Auntie. Roll ourselves back after the amount of food you've given us. Not to mention the sherry you've poured into my girlfriend. I'll have to carry her back."

I feel a thrill at his use of the word girlfriend. Bea nods and makes a comment about me being light enough to throw over his shoulder. I think she's enjoyed the night. I know she has. But she's tired. It's definitely time to go. She packs some roast beef in foil for us, along with our spare apple pie.

"Not so long next time Adam," she chides him. "And look after that beautiful girl."

Adam embraces her as we're leaving. He slips the food into the rucksack he's guarded all day. My rucksack has the standard overnight kit. Toothbrush, knickers, toiletries, some fresh jeans and a top for tomorrow. He takes my hand as we stroll. We decide to walk back rather than taxi or tram. It's a couple of miles. Adam says we can walk the tonne of roast beef and apple pie off. We even have a picnic or breakfast if we get lost. I giggle. I still feel a little tipsy.

"Do you think Aunt Bea's ok?" I ask him.

"How'd you mean. I thought she was great tonight. Packed away more booze than either of us."

"She did. It's just, well, she'll not live forever. She's had a couple of strokes. Her memory isn't what it used to be." I worry for Adam. He's had so much loss.

"She's fighting fit," he brushes it off. Auntie Bea's made of stuff that will outlive both of us. As long as she's got her car and her garden. We should make more of an effort to go over though."

It takes us around 45-minutes of a leisurely stroll to get home. Adam takes himself off immediately for a shower, claiming a long day and needing to freshen up. Something about not wanting to take me to bed smelling bad and wearing the dust of the day. I have a double flutter. Triple, quadruple flutter. I'm sure that's a sex-bomb, he's just dropped. I make tea. Sober us both up. He has an extra-long shower, coming back looking flushed from heat and scrubbing.

"Cutely tousled," I run a hand through his damp hair. It's been years since we've actually had sex. I'm nervous. I hope it all still works. He downs the tea I made for him in three gulps. He's wearing a dressing gown with some boxers underneath. I undo the dressing gown belt and press in.

"You called me your girlfriend tonight," I bring my hands behind his back, stroking.

"I did, didn't I." He runs his hands through my hair.

"I liked it." Am I doing this right? It's been so long.

"So did I," he said, and he kissed me. Proper, long, lovely kiss.

I melt into him.

"I hope things still work," he looks at me ruefully, "I'm older than I used to be."

I giggle flirtatiously and slip a hand down. "I think it's like riding a bike." I whisper. "Literally. I think I can help you remember."

He gasps. I lead him upstairs. I feel like I'm in control of this. He lets himself be guided.

"Condoms?" he manages to say between breaths. I pretend I haven't heard and slip on top. Long, slow, beautiful, romantic, healing. Apparently after five years, everything does still work. I know what I want. I lie back, happy. Content. Sated. I feel complete. I hold him as he falls into a deep post-coital slumber.

19 RACHEL: Walking with a Map

I flop on the bed on my stomach, with my laptop open in front of me. The Wi-Fi is great here. You wouldn't have thought they'd have superfast broadband on the Isle of Arran. It's the middle of nowhere.

Guy is in the shower. He says he's aching all over. I think I've proved I'm fitter than him. I packed so much into our first mini-break together, I may have broken him. Today's task was climbing Goatfell. I mean, c'mon it's less than 900 metres. Not even a Munro. A tiny wee Corbett. Still the highest point on Arran. Still a scramble on all fours at the end to the top. But man, what a view. Magical. Such a lovely clear day too. I'm sure that was Ireland we could see in the distance. I mean I could have taken him the steep way by Corrie. I was kind for our first weekend away together. Didn't want to exhaust the poor guy. Ha! I thought he was going to die when he realised we had to all-fours scramble to reach the summit after a 10km amble through the forested grounds of Brodick Castle.

As I keep telling him, you only get to enjoy the utter indulgence of a spa when you've broken yourself on mountain climbs, bike rides and wild water swimming first. Spa booked for 5pm. Wondrous hotel dinner booked for 8pm. I love this place. Arran's always my 'go to' for a few days away. Indulgent spa hotel, tranquillity, fine food, magical views, mountain biking, Glen Rosa and the emerald pools for swimming. Who says I'm not good to my men? I treat them very well.

I'm not sure why I search 'Sarah Emmerson' idly on my laptop. I'm not even thinking about Adam or Amy. Maybe I'm a stalker. A sub-conscious stalker. Maybe it's a cyber-tick that makes me search ex-boyfriend-related people. Boredom? Curiosity? It amazes me how many Sarah Emmerson's there are. I mean look, there's one in Glasgow. She looks about 14. There she is, Sarah Emmerson, INSpire, New York City. When I hit 'images,' several pictures of her fill my screen. They all look the same. Corporate, leggy, confident, American blonde. The usual ones, A Connect2Me profile. Well, we know she's there. Lots of Sarah Emmersons on Social Media. Try typing 'Sarah Emmerson' and 'New York.' There she is again. Several links to INSpire. There she is on an 'Our Staff' page and a biography. Harvard Graduate. MBA. Voted New Yorker most likely to succeed in business. Women in Business Award. There's a picture with some bloke. Her husband, I presume. Business Awards. Handsome looking chap. A recent New York Times link catches my eye 'missing businesswoman.' Interesting. I click on it.

'International businesswoman Sarah Emmerson, 42, Head of Product Design and Product Management at INSpire, mysteriously

disappears following major financial transaction. Ms Emmerson was expected back in New York last Sunday, following a business trip to the UK. She didn't return. It is unclear at this stage whether her disappearance warrants criminal investigation.'

That's all it says. I read it again. Then again. Major financial transaction? Criminal Investigation? FUCK! Wow! She's embezzled company funds. None of the other newspapers are carrying anything. None of the news channels. None of the UK papers. That's it. Just that one paragraph. International businesswoman and International criminal. Wonder how much she got away with. Wonder if Adam knew anything about it. Surely not. He's a twat. A selfish, self-obsessed twat. He's not a criminal though. Not embezzling company money. That's not his style, is it? I check back my Connect2Me messages with Sarah. There's nothing remotely suggestive of a criminal mastermind. She's quite open about her trip to London and Manchester.

If Adam wasn't such a narcissistic twat, I'd message him and ask him. I don't want to open that Pandora's Box though. You never know what evils or unwanted mail it will generate. Especially not when I'm away for the weekend with Guy.

There's been no activity on her Connect2Me account for a couple of weeks. That's unsurprising. She'll be hiding in an anonymous hole. She's probably not even in the UK anymore. If she even came here. She's most likely fled to some white-collar criminal gangster's paradise to live out her days. I check back her profile:

Wife and mom to two junior-school-sized Rugrats

Really? Wow! It's a cold fish that embezzles company funds and leaves their husband and kids behind. Smiley, corporate, beautiful and hard as nails. Guy comes out the bathroom.

"Hey, you. Bear Gylls' adventuring twin sister. Have you SEEN the state of my knees. LOOK. That's what a rock-face scramble does to soft, tender, uninitiated knees." He points to his angry red scrapes. He's standing by the bed, naked. I can lean off the bed and just about reach him. I projectile my head at his knees to kiss them and miss. The gap's too big. I bang my face into them instead.

"Ouch. Glasgow women are hard. Why are you head butting my knees?"

"You need a doctor to take a look?" I look for 30 milliseconds. "You'll live."

"So much sympathy and compassion. Your patients must love you. I prescribe a good knee scraping for your unfitness, Guy. Take all the skin off them. That'll help."

"Look at this," I say, not really listening. I click on the New York times link and enlarge it for him to read. He reads.

"Some American businesswoman has absconded

with a shed-load of dosh?"

"It's not some random American businesswoman, it's the business associate of my ex-boyfriend that she was coming over to meet."

"Wow! You think he could be involved? Maybe they're holed up together somewhere. His loss." He lowers himself over me and hovers, kissing me, "I got the bigger catch. The fool."

"Adam's a selfish arse. He's not a criminal. He'd sleep with her, then block her. That's his level. Amoral asshole. I don't think he'd steal money. Would he? I don't know anyone that would embezzle company funds."

I shake my head. None of it makes any sense. I click on her Connect2Me profile again. I click on her messages again. Before I can help myself, I type:

'Hi Sarah. Been a while since we messaged. Hope you're ok.'

I hit send, without thinking.

"You do realise the police are going to be monitoring all the traffic to that account. 20 seconds since you sent? You'll be on an FBI Wanted list by now."

I look at Guy in horror. "Shit. I never thought."

"Daftie." He flops on top of me, lifts my laptop,

places it on the floor and slides in under the bed, so it doesn't get squashed or cracked, "I think unless you've actually handled any of the stolen money, know where it is, know where she is or actually killed her for it, you're pretty much in the clear. Dr Donaldson? You have way too many clothes on." He starts pulling my top up to explore what's underneath.

"And you have way too few, even for a spa appointment. Minimum requirement is at least some swimming trunks, a white fluffy robe and some white fluffy slippers."

"We don't have time for hanky-panky first? Boooo. Can we be late?" He looks crestfallen. I laugh and shake my head.

"Absolutely not. I promised you a spa break. So spa-ing we must go. It's ten to five. I think not even you can achieve hanky-panky in ten minutes. Spa treatments are designed to alleviate all that tension. Besides those knees need a break. Look at the state of them."

"Question is, did I pack my swim trunks. Otherwise I am commando spa-ing." Reluctantly he lifts himself off me.

"Tell me you packed swim trunks," I cry. "Who comes on a spa break without swimming trunks?"

"Never fear, Dr D. I packed trunks. You deny me hanky-panky. I am at liberty to tease you mercilessly."

"I did NOT deny you! You took forever in the shower. Even though, as I pointed out at the time, you have to shower before you get in the spa ANYWAY. Double shower, plus a spa pool. How clean are those knees going to be? Fair warning though, my expectations of hanky-panky later are very high." I hand him a white fluffy robe, whilst stripping out of my own clothes in exchange for my cozzie. I didn't tell him I'd bought a new one for the weekend. Push-up, suck-in and as sexy as it was possible to find and get delivered four days before we were setting off. Well, you can't come on your first mini-break to a spa hotel with an old cozzie, can you. I hadn't seen his either. You can tell a lot about a man from his swimming trunks. I am praying for neither tight budgie smugglers nor long, tropical surf-boy baggies. Fortunately, I'm rewarded with sensibly-sized, black swim shorts.

"Sensible Swim Shorts Test passed." I smirk. "They can come to South America."

"Arran was just a test then? Never realised that. Your costume can similarly make its way into our suitcase."

"Thank you, kind sir."

I throw a fluffy robe at him and take the second for myself. It's nice being away. I'm having the best weekend I've had in ages. Guy is so straightforward. No games. No manipulating. No gaslighting. We just have fun. He's interested in me too. He listens. He asks questions. He's normal. So far anyway. I'm more guarded this time. Healthy relationships take time to develop.

I'm bothered by the New York Times article and Sarah Emmerson's disappearance. It feels like a book with some sinister plot leading me back to Adam. A never-ending maze with no exit. I hope Amy's ok. I hope she's kept as far away from him as possible. She deserves peace and a chance at life. What woman, already successful, well-paid with prospects and a seemingly happy life leaves it all for dirty money. It doesn't make sense. I hope she's not with Adam. How many lives can he ruin?

I'll go see Amy again when I get back. I'll take another coffee trip down to Manchester. See how she's doing.

"You coming then?" Guy is all robed up and looking adorable.

"You suit a fluffy robe and slippers."

"Uh-huh. Now she wants hanky-panky. Uh-Uh. Nope. We have a Spa date. I'm on a promise for later. Right now, my body needs de-tensed and recovered from the massive mountain you dragged me up."

"Corbett," I mutter pulling the door shut behind me. "It was just a Corbett."

Should I have messaged the disappeared ghost of Sarah Emmerson. Probably not.

"Think I should tell the police?" I ask Guy as we walk down the corridor.

"What about?" Jeez he has a short memory.

"Sarah Emmerson. Think I should let the police know that she told me she was coming to Manchester to meet with Adam Waters about investing in his conferences?"

"You don't think they'll know that already? Will they not have already looked at all her Connect2Me messages?

"Probably. I just have this feeling that if bad stuff's gone on, maybe I have a bit of the jigsaw. Is it my civic duty to pass it on or to just stay out of it?"

"Maybe we do it tomorrow if you still feel you should. Ponder it for a night."

"You're right. The Guy who's always right." I knock him with a hip bump as we walk. "First one there gets the big towel," I sprint off down the corridor. I hear him murmuring something about scraped knees and mountains behind me. "Corbett" I call back, "It's a Corbett. Wait till you see where I'm taking you tomorrow. Mountain bikes. That's all I'm saying. Hope your bum's tougher than your knees."

20 ADAM: The Biggest Risk is Not Taking the Risk

"It's only fair that we share the risk, Adam. 50:50. We're equal business partners."

My head hurts. My throat's dry. Had a shit night's sleep, full of weird dreams again. I can't be arsed with this.

"Steve, I'm not taking a loan out against the house to cover the conference. Absolutely not. This house is all I've got. You were the one that booked the Premier Hilton Deal and paid first class air fare for the keynotes."

Steve's voice ratchets up ten octaves. He's a screaming whirlwind.

"Fuck's sake Adam. So it's ok for me to risk my house. Two kids at university, two kids at school. You on your own. In what way is that fair? What do I say to Stella? Yeah, babe. I carried the whole can, lost the house, bankrupt, can't feed the kids. No, my business partner put fuck all into the deal."

I can't be arsed with this. I should just walk away. The finances are all in his name. I just work the spreadsheets. Currently we're operating at around a £100K loss, unless we can boost ticket sales or net another sponsor.

"You fucking lost INSpire. I met the woman. That deal was in the bag. What did you do? Flash yourself on camera or something? How could you lose it? It was a cert. £980K. Asshole." He rants on.

I feel the urge to open a beer. I'm not even listening.

"It's less than £100K, Steve. There's still two months to go. That's loads of time to net a new sponsor and drum up sales. I've been thinking. A Group Offer for big businesses. Buy six tickets, get four free. Something like that. That's £10K per group sale. Ten group sales and we're in the clear. I'll run another group promo through all my Connect2Me contacts. We'll be fine."

"But not fine enough for you to cover our asses with a loan?" He's still raging.

I've found the more he screams, the quieter and more calmly I speak. It's a well-known strategy for managing histrionics. Years of dealing with Amy taught me that. I'm a master. Keep calmly selling solutions to get him off the phone. Then I'm walking away. I don't need this shit anymore.

"We'll be fine, Steve. All businesses go through this kind of panic in the run-up. Our brains are primed to think of worst-case scenarios. Evolution. That's what this is. Evolution makes us pull our fingers out so we turn a profit over. The business model is a sound one."

"We've not sold a single fucking ticket in a week, Adam. How is that fucking sound."

He swears too much. I imagine him red-faced, swearing, sweating and flailing his arms around. I'm glad he's several miles away. He's got high blood pressure. No wonder. He'll pop an aneurysm at this rate.

"Calm down, Steve. You employed me to do the leg work. Let me do the leg work. We'll re-energise with some new offers on ticket sales and I'll do another whole network promo. I'll action all that this afternoon. I'm on it, right? I'll message some potential investors too. Put the feelers out. There must be other INSpire's out there. We just need to find them."

Meanwhile I'm thinking: 'I'm so walking from all this shit.' 'I don't need it.' 'Steve's a fruit loop.'

"You're not getting it Adam, are you? This is serious. Stella's gonna go ape when she finds out. We could lose everything. I've got kids, man. Kids. Kids I can't feed, clothe, who can't finish university. We might not have a house. Please, I'm begging you, take a share of the risk. Put a safety net in place. Or Stella will kill me, then leave me."

He's over-reacting. He forgets I know he owns his house outright. Big 5 bed villa in a decent part of Manchester. Worst case scenario, he ends up downsizing. No biggie, is it? Kids are almost up and away anyway.

"I'm not taking a loan out against my house, Steve." How many times do I have to tell him? Absolutely not. I'm not mad. "But I will work my socks off to turn a profit. You know I will. We'll be fine. I promise."

"Asshole, Adam. You're a total Asshole. You've got no dependents, no wife, no kids, a paid off house. We're both company directors yet I've got all the risk. Asshole." Steve sounded like he was close to tears. He can be overly dramatic.

"I've got health shit going on, Steve. It's unlikely I'd get a loan." I don't know if that's true but it sounded good. "I've got diabetes."

I wait on a response to the revelation, but don't get one.

"It's serious Steve. Heart disease, kidney problems, blindness, early death. I've already got heart irregularities. I'm due at the doctors for a full physical work up. High risk for a lender."

"You need to lose weight and stop drinking, mate."

"It's not as simple as that. The damage is already done. I feel shit. But it doesn't stop me touting for ticket sales and drumming business. You get the website updated, the new speaker bios up. I'll hammer Connect2Me. £100K is nothing. In two months we'll turn a healthy profit."

"We HAVE to turn a profit, Adam. There can't be an 'if' here. We've got no savings to fall back on. We lose the house, Stella never forgives me."

Stella. A pint of Stella. Ice cold. Condensation dripping sexily down the glass. My mind is wandering. I can't take any more ranting. It's just bouncing off me. For all his talk, I'm the one that always brings it home. Ideas Man AND Legwork Man. I'm absolutely shattered. The last few days have taken their toll. My Ikea visit to the Isle of Man was exhausting. Almost as tiring as playing perfect boyfriend to Amy. Ironically, I was more worried about being able to 'perform' with Amy than I was about what happened on the Groudle Glen clifftop. Groudle Glen was always within my control. The biology of sleeping with your unhinged ex so she'll cover for you, that's a less reliable ask. But just as crucial to the Masterplan. Genius, Adam. You're genius. You pulled it all off. Just a whinging Steve to go.

"ADAM! Fucking pay attention. I'm trying to summarise what needs doing."

Damn, I drifted off.

"I'm here, Steve. I'm listening. Just making a list of all the things I've got to do this afternoon. I'm doing a network promo-drop. I'm targeting some of the bigger businesses. I'm getting our group ticket offer up and running. I'm scoping potential investors. You're updating the website, bios and programme. Make it snappy. Re-invigorate and re-launch. Wouldn't do any harm to target some personal contacts and contacts of contacts. Personalised messages selling it. It can't just be me doing the marketing. Yes?"

Just get him off the phone. I need to sleep.

"You want to come round here this afternoon? We could work together and bust it all this afternoon."

He's pleading. No. I absolutely do not want to sit in Steve's room for the afternoon. I can't imagine anything worse.

"I need some of the tech I've got here. I'm probably fastest just getting torn into it myself."

"Ok, shall we touch-in again this evening and review progress?"

I groan inwardly. He's such a pain.

"I'm feeling anxious, Adam."

"I can tell." Sarcasm probably not helpful. "Try not to worry, Steve. We've got this. I've got Amy popping round at some point. If my phone's off, that's why. Don't worry." Anything to get him off the phone.

"What happened with Sarah Emmerson anyway? That was in the bag. She was as keen as mustard."

I jump at the sound of her name. An unpleasant flashback. I'd rather she didn't have a name. I'd worked hard to forget. Sarah Emmerson was a lifetime ago. Done and dusted. Chore ticked off.

"Ach. I'm not sure she had as much influence over the company directors and allocation of funds as she led us to believe. She was a minor cog. We were strung along. Unfortunate waste of time. Sometimes it happens. There are more Investor Fish in the sea. We just need to net one."

"Seems odd. To be so sure about sponsoring us, then to back out."

"Maybe it fed her ego. Narcissism. Fantasist. People are strange. C'est la vie."

I want to get off this topic. I want him off the phone.

"Ok, Steve. I'm going to go and get stuck into what we agreed. Website, updates and personal messages, yes?"

Phew. That wasn't fun. I'd been avoiding him for days. Hopefully that'll tide him over for another week or so. Meanwhile I'm disentangling and backing out.

Our partnership is over. I'm tactfully disengaging. I'm not as hopeful of making up the £100K shortfall as I make out. Not my problem anymore. I look at the time. 11am. Too early for beer? Fuck it. I think I deserve one. That was hard. It'll help me sleep too. I need to sleep. Beer. Wank. Sleep. In that order. My phone buzzes.

AMY: 11.04: Good morning handsome! I can't stop thinking about you. Don't know if you're up yet, but I have cake! Pop round for cake, coffee n fun?

Double groan. Triple groan. That's all I need. Amy madness. Nope. Just nope. I've done my duty, now I need a break. Amy reminds of me of my relationship with beer. The more you give her, the more she wants. I always have to temper her with a bit of negativity. Otherwise, she's all over me. I'm constantly having to educate her. It's tiring. Tricky just now, because I also need her for the Masterplan.

ADAM 11.21: Shit Amy, more cake? Diabetic Overload. Maybe tomorrow. Text you later.

And it's a wrap. Chores done. I am so dry. My head's beginning to thump. I head to the kitchen and crack open a bottle of beer, downing half the bottle in a one-er. Better. Another two gulps. Even better. Phone's ringing. Withheld number. Everyone wants a bit of me this morning. I stare blankly at the phone, letting it ring out. I take another slug of beer. It clicks onto voicemail.

"Hi Adam. This is Jim Walker, Consultant Psychiatrist at Wythenshawe. It's 11.40. I've been trying to get hold of you for a few days now to see how you're doing. Please give us a call so we can arrange a convenient time to meet. I can also drop by and see you at home if that's easier. Hope you're doing ok. If things have gotten worse, please phone straight away and we can arrange something quickly. The number here is........"

He reels a number off and tells me he's looking forward to seeing me. The feeling isn't mutual. My phone talks to me, using its automaton tone.

"To hear the message again, press 1. To save the message, press 2. To delete the message, press 3."

I press 3 and wave him goodbye. Farewell Dr Walker. I'm not sure you can help me. Everyone wants a bit of me. Beer. Wank. Sleep. Being left alone. Best therapy. Cheaper and more accessible too. It worked before and seems the only way to stave off these awful dreams. Amy, Sarah, childhood things I'd buried, morphing monsters, sliced flesh, too much blood. The least helpful thing I can think of doing is reliving them through discussion with my psychiatrist. Wanking works far better.

21 AMY: Fall Seven Times, Stand Up Eight

The contents of an 'ovulation kit' are strewn on my bed. Silly, I know, but I'm scared to look at it. Ten sticks, a holder and a set of instructions. They could be made of lethal uranium or stinky fish the way I'm giving them a wide berth. I didn't even know what an ovulation kit was until a few weeks ago.

Getting pregnant was to be avoided at all costs. Take all precautions. Belts and braces, twice over. I know how Adam feels about it. He doesn't do babies. Because he doesn't do babies, I convinced myself I didn't either. I couldn't entertain the notion that I'd be capable or that I could foist something so awful, stressful and tying onto a partner. I took a bus into Altrincham to buy the kit a week ago. An hour's bus journey. I didn't dare buy one locally. I don't know anyone in Altrincham and I never go there, so it seemed safe. I would die if anyone I knew saw me. How do I explain standing in a queue with an ovulation kit? It's not as if you can say you mistook it for tampons or moisturiser. Everyone would know how awful I am. How I was contemplating tricking my boyfriend into parenthood. I don't deserve something as precious as a baby. I'll never be good enough. I had to fight a panic attack in the chemist. Holding on, breathing, grounding and 5 things, 4, 3, 2, 1 again. Mindfulness training, I've been using it for years to get by. People kept asking if I was ok. I was trying to hide the box without making it look like I was shoplifting. That would be all I needed, the police. I bought it, scarlet-faced and stuttering like a loon. I put it in two bags to get it home and stashed it in the wardrobe. I've been too scared to acknowledge its presence since.

Everyone's out. I'm here on my own. So, I empty the box contents onto the bed. I read the instructions.

'Over 99% accurate' 'Get pregnant faster. At home urine test which pinpoints your two most fertile days to maximise your chances of getting pregnant.' 'Once your LH surge is detected make love at any time during the following 48 hours to maximise your chances of getting pregnant.'

The deal is that I pee on the stick. 5 seconds in the stream. If a smiley face comes up in the digital window, I'm fertile. If no face comes up, I'm not. I may not be the most regular in terms of menstruation, but I'm old enough to have a sense of when it's likely. My best guess for this month is around now, two weeks since my last period. The magazines all say that's likely when an egg is released. I'm crapping it. Do I really want this? Is it ridiculous to think I could ever be good enough? What will Adam do?

About a month ago, I sat down with my doctor and had this discussion. She went through all the risks. Every single one. My age, my mental health, my previous suicide attempts, the biology of pregnancy and all the hormonal changes, the stress of pregnancy and child birth, the strain it puts on relationships, Adam, the risks to my health, the expense of raising a child. All of it. I was there for over an hour. It should have terrified me, but it didn't. What amazes me is that she didn't rule it out either. She didn't tell me I was ridiculous. That I was stupid or selfish. Or that I'd be a terrible mother and screw myself and my baby up. On the contrary. She talked risks and how we would counter them together. We talked about more frequent appointments, self-care and monitoring. Healthy living, good food, sleep, exercise, folic acid and vitamins. Minimising stress. No alcohol. The possible reactions of prospective fathers. She told me that 30% of domestic abuse starts during pregnancy. She also said women have a remarkable ability to cope. That motherhood can be a strength. That looking after a baby can make you more resilient that you knew you could be. We were warriors. Goddesses. She also told me she'd be there for me if this was a choice I made. She didn't leave me steeped in shame for the terrible person I am. She understood why it was so important. Why it was everything. I've been repressing who I am and what I need. I'd expected to feel foolish. I didn't. I felt listened to. Understood. Two grown-ups having a sensible, grown-up conversation. Precautions, risk, monitoring, self-awareness, safety planning. We agreed to make changes to my medication. I came off one medication totally. I swapped one for another at a low dose. She said the risks of abnormalities were low, but the changes made it even safer. We agreed to more frequent appointments. She gave me a list of organisations and support lines to contact if I wanted to talk things through with people who understood. She also warned me that fertility declines rapidly with age, particularly for women and showed me some charts. What she's implying is that I can't wait too long. I cried as I was leaving and she hugged me. I told her they weren't sad tears, they were tears of happiness. For the first time in a long time, in years, I felt happy. I felt heard. I felt like I wasn't crazy. I wasn't repressing my own needs by absorbing myself in someone else's. Loving myself is important too. One of the things she asked me. She said, if the absolute worst-case scenario is that your relationship breaks up, for whatever reason, he leaves me or hurts me or I want something else, could I bring a child up on my own? She told me not to answer that question straight away, but to think about it. I did think about it. Yes. I think I could bring a child up on my own. That's a massive step.

I look at these ovulation sticks strewn on my bed. I pick one up and turn it around and around in my hand. I already know I'm likely to see a 'go for it' smiley face. I also know that if I don't do it now, I'll have another month to wait. I'll be another month older. So will Adam. He said yes to the Labrador. We've been so loved up. We're having sex. I stopped taking the pill months ago. Neither of us are getting younger. Peeing on a stick is never elegant, especially as I want to make absolutely sure the tip of the stick spends the maximum amount of time in the stream. I turn it face down for the required three minutes, and walk away. I don't want to watch for a face. I give it 6 minutes. Just to be sure. There it is. The 'go for it' smiley face. I knew it would be there. My stomach is knotty. I have 48-hours to bed him. I'm not sure where this determination has come from. The fabled biological clock? A new inner strength. There's no time like the present. Clock's tick. I take a deep breath. Shower, shave legs, dress, don best underwear, go round. I can do this.

Two hours later. EEK! I'm driving to Adam's. He doesn't even know. I should be terrified. Weirdly I'm quite calm. I've just gone for jeans and a top. Casual, popped-by, no-big-deal look. The 'this wasn't planned' look. What turns Adam off is drama and emotionality. Here's hoping the opposite does, well, does the opposite, I guess. Girl-next-door, no drama booty call. As I stand on the porch, I realise I hadn't considered the possibility that he might not be in or that he might not answer the door. Worse still I hadn't considered the possibility that he might have people round. 48 hours. Tick-tock. Fortunately, none of that applies.

"Amy," he stands behind the door, looking surprised. "I'm working."

"I know," I say smiling, "I don't want to disturb. I need some time out the house. A break from the well-meaning but sometimes intrusive, sometimes annoying sister. Just a familiar face."

"It's good to see you, but I've got loads of work to do."

"I'll blend in. You'll hardly notice me." I walk in. I don't wait for an invite. Empowerment. Feet over the threshold. "Honestly, work on. I just need some peace and quiet. This is perfect."

He looks sceptical, confused maybe, but accepts it and disappears upstairs. I make two mugs of tea and take them up. He's sitting at his desk in the spare-room-office-bedroom, working with his MacBook on one side and his PC monitor on the other. He flits between the screens comparing spreadsheets.

"Looks complicated," I say. I put his tea down beside him and kiss the back of his neck, before flopping on the bed behind and closing my eyes. Silent mindfulness. 5 things, 4, 3, 2, 1. He works on. I lie in peaceful silence. It's nice. I must lie for half an hour, listening to him tapping away on his keyboard.

"Steve's a fruit loop," he pipes up unexpectedly, "he complains about the budgets being overspent, but he's overspending unnecessarily on all of them."

"Steve's always been a fruit loop." I respond gently. "I don't know how you can work so closely with someone who stresses you out so much."

"I know. I've been thinking for a while that I need to disengage. He gets so wound up. Then he gets unreasonable. It's stressful. I mean, like here, he's worried about breaking even on costs, but pays first class flights for all the keynote speakers, as well as executive rooms at the Hilton. Speakers don't expect that kind of luxury. They don't need it. Not when costs are tight. Hot sit-down lunch when we're also having a big sit-down dinner. Delegates won't want that. They'll want a casual buffet and a mingle."

"Yup. Agreed on all counts. I'm not sure anyone needs the indulgence of first-class travel these days. Climate reasons alone. And I'd explode if you gave me a hot sit-down lunch and dinner, plus all the pastries, snacks, biscuits and chocolates they do with coffee breaks. You should put a woman in charge of the finances."

"Or anyone bar Steve. No wonder he can't balance the books. He needs to control himself."

"You sound stressed. It's not worth it. Seriously. Take a break. Come and chill for a bit. Lie beside me."

He surprises me by doing as I suggest. I didn't expect it to be that easy. He gets up from the desk and lies down beside me. He puts his arm around me. I mould against his chest.

"Anything I can do to help?" I ask, thinking, go gently, this is nice. "I used to be a dab hand with a spreadsheet. Fingers of fury," I wiggle my fingers in front of his face. He shakes his head.

"Flights are non-refundable. Might be able to do a deal with the hotel on the rooms, but I don't think we'll get much of a discount. It's the Hilton. They don't need to pander to us."

"You can only do what you can do, Adam. No point in agonising over things that can't be changed.

Steve's mess. Not your fault."

"I know, I keep telling him the only solution is to drum up more ticket sales and try to find another sponsor. As always, I do all the legwork whilst he runs in circles whinging."

"I don't like seeing you so stressed." I've slipped a hand up his t-shirt and begun to massage. He doesn't resist. Way easier than I expected. I take that as an invitation. "Take 10-minutes out for a de-stress. It might help. Go back to the spreadsheets in a bit. They'll still be there." I know there's some body lotion in the bathroom, my old stuff. But I think if I get off the bed, he'll get up too and go back to the desk. I need to work with what I've got. It's like walking up a hill. Keep the momentum going. "Let me try something. Ten minutes." I flip on top of him, so I'm straddling him and pull his t-shirt off. He obliges. Good start. "Close your eyes," I tell him. "No peaking. Go on. Trust me." He frowns slightly. I laugh and lean back in the straddle, so I'm pinning his legs down. I arch my back. I'm hoping it's a good view. "Close your eyes, I'm not going to hurt you." He feigns a bigger frown and pulls a face.

"Promise?" He's teasing me.

"I promise," I say and I brush my hands lightly over his eyes, like I'm closing his eyelids. He can't help closing them. Automatic response. I start with hands on his body. He opens his eyes, when I switch to roaming my lips over him. "Uh-uh. Close eyes." I brush my fingers gently over his eyes again. I nibble on him. Just where it's sensitive. Ultimately, I slip a hand down his shorts and am rewarded with a gasp and a groan. I'm feeling pleased with myself. It gives me confidence to go further. More with the lips, tongue and mouth. Like many good massages, it crosses an inevitable line from gentle and sensual to lustful and urgent. It's been a very long time since I've exercised any kind of control or skill like this. I've never had the self-confidence. I'd always be terrified of a crushing rejection. Nothing breeds shame and destroys self-worth more than a thwarted lustful advance. My best chance of success is to go with hands and lips, until I'm certain I'm past the threshold and he can't stop the climax. I've picked up that he's begun to fret about performance. An age and weight thing. It seems to be working anyway. He seems to be enjoying it. Woah. That's an understatement. I'm definitely getting there. I've somehow managed to slip my clothes off without breaking momentum. I am indeed a goddess. My once-in-a-month opportunity, I need to make this good. I throw myself into the cause, slipping on, grinding, twisting, squeezing, leaning back and finding a rhythm that works for him. I can feel conclusion building and make sure he's as deep as I can get him. With a deep groan and an expletive, it happens. I hover for a moment or two, just to make sure, before lying back and making sure nothing escapes.

"Wow!" he says sleepily, "that was kinda awesome. You've not done that for a long time. You were persistent. Enthusiastic."

"Shhh...... lie still for ten and hold me. De-stress.

Spreadsheet antidote. Let me lie here for a bit with you, then I need to get back. Before I'm missed. I can't stay long." We both doze off. Actually, for a couple of hours. Perfect.

"Damn spreadsheets," he says groggily on coming to. "Want a beer?"

"I'm fine," I say stretching. When I press my legs together, I can still feel it. Glorious success. "I should get back."

"Plenty hot water if you want to shower."

"I'll be fine till I get back. Gotta go." I pull my underwear and jeans back on. "I kiss him, leaving him lying there. "Text you later." Then I slip out quietly. No drama. Yup. I can do no drama and understated if that turns him on.

I jump into the car. I can't believe I jumped him and left. I giggle to myself. New Amy. I plan on holding off showering until tomorrow. Maximise the chances. Maybe we can do a repeat. 48-hours the box said. WOOP!

22 ADAM: I'm Not Ill, My Pancreas is Just Lazy

Amy's face. We're having sex. I'm watching. Not from my body. Above my body. Around Amy's body. Fusing with her body. Fusing with her face. Ugh. Morphs into Sarah Emmerson's face. She's on top of me. Her long hair wraps around my throat. Tightens. Writhing snakes. They hiss menacingly. Amy's going for it. No, Sarah. Fuck, there's a knife. Get the snakes. She's plunging it in me. No, in herself. It's a ritual fucking sacrifice. My mother watches. She slits her throat. Ear to ear. Gurgles. Morphs. Amy-Sarah-monster. A giant. Disintegrates. Millions of bloodied ants. A sea of gushing blood and entrails and ants. Fills my nose, mouth, throat. Smeared on my chest victoriously. Killer Amy-Sarah-ants everywhere. I can't see. It's a red, pulsing blur. It's pulsing in my head. Covering my hair. I'm drowning in Amy's blood. Sarah's blood. Amy's blood. No, it's mine. My blood. My ants. My mother in a grave covered in ants. She can't breathe. I can't breathe. Holy shit. I can't breathe. Really, I can't breathe. I can't fucking breathe. Wake up, Adam. Shit. I can't breathe. Holy fuck. WAKE UP. I'M DYING. I CAN'T

BREATHE.

Shaking, drenched in sweat. My heart is racing. I'm soaked. Dripping. I can wring my body out. The sheet is saturated. I ooze off the bed in a sweat-water-slide. What the fuck is happening to me? I can't see. I can't focus. Everything is floating. Foggy and blurred. Eggy and furred. Words won't even form right. I'm so scared. If I could breathe, I'd cry. I'm not thinking straight. Panic attack? Not panic. Absolute terror. A crescendo of absolute terror. I'm about to explode and splatter the walls in gunk. Amy, help me. I need you. Amy, please. AMY. I'M FUCKING DYING. WITCH! You left me. Selfish cow. I'm so scared. I don't want to be alone. Everyone leaves me. Then I die. The words hit. THEN. I. DIE. I promise mummy. I'll be good. Don't hurt me. I don't want to die.

I reach for my phone. It's on the bedside table. Shit, I knock it off. Where the fuck is it? I'm half in bed, half on the floor. Do I die like this? In my underpants? Amy's number, Amy's number, Amy's number. How do I dial? Who do I want? Why don't my fingers work? I can't stop shaking. I drop the phone again. Blind panic. Three blind mice. Fuck's sake. Fucking-shitting-sake. I'm fucking dying. Here. Alone. Drowning in fucking sweat. My heart. I start crying. Gulping and crying. A hand is gripping my heart and squeezing hard.

My father. I knew he'd kill me.

My heart doesn't feel right. Two small beats. A gap. It's stopped. A giant beat. Three fast beats. A gap. A monster beat. Hundreds of fast ones. I can't breathe. Heart or panic? Breathe. Force my heart back into a steady rhythm.

"Adam? It's four in the morning. What's wrong?"

Speak up Amy, faster. Why are you whispering? It's an emergency. Don't be useless. Not now. Why are you so useless?

"Heart attack. Fuck. Amy, help me." I'm gasping and crying.

"Phoning an ambulance NOW. Adam, listen to me. I'm phoning an ambulance. I'm putting the phone down. I'm phoning an ambulance. Then I'm phoning you straight back. Pick up. Ok? OK?"

She sounds faint. What did she say? Is that my phone ringing? I reach out. I don't know. Where is it? What am I doing? Floating in space. It's light up here. A bang brings me to. What's that? Someone's in the house. People? An army. All running up the stairs. The army's here. Hallelujah. They're in the room.

"Adam….. Adam." Someone's got my hand. "Adam? Adam, can you hear me?"

I can, just about. But you sound very far away and the words don't make a lot of sense. Who's Adam?

"Adam, can you tell us what happened?"

I start to tell them. The words aren't coming out. I'm jumbled. Why won't the words come out? What did happen? I don't fucking know. Why ask me? My mouth doesn't work. I've got things on me. My chest, my arm, my finger. Why are they covering me in things? Am I dying? Maybe I'm already dead.

"Adam, do you know where you are?"

That doesn't even make sense. You're not even in the room. I'm not in the room.

"Sarah. Find Sarah. Sarah Emmerson. Blood everywhere. My mum……she's there. Keep dancing. Get Sarah. Mum's not good."

"Who's Sarah, Adam? Amy's here. Your girlfriend Amy."

Sarah. Amy. Sarah. Amy. Jo. Whose face is who's. Who's Amy? Amy Who? Sarah Who? Jo's dead.

"I'm here Adam. The paramedics are here. They're wondering when you last ate."

Fairy cake. Ferry cake. Keep dancing. "Sarah?"

"It's me, Amy, Adam. I'm here. Everything is going to be ok."

Someone is crying. Who's Amy? "Sarah?"

"Your blood sugar's really low Adam. They're going to give you something."

I had sugar in my pocket, on the ferry. "Sugar on

the ferry. Don't die Amy." Is that pear drops?

"Adam? Adam? Stay with us Adam. Stay awake. Listen. Adam? Can you hear me? Stay with my voice Adam. Focus on my voice."

Why is everyone still in the next room. I can hardly hear them. Did I hide the knife? Fuck, did I hide the knife? They're looking for it. They know.

"We're going to lift you on to the stretcher Adam. Listen to me. We're taking you to hospital. They'll sort your blood sugar out. Check you over. How much alcohol has he had? Drugs?"

Who are they asking? I need beer. I can't see who's here. How did they get in? Did I let them in?

"Ok, lifting now, Adam. On three. One... two... three.... LIFT."

Are they putting me in a straitjacket? They're fastening me down. They fastened dad down. In the care home. He never came out. Bump. Bump. Bump. Bump. Sliding doors. Slam. Sinking into the ground. Everyone is disappearing. Is Sarah dead? Tie rocks around the clothes. Shhhh....... Beep. Beep. Beep. Beep. Nothingness. They've all gone. Everyone leaves me. Darkness. Silence. Death is quiet.

"Well. Hello Adam. Welcome back!"

I blink. It's very bright. My eyes take a few moments to adjust. A woman is holding my wrist.

She's smiling. Is she looking at me? She has a stethoscope round her neck. This isn't my bed. Where am I?

"You're in hospital, Adam," as if she read my mind. "You're safe. I'm Dr Russell."

Beep. Beep. Beep. Beep. I'm wired to a machine. And a drip stand. It smells like a hospital. I hate hospitals. I feel my stomach lurch. Antiseptic, infection and death.

"You've had a hypoglycaemic attack. Low blood sugar. Your body went into shock. You're lucky your girlfriend called an ambulance or you might not be here."

This woman can definitely read my mind. Another witch. Witch Doctor. My girlfriend?

"Is your girlfriend's name Sarah?"

I shake my head. "Amy. Amy Hawes." My voice is dry, crispy, sore. It's all cracked. A toad's grunt.

"Ah, you were talking about someone called Sarah. We couldn't understand what you were saying."

Fuck. Fuck. Fuck. Fuck. What did I say?

"I was to tell you that she's securing the house for you, then she's coming over. They had to bust your lock to get in. She's found a joiner to sort it all, so you're not to worry. Everything's secure again. Glad to say it looks as though we've stabilised things. Your stats are coming back to normal. You gave us all a scare."

"I can go home?" I knew that was hopeful. God, I hate hospitals. No beer, shit food, bright lights and sub-tropical temperatures. Too many nosey nurses. Peeing in bottles. The incessant, bloody beeping. The smell of death. I feel claustrophobic. If I could jump up and run away, I would. Escape this terror. Hide and breathe. I'm a specimen, pinned out on open display. About to be gutted.

"In a couple of days. We need to make sure you're stable Referrals to endocrinology, dietetics, cardiology. Diabetes is serious. You've been lucky this time. You were moments off a diabetic coma."

"I feel fine, now," if I try an optimistic tone, it might work. It's hard to charm a doctor with a hospital gown on. Cheeky smile? Wink? Hello doc. Want to check everything's working again down there? Wrap a hand round?

"Good. We want you staying that way."

Damn, I'm getting nowhere. She's tough. Wonder if I can get Amy to sneak some beer in. My MacBook. I don't like being separated from it. Too much sensitive stuff. She's a snoop. She can't help herself. Annoying cow. Maybe I could sign myself out.

"You're going to have to monitor your blood sugar properly, Adam. No skipping meals and you need to cut down on alcohol. Seriously. This is an alarm bell. The team can help you put plans in place to prevent long term complications. You've been very lucky this time."

I just need to be home. I don't like the idea of Amy snooping about when I'm not there. She'll have keys again now. That's inconvenient. Snooping witch. No respect for boundaries. I need to get home.

"Rest up. Your body's been through major trauma. Sleep and rest are best things for now. Try not to worry. Everything looks ok. You'll be able to go home in a day or two."

"I *have* to stay?" pleading look, charm offensive. She has nice eyes. Red hair. First year sociology student. The virgin.

"Well, technically you can sign yourself out. We can't keep you here against your will. But I really wouldn't recommend it. It's just a day or two. The nurses will take good care of you."

I sigh. No MacBook. No phone. No clothes. Amy rampaging through the house looking at God knows what. Great. Bloody great. I'm trapped. Prison Hospital Hell.

"Try to relax," and with that she left me to my own devices. As much as you can be when you're hooked to a drip stand, a catheter and a beeping machine.

"You up to a visitor?" one of the nurse's breezes in with a bedpan in her hand. I really hope that's not for me. "Your girlfriend is here."

Bloody Amy. She didn't wait for a response. Moments later, Amy bounds up to the bed. Why can't she be miserable. It's a prison.

"Hey," she takes my hand, "you gave us a fright."

"Hey." I'm not in the mood for her chunter. "Who's *'us'* anyway?"

"I've had the door sorted. The joiner's fitted a new lock. I've got two keys." She fishes in her bag and brings out two sets of two keys. "I'll put one in your drawer. Shall I keep a set? Just in case?"

Jeez. I can't actually say no, can I? No. There you go. No, you fucking can't, you snooping bitch.

"That's great, Amy. You're a star. Thank you. Doctor says without you, I'd probably not be here. Thank you. Thank you for everything."

She looks as if she's about to cry. No. Please, just no.

"I'm fine, Amy." I keep it bright and breezy. "Doctor says everything is just fine. Everything is stabilising. There's no damage. It's just a warning. Don't skip meals, good food, more exercise, less beer. That's all. I'll be fine. *We'll* be fine." Nope. That starts her crying. That's what I didn't want. Stop it, woman.

"I thought you were dying Adam. I thought that was it. You looked so bad. Grey and sweaty. You weren't making any sense. You kept talking about Sarah. You didn't even recognise me. You didn't know who you were."

Fuck. Fuckety-bloody-fuck.

"Why were you talking about Sarah? Do you….. " she pauses and licks her lips. She's trembling. "Do you like her? I mean, it's ok if you do."

"Fuck's sake, Amy. My brain was fucked. I was jibbering nonsense. I don't even know what I was saying. Course not. Don't be ridiculous. I phoned YOU. I wanted YOU. When I thought I was dying, it was YOU I needed. Crazy girl. Doctor says everyone jibbers random nonsense when the brain blips. Random people we barely know. She was some electrical brain misfire. The people you love are people you are least likely to jibber about. Everyone knows that. Brain sparks random shite."

She nods. Looks relieved. I think I got away with it. Thank fuck. Get off topic. Give her something to do.

"Would you be able to bring me some things in? I don't know who else I can ask. Or trust. You're the only one I have. I love you."

"Of course, Adam. Anything. I love you too. Give me a list. I'll do it now."

Dare I ask her to smuggle some beer in? Step too far maybe? Or will I? "This hospital gown is a nightmare. It's got no back, just ties. My arse is hanging out for the world to see. Can you bring some pyjamas? I don't own any. You'll need to buy a set." She nods, writing it down.

"Yup, that's fine. Pyjamas. What else?"

"Some boxers. Jersey ones. Loose. Not the fitted, jockey ones. Some clothes. Shoes. Socks. My MacBook. Charger. My phone."

Beer? Beer? Go on.

"Would you sneak a couple of beers in too?" This place is the pits. Depressing. I'll never sleep. It's too bloody hot. And the beeps drive me mad."

She looks at me anxiously. "Are you allowed beer in hospital?"

Stupid, bloody woman. Of course not. It's a hospital. "Yes. It'll be fine. Anything which reduces stress is good. And a couple of bottles is nothing. Doctor says reduce, not stop. Stress is worse for my health than a bottle of beer."

"Ok, if you're sure."

I'd kill for a fish supper too. The grey food will kill me. I think Amy may actually pass out if I add a fish supper to the list.

"Some decent food. The food here is shocking. Inedible. Grey. Maybe some decent snacky things from Marks and Spencer's. Sandwiches and stuff. Biscuits. Jelly babies. Juice too."

She scribbles it down. "Shall I let Cal know? What about Steve?"

"It's fine. Just bring my phone in. I'll do the calls." I really don't want Amy telling my brother or my business partners about my near-death experience. I'd rather temper that one myself. Maybe in a week or two. The last thing I need is Steve turning up at my hospital bed where there's no escape from the harassment. "No visitors, Amy. Just you. You're the only one I want to see. The only one I need. I love you."

She nods and looks pleased. Score. I am good. I am very good. I even believe myself.

"I think I got everything," she reels through her list.

"Want some money?" I offer, knowing she'll refuse. There's quite a lot on the list though. She'll need to buy pyjamas, pants, socks and do a Marks and Spencer's run. Courtesy to at least offer. She shakes her head. I know she's pleased to help. "Be careful with my MacBook. It's got all my work stuff on it. Don't leave it anywhere. Use the laptop bag. I'm dead if that goes. My life is on my MacBook."

She nods again. "Got it." She pauses. "Adam….?" I wonder what's coming. "I was looking for your house keys… for the joiner. He wanted them to get the old lock off. I found these." She takes two crumpled pieces of paper from her bag.

What are they? I can't see.

"Isle of Man ferry tickets. They were in one of your pockets. That's the day we were at Aunt Bea's for dinner."

Shit. And fuck. Quadruple fuck. Anger hits like a tidal wave. I am so fucking angry. How dare she. Unbelievable, useless, snooping witch. No right. She has no right. Searching my pockets? Disloyal cow. She knows.

"Really?"

I keep my voice level. Uninterested. It's an effort. I want to slam her hard against a wall. She deserves it. Useless, snooping harlot. I perfect nonchalance. I take the tickets from her, screw them up and toss them in the hospital disposal bag for tissues.

"Must be a printing error."

That's believable, isn't it? Best I can come up with on the spur of the moment. Not bad at all. Plausible. Definitely plausible.

"Happens all the time on these crappy ferries. As long as they give you a piece of paper, they don't really bother what facts or fiction is printed on it. Wrong date. Mickey Mouse outfit. Not been to the Isle of Man in ages."

I've got away with it. She's shut up.

"You sure you don't want some money, honey. I don't want to put you out." Gentle and loving sorts everything with Amy.

"It's no problem. I'll go get everything now."

"Give's a kiss then sweetie. I nearly died. Remind me what I could have lost." I know how to work her. Of course, she leans in for the kiss. I make it a good one. "I'm sorry for scaring you. You saved my life. I owe you the world. And I promise I'm going to give it to you. Starting with all my love." Another decent kiss. I'm feeling sick. Too many close calls. Too much stress. I haven't brushed my teeth in a couple of days. Oops. "I love you," I squeeze her to me. She'll not let down. Thank goodness. Must be more careful. She relaxes into me and kisses me back. Perfect. I feel bile rise.

"I love you too." I know she does. "Everything is going to be ok, isn't it?"

"Everything is going to be bloody brilliant." I wink at her. "Starting from right now, beautiful girl. I promise. Just remember, I love you. And always will. Without you, I have nothing. You saved my life. That means something. Forever."

23 RACHEL: An Apple a Day Keeps the Fairies at Bay

"Congratulations, you're most definitely pregnant."

I look at the stick in my hand indicating the presence of human chorionic gonadotrophin, a sure-sign marker of pregnancy. As far as medicine goes, they may be simple things, but urine sticks rarely lie. One of the few constants in the life of a family doctor.

"When was your last period?"

The woman in front of me beams. Literally glows. She rubs her belly protectively, almost with an air of wonder. It's just lovely to watch. I smile. I can't help myself. I think I might be beaming as much as her. Moments like these make it all worthwhile. So much sickness, poverty, poor mental health, older adults fading away, day in, day out. A longed-for pregnancy is a joy. This is why I became a doctor. These life changing moments of pure ecstasy. A happy twosome becomes a three.

"It was due two weeks ago," she tells me happily, "I did three home tests, but I didn't dare believe. I thought, if the doctor says I am, I must be. I can't believe it."

I beam at her and rub her shoulder. Doctor-Patient, Woman to Woman solidarity. I had referred this couple for IVF about six months ago. They'd fallen pregnant before the assessment came through. It so often seems to happen that way. Like you're testing fate, daring it to defy you, until it finally gives in. Ok, fate says, have the baby.

"I think you can believe it. Four tests don't lie. There's definitely a baby in there." I'm glowing as much as she is. We could jig round the room together. "Have you told Eddie yet?"

She shakes her head. "I was scared to. In case it wasn't real. He wants it so badly. I even told him to leave me and find a woman who wasn't broken. A woman who could have his children."

"YOU are having his child. YOU are his perfect woman. Just takes some couples longer to get there than others. Congratulations Mummy-To-Be! Now…." I bring some forms up on the PC. I also pull a checklist from my drawer for her to take away. "Things to do. We want to monitor you closely, given the problems you've had conceiving. First step is to make an appointment with the surgery midwife. Do it at reception before you leave. She'll book your first scans. Keep taking the folic acid for another two months. Eat well and often. Keep exercising. Oh, and tell Eddie." I wink at her. "I think you're going to have one excited dad-to-be. Maybe slip a baby sock in his dinner tonight."

I glance at the clock. I'm running late. It's been a busy morning clinic. It's going to be a very quick lunch. I usher my last patient of the morning out the door, reminding her to book her antenatal appointment at reception. A nice appointment to end on. I slip my shoes off under the desk and wiggle my toes. The modern, practical laminate flooring is cool underfoot. Mixed bag this morning. My first patient had been a teen who didn't want to see her pregnancy through. The penultimate patient had been a lovely 82-year-old woman who'd had her third TIA and who I'd devastated by telling she couldn't legally drive any longer. That had been preceded by the young guy in so much debt, he thought the only way out was to drive his car into a tree. At least he came to see me and didn't just do it. I need to do some secondary referrals and sign the repeat prescriptions before the afternoon clinic.

My lunches have become grabbed porridge pots. Just add hot water. Hot. Vaguely filling. But less than satisfying. Gruel for the workers. I grab a pot from the drawer and head for the kitchen. No-one else there. It's been so busy lately. We've become ships that pass in the surgery. I can go all day without seeing anyone. Everyone trapped in a consulting room conveyor belt of never-ending problems. That's modern general practice for you. The radio fills the space as the kettle creaks and clicks, mid-way to a stuttered boil. The familiar jingle.

'Now for the latest news. It's one o'clock.'

What is it they say, a watched kettle never boils? I glare at it. Time ticks on.

'A body has washed up on the West Shore Beach of the Isle of Walney in Cumbria. A dogwalker made the gruesome discovery at around 7am this morning.'

I've never even heard of the Isle of Walney. The Isle of Walnut. Walnut Island. I turn the radio up from its barely audible level to listen.

'Walney, primarily a nature reserve administered by Cumbria Wildlife Trust is an 11-mile-long Island in the Irish Sea, linked by bridge to the town of Barrow-In-Furness.'

Well, there you go, my questions answered. I think I've been to Barrow-In-Furness. It's just on the edge of the National Park. There's an abbey there. Years ago. Maybe camping? A Lake District walking holiday? A vague memory. I wrinkle my nose, trying to think.

'The body looks to be female, but is as yet unidentified. It's not known how long it's been at sea. A forensic team has been deployed to the area.'

The kettle clicks off, just as the Practice Nurse comes into the kitchen and gets a Tupperware box of salad out the big, double-door white fridge.

"Hey Rachel. Busiest morning ever, eh? I've not even had time to go for a pee. How's you?" She clicks off the lid of her box noisily. "What I wouldn't give for a giant slab of cake. Slimming World tonight though. Almost a stone. Gotta keep going."

"I know, I'm on the hot water gruel." I hold up my porridge pot for her inspection. "It's not much of a reward after a packed clinic. Food is fuel and all that."

They're interviewing the dog walker on the radio now.

'Nothing ever happens here. It's horrible. Milo started sniffing and barking. I thought it was a washed-up seal, or a whale. The last thing I expected was a naked woman. All bloated and rotten. The birds had been pecking at it. Horrendous. Rocked our community. Poor girl.'

"What's that?" Chris motions the radio between mouthfuls of lettuce. "What's happened?"

"Body of a woman washed up. Beach on an Island just off Cumbria. They don't know who she is or how long she's been at sea. Dogwalker found her."

"Ugh," she shudders, "now that's a find when you're out walking your dog that'll give you nightmares. Not pretty."

"It is." I stir the porridge round and round, concentrating on breaking up the clumps. "S'cuse me Chris. I think I'll eat this in my room. I've got a load of paperwork to do before this afternoon."

I turn the radio back down to its barely audible level before exiting the kitchen, gingerly carrying a pot of burning porridge lava by the lips of the pot top. This stuff removes skin. I google the news as I blow on the burning spoonful and eat, and read some more. There's not much to add to what I heard on the radio. A body has washed up on the beach. The Irish Sea has mad and constantly changing tides, or so the experts say, so she could have entered the sea anywhere. There's a whole science around tides and directions and seasons. They change daily, apparently, and the Irish Sea is particularly wild. My search tells me it's female. Yes, I knew that. They don't know who she is. Knew that too. Some horrible stuff around the decomposition of bodies at sea and what happens to them, making them difficult to identify. Apparently even weighted bodies float to the surface after three or four days. They get eaten by birds, buffeted madly by waves, and if that's not enough indignity, putrefaction and scavenging creatures dismember the corpse in a week or two and the bones sink to the seabed. Does that mean she's been in the sea less than two weeks? I like living people. Forensics freak me out. All dental records, fingerprints and DNA. Another article says most bodies that wash up are suicides rather than nefarious murders. Poor girl. Was life really that bad? Makes me think of my patient who'd been fantasising about driving into a tree. Buffeted by her wild, watery grave, instead of an imposing, immoveable oak tree. From nature, back to nature. Dust to dust and all that. On a whim, I ring Guy the guy.

"I am privileged, Dr Donaldson. During clinic

time too. I got a lecture in twenty. What's up? You ok?"

"Nice to hear from you too." He's so normal. Instant comfort, like a hot porridge pot when you're starving. I can feel his voice work its magic.

"Sorry, hun. I meant to say… darling Rachel, how wonderfully unexpected. I love hearing from you at any time of the day. You just calling to say you love me?"

"Kind of. I miss you. Just wanted to hear your voice. You seen the news?" Maybe I should have stopped reading about the scavenging of bodies at sea and that poor woman.

"No, why? I've not stopped this morning. Us University Lecturers, overworked and underpaid. Not like the elite of NHS medics."

"A woman's body washed up on a beach in Cumbria. A dogwalker found her. Horrible. Tiny Island Community. They don't know who she is. It knocked me off-kilter. News says most bodies that wash up like that are suicides. What could be so bad that you toss yourself off a cliff? She was all bloated and rotting."

"You may be a brilliant doctor, but you can't save everyone in the world."

"I need to stop reading about seabirds, scavenging, decomposition and the battering tidal currents of the

Irish Sea."

"Yes, you do. Want me to come over tonight? I could make dinner for you, or we could go out? Whatever you fancy. If it distracts you from decomposing bodies, it's well-worth the rail fare. I can afford to be late in tomorrow too."

Yes, yes, yes and yes. That was exactly what I wanted. This Guy was a keeper.

"Actually, I would LOVE that, Guy the guy. What time can you get here?"

He laughs. "You're that keen to jump me, that keen to be distracted or that keen to experience my home cooking. I warn you, it's nothing special."

"I've jumped you before. You underestimate yourself. I thought it was quite special." I like this talk. I don't want the call to end. Light hearted nonsense is just what I need.

"HA! You got me, girl. I can probably catch the 6pm train, be through for 7? Pasta and jumping, in whatever order you fancy. Just steer off the dead body talk."

"What's the use of dating a microbiologist if you can't ask them about decomposing bodies?"

"If she was a fungus, I'd be your man. Don't you have forensic buddies for this kind of weirdly morbid curiosity?"

"Most of my buddies, prefer working with the living. Speaking of which…." I glance at the clock and sigh. "My next patient is due in ten."

"Yup, you got clinic. I got a lecture. 7pm for seafood pasta extraordinaire?"

"Guy, you're perfect. Want me to pick anything up?"

"Nup. Just your good self. I'll do the shopping. Send you into a fish shop and you'll just go all dead body and 'scavenging sea creature' on me again. We'll get weird, flesh-eating molluscs for dinner. See you in a bit, hun. Love you."

"Love you too, Guy." I really think I do. Reliability, constancy, love, feeling wanted. Sincerity and integrity. Someone with integrity and morals, not like….. well…. whatever.

Guy's hung up. But I feel so much better. Don't know what got into me. Focus. First patient in ten minutes. I can get a couple of referrals typed and these repeats signed. I pick up my phone. Type a text to Amy. Nothing like procrastinating over paperwork. I don't like thinking about suicides.

RACHEL: 13.41: Hey Amy. Been a while. How are you? Have you seen the news today? Some poor soul has washed up on a beach in Cumbria. Hope all is well with you. We must catch up properly soon. Xx

245

Quite often Amy picks up and texts back quickly. She must be busy.

RACHEL: 13.58: Let's catch up soon. It's been too long. How about a coffee and cake meet-up when I'm next off? Give me ring later and we can arrange something. Hope all is well. Xx

I press send and switch my phone off for the afternoon.
I'm so glad Guy's coming round tonight. I have this horrible feeling of foreboding. A sort of dark, complex cloud that won't shift. Wish I knew where it was coming from. Must stop researching how to identify decomposing bodies. Do you still have fingerprints after a week being pummelled at sea? Teeth and DNA?
I'm just being daft. 2pm appointment is an emergency. Screaming toddler with earache. I don't need reception to tell me they've arrived. I can literally hear the screaming from the waiting room. I may not be able to sort the world. But thankfully screaming toddlers and earache is within my gift.

24 AMY: The Biggest Gamble in the World

OMG

OMG, OMG, OMG

I can't bear to look. I can't bear not to look. My period is late. I've peed on a stick. It's now sitting face-down on top of the lavatory. It's been sitting there for 8-minutes 36 seconds. I can't bring myself to turn it over. Just stare at it. I can't explain it, but I *feel* pregnant. I mean, if I am, granted it's no more than a few cells away from being sperm and egg. Actually, that's not true. It's already got a back, a neural tube, and the beginnings of a heart, eyes and ears. I've looked it up. I run my hands over my tummy. Where is she? I always imagined if I had a baby, it would be a girl. Right now, she's the size of a blueberry. I can't turn it over. I'm scared.

If it's positive it will change my life forever. I will have to contend with the guilt of never being a good enough mother, along with everything else. If it's negative, it will crush me more. I'm not even capable of falling pregnant. I can't do that. The most basic of human functions. C'mon Amy. A good mum doesn't cower away from a stick. Turn it over. I can't. Turn it over, stop being ridiculous. My heart is racing. This feels like the biggest thing in my life. It IS the biggest thing in my life. Turn it over, Amy. TURN IT OVER. I need to breathe. I can feel panic rising. Ok, sit down on the lavatory. And breathe. I'm doing it. I blink. There are two windows. One has one line, one has two. I think two means I'm pregnant. But I'm not sure now. Where are the instructions? Fuck, where are the instructions? They are still on the bed.

Calm down. I smooth them out. There are the pictures. One line in both windows = NOT PREGNANT. One line in the 'Control' window, two lines in the 'Results' window = PREGNANT. I look at the stick again. One squinting eye at a time. One line in the control window. TWO LINES IN THE TEST WINDOW. I sit and look at it.

I'm pregnant. Adam's baby is growing inside me. Now I've done it, I feel surprisingly calm. I think I knew. It feels right. I feel a warm glow spread. Anticipation? Nerves? No. I think it's happiness, fulfilment, purpose. I'm going to be a mum. I'm going to do my best to be a good mum. I'm going to cherish this little, growing bean. She's going to be loved. With all my heart, she is going to be loved. This is something, I have to be good at.

The packet has three tests, should I do another, just to be sure? I mean, I know it says 99% accurate, but someone has to be the one person in the hundred, right? I take out another test. Peeing again is hard work. I used it all up last time. This time I have to pee into a glass and hold the stick in it. I can't trust that there's enough of a 'mid-stream.' So maybe this one won't work. I turn the stick face-down again. This time, I don't agonise. One line in the 'Control' window, two lines in the 'Result' window = PREGNANT. Test number two confirms it. So does test number three, with even less pee. This baby is determined. She's announcing her presence.

I need to make a GP appointment. I need to make an appointment with my therapist. I need to tell my sister – oh fuck. How do I explain that one? I need to tell Adam – quadruple fuck. How's that going to go down? You and me, a campervan, a Labrador, and…… A BABY. He'll be a good dad. It'll give him focus. Something to love. I want to see his face when they put his baby in his arms. The look in his eyes. The softening. The love. I know it's there. You are driven to adore your offspring, to put their needs before your own. It's what couples do. All that can wait. There's no hurry. I need to get my own head around it first. I lie on the bed. T-shirt pulled up, leggings pulled down, letting my stomach breathe. Letting her experience the world for the first time.

"Welcome to the world, little one. I might not get it right every time. To be honest, at times, I'm a complete fuck-up. But we'll learn how to do this thing together. I love you. I'll look after you. I'll protect you. You might be no bigger than a blueberry. But already you mean everything to me. You make my life worth living. Your daddy and your auntie are going to feel the same way."

My phone buzzes on the table beside me. Who's interrupting me? Is it Adam? Daddy Adam? No, it's another text from Rachel. I feel bad about ignoring her last few messages. It's not that I don't want to reply. It's just that I have other things on my mind. I gently stroke my tummy. Round and round, massaging. The lightest of touches.

"Can you feel that, baby?"

Can she feel me? Can she hear me? Everything I've read says yes. From the earliest first few weeks, she's affected by your stress, your happiness, your voice and your touch. Everything you feel, they feel too. Darling little blueberry. Little Blue. She can be Little Blue for now. Rachel will understand. Maybe we can take a trip to Glasgow, show her the sites. Maybe Rachel can be Godmother. Although that might be a bit weird. Maybe not. Not after the me, Rachel, Adam thing. Try explaining that to Little Blue later on. But we can go to Glasgow, show her the sites. I can carry in one of those little papooses, slung across my chest. Breast feed her in a Glasgow café or a museum, like all the mother earth Goddesses do. Just wop them out naturally, unashamedly, determinedly, whenever she needs them. This is a new era. She'll grow up strong, confident, unashamed. That's my role now. I feel ok about it. It's the first time I've felt ok about anything. Nothing is going to harm or upset or do anything other than cherish my baby. I wrap a bubble of protection and love around my tummy. I've found something worth living for, and it isn't Adam. I need to make the phone calls. There's time enough for all that. Just savour the moment.

There are some woods just down from my sister's house. It's only about half a mile. That's what I feel like. Mother Earth. Just being at one with nature for an afternoon. The two of us. Me and Blue. I put my old trainers on, fill a bottle of water, stick a banana, a peach and some raisins in bag (eating healthily for two, right?) and head out for a walk. Psychological or pregnancy hormones, who knows? Everything feels, sounds, looks, smells more intense. Birds singing, sweet honeysuckle on the air, fluffy white clouds in a blue sky. I can't remember feeling happiness like this. Nature is an amazing thing. I've been scared of my shadow for so long.

I don't see a single person on my walk to the woods. Everything is so green. I want to take my shoes off. Feel it springy beneath my toes. The pine needles on the path mark my way. I'm sure if I walk for a mile or so, there's a fork off which takes me to a waterfall. There is something magical about a forest. I can't put it into words, but I feel it deep within. For years, therapists would tell me nature could make me feel healed and restored, give me strength, drain away negative energy, fill me with positive energy. I just had to open myself to it.

I remember reading that Buddha left his palace at a young age to seek liberation in the woods. He even advised his pupils to meditate in the jungle to achieve higher states of consciousness. A therapist once told me that the Japanese practice of forest bathing, which is basically just being in the presence of trees, is proven to lower heart rate and blood pressure, reduce hormone production, boost the immune system, improve overall feelings of wellbeing.

Maybe I'll bring Adam here to tell him about Blue. We'll bring Blue here in her papoose when she's born. We'll take her to Forest School, forage for wild garlic, mushrooms and berries, build dens and hideouts from sticks. Did Hippocrates not say that nature was the best doctor? I must ask Rachel. Nature's peace. Aha. Here's the waterfall turn off. I can hear the rush of water. The smell is heady. Crashing forest water, pine needles, damp moss, rotting tree stumps creating new life, magic. I take my trainers and socks off. Screw it. I take my leggings off and shove them all in my bag. The pine needle path is like a spongey, living carpet. A sea of deep, green plant life. Cool and soothing. It seeps upwards. This little clearing is dappled with sunlight peeking through the gaps in the leaves. Rays of sunlight filtering through the verdurous canopy. There is something about fertility, rebirth. Nature does not ask permission. It does not cower away in fear or anxiety or shame. It blossoms, births and rebirths when it feels like it. A fallen tree hangs over the water. It makes a perfect, peaceful sitting place, where my feet and ankles can dangle into the water. It's freezing. Breathtakingly freezing. I imagine the cool healing travelling up to Little Blue. I can do this. With or without Adam, I can do this. Today, I am Persephone. Pregnant and Powerful. Lady of Light who brings life and possibility back to the Earth, in my knickers. Sex Goddess. Me and Little Blue rule innocence, beginnings and rebirth. I need this. I deserve it. No more shame. My baby deserves better. It's so peaceful here. The water bubbles and flows, ice-cold over my feet. I swear I can feel Little Blue smiling. Shall I phone Adam? Shall I, shall I, shall I? Nothing bad can happen in the magical place.

"Hey Amy, how are you?" He picks up straightaway. I wasn't expecting that. "I was going to give you a ring later. Got a question for you."

He sounds happy. He jumps in before I get the chance to.

"Go on," I smile. I love this Adam. Happy Adam.

"Come on an adventure with me." He's excited. It's sweet. "I want to go look at Campervans tomorrow. I want to buy one. For us. Come with me. Go on. I'll even buy you lunch out to celebrate. Go on. Please say yes. I want someone to come with me. A campervan for us."

I laugh. "Ok, ok, we can look at campervans tomorrow." Is it sensible to buy a campervan when you're pregnant? I need to tell him, don't I?

"This company is awesome. You'll fall in love with them. We'll be intrepid adventurers in search of wide-open spaces. They can do a conversion specially for us, to our spec. Or we can buy, ready to go. They're so beautiful."

"So expensive, Adam. I have some savings. I have a few thousand saved up. Shall I contribute?"

"Nope, no need. Business came good. I had a windfall. This is my gift to you."

Baby, baby, baby, baby. Babies are expensive. Babies are more expensive than campervans.

"So, you'll come? Look at campervans with me

tomorrow?"

Should I tell him now? I don't think I can. He's all full of campervan happiness.

"Where are we going to? Where's the company."

"Em, yup. Was getting to that." Adam giggles. "Bit of an adventure. Trip to Kent tomorrow?"

"Kent!! The other side of London?! That's miles away."

"Four hours-ish. It's a nice drive. We can have dinner out. It'll be fun. Specialist company. Best conversions in the UK. It'll be an adventure."

"I guess I can escape for the day."

What will I tell my sister this time? Just off to buy an outrageously expensive campervan with the boyfriend, you hate. Oh, and by the way, I'm having his baby too.

"Can you drive, sweetheart?"

Typical Adam. Invites me out for a day of adventure, then asks me to drive. I don't mind, sounds like it will be fun. I wiggle my toes in the water. It's so cold, they've gone numb. Sitting in a car together, heading off on an adventure. It's a golden opportunity to tell him about our other adventure.

"What time do we need to head out. It'll need to

be early, if we've a four-hour drive there, and four hours back."

"I was thinking if we set off about seven, we can stop for breakfast on the way. Get there twelve/one-ish. Then have a nice dinner when we get back. Could hit the Nepalese. You could stay over, after all that driving?"

Gosh. He'll know by then. Our first night together as parents. Best to tell him tomorrow.

"Sounds like a plan." I confirm. "I'll swing by at seven and pick you up."

I can hear him grinning. He's like a small boy. "I'm excited," he said, stating the obvious. "I've always wanted a campervan. These conversions are soooo cool. You're going to love them."

"I think I will," I tell him. His enthusiasm is infectious. "It'll be fun to spend the day together."

"OK, seven it is. I'm going to struggle to sleep tonight. Tomorrow night we might own a campervan. First stop, Aunt Bea's. Then Anglesey. Then Penzance. Then Europe."

I don't want to think about toilets, showers, pregnancy. What's worse than camping. Most likely, camping when you're pregnant, closely followed by camping with a baby. It'll be fine. I need to phone the doctors and make an appointment. I should do that today.

"I love you, Amy. You're the best."

"Love you too, Adam."

I don't want to think about his windfall. I'm sure it's in the bank. Adam can be a bit 'optimistic' when it comes to finances. It'll be fine. We ring off. Well, that didn't quite go as expected. At least I've set it up for tomorrow.

"Hello, Woodlands Surgery, how can I help?"

"Hi there, I'd like to make a doctor's appointment please."

"Name?"

"Amy Hawes."

"Date of birth"

"Can you tell me what it's in relation to?"

I can feel her eyeballing my recent appointments and medical history as she speaks. Amy Hawes, suicide risk and regular nutter. We keep an eye on this one. Red flagged. I want to tell her to mind her own business. I want to tell her to get out my notes, but that will just confirm the red flags and resident nutter status.

"I think I'm pregnant. Dr Roberts likes to keep an eye on my mental health. She'll want to see me."

"Have you done a test?" Really, is this any of her business?

"Yes." Three actually. "It was positive."

"Perfect. Friday at 3pm? Dr Roberts has a cancellation."

"That would be fine. Thank you." I breathe a sigh of relief. That's that booked. Something ticked off the list at least.

"Excellent, we'll see you then Amy."

Rings off. Done. I close my eyes. Circle my ankles in the soothing icy water. Ten minutes here, where nothing bad can happen. Where all is good with the world. Peaceful. Magical, *Motherly*. I'm leaving this fairy pool energised and ready for what lies ahead. The next chapter in the Book of Adventures.

25 ADAM: You Only Regret the Roads You Didn't Take

"BEEEEEEEEEEEEEEP"

What the fuck is that? Slowly the car horn permeates my foggy, sound-asleep brain. Wankers! Who the fuck is beeping a horn at this time in the morning? Ugh. My mouth's all tacky and my eyes are glued. I grab my phone from the bedside table and almost drop it, peering groggily at the screen. Eventually I can almost focus on the numbers.

7.20am.

Shit. It's Amy, isn't it? She said she'd pick me up at 7am. How very Amy to be on time. Normal people aren't on time this early in the morning. I struggle to my feel, scratching. Wander over to the window. I really must get some curtains at some point. I'll get Amy to sort it. There she is. She's hanging out the window.

Noooooooooo, Amy, don't beep again. Fuck's sake woman. I motion '5-minutes' to her, by holding my hand up and moving it back and forward. I think she's got it.

Twenty minutes later, I'm sorted. That's not bad, is it? I've even showered and brushed my teeth. We'll stop for breakfast soon. I need coffee.

"Hey sweetheart," I open the passenger seat and jump in, leaning over for a kiss. I'm rewarded by a response. Good, she's not too annoyed. "Blooming alarm clock never went off. I know I set it. No matter, plenty of time. You ok?"

I'm out of breath from rushing. I lift myself off the car seat to loosen my cargo shorts and make myself comfortable.

"I'm good," she says, smiling.

That's good. Old Amy would have ripped my face off for being made to wait. She'd had exploded my ear drums with shrieking by now. She's being uncharacteristically chilled.

"Excited?" I raise my eyebrows and grin at her. She puts her hand on my knee.

"I am very excited. This is fun. But I have no idea where I'm going. You have to navigate. Which way?"

"Right at the bottom, head for the ring road. Down the M6 towards Birmingham." I'm using my hands to point, which I know is pointless. "Breakfast at Knutsford? I'm dying for a coffee and a proper breakfast. I think there's a pub restaurant type place that does breakfasts. Before I die. Caffeine."

"Gotcha."

I start fiddling with the stereo. Amy's choice of music is generally shit. Her driving also depends on her mood. You don't want to get into a car with her when she's going off on one. You fear for your life. Everyone gets the venom. The innocent passenger as well as the fellow drivers and the non-existent, but deeply personal slights as they don't cut out in front of her, the way she's sure they always do. She takes a mouthful from a bottle of water in the cup holder.

"There's a spare one in the back, if you want," she says tilting her head back to motion the bottle of water on the back seat. Water. How very Amy. Who even drinks water at this time?

I've found a best of Bowie CD in the glove compartment. That's inoffensive. 'Rebel Rebel' starts blaring out. Amy starts singing along at the top of her voice. We both know the words. Bowie used to be a regular shared listen. Before long, I'm yelling along too. It's a long time since we've been so comfortable and she isn't yelling at me for taking up space. Or breathing. Or not having had a shower. It seems like Campervans and money sort everything out. I knew they would.

It takes us about forty minutes to get to Knutsford. And yup, they're serving breakfast. Score. It's a buffet-stye one too, where you just help yourself. Double-score. I down an orange juice and refill at the drink dispenser, down again, then refill and walk it back, with a mug of coffee for good measure. I load four sausages and a mound of bacon on the plate. Two fried eggs, fried bread. A bath of beans. These places are such good value. It occurs to me that I don't need to worry about money. I can dine anywhere now. Anywhere I want. I suspect there will always be an attraction in eat-all-you-can buffet style breakfasts. Real money doesn't need to flaunt it. You know where you are with a buffet style mound of sausages and overcooked eggs. It's a British institution that sets you up for the day when you're on the road. Amy is helping herself to an Amy-style breakfast. Muesli and yoghurt or some such shit. What is it with women and muesli?

"These sausages are great," I say waving half a sausage on a fork at her. "You want to get some sausages down you. Set you up for Campervan-Fest."

She's got some sort of weird, red, fruit tea. It smells nasty. Weird how the smell of hippy tea drowns out good old sausage, bacon and eggs.

"Adam?" oh-oh. Something's brewing. She sounds serious. "Adam, there was something I wanted to tell you. Have to tell you, really."

Shit. Drama. Amy-drama. I load a wadge of beans on half a sausage and pop the whole thing in my mouth, losing a couple of beans to my cargo-shorts.

"Go on," I mumble sausagily. "What is it. Sounds serious."

"No easy way to say it. I'm pregnant. We're going to have a baby."

The words take a few moments to register. They're alien. I lose some more beans to my shorts. I don't do babies. I don't do children. I don't do pregnant women. She knows that. I'm a free spirit.

"Say something Adam." I must have been staring at her. I cut a piece of bacon in half, deliberately slowly.

"I'm just going to get some more sausages. Some coffee." I get up from the table and walk to the buffet. Two more sausages. Two bacon. Another egg. Then to the coffee machine for a refill. I open three milk pots and slowly stir them in. Pop some toast in the toaster and wait on it popping. By the time I come back to the table, fully laden. It's processed.

"It's mine?" Are the first words that fall out my mouth. A little bit more dryly than I meant.

"Of course it's yours. The last few times, we didn't use anything. I thought I was too old to bother. I thought we were too old. Against the odds and all that. It just sort of happened. You're going to be a dad." Her voice is ratcheting up. We're on the hill. I recognise the signs.

"I'm going to be a dad?" I repeat the words to help them process. "You're pregnant?"

What are you meant to say in these moments? The biggest part of me is raging. I want to throttle her. Pin her against a wall, hands round her neck, yelling stupid cow, you know how I feel. Manipulative, stupid cow. Tying me down. I'm a free spirit. You know that. Babies are lead weights. Tying you to the spot, killing spontaneity. Fuck's sake they are a *commitment*. Commitment is the polar opposite of free spirit. I look at her. She's smiling at me. She takes my hand and places it on her warm belly, under her shirt.

"It'll be fine," she says. "We'll be fine. She'll be fine. Two can become three. Plus Labrador and Campervan. Now we've got a reason to buy it. To show her the world."

I almost believe her. This is so confusing. I was so sure. Now there's a baby under my hand. We've made something. Something of mine. Now I'm not so sure. That bloody song. It's there, in my head. That song is coursing through my brain. Who's sorry now. A baby? What would my mother say? I know what she'd say. She'd be thrilled. Another generation. I saw what she was like with Cal's two. She adored them. A whole new generation to educate about fairies and changelings. Bedtime stories to terrify and fuck you up.

"Who's Sorry Now?" it pops out.

"What," Amy looks confused. My hand is still on her belly.

I laugh. I think I've gone insane. Amy thinks I've gone insane. Insanity has always been her prerogative.

"You've thrown me, Amy Hawes. For once, I am

speechless. It was my mother's favourite song, Who's Sorry Now. You made me think of my mother and what she would say. She'd be thrilled. She loved babies. It popped into my head. Madness."

"We could call her after your mother, if you wanted, and if it's a girl."

"You keep calling it a girl. You know it is?"

Amy shook her head, still smiling. "No, I don't know. It's just a feeling. Either way, we'll love it." She takes my hand and holds it. "Adam, we'll be fine. I want to be a mother. I want us to be parents. Campervans, adventures and a baby. The three of us. It feels right, doesn't it? Speak to me, Adam."

"When? I mean, when did it happen. How pregnant?"

"I think about a month. I'm seeing the doctor on Friday. I'll have a better idea then. Are you ok?"

I can see that she's nervous. She wants me to be happy about it. I've got that bloody song going round my head. I'm raging. I'm happy? Fuck. I wish that song would switch off. Am I happy, stressed, angry? Confusion is all I feel. I'm waiting for a surge of love. That's normal, isn't it. You don't feel empty. You feel a biological surge of love. For mother and baby. My baby. Empty isn't meant to be your overriding emption.

"I'm thrilled Amy. Truly thrilled. A baby. Wow!

Really, I'm good. I'm amazing. It's bloody fantastic."

I get up, put hand around her shoulders and kiss her. I honestly don't know what to think. I'm angry and pleased at the same time. I want to hit her. I want to protect her. I want to pace the room and bang a wall with my fist. I want to lie on a bed and hold her. Hold *them*. She's ruined everything. She's made everything right. Fuck's sake. I bang my head. Who's sorry now?

"You think you're good enough to be a father, Adam? You're a killer. *YOU* ruin everything."
My mother is standing behind Amy. I thought she'd be pleased. I thought that was everything she wanted for me. I don't understand.
"Run a knife through her soft belly."
"You had your way, now you must pay. Who's Sorry Now?"
I shake my head. Get out of there. I can be a father.

"Hey, hey, sweetheart. Penny for them? I swear I have just seen every emotion in your face." Amy cups my face with her hands. "Don't worry. We'll be fine. More than fine. You got this. You'll be a great dad. We got this."

She sounds so gentle. I like this Amy. This is pregnant Amy. Pregnant Amy. Amy with baby. My baby.
"Run a knife through her soft belly. Two for one."

"We shouldn't call her after my mum. Or anyone.

She's going to be her own person. A new start. Free from everyone's past." This is it. This is the new beginning. I didn't know until now how much I needed it.

"I like Leda, Queen of Sparta. Greek Mythology. Our own Goddess. Or just Helen. Legendary beauty of Troy."

Amy rubs her hands over her belly as she talks. I can almost see a baby there, curled up, sleeping.

"She's only the size of a blueberry at the moment." It was as if Amy could read my thoughts. "But she's got a heart, the beginnings of arms, legs, a brain. She's us."

Her eyes are shining. Inexplicably I bend over and kiss her belly. She runs a hand through my hair. It's nice. "I wish I had been on time this morning." I say ruefully.

"Daftie," she laughs. "You wouldn't be Adam if you didn't tip out of bed when I beeped the horn. C'mon. Finish those sausages. Let's go buy a campervan for a little girl."

Suddenly, sausages have lost their appeal. I open the restaurant door for Amy, then the car door.

"We should get married," I say, jumping in the car.

"What?" Amy sounds incredulous. "You hate marriage. You're a free spirit, remember?"

"I know what I said, but we should all have the same name. I don't want Blue Helen Leda having a different name to me. Or to you. We should all have the same name. Waters. Blue Waters. Sounds like an Indian legend."

In that moment, I actually mean it. I have money, a future, a family. A new start. A way to end the nightmares. Silence her. Put it all behind us. We sing our way down the M6, skirting past Birmingham, with another two stops before reaching Kent. I use the sat nav to direct Amy through the streets of Ashford. I didn't realise it was so far south or so far East. Jeez, we're only about 20 miles from Folkstone. We've been driving for hours. My back's all sweaty from the car seat.

"Think we should just stay here tonight?" The idea occurs to me. It seems quite nice. Kinda historic and old, for being so close to London. "It's such a long way back. Just thinking maybe we should rest up. Have a night away. Make the most of it. You should rest."

I wish I'd thought of it before. Honestly, sometimes I have no concept how far things are away from each other in my own country.

"We could get a nice meal, go to a pub, just chill out. Don't worry about money, I'll pay." We can stay anywhere we want.

"That sounds awesome. I'll just need to phone

home and think of some excuse."

"Erm… how about you're buying a campervan, planning a wedding and trying out baby names?" I wink at her. "I wouldn't, she'll just be jealous. Some people have no sense of adventure."

"She'd have a heart attack! My stuff would be packed in black bags and pitched on the street for the betrayal."

"She won't do that. She's going to be an Auntie. She'll get used to me. You'll see. Look. We're here."

It's true. There's the Campervan business showroom. It's unremarkable for the extent of the drive it's taken us to get here. You'd have driven past it, if you didn't know.

"We're here." Amy exclaims. She indicates to turn in. "Campervans, campervans everywhere."

We park up in the customer parking. We'd been wandering less than five minutes, trying to get bearings when a guy in jeans and a t-shirt approaches.

"Can I help?"

"Let us just have a browse for a bit mate. Then we'll come find you."

"No problem. Just over there. Any questions, just ask."

"The VW California," I whisper to Amy, taking her hand and leading her to the campervan I've been eyeing up online. "It's the daddy of all campervans. Sixth generation, produced in-house by Volkswagen. It's very cool. Impressive build quality, high grade doors and all fold-out equipment. Top for safety. I think that's the one we want."

I run my hand down the outside of the shiny new van. I think I'm in love. The pop top is open and the roof top bed made up. The new version has plastic springs instead of wooden slats, making it even more inviting.

"It comes in different colours." I don't know if I'm speaking to myself or Amy. I want her to be as excited as I am. All white. Or this two-tone.

"I really like this one," she says, also running her hand down the side. It's stunning."

The van we were admiring was a two-tone red and white. It was modern, but the colours also gave it a retro vibe.

"Get up top," I say giving her a nudge. "Give it a try." I swing up the ladder to the top bedroom in the pop-top. I extend my hand down to pull her up.

"Can we?" She looks around nervously.

"We can do anything." I give her a pull as she starts up the ladder. We both lie on the mattress in the roof. "How awesome is this?" I put my arm around her as we lie on our backs. "Imagine we're on a beach having watched the sunset, swam in the sea, drank prosecco on the shore."

"It feels expensive," whispers Amy, "how much?"

"About 65K, new."

"ADAM! No way!

"Helluva lot cheaper than a house! Most up-to-date infotainment unit. It's perfect. Everything you could need. Double gas hob, built in table, fridge. An awning, hidden picnic tables. Plenty of space for a cot." I squeeze her. I have the money. I can buy it outright today. Heck I could buy three of them outright today.

"Are there any cheaper ones?"

"I told you, Amy. Business came good. I have the money. I can buy it outright. Right now, if you like it. We just go up to the guy and we buy it. We deserve it." Amy giggles. She's in awe. She respects me.

"What will Aunt Bea say? I don't think it's quite the retro battered camper she was expecting to roll up."

"It's perfect. Perfect for the three of us. Perfect for our new adventure. We don't need to worry about money. Shall we carry on looking, or will we just buy this one? There's a Ford version and a Mercedes version too. I just like the VW. If you're going to buy a camper, you should buy a VW."

"Are the others any cheaper?"

I roll on top of her as a reprimand and press my face into hers. "Nope. No money talk. For once, money doesn't come into it. We buy what we like. You like it?"

"Adam, I love it. It's just…" she looked for the word. "It's just so extravagant. We don't *need* it."

"Exactly, we don't need it. But we want it. Which is exactly why we should buy it." I unzip the pop top at the front, so it's entirely open view. We sit cross-legged looking out over the garage showroom. "Imagine we're on a mountain. Or on a clifftop overlooking the shore. We're in Tuscany, the South Coast of Italy, South America. C'mon Amy, we have to, don't we?"

"We should look at the others. It's such a huge purchase. I don't think we can buy the first one we lie in."

I laugh. "Your wish is my command, princess. Let's look at others before we buy this one." I help her down from the ladder and lead her to another campervan, all black, with dark windows.

"This one looks like a gangster van," she says peering into the inside. "I don't think it's us. Looks like a van for dodgy dealings."

"This is the Mercedes. The two front seats swivel to make the downstairs bedroom, and there's a pop-top, like the VW. There's an awning, like the VW, but not as much smart space."

"It's darker inside. I prefer this first one. Is it cheaper?"

"Nope, they're all the same sort of price. Want to look at the last one?"

Amy nods and climbs out the Mercedes van, stroking the side of it.

"Doesn't feel as nice. Feels like we'd be dealing drugs or burying bodies in this one."

I take her hand and lead her to the third van. It looks like a Ford Transit.

Amy wrinkles her nose. "Looks like we'd be doing the cash and carry run in this one. It looks like a Transit van."

I laugh. "It is a Transit van. Quite a cool conversion though. This one has its own freshwater fill up supply connector and an outdoor shower facility with a fuel fired heating system."

I've lost Amy, she's wandered off as I was talking spec. She's gone back to the VW. She's back upstairs in the pop-top looking out.

"Can we really afford this?" she says as I heave

myself up. "I don't think I've ever seen anything so beautiful."

"You are beautiful, Amy. You are pregnant, You are beautiful and yes, we can absolutely afford this. You want it?"

"You're sure Adam? It's not worth getting into debt over or worrying about money. I will love you and we will have endless adventures whether we have a campervan or not."

"I'm sure Amy. We can afford it. You want it?"

She nods. "I want it. It's beautiful. But only if we can afford it and we're not getting into debt."

"Then let's go buy a campervan, honey." I've never bought anything so expensive before. It's a good feeling.

"Will you be taking one of our competitive finance deals, Mr Waters."

"No, it's an outright cash purchase." That feels so good. I want to say it again.

"Very good, sir."

I swear that changes the tone of how he speaks to me. Respect. Respect and courtesy. Suddenly I am someone important. I'm a Sir. How about that, mum.

"Now, we have several packages that you can add

on. Would you like our air conditioning package? Vital if you're planning travelling out of the UK."

"I don't think we can buy a new campervan and stay in the UK. I think we should add that on, yes."

Amy has wandered off, stroking vans. I know she finds conversations about money worrying.

Spending just shy of 75K turns out to be surprisingly easy and surprisingly quick.

He's thrown a VW hoodie for both of us into the bargain. We get to take those away with us today. Cool.

"A small for your wife?" he says, getting up to go into the back room.

"I'd go for a medium, we're having a baby. Extra, extra-large for me."

"Wow!! Congratulations mate. A top of the range VW Camper, a stunning wife and a baby. Some guys just have it all. Good on yah."

Some guys have it all. Hear that, mum? I'm not a failure. I find Amy sitting on the picnic table, under the awning of the VW. She's googling hotels in Ashford.

"I'll get the hotel, and dinner tonight. It feels like the least I can do. So much money." She frowns.

"Nope. This is all my treat. What kind of husband would I be if I let my stunningly beautiful, pregnant wife pick up the tab. Wotcha found?"

"Well, there are some cheap and cheerful's in town. We could hit Ashford centre for a meal somewhere. Beer in a spit and sawdust pub. Or there's a Champney's Manor just outside with a pool, spa, luxurious rooms and a four-poster. I'll shout for Champney's if you fancy. We could pick up some swimming stuff in the supermarket."

"*I'll* shout for Champneys. You look exhausted. I told you, don't worry about money today. Special day all round. I think we deserve a spa and a four poster. Make the most of it, girl coz in two weeks, it's all going to be about the upper bedroom springs, the starry skies and the pop top. The prosecco may have to wait a few months though whether we're in Champneys or under the stars."

She smiles at me, stands up and gives me a hug. "I love you Adam Waters. Let me give them a ring and see if there's a room. Spa and a four-poster sounds just perfect. You're just perfect."

"Almost as perfect as my pregnant wife."

26 DR JIM WALKER: An Inspector Calls

"Good to see you looking and feeling so much better. Make an appointment with Shona on the way out. Two weeks. Keep up the good work, everything we talked about. Stick to the plan. We'll see you again in two weeks, yes?"

I get up to escort the young female patient from the room, warmly shaking her hand.

"Remember and see Shona. We'll see you in two weeks."

It's always a relief when a young woman responds quickly to treatment for postnatal depression. Close monitoring and early intervention. You can't muck about with these things. Not when there's a baby at stake. She looks much brighter than she did a fortnight ago. Definitely on the up. She's been gone less than five minutes when Shona buzzes through. I am sure I've got a break before the next appointment. I'm counting on it.

"Dr Walker, the police are here to see you. They

need to see you urgently about a patient. I've told them you've a busy schedule, but they say it's important and that they need to speak to you now."

It's funny how, even as a seasoned professional who's seen most things in life, still the mention of the police gets the adrenalin pumping. What now? Who now? What's happened? A suicide? My heart sinks. It's usually a suicide. A failure. Another critical incident review.

"Very well. Show them through Shona."

The door opens. Shona looks flustered. She shows two men into the room. Plain clothes. Not even uniformed cops. Must be serious.

"Thanks Shona. I'll take it from here."

I dismiss the flustered secretary. It's not the first time the police have insisted on the need to interrupt a clinic, but it's not a regular occurrence.

"Sit down gentlemen. Can I get you a tea or a coffee?"

They look at each other and number one answers for both of them.

"We're fine. Thank you. Dr Walker. We'll cut straight to the chase. A woman's body washed up on the coast of Cumbria a few weeks ago. You may have seen it on the news. On the Isle of Walney. Western end of Morecombe Bay in the Irish Sea. Discovered by a dog walker. A shocking discovery for a quiet Island Community."

Why did they always sound like they were playing out an episode of a Forensics drama. Will they get the pictures out next?

"Yes, I remember seeing it on the news. Quite a shocking find. Distressing for the inhabitants, not least the dog walker who found her I shouldn't wonder. Traumatic."

"Indeed it was. The body was in some state when she washed up. Multiple, frenzied stab wounds and a two-week battering in the surf. It wasn't pretty."

They pause for effect. I think I'm meant to express some horror.

"No. I can imagine. How do you think I can help? Cumbria will have their own trauma counsellors surely." Walney Island seems a million miles away from Greater Manchester.

"It's taken forensics a couple of weeks to identify the body. Partly because of the decomposition. Buffeting from the waves, putrefaction and scavenging by sea creatures left little for us to identify. To complicate matters further, she wasn't British. She was an American citizen. A businesswoman from New York. Married with two small children."

I'm pleased that Shona's not here. She doesn't have to listen to this.

"You think she might be connected to one of my patients? Do you have a name?"

"We don't know yet. These are just initial enquiries, Dr Walker. Her name is Sarah Emmerson. We understand she was travelling to Manchester to meet one of your patients, Adam Waters. She had two meetings in London prior to. We still don't know whether she arrived here or not. She had her two London meetings. We know she was alive then. The last sighting was her checking out of her London hotel early morning on the 18th June. We know she checked out at around 6am. No-one saw her again. She was due to fly back to New York on the 21st. She never returned."

Adam Waters. Adam Waters. Adam Waters. The name is familiar.

"I have a big caseload, gentlemen. Let me check my notes."

I know how this goes. Doesn't matter what I say or do. They're leaving here with my case notes in an evidence bag. They'll unpick every word I've written. It's not just Adam Waters they are scrutinising.

Early on in medical school, you're taught case notes don't belong to you. They are legal tender. Open access in criminal situations. Even the most intimate of details. From childhood abuse to innermost fantasies told in confidence. They can be lifted as evidence at a moment's notice. Hence they always need to be up-to-date, accurate and professional. It used to put the fear into us as trainees. One of those things they warn you about and you believe it will never happen to you. Not unless you were psychiatrist to the mob. I'd moved to a system of minimal, factual documentation.

Waters is under W, obviously. Shona's filing is top notch. Bottom drawer of the locked filing cabinet.

"I'm old school," I say apologetically, "I still keep everything in a paper file. You know where you are with paper files. I haven't quite embraced the digital revolution yet. Fortunately, my secretary is similarly old fashioned."

I find it. Please let it be up to date. No gaffs or gaps. Let's hope everything stands up in court. Sigh...... There's always a back story. The legal system is rarely interested in anything but a conviction. Whether they're guilty or not. Childhood trauma has a lot to answer for. So does our lack of understanding and empathy. Even mostly good, mainly fragile people can do bad things. It's our job to understand them. Yes. Adam Waters. Saw him twice and he dropped out of treatment. Phoned him half a dozen times. Left messages. Wrote to GP, asking them to follow up. Case still open.

"Here it is. Adam Waters. 52-year-old chap referred for depression. Drinks too much, borderline diabetic. Saw him twice about three months ago. Prescribed some antidepressants, sertraline, which I believe he never took. He never came back. I phoned half a dozen times, wrote to the GP, even attempted a home visit. Not home. No answer. Case still open."

"Any evidence that he was a risk? That he was dangerous?"

"To himself or to others? Memory is, that he was a biggest risk to himself. His life was crumbling around him and he felt a failure. Sad, scared and a fragile ego, rather than bad, mad or dangerous. But I only saw him and twice and it's been a while."

They both jot things down in their notebooks. Pointless when they'll be taking apart every word in the notes later. I flick through his notes.

"He was stressed, depressed, having bad dreams. He'd just had a relationship break-up, he was worried about money and there was evidence of childhood trauma. Multiple bereavements which he never properly processed or grieved. Failing business. Weak sense of self. Lacked empathy. A degree of narcissism. When things were going well, he was king. When things started to fail, he took it badly. When he was acutely stressed, he sometimes heard his mother talking to him. Auditory hallucinations."

I knew that last bit would be a golden nugget for them. Evidence of insanity. People rarely understood how common auditory hallucinations were during episodes of acute stress.

"His dead mother? Saying what to him?"

"The usual things. That he was useless. That he wasn't good enough."

I read verbatim from my notes. "I've written here: *Psychotic features. Auditory hallucinations. Negative content. Depressed presentation. Alcohol – 6 beers daily. Not actively suicidal. Low risk to self and others. Unresolved, complicated grief (mother). Money worries/risk to house.*"

The two police officers look at each other.

"Sarah Emmerson transferred a significant amount of money to an offshore account before she disappeared. Just shy of a million. When she disappeared, the company assumed embezzlement. A British lover. A partner in crime."

"Adam Waters is a fly-by-night. A chancer. Charming but not an academic or a criminal mastermind. It's hard to see him engineering a corporate white-collar crime to the tune of a disappearing million. He's also not a well man. When I last saw him, he looked a mess. An uncontrolled diabetic and a habitual drinker. I referred him back to his GP for a full physical work-up. He'll end up having a heart attack, stroke or a diabetic coma."

"Is he well enough to launch a frenzied knife attack on a slim, attractive mother and toss her body into the sea? Physically strong enough? Stressed enough? Desperate enough? Hearing voices telling him to do it? I'm afraid he's our prime suspect at the moment. Her other two business contacts have cast iron alibis. All the evidence is that she left London for Manchester on the 18th June."

I flick backwards and forwards through the notes, searching for nuggets that absolve him of the possibility of wrong doing. Of course, I find nothing to either exonerate or incriminate him. Psychiatry is as much an art form as a science. There are no absolutes.

"I'm afraid I can't answer your questions definitively, gentlemen. All I can say is that at the time I saw him, I noted that he posed a low risk to himself and others. That was my professional opinion at that time. But I only saw Adam Waters on two occasions before he dropped out of treatment. I was worried enough to follow him up half a dozen times. I tried to visit him at home and to alert his GP to the state of his health. But he categorically did not meet the criteria for sectioning or for enforced treatment. Unfortunately, we can't force people to accept treatment, even when we think they would benefit from it. As I said, my professional opinion at the time was that he posed low risk to himself or others."

It's not like me to get flustered. I can feel the beads of sweat on my forehead and a small trickle down my back. I remember Adam quite clearly now. A dishevelled charmer. Unkempt. The sole of his shoe was hanging off. In need of a shower, a scrub and some tough words. Smiling, but tragic. I had queried a narcissistic collapse. Someone who thought he was the tops at everything. Always waiting for the next big break. Until everything unravels and there's no escaping the missed opportunities and the failures. Life has passed him by, and he's not where he thinks he should be, where he deserves to be.

I'd flippantly referred to him as Gangster Adam. Our Good Time Gordon. Typical Mancunian Cheeky Chappy. Ducking and diving and cutting the next deal, which nine times out of ten was destined to fail. Manchester is full of them, so is my clinic. They tend not to launch frenzied attacks on young women. Or be capable of successfully embezzling a million quid.

Truth is, I'm not convinced that he isn't capable of corporate corruption or of a frenzied knife attack on an unsuspecting colleague. He was acutely stressed. Childhood trauma. Psychotic breakdown. Hand on heart, I don't know. But I'm worried for him.

Groudle Glen and the Isle of Man keep popping up in the notes. Over and over. I keep noting it. It's obviously significant to him.

"Where did the body wash up, again?"

The more dominant one consulted his notes.

"Biggar Bank Beach, West Coast of Walney Island."

He's reading from his notes. He'd clearly never heard of the place until an American businesswoman's decomposing body washed up there.

"Walney Island is an 11-mile-long Island in the Irish sea at the tip of the Furness Peninsula. Biggar Beach is located on the more exposed West Coast. Most remote part of the Island. The beach is backed by a caravan site and a large area of salt marshes. She was found early morning by a dog walker from

Biggar. Traumatised the poor woman, a find like that. Not much left of her."

My geography's not great. I'm resisting the urge to download a google map to get my bearings. I need a visual to work it out.

"And you reckon she'd been in the water for about two weeks before she washed up?"

He checks his notes again. "We're pretty sure she died on the 18th June. She was alive when she checked out of her London hotel in the morning, but never checked into her Manchester hotel that night. So something happened to her between London and Manchester."

"But Manchester's not on the coast." I know my geography's not great, but even I know Manchester isn't particularly close to the sea. "So London to Manchester would be in-land."

"Exactly," he nods seriously and closes his notebook over. "It's a mystery."

"But if you know when she dies, and where she washes up, can't you work backwards. There must be a record of the tides. An oceanographer would tell you. You should be able to trace back to where she was killed, no?"

"You'd think, wouldn't you. But s'not that simple. Apparently, the Irish Sea tides are mental." He realises where he is, and what he's saying. "Sorry, I mean the Irish Sea tides are some of the most erratic and changeable in the World. The tides could have pulled her in any of a hundred directions. Apparently, she could have died anywhere that borders the sea. Just to narrow it down. Proverbial needle, haystack, haven't got a clue where to start."

I can't resist it any longer, I've pulled a map up on my PC screen. I'd been itching to do it. I poke at the map and trace the sea with my finger. Isle of Man to Walney Island. It's a plausible story.

"When you go through the case notes, you'll see that the Isle of Man features in our discussions. It's important to him. It's where his mother took him when his parents split up. He was a traumatised four-year old, she was a survivor of domestic abuse. When he's stressed, he hears his mother. It's not uncommon. But he most often sees her with the backdrop of the Isle of Man. One bit in particular. Here, I wrote it down, Groudle Glen."

The plods are scribbling furiously. "How you spelling that?"

I spell it out for them. "It's a couple of miles from the capital town, Douglas. The Glen leads to the sea at Port Groudle." I point at the map on my screen, reading the names out. "It used to be a Victorian tourist attraction."

"You think Adam Waters may have killed Sarah Emmerson at Groudle Glen and tossed her body into the sea?" Both plods look animated now. They think

I've solved their case.

"Woah. Big 'ifs.' I'm saying that IF Adam Waters is a suspect, and IF you think Sarah was coming to meet him, then Groudle Glen is place that holds particular significance to him. You'll see from the notes. We talk about it. The map puts Groudle Glen as straight-ish line, 'mental' tides pending to Walney Island. It might be worth sending a forensic team and a dive team to take a look. At least to rule that particular needle out the haystack."

Mostly it will ease my own mind when they find nothing. I really, really hope they find nothing. Thirty-odd years in the game and still you're never really prepared for days like these. Hopefully it's nothing. The poor girl. Her last moments in a foreign country and the hands of who knows what. Psychiatry is never about the mad, bad, dangerous and always about the traumatised sad who torture themselves and hide from everyone else. Poor Adam. Goodness knows what trauma lies ahead for him. Whatever way you look at it, it's tragic. This doesn't feel like it will end well.

"Please remember that Adam Waters is still my patient. He's experienced significant trauma in his life. He was suffering acute stress alongside physical poor health when I last saw him. I'd like to help if I can. Minimising distress will help us find answers more quickly. Please keep me updated so we can work together."

Both men nod, but I know the mental health of a

suspect is often the least of their concerns.

"Of course, Dr Walker."

"I mean it. I'll give you my personal mobile number so you can get hold of me anytime. Someone's who wasn't a risk can quite easily become a risk if they feel cornered. As soon as you have any information, call me. Whatever happens, Adam will need some support to get through what's ahead."

"He killed a woman, Dr Walker. A wife and mother of two young children."

"With all due respect, gentlemen, we don't know that yet. Minimising distress and risk will hopefully help solve our unknowns. That will help the family as much as anything. The last thing anyone wants is the suicide of a suspect."

I can see by their faces how important they feel psychiatry is. Not important in the slightest.

"Have you interviewed him yet?"

"Hmm?" They're looking for an evidence bag for my case notes. Job done, as far as they're concerned. Patient is guilty and they have a lead.

"Adam Waters, have you interviewed him yet?"

"Not yet. We've wanted to speak to you first. We've got a couple of leads to follow. Then we'll pull him in. The girlfriend too. See what she knows. The women often crack first."

I can feel my heart sink. These guys don't do mental health.

"It might be good to have some medical or psychiatric support on-hand for the interviews. If you let me know when they are, I'll do my best to be available."

"We'll do our best doctor. We'll need to take the case notes away, of course. Evidence." The dominant one pointedly puts some gloves on and holds the bag open for the notes.

I'd expected it. I don't even get the chance to check everything is filed correctly. "Of course." I bid goodbye to the blue medical file and pop it into the bag. Goodness knows when I'll see those again.

Number one makes a point of ceremoniously sealing the evidence bag off, removing his gloves and depositing them in a separate bag. It's a practised routine. I'm too old to be intimidated. It's just annoying.

"Hopefully everything is in order, but if anything requires clarifying, you have my number. Don't hesitate."

"I'm sure we'll find everything we need."

I sigh inwardly again. Life feels heavy. "And please, do keep me up to speed. I'd like to be there when you interview Adam. His girlfriend too. I don't know what kind of state they're both in."

"We've noted it, doctor. We have your number."

They've got what they want. They stand up and adjust their trousers. If it wasn't so tragic it would be a comedy routine.

"I think that's us, Dr Walker. We'll not take any more of your time."

"You know where I am. Really. Anytime." There are only so many times I can say it. Deaf ears, fall on, I'm afraid.

"We do, thank you."

I open the door. My next appointment has been waiting for ten minutes.

"I'm sorry." I'll be right with you. "Shona. I think our colleagues have everything they need. If you'd be good enough to see them out."

"Two minutes," I mouth to my patient, holding up two fingers to confirm. I need to compose myself. She smiles and nods, thank goodness. I sit at the desk, deleting the Isle of Man off the computer in one move. I close my eyes for two minutes and just breath. I need to park the last half hour to somewhere barely conscious for now. Adam Waters. I knew something wasn't right. Shona opens the door and brings a coffee in. Bless her.

"Thought you might appreciate this," she puts the coffee on the desk. "Everything ok?"

"Just one of those conversations you hope you'll never have Shona. I'll be fine."

"I've phoned your one o'clock and told them you're running late, and your two thirty has cancelled. That should give you a bit of time. Let me know if I can do anything else. You look pale."

"You're a star Shona. I don't know where I'd be without you. Sometimes the job just gets you down. Maybe it's time for us both to retire, eh?"

27 ADAM: Reverie is the Groundwork of the Creative

"I can't believe you're leaving me in the lurch, Adam."
Steve is always so plaintive. Makes a drama out of everything.

"Steve, I almost died mate. ALMOST DIED. I nearly corked it. If Amy hadn't phoned the ambulance, I wouldn't be here. Doctor said I was moments from death. Puts things into perspective that does. I just need some time out. That's all. To get my head straight."

Truth is, I can't be arsed with the conferences. Too much effort. I can make all the money I need from investing my off-shore assets. No need to pour over spreadsheets, wave at the masses on Connect2Me or put up with Steve's melodrama anymore.

"I mean, you're all right now, aren't you? Diabetes is manageable, isn't it? Lay off the beer and takeaways. I don't understand why you have to pull out."

"Doctor said I was lucky to survive without brain damage or heart failure. Lucky to survive at all. Said it could happen again anytime. It's weird staring into the black hole of death. It's like the Sword of Damocles hanging over your head waiting to strike again. I could go anytime."

"Can't you just see this conference through. I've clawed back about £80K I think, but it's touch and go. Need a final drive on tickets. Got all the merchandising and audiovisuals to set up to. Stella's going off her head. I'm doing like 15-hour days. She still doesn't know how close we are to not breaking even."

I'm not even listening. Something about Steve's voice makes me want to crack open the beer and have a wank. Must be the stress. So tempting just to tell him to fuck off. Problem is Steve doesn't just fuck off. He phones a million times, then drives round and sits in my drive like a jackass.

"Amy's pregnant, Steve." That stops him in his tracks.

"What the fuck?! Yours?"

Who else is she going to be pregnant to? "Of course it's mine, pillock. We're having a baby."

"You and Amy?"

"Er…. Yes. Why is that so difficult to believe?" I'm almost annoyed at the insinuation. Does he think I'm not capable of impregnation? He did it, after all. Four times. I can manage it once.

"Wow! It's just…. well…. I never had you down as the paternal sort. You hate babies! And Amy? It's always sort of off-and-on-and-off again."

"Congratulations might be nice." At least it's got him off the topic of conferences and bleating about risk and his house.

"Yeah. Congratulations and all that. Big change for you. Fewer nights down the pub, eh. More nappies and night-time feeds. When's she due?"

"Dunno. She said she was about a month, so I guess eight months' time? When does that make it? Sometime in March?"

"How she doing? You guy's sorted your differences?"

My differences? I mean really, is this any of Steve's business. Beer and a wank. It's what I crave. I just wanna get off the phone. I'm done with all this shit. A million in an off-shore account clarifies the mind.

"Amy's just Amy. Well up for it. Happy to be carrying a chip off my old block. We both are. But it's been a lot to take in. Escaping death, creating life, Amy and parenthood. All change. I just need some time and space to get my head around it. We bought a camper. Been thinking about it for ages. Thinking we might just head off for a few months. Get our shit together on the open road."

"I thought you were strapped for cash?"

I can hear the annoyance in his voice. I brace myself for the 'I'm risking my house' tirade.

"I'm worrying about keeping the house and my marriage, you're swanning off buying campervans."

My finances are absolutely none of Steve's business. Seriously where does he get off. I do the spreadsheets for his conferences, the marketing legwork and keep us in the black. If it wasn't for me, he'd have lost the house three conferences ago. Some people don't know how lucky they are.

"They're not as expensive as you might think. We've been saving for ages. Now we've got the baby to think about too. We need to create some space for ourselves. You understand? It's a parenthood thing, mental health. I've got other people to think about now. I can't focus on conferences."

"You're an asshole Adam. Always have been. You let me take all the risks. I sign all the finance. You bale out. Asshole."

"I understand you're annoyed, Steve;" that sticks in my throat. I'm not the rude, manic, unhinged asshole here. "The spreadsheets are all done. All you need to do is the marketing and audiovisuals. Keep the sponsors happy."

"That's the whole fucking conference, then."

He's so emotional. He needs to get a grip. I can hear the beer calling.

"Stella's going to fucking kill me. She always said you were a selfish nob."

That's rich. I always thought Stella liked me. Plenty of times I could have slipped a hand down her panties when Steve was otherwise engaged. Must be tough living with the manic-meister. She went through a phase of seriously giving me the eye. I assumed she wasn't getting it at home. I slip a hand down my boxers. These confrontations with Steve are always so stressful. I close my eyes and let him prattle on about Stella, the house, the spreadsheets, audiovisuals. Not my problem if the conference flops. It's all in Steve's name anyway.

"So are you saying our business partnership is over, Adam? That's it?"

Yes, Stevey-Boy, that's exactly what I'm saying. I have a million sitting in an offshore account to invest. I bloody hate confrontation and you're a manic nob-end.

"Of course not, Steve. I just need a break. A few months away from the rat-race. A re-charge and re-boot. I need to make sure Amy's ok, sort my diabetes, sort my mental health. A few months on the road. I'll be back. You'll see. Stella will love me yet."

"I don't think Stella will ever love you. She blames you for half-arsed investments and leaky sponsors. Don't mess with a mother and her ability to fund her children's education."

"Just as well I got 18 years to plan for all that, eh."

"Fuck you, Adam."

And that's it. I'm out of the conference malarky. No more stress. Sweet campervan adventures. Hopefully he'll find some new mug to do his legwork for him. I was too good for this nonsense. Money makes money. You only need a bit in the bank to make more. And baby, I got that sorted.

Would it be bad to crack open a beer, phone Amy and have a surreptitious wank whilst she's talking? Weirdly I'm finding the fact she's pregnant quite horny. Saves my life and has my baby. What a girl. I go to the kitchen and open the fridge. Running low on supplies. I need to do a beer run. I take a bottle, crack it open and slug a third of the bottle in one.

Arsehole Steve. How dare he make me feel bad about his crappy business. I'm stressed. Out of it now though. I leave the world of corporate conferences behind me. Bigger, better, money, open roads and babies. I open another beer and take both bottles upstairs. I lie on the bed to phone Amy. She answers after a couple of rings.

"Hey babe," I lie on the bed, bottle in one hand, phone in the other. At times like this, I could do with a third hand.

"Hey Adam." She sounds surprised. "Everything ok?"

"Yup. Everything's fine. I just miss your voice. Love you, baby."

"Aww… I miss you too, hun."

"Just had Steve raging at me down the phone. Going off on one. Completely unreasonable. The conference is all organised. I've left everything perfect. A trained monkey could see it through. So I tell him, I just need a bit of head space, to get back on track after getting out of hospital, to look after you, the baby, everything. Fuck's sake, I nearly died. You think he'd have a bit of compassion. Wanker."

I finish the remains of the first bottle and feel grateful for having brought a second one upstairs. I swap the empty for the full one. I take a swig and continue on.

"I can't take Steve having a go. Not after everything I've done for him. I've run these conferences. All he has to do is to sort the audiovisuals and sell a few more tickets. I just need to hear a loving voice. Have someone be nice to me. Calm me down a bit."

I put the bottle down and slip a hand down my boxers. Now Amy, speak now. Just let me close my eyes and listen. I love listening to you.

"Shall I pop round? I could be there in half an hour. Calm you down in person. We could just lie and chill for a bit."

Fuck no. I don't want her to actually come round. I'm happy with a phone-wank, then sleep. She'll only keep wittering on.

"Just talk to me darling. I'm going to speak to you for a bit. Catch some shut eye. Then maybe go out for a walk or something this afternoon. Kick this diabetes thing into touch. I'd like some head space just to sort myself out. Steve gets me so wound up."

"Steve is a pain in the arse, Adam. At least it's done. You got yourself out of the conference. Don't feel too bad. You're what's important now. And us. Steve can do one and jump in the lake. You've set it all up for him anyway. What's he complaining about?"

"Mmmm…." I'm barely listening to the words, but the drone is pleasant. "I love listening to you Amy, you're so good for me. I'm glad you think I'm doing the right thing." Talk some more, baby.

"I've always thought Steve put too much pressure on you. You should just ditch the whole internet conference thing. You've paid the mortgage off. Get something normal. Just a regular, manual thing to give you a bit of structure. Gets you outside, something that gets you fitter. Delivery driver or something. The supermarkets are always looking. Nine to five. Low stress. We don't need much to live off. I don't care what you do, as long as you're happy and we're together."

"Definitely something I should look into. We don't need to worry about money though."

"You sure, Adam? I mean, you've never really talked about the windfall. How much or how long before it runs out. We bought the camper. Is there much more left? Where did it come from?"

"Just a business deal, baby. Sometimes these things happen in corporate finance. You just happen to be in the right place at the right time. I got lucky."

"But what actually happened. How do you suddenly get money to buy a camper?"

"Working with an investor over the sale of a company, that's all. Corporate finance stuff. Boring stuff. Talk to me about nice stuff. Where's the first place you want to go with the camper? We should have it in a fortnight."

"Ooooo. I've been thinking. North Wales for starters. It's close enough as a starter adventure, not far enough away to be scary. We can build confidence and know we can get home if we need to. It'll be quiet. Beautiful. Not touristy. Still a bit wild. Colwyn Bay. We should go to Colwyn Bay. Beautiful beach, ice cream, long walks, pretty sunsets. It's blue flagged for swimming. Enough restaurants and pubs for the nights we don't want to cook. Perfect."

I'm sure Amy has no idea what I'm doing on the other end of the phone, but it's exactly what I need. I'm careful not to make a sound. The challenge is almost thrilling. Keep talking. Yes. Oh yes. I hold my breath to finish. Mmmm. Oh yes, baby. Nice. I need her off the phone now.

"You sure you don't want me to come round? We could chat about Colwyn Bay."

"That would be lovely, Amy. I sort of set today aside as self-care day. Get some exercise, sort my head out. Sometimes you just need some time to retreat into yourself for a bit. Maybe tomorrow?"

"I understand. I get it too. Time to recharge, reset."

Good, she gets it. I can't face her in person. "Thanks Amy. I needed that. Your voice, I mean. I needed that. I think I'm going to catch forty winks of good, health promoting sleep. Then do something productive with the rest of the day. You've helped so much. Thanks for talking."

"Anytime, Adam. I'm always here for you. I love you."

"Love you too baby. Feeling sleepy. Speak soon."

I swear I'm asleep before she even puts her phone down.

28 AMY: Assisting with Inquiries

Those awful police drama's that people get addicted to. The ones old people watch. A shabby detective in a dodgy coat. I'm playing a part in an episode of one. No-one has given me the script. I'm expected to know the words, know the ending. It all sorts itself out. The innocent are innocent. I'm vindicated. It wasn't me.

The room is dingy, there are no windows. It smells sweaty and unpleasant. Like a lifetime of bad people have been interviewed here, drug addicts, alcoholics, criminals, psychopaths. All sweating guilt and avoidance. None of them smelling sweetly of innocence and shower gel. I wonder if anyone has ever urinated in the corner. Why don't they at least put some carpet down, rather than this concrete hard stuff. Soften it a bit. Or do we not deserve that? If you're here, you're obviously bad and you don't deserve any kind of soft furnishings. Bad people only pee and sweat into them.

God, I feel sick. Sick and woozy. The lights are eye-searingly bright. The seat is hard and plastic. Even the table is a basic affair. Metal legs and a Formica top. I run my finger along the table top. It sends a shiver down my back. How many sweaty, guilty fingers have done the same thing. Maybe you can absorb badness-DNA through your fingers. Badness osmosis. The set-up makes me think psychological torture. Waterboarding. Sleep deprivation. Plain clothed policemen getting in your face and screaming at you. Then being nice and offering you biscuits.

I look at the two officers sat opposite me. Which one was nasty? Who was the nice one? Screamer and Biscuit. Sounds like a band. Do I not look out of place here? I have a pink silk shirt on. There will soon be damp stains of perspiration under my arm, down my back. Proof of guilt, they'll say. Innocent people don't perspire.

I think of Adam's house. I'd worked so hard on that over the years. My sanctum. I live and breathe that house. Edwardian wallpaper, unique and meaningful pieces of old furniture I pick up along the way. The cool, huge giant silver antlers I got Adam to put on the living room wall. Throws and cushions at every turn. The artwork we buy from holidays in special places. An oversized squashy, worn leather sofa to collapse into. Fluffy blankets to wrap yourself in. A tub of slippers and comfies by the fire. Low calorie hot chocolate in the kitchen. Scented bubble bath. I mean, I know I spend much of my life rearranging it all, but that's because it's mine. That control over my immediate environment gives me peace.

I am not at peace. I am bewildered, scared. I can't think straight. I don't understand what's happening. Maybe it's a lifetime of fear I can smell in this room. Maybe I smell like it too. Fear and urine and pheromones. Terror. We're all guilty before we even know why we're here. I wish there was a window.

"Thank you for coming in Ms Hawes. Or would you prefer Amy?"

I jump. Of course I jump. Look at me and I jump. I want to be invisible. It's the man. It's always the man who starts, isn't it? That's the script. The woman is there because I'm a woman. In case I cry. Or collapse. Or have some sort of breakdown. She'll have a special name, like the woman's support officer, or something. She'll have done the training.

"Amy is fine." Damn the words won't come out. Numb, cardboard lips and a disconnected windpipe. It's not my voice. There's not even any voice. I feel my head swimming and everything becoming distant.
The female support officer (if that's what she is) pours a plastic cup of water from a jug and places it in front of me. She smiles (they must teach you that). She's the nice one, Biscuit He's Mr Nasty, Screamer.

"Some water," she says as she places it in front of me. "Take your time."

I take a sip of the water. It's lukewarm and unpleasant. It tastes like the room. Like someone has peed in it. I breathe. In and out. Slow. In. Hold. And out. I take another sip of water.

"I'm sorry." I sound like a mouse. Small and squeaky. "I suffer from chronic anxiety and panic attacks. Depression too. I take medication." I take another sip of the warm water through cardboard lips.

"I'm pregnant too."

The man and woman glance at each other. I knew it would be the woman to speak. Women's Support Worker.

"As we said before, Amy, you can have legal representation sitting in with you, if you would like. We can also ask our doctor to sit in, to give you some support, if you would like. You're not in any trouble. You're here voluntarily to assist with our enquiries. We just want to ask you some questions, that's all. What we don't want to do is stress you or make you feel unwell."

I nod shakily. I'm gripping the edge of the plastic seat I'm sitting on. I'm gripping it so hard my knuckles are white. Harder still. The pain gives me something to focus on. Five fingers, four, three, two, one. Attached to four limbs. Four leg, three leg, two arm, one arm. Three of us in the room. Me three, her two, him one. Two thumbs on the underside of the chair. Press hard. Two, one. One cup in front of me. Focus on it. One. The sickness is passing.

"Amy, would you like someone to sit in with you? We can arrange a legal representative or a doctor."

"No. It's fine." I've done nothing wrong. They've just said that. "I have some breathing and focusing exercises that I do to help my panic attacks."

"Take your time. We can stop at any time. Just say. If you don't feel well, just say. We can have a break anytime. We can also get our doctor at any time to give you support. Would you like him now?"

"No, I'm fine." If I just keep saying that, maybe it will come true. Maybe I will be fine.

"Just let us know Amy. We go at your pace, ok? You're not in any trouble and our first priority is looking after you, ok?"

Hard to believe in this awful, dingy, smelly room of guilt, but I nod. Why does she keep asking if I'm ok? I'm obviously not. This room is not ok. I think of Rachel. She's a doctor. Of all the people who could sit here with me, I'd feel ok, I think, if it was Rachel. She'd know what to do. She'd sort them out, tell them I'm innocent.

"Amy we're going to record our session today. Just so we have an accurate record of everything. Is that ok?"

I stare blankly at them. The words don't register. I'm sitting watching TV. This is what happens on TV. You sit in a dingy room, they record the interview, then they send you to prison. I don't even know what I've done. Did I not tax the car or something? It's fine, I'll pay it now. I've got money. I'll pay twice. Cover the inconvenience and everyone else's time. Pay for the biscuits.

"Amy, do you want anyone to sit with you?"

I shake my head. Didn't I already answer that?

They think I'm mad. Everyone thinks I'm mad. A half-wit who can't speak.

"I suffer from anxiety. Sometimes it takes me longer to process things." My therapist taught me to say that, to explain why I'm weird.

"Ok, you've not done anything wrong Amy. We just want to ask you a few questions. It's easier if we record things. My writing is terrible. If I have to write it down, no-one can read it, not even me!" He smiles. He's trying to crack a joke. It's really confusing. It's like when you're feeling rubbish and someone being nice to you is the thing that tips you over the edge. I begin to cry. I'm crying and gulping. They just wait. This isn't going away, is it? If I squeeze my eyes shut and will it, I can open them and be somewhere else. Like the cartoon of the man who goes into the shop changing room and comes out somewhere else.

"I'm sorry." My therapist tells me I apologise too much. I apologise all the time. To everyone, for everything. I apologise for my presence, who I am, the fact that I can't do anything.

"It's ok," it's the woman again, "whenever you feel able, we can start again."

"I'm ok. Ask me what you need to ask me." Squeaky mouse voice. I'm 8 years old again.

"Ok, Amy. Is it ok, if we record our discussion this afternoon? It makes it easier for us and means we have an accurate record of things. Would that be ok?"

I nod. Have we not used up our daily supplies of 'ok?' yet?

"I'm sorry, Amy." Suddenly everyone's apologising. "We need you to say it. Answer with a yes or no. Is it ok for us to record our discussion this afternoon?"

"Yes."

I can feel myself drifting off. Floating towards the grubby ceiling with the bright lights. They've turned the recorder on. The woman is telling the recorder who we all are. I'm Amy Hawes. They ask me to confirm. I have to give an address. I give my sister's. Date, time. It's all official. They tell the recorder that I've declined legal representation and that I don't want the duty doctor to sit in. They say I'm pregnant and that I can ask for a break, or to stop the interview at any time. Is this a drama or a comedy? I'm floating round the room. A tragi-horror. I wish I'd read the script. Even the TV blurb that tells me what it's all about. Are we pre or post watershed? Violence or swearing?

"Amy we'd like to ask you some questions about your boyfriend, Adam Waters."

This is about Adam? "Is he ok? Has he done something wrong?" They don't answer me. "He had a diabetic attack, almost died. I had to call an ambulance." I'm rambling. Maybe he's dead. Please no, don't let him be dead.

"Do you know what he does for a living, Amy?"

"He organises conferences. Business design. Product design. User experience. Stuff like that. Works with google, amazon, some of the banks, anyone. He brings people together to share ideas. Inclusion. Iterative development. Agile working." I use words I've heard Adam use but never really knew what they meant. Just words. Clever stuff.

"He was due to meet a woman called Sarah Emmerson on the 18th June, Amy. Do you know who she is, Amy? Has Adam ever mentioned her?"

I squint at them. My head hurts. I can't see people, only blurry, disconnected shapes. Sarah Emmerson? The name is familiar. I think I've heard it before. I shake my head.

"For the record, Amy has shaken her head to indicate that she doesn't know who Sarah Emmerson is."

I have brain freeze. Who is Sarah Emmerson? I have heard that name.

"Amy, Sarah Emmerson is a businesswoman from New York. She was the Head of Product Design and Product Management at an American company called INSpire. She was also wife to William Emmerson, a New York lawyer and mother to two small boys."

I look blankly at them. My brain is thinking of

Connect2Me, the business networking app that Adam is obsessed by. Sarah Emmerson, INSpire. Connect2Me. She feels like a very long time ago. So much has happened since then. She comes from a distant life I can barely remember.

"Sarah Emmerson was visiting the UK. She had a meeting scheduled with Adam Waters on the 18th June in Manchester. She left London early morning, but never made it to Manchester. Her body washed up on Walney Island in Cumbria a few weeks ago."

"Cumbria? Adam's never been. Not that I know anyway." I breathe a sigh of relief. Cumbria has nothing to do with me and Adam.

"Sarah wasn't killed in Cumbria. She was killed at Groudle Glen on the Isle of Man and thrown into the Sea. Her body was battered about for a few weeks before washing up on Walney. A dive team found her bag, weighted down with rocks in the sea at Groudle Glen. They also found traces of her blood on the cliff top. She was stabbed repeatedly before being thrown into the sea. Her bag was weighted down with rocks so it would sink."

The room is swimming. I think I'm going to be sick. I am. There's a thumping in my head. I've got the out of body thing going on. I'm burning up and can't breathe. I'm all around the room. In bits. I'm dying. Gasping. Gulping for air. Someone is trying to put water in my hand. I can't focus. I can't breathe. Can't breathe. Help. Oh my god, help. Please help my baby. She can't die here. I curl up around her. She can't die. Not here.

"Amy, I'm Dr Williams. I'm the duty doctor."

Who? Where? How did he get here? Where am I? I look at him blankly. I see through him. My face burns. I'm gulping, gasping, grabbing for oxygen. I can't hear him. His mouth is moving, but I can't hear him.

"Amy, listen to me. Focus on my voice. We think you're having a panic attack. Listen. We need to slow your breathing right down."

The words are all jumbled. Nothing makes sense. I start to cry. Tears stream down my face. It makes it harder to breathe. This is where I die. Me and Blue. We die here in this airless room. My nose runs into my mouth.

"Close your eyes Amy and listen to my voice. Close your eyes."

He's holding my wrist. Is he feeling for a pulse? I'm already dead? His hands burn my flesh. My skin is super-sensitive. It hurts. I wouldn't feel that if I was dead. The feeling from his hands on my wrists travels up my arm. A numb tingling. A rotten-ness. Black mould, rotten to the core. Leave me to die.

"Listen to me Amy. I'm going to help you. Close your eyes."

The veins in my eyelids will go black, mouldy

rotten. Like Sarah Emmerson. Oh my god, Sarah Emmerson. A new flood of tears. I grab the air as I drown. Red blood gurgling and spewing.

"Close your eyes, Amy. Good girl. Now close your mouth. That's it. Excellent."

The black-vein-death spreads over my face. Now I'm freezing. Ice cold. The black death is icy cold.

"Breathe in through your nose, Amy. Breathe in slowly as I count to four. Ok, breathe through your nose. 1……….. 2………. 3……… 4…………. Good girl."

I'm going to explode. Spontaneously combust. Splatter Amy-blood and entrails over everything. Dripping down the walls.

"Hold your breath, Amy. Don't exhale. Hold it for seven. No breathing. 1…….. 2……. 3……. 4……..5……...6……….7. That's excellent. You're doing really well."

My head is going to pop. Focus on the voice. Do what the voice says.

"Now let it go Amy, whoosh it out. All the air. Exhale to the count of eight. 1……2……. 3……. 4…….. 5…….. 6…….. 7………. 8………. Perfect. Good girl. Keep listening. Keep your eyes closed. We're going to do that all over again. Ok? Close your mouth and inhale through your nose to a count of four. 1………. 2………. 3……….. 4. And hold your breath. Seven counts."

I follow the instructions. The black mould is receding. Slowly, it's losing its alternate burning and icy grip. I listen to the voice.

"Keep your eyes closed, Amy."

We do the whole thing another four times. I think, when I open my eyes, I'm going to be back in my bedroom, at my sister's house. My dressing gown on the back of the door. The cosy grey, furry throw on the bed. The Monet print on the wall. That's where I want to be. As far away from the nightmare as possible. That bedroom is safety. Please, I don't want to wake up in Groudle Glen. I afford myself the luxury of stroking my stomach. She can't know the black mould.

"When you're ready Amy, open your eyes. Gently come back to the room."

I don't want to. Only if I'm in my bedroom. I open my eyes. There is no dressing gown, furry throw or Monet print. Of course there isn't. There is Room 101. Place of nightmares and dead people. Tortured and ravaged. Dead and bloated.

"Have a drink, Amy." The woman is shoving the plastic cup at me. "I'm sorry for having to put you through this. I know it's not pleasant."

'Not pleasant' might be the understatement of the year. I remember who she is, Sarah Emmerson. She's tall, beautiful, model-like, blonde, clever. She's mom of two rug-rats. Now she's bloated and ravaged. The stuff of horror films. I fight down the bile.

"We just have two questions to ask you Amy. Then I think we should stop for today. They're important ones. Things we have to ask you. Are you ok to carry on? Just two questions."

She looks at the doctor. He gives a tiny shake of his head and a shrug. He thinks I can't see him. Everything is so intense, it hurts. She's going to ask me something about Groudle Glen, I know she is. I've been there. I've been there with Adam. We've taken the train, walked the path, watched where the sealions and polar bears used to be. I know what it means to him. Childhood and fairies and his mother. The red water wheel, the little white house. He used to try and make me dance, so the fairies wouldn't come and get me. It's all too much of a coincidence. I brace myself.

"Amy, we think Sarah died on Wednesday 18th June. Adam tells us that was the day the two of you went to Ikea in Leeds. Then you went to his aunt's house for dinner." The woman consults her notes, "Aunt Bea. You went to Ikea, then you went to Aunt Bea's. He was quite specific. I know it's a few weeks ago now, but can you confirm you and his whereabouts on Wednesday 18th June?"

I look at her. Ikea. Drawers and kitchens. We went to Ikea to look at drawers and kitchens. He had his shirt on inside-out. He went to the gents to change it.

Then we had roast beef and sherry. He wasn't on the Isle of Man. We went to Ikea to look at drawers and kitchens. The beginning of nice Adam. Our new life together. There was something about Isle of Man ferry tickets. Was there? But that was all a mistake. My Adam was in Ikea.

"We were in Ikea on the 18th. Things for the baby. Getting the house ready. Chest of drawers and kitchens. I remember because he had his shirt on inside-out and had to go to the gents to turn it the right way. Drawers and kitchens. Then we went to Aunt Beas. She'd made roast beef and Yorkshire puddings. Two apple pies. We ate one and took one home. We walked home. He'd had a couple of bottles of beer. Bea kept filling my glass with sherry."

We made love that night. I remember. That was the first time in years. The start of the new Adam. The start of our lovemaking. The start of Blue. That proves it. He couldn't have been on the Isle of Man. You can't kill someone on the Isle of Man, dash back to Chorlton, eat Yorkshire pudding, then make love to your girlfriend. That would be utterly psychopathic.

"You definitely remember going to Ikea on the 18th. Then dinner in….." she consults her notes again, "dinner in Chorlton."

"Yes, with Aunt Bea. She'll confirm it. She cooked roast beef and apple pies. We decided to walk home after dinner. I remember."

"And did you buy anything in Ikea? Did you

purchase anything? Use a credit card? Get a receipt? A ticket for the car park?"

I racked my brain to remember. "Drawers and kitchens. We looked at chest of drawers and kitchens, but didn't buy anything. We were going to go back again."

"So there won't be any receipts or credit card purchases? Did you stop for fuel, for lunch? Did you buy anything on the way there, on the way back? Did you go to the café?"

It's all really foggy. I don't remember any of that. My brain won't retrieve it. I briefly see ferry tickets, but it's quickly closed down. I shake my head.

"We just looked, then we went to Bea's. I don't think we needed to buy fuel. Adam doesn't like the Ikea coffee so we didn't go to the café. Lunch out would have ruined our dinner."

"But you were definitely in Ikea on the 18th June." I nod my head.

"Yes."

"You're sure?"

I nod my head again. "Yes."

"What time would that have been Amy?"

"We left Manchester mid-morning. Spent all day

there. Went to Bea's at around 6pm. Got the metro so we could have a drink. There's a big visitor information sign by the metro. All about Chorlton."

I'm definitely remembering bits through the fog. I remember Adam's inside-out shirt, and reading the visitor board with him. He wasn't on the Isle of Man. I feel pleased with myself for remembering. Maybe I'm not so bad.

"Ok Amy, the only other question that's important to us is about Adam's finances. Sarah transferred a very large sum of money before she died. Almost a million pounds. That money has gone missing. It may be the motive for her death. Has Adam made reference to money? Has he been spending more or made plans around money?"

The campervan. But that's not a million pounds.

"We bought a campervan last week. But we'd been planning that for ages. The baby just motivated us to finally do it. Honestly, we've been saving for a camper forever. He wants to take me and the baby on open road adventures. That's all."

"He bought a new campervan?"

I nod. "Yes. But he's wanted one and been saving up for ages. He owns the house outright, so we've no bills. He's giving up the conference business, but he still wants to work. Needs to work. We were talking just the other day about him doing something simple like delivery driving. Just to keep us going. I'd know if he had a million pounds in the bank. We don't need that kind of money. Money doesn't make you happy."

"So he's never talked about coming into some money? A business deal, windfall, an offshore account?"

I shake my head. "No. He was just really proud that he'd saved up enough for his camper. We both are."

I stroke my stomach. He bought the camper for me and Blue. I remember how happy he was when he found out about her. He bought it for us.

"He wouldn't be applying for delivery driver jobs if he had a million pounds in the bank. We don't need that much money to live on."

"Ok, thank you Amy. I think that's probably enough for today. We don't want to stress you or the baby any more than we need to. You've been very helpful."

I nod. I could weep with relief. I am weeping. It's too much. I look at the duty doctor chap. He's nice. I thought I was dying. He saved me. He looks concerned.

"Amy, I'm worried about you. I think we should get you to a place of safety. Somewhere you and the baby can feel safe. That's really important. Can you hang on here a moment, whilst I have a word with the officers."

He disappears out the room with the man, leaving me with the woman. She smiles at me.

"That was quite an ordeal," she says gently, "I'm sorry we had to put you through that. When's the baby due?"

"March." Talking about Blue always makes things better. "We've nicknamed her Blue. She was the size of a blueberry when I told Adam I was pregnant. She'll be a bit bigger now."

"You know it's a girl?"

"Just a feeling. I've always felt like she's a little girl. Adam was so excited when I told him. I know what you think of him, but he's a good person. He loves us."

"We're just doing our best to get to the truth Amy. I hope you're right."

The doctor and the male police officer enter the room again.

"Amy, Dr Williams and I both feel that we should organise a place of safety for you and the baby. We're both telling you, that for your own safety we strongly advise against any contact with Adam. We can protect you and the baby if we arrange for you to stay at one of our safe houses. We can arrange for a female officer to keep you company. Just for a few days until we can get to the bottom of what's going on."

I feel my heart begin to race again. I'm prickling. All hot and cold. My breathing quickens.

"Calm down Amy, it's ok." It's the nice doctor. "It's just for a day or two. Just to be safe. We need you and the baby to be safe. You are our priority. You've been through a lot."

I know what's best for me. It's not a strange house, with strange people and nothing I know. The mould is coming back. Terror. I need my dressing gown, my furry throw. My cosies. My life. Control is safety. So is familiarity.

"No. I want to go back to my sister's house. That's my safe place. She'll keep me safe. She always does. I won't go to Adam's. Please don't make me go somewhere I don't know. Please. I need to be somewhere I know, with people I know." I beseech Dr Williams. The policeman too. "Please. I can't go somewhere I don't know. My mental health won't take it. My sister always looks after me." I'm sobbing. I can't stop.

"We can't make you go, Amy. That's your choice. Personally, I'd feel better if we were looking after you in one of our houses and keeping you safe. But I can't force you to take that decision. Please stay in the house. Make sure others are around. We'll need to speak to your sister."

"Please I need to be somewhere I know. I won't cope if I'm not." I'm crying so hard, the words are jumbled and they can't understand me. It's been a long day. I just want to go to bed. I want to curl up into a ball and sleep forever.

"Ok, we'll speak to your sister. No contact with Adam, Amy. Please. Just until we get this sorted. You've been through enough. We need to make sure we get you access to the right medical and psychological support."

I need my sister. I need my bedroom. I can't think straight. What are they suggesting? Adam would never hurt me. He loves me. I'm carrying his child.

29 RACHEL: Where is She?

I stretch luxuriously in the bed. No work. No on-call. No nothing. This could be the perfect Sunday. I look at the clock. Six am. It's early. The sun is streaming through the bedroom window and bouncing joyfully off the bed. Why is it so hard to get up in the morning when you've got to get to work and you crave another fifteen minutes under the covers, but then a lazy Sunday and PING? A bit of sun and I'm awake with the larks. Guy the guy snoozes beside me. Nope. No snoozes. I launch the attack, cosy in and nibble his ear. Then I stick my tongue in for good measure.

"Get off me, woman! What time do you call this? Can't a man sleep on a Sunday off?"

"Nope. I'm awake. Sun's out. Wake up, wake up WAKE UP."

I climb on top of him, straddling his broad chest, letting my hair dangle down onto his face. I run my hands through his dark chest hair.

"Oh, I see. It's like that is it?" He flips me over, like a doll and pins me down with his body weight. "HA! Wake me up at the crack of dawn, wench, would you? I'll show you who's boss. Why are you so full of beans?"

"Sun's out. Sexy man by my side. Day off. Too nice to be wasting it sleeping. You're awake now though. I done my job good. I deserve a reward."

"Reward? You'll pay royally for it!" He kisses me, deep and longingly. "Just as soon as I pee."

Men are so romantic! Victims to their biology. He hops off me and nips to the lavatory. I hear him brushing his teeth too. Maybe I should too. Morning dog breath and all that. I pick my phone up from the bedside table. No messages. I was hoping to hear back from Amy. I've sent her a few messages now and had no response. It's not like her. It's niggling me. My final message was just last night. She's not opened it. Likely she's busy. That's a good thing. Getting on with life. The niggle is there though. She's always picks messages up quickly and nine times out of ten, I get a response. I check again. Still no response to last night's text. On a whim, I dial her number. The phone rings. Shit Rachel, it's like six o'clock in the morning. What are you doing? It only rings once before I cut it off. Who's need am I meeting? Mine, not hers. Guy kicks the door open. He's got a mug of coffee in both hands.

"Coffee in bed for the beautiful lady. Caffeine to wake her adoring sex slave up." He sets the mug down on the bedside table next to me. "Voila, Mademoiselle. We aim to please."

I'm still holding the phone. I wave it at him. "Fancy a trip to Manchester?" I say as if waving the phone explains everything.

"Manchester? Why? I thought we were all about the mountains, the lochs and the paths less travelled?"

"I'm worried about a friend. She struggles with her mental health and she's had one Hell of a year. I'm not getting an answer. I've been trying to contact her for days."

"Busy? It happens you know. People have lives."

"I know. Something's up. I can't explain. It just doesn't feel right. I hope I'm wrong."

"And you don't have enough to do, looking after the mental health of the Glasgow population without taking on Manchester too?" he leans over and kisses me on the forehead. "I'm teasing you, beautiful. You want to go to Manchester to check on a friend? Wherever you go, I follow. Lead the way, Mac-Rachel. I love that you care so deeply about everything. My job to make sure you're both ok? Today?"

I look ruefully at him. It's hardly the lazy, relaxing Sunday we'd planned. "Do you mind?"

"Anywhere with you is an adventure, why

wouldn't I want to squeeze in a few domestic ones before we jet off to Argentina."

I shiver in anticipation. Over the past month, we'd begun to make the talks about travelling to South America, more of a reality. Guy had applied for a year-long sabbatical. I had begun to investigate short term, locum work.

"What's the story anyway?"

"Hmmm?" I was jolted from a mind wander.

"Your Mancunian friend. She from Manchester that you're worried about. What's the story?" For a moment, I wondered how much information to give him. It was an unconventional backdrop. The whole love triangle. What the heck. No point in lying. It was before we met anyway.

"It's a weird one. We both dated the same bloke. A narcissistic, abusive asshole who took the piss out of both of us. Neither knew the other one existed. Mine was short-lived before I realised something wasn't quite right. She got gas-lighted and manipulated for years. It damaged her. I feel a bit responsible. He sucked me in good and proper."

"But you didn't know about her?"

"No. He told me she was an ex, that it had been over for ages. Spent two years telling me how mad she was and how much he hated her. I believed him. I even called it his 'comedy routine' of girlfriends past.

He had a string of unsavoury anecdotes."

"A love triangle?" His eyes were smiling.

"No way. A selfish wee prick who lied through his teeth so he could have his cake and eat it. It almost destroyed her. A guy with no morals and no respect for other people. And that's putting it mildly. Destroys women for fun."

"And you dated this prick? Given your current choice of man, an excellent choice if I may add, I assumed you had better taste."

"Oh, I do. Believe me. It was short-lived. But these bastards can be charming and spin a good yarn. That's why I want to check on her. He's incapable of being on his own. He'll destroy her. She's already tried to kill herself because of him."

"Have you tried phoning?"

I wave the phone at him again. "Been there, done that. No response. She's fragile. If he's love bombed her. Played the victim. Manipulated her into going back, she'll crumble. It's taken her months to get to the happier place she was in."

"She's not your responsibility, Rach. You can't take on everyone. What happens when we're in South America?"

South America. We talk about it all the time. As if it's….. well as if it's like popping down to

Manchester.

"I know. Just this once. I can't explain it. Something in my gut. A bad feeling. Down and up in a day. We'll have fun. Lunch out. My best Guy the guy Mix Tape. It's only a couple of hours away."

I straddle him again and pin his hands down on the bed above his head. I grind my hips on him simultaneously.

"Hey," he protests, "no fair."

I grin. Seriously, he's so much fun. "So, tell me you love me." I grind deeper.

"Nope," he exaggeratedly shakes his head from side to side to side on the pillow. "No way."

"Tell me!" I can feel the movements having the desired effect. I respond accordingly.

"Make me!" He squeals as I nibble on a nipple. "I play hard ball."

I nibble harder on his other nipple. He squeals louder. I got this boy. I so have this boy. He's all mine.

"Ok, ok, ok, ok. You got me. Yes, yes, YES. Dr Davidson. I LOVE YOU. Now finish what you started, then take me to Manchester, you mad woman. Let's go rescue a damsel who may or may not be in distress."

I am caught off guard and he flips me over so I'm lying on my tummy on the bed. He pins me down this time.

"M'wah ha ha! See! You only think you're in control because I let you." I love this man. I truly love him. I love the way we are together. "And for the record," he whispers in my ear, "I love you. I will always love you, and I will follow you to the ends of the earth, wherever you want to go."

Making love to Guy is always a delight, a wonder, beautiful, loving. I can't wait to go to South America and start a life. With Guy you know nothing bad will happen. He's programmed to love and protect. We doze off, it's after nine when we wake again. Guy wakes first this time.

"My coffee's cold." The mug of coffee on the bedside table is undrunk and cold.

"I don't know….. your willing slave makes you coffee……"

I pick up my phone.

"Any news from the missing Mancunian?" he asks. I shake my head.

"Absolutely nothing. She's not even opened the two texts from yesterday. It's not like her."

Guy sits up. "Ok, let's do this thing. We set off

now, the roads will be quiet. We'll be there by lunchtime. I'll drive. You navigate."

Guy had driven through on Friday after work. It wasn't like him, he preferred public transport, but he'd had a meeting out of town and had just carried on through to Glasgow. It meant his car was sitting outside.

"Sure? We can take my car if you like." I am very aware that this is my folly, and not his. I shouldn't be putting him out on our supposedly romantic time together.

"Don't be daft. At least let me pretend to be the superhero that rescues everyone. It's good for my ego to rescue damsels in distress." He grins at me. "At least pretend to be vulnerable."

I flutter my eyelashes….. badly, and pretend to swoon. Before long we're on the road, headed South out of Glasgow. I can't shift this impending feeling of doom. I send Amy another text.

RACHEL: 9.29: Hi Amy. Haven't heard from you in a while. Hope all is well. Will admit to being a little worried. It's not like you not to reply. I'm going to be in Manchester this afternoon. Let me know as soon as you get this?? Thinking of you. Xx

I hit send. That one remains unopened too. I put my hand on his leg as he drives, just to feel the connection. It's just as well he's driving. I'd be fighting the urge to floor the accelerator and speed up. Black clouds gather over us as we speed down the M74. Rain begins to fall on the windscreen. The windscreen wipers slosh backwards and forwards, backwards and forwards, backwards and forwards. Like a metronome, ticking off the moments till Armageddon, every mile. I'm not even sure why we're going down, or what we're going to do when we get there. I don't even have Amy's sister's address. Would I go to Adam's? The thought of that makes my heart beat faster. I've not been there since before we broke up. The happy times when we supposedly had our own fairy tale. The lies, the duplicity, the shadow of a fragile ex, who never was an ex. Surely she's not gone back there. That would be madness. The oppression of it hangs over the car, like the black clouds we're driving into.

"So, what's the plan Sherlock? We go to Amy's house? Whereabouts in Manchester is she?"

Guy will think I'm nuts. A four-hour drive on a Sunday off when I don't even know where she is. Rachel saves the world, one ghost at a time. I'm so glad of Guy's company, his strength, his *normality*. His presence means I don't get sucked back into that alternative reality. Adam's world is a strange and scary place. One foot in everyone else's reality, one foot in some fucked up dreamworld of fairies and abuse. To think I thought it was romantic, unconventional, special when we were dating. Certainly was special, but not in a good way.

"Guy, I have a confession." I'm glad his eyes are on the road. "I don't actually know where Amy is living. I mean, I know she's at her sister's, but I don't know where her sister lives."

"A wild goose chase? Needle in a haystack? Find a troubled girl in Manchester somewhere. What could go wrong? So we may end up having to go to the mad ex's house, if all else fails?"

Yup. He's called it. That's why I'm glad he's here. He puts his hand on my knee and leaves it there. Turns out we both need the connection.

"I'm teasing you, darling. Don't worry. We'll find her. I'll not let anything bad happen. I love that there's never been a dull moment since I met you. I love that you save the world. I love that you care. I love you. I'd do anything for you. Now if you would be good enough to find the bag of jelly beans that are in the glove compartment. Open them, mine out the red ones, just the red ones mind, and feed them to me, I would be most obliged."

I squeeze his knee before hunting out the sweets. I find four red ones. I find his open mouth.

"So how come an intelligent, gorgeous, switched on, all-round fabulous girl like my girlfriend finds a dangerous nutter to date? Do you only date nutters? And yikes, eeek, are you just about to head to South America with another one? Hmmm?" He pokes my side. "More jelly beans." He proffers his hand.

"Let's just say he presented as very sane, very normal, very charming, very loving, very kind, very single – having told his ex that it was over between them. He turned out he was none of those things, just a very good liar and self-obsessed fantasist. You know what they say, clinically it's a fine line between narcissistic, psychopathic and borderline personality disorders. His charm was a well-rehearsed script. Amy's had years of the gaslighting and abuse. He's done his best to destroy her. I didn't realise he'd been lying to both of us. When she found out, she flipped, took an overdose and I felt pretty shitty about the whole thing."

I dig out another handful of red jelly beans and put them in his hand.

"But she's left him. Yes? She saw the light?"

"I think so, but I'm not sure. She's a lot stronger than she was, but still fragile. And he's a manipulative bastard who can't face being on his own."

I know it sounds irrational, even to me. I just have this horrible feeling in the pit of my stomach that I just can't shift. If it's a wasted trip, so be it.

"I can't explain it Guy. Adam isn't like anyone I've met before. He's fractured. One part, Prince Charming. Another Freddy Kruger. One foot in this world, one foot somewhere dark, fucked-up, psychopathic. He fucked us both over, me and Amy, and ended up with neither of us. Adam doesn't do being on his own. The darkness subsumes him. I actually don't know what he's capable of. It terrifies me. It should terrify Amy, but the years of abuse, they've destroyed her. Stockholm Syndrome or something. Sometimes he's like this wee troubled boy, desperate for love, clinging on to life. She can't resist going back, making excuses, letting herself be sucked in again."

The car speeds down the motorway, headed for the M6. We are approaching Gretna. Almost out of Scotland. My palms are sweaty. I wipe them down the front of my jeans. As if I'm trying to rid myself of something noxious. Thinking of Adam made my skin crawl.

"Want to stop at the services?" Guy says, stealing a sideways look at me.

I shake my head. "Let's just get down there as fast as we can. I'll try ringing her again."

I am getting the feeling perhaps Amy doesn't want to be contacted.

30 CAL WATERS: Brothers Don't Walk the Dark Alone

"If you're asking if I think my little brother is capable of killing anyone, then categorically NO! Adam is vulnerable. Plays the big man 'cause he's scared of his own shadow. I'd pledge my bloody kids' lives on it. You've got the wrong man. I know my brother. He's not capable of hurting anything or anyone."

I'm getting wound up. It never helps. I want to wrap my arms around Adam and let him know that everything will be alright. Cal's here. Cal will sort it. They're just playground bullies. I know I've neglected you lately. Life got busy, but I'm here now. I've been in this Goddamn room for hours. No windows and it stinks.

Tweedledum and Tweedledee-Bully over there. Overpaid, officious, supercilious, ignorant twats. They think they're streetwise. They know fuck-all. I ran with the real bad boys. I know what I'm talking about. I'll always be there for you, bro.

I was meant to be meeting mates for a cycle. Bits of the Pennine Way. Fuck's sake. Our establishment is a piece of piss. It really is.

"Will we be much longer?"

I'm struggling to keep the irritation out of my voice. Actually, I'm not even trying to. I need a beer. I need to see my brother. The establishment can go fuck itself. It makes up what it wants anyway.

"Just a few more questions, Mr Waters. We won't keep you much longer. When was the last time you saw your brother?"

"I spoke to him on the phone last week. He was in good form. Been saving up for a campervan. Always wanted one. From when we were boys. And Amy's pregnant. He's going to be dad. He was over the moon. Happiest I've heard him in a long time. He deserves a bit of happiness."

"What makes you say that?"

"We all deserve happiness, don't we?"

I feel defensive, angry at their stupidity. Happiness is reserved for the official twats?

"He works hard."

They really are arseholes. Black and white, villains and heroes.

"It's a tough world. Amy's a nutter. She's exhausting. A baby will make him a man. Wish it wasn't Amy. Girl's too high maintenance, too highly strung for my liking, but it's exactly what Adam needs. Distraction. A bit of purpose."

It's a joke. He's a normal bloke doing normal things. The only thing Adam is guilty of is a bit of ducking and diving on the internet selling over-priced conferences that lack substance, and having a wacky girlfriend that puts everyone on edge. Hardly criminal activity.

"When's the last time you saw your brother, Mr Waters? Face to face?"

They spit out the words 'brother' and 'Waters.' They think they've got their man already. They just want to twist my words to confirm it.

"Not since last year. Adam was the wing man on our cycling tour of Northern Scotland. Haven't seen him face to face since."

A stab of guilt. Adam doesn't do well on his own. Should have made more of an effort.

"I don't exactly get on with his girlfriend. Truth be told, she doesn't get on with us. The house *he* bought with *his* money? She made it her own. Everything. Constantly redecorating, rearranging, never at peace. The space he occupies gets smaller and smaller. It's all her. Pervasive essence of Amy seeps into everything. I stay away from the house. He knows where to find me."

It's all excuses. He knows where to find me. He'd

just never come looking. He's built a wall around himself. It's all about appearances.

It's hot and stuffy. My trousers are stuck to me. They've gone tight and I'm tired. I feel the urge to pace. It's a hard, cement floor. I could tap dance. Set their inane words to it. Serenade of the innocent. Wonder where Adam is now. At home most likely. Does he know we're all being interrogated about his movements? About whether I *really* know my own brother.

"Do you know if Adam had any financial difficulties? How was work?"

"Doubt it. He owns his house outright. Bought it after our mother died. We had a wrangle after the funeral. She ended up leaving me and the two kids the biggest share of her assets. Her house on the Isle of Man. What could I do?" I shrug. "It's what she wanted."

Reality was that Paula and me looked after her for a year before she died. Had the downstairs converted. Hospital bed, commode and wet room. Adam wasn't into all that. He couldn't cope. He doesn't do stress. Didn't want to see her when she was dying. I'm not telling these twats any of that. Adam's a topper. Heart of gold.

I can't sit any longer. I'm going to explode with the pointlessness of it all.

"Look, do you mind if I stand up and move about? I'm getting cramp. It's very stuffy in here."

"I'm sorry, Mr Waters. Just a few more questions, that's all. By all means, get up and stretch your legs. Would you like a break?"

I shake my head. I want this nonsense over and done with. I want to see Adam. I need to know he's alright. This place makes you paranoid. It's my fault, I'm responsible. I' overwhelmed. I need to hug my little brother. I'm so sorry Adam, I should have been there for you. I wish I'd made time. I wish I could go back in time. I wish I could see you now.

I stand up and straighten my trousers. I feel sticky and damp. This place is so goddamn airless. My legs feel wobbly.

"I'm fine. Just keep going. You said you just had a couple of questions for me?"

I hate these guys. It's hard not to visualise leaping across the table and punching the face off them. Starting with the tall, thin one with the mean face.

"Yes. Just a couple, Mr Waters. What was the state of Adam's finances? Did he have any financial concerns that you know about?"

Financial concerns? Adam had a big five-bedroom house, paid outright, in a leafy part of Greater Manchester. Not bad for a 52-year-old guy. They've already asked me that, haven't they? What did I say? Keep it consistent. They're trying to trick me.

"As far as I know, Adam had his house paid for outright. No children. Few outgoings. He made his beer money organising business conferences. He had no concerns that I knew about."

Surely Adam would have come to me if he was worried about money. I'm the only family he has. We've got each other. He knows I'd have helped.

"Sarah Emmerson transferred a large sum of money before she disappeared. Almost a million pounds. She was due to meet Adam the day she died. Had Adam mentioned a windfall or a business deal? Did he appear to have more money than usual?"

I shake my head. "Nope. He'd just bought a campervan that he'd been saving up for. It's hardly a bolthole on the Gold Coast. Adam was as Adam always is. He has a big house, but lucky if he has a fiver in his back pocket. I always got the drinks in." The sarcasm sneaks in. "I don't think he has a cool million stashed somewhere that we don't know about."

The idea seems preposterous. My brother couldn't afford a new pair of shoes. They are consulting their notes. I arch my back to stretch it and pace another furlong of the room. I'd be ploughing a furrow in the carpet, if it wasn't a depressing, grey cement floor.

"Mr Waters, what can you tell us about the family connection to the Isle of Man?"

Eh? The Isle of Man. I look blankly at them whilst the question registers.

"The Isle of Man?"

"Yes, what was Adam's connection to the Isle of Man?"

"I own property there. Rent it out. My mum's old house. It's where we grew up. For a few years anyway. We moved there with my mum after she left my dad. Why?"

They ignore my question and plough on.

"When would that have been?"

"When we stayed there? Jeez. Years ago. Years and years. I was eight, so Adam could only have been about four. Is this entirely relevant?"

"Bear with us, Mr Waters. It's a line of enquiry. It may be relevant, it may not. We don't know. What was Adam like at the time? We understand he was cited in the divorce papers." They consult their papers, reading out: "Enuresis, night-time terrors, self-harm, attachment issues, developmental delay."

"Enuresis?" I don't like this line of enquiry.

"Bedwetting."

I know that. I just don't want to remember. Memories I don't want to revisit. The Isle of Man, a loopy, post-separation, abused and broken mother and a traumatised brother who kept trying to cook himself. Fairies, dancing and walks to Groudle Glen at three o'clock in the morning. Adam and his habit of putting bits of himself on the cooker. I can still smell his burning flesh and feel the terror. Yes, he wet the bed for years. Smeared shit on the walls too and didn't speak for six months. Eventually the nightmares stopped. Or at least, he learned to bottle them up and not tell anyone. I should have been a better brother. I should have looked after him. It's my fault.

"I think most families struggle with separation and divorce." Keep it neutral, Cal. They don't need to know the detail. "My parents didn't like each other by the end of their time together. My dad had a temper. My mother irritated him. There was no love lost between them. Countless other families go through it every day."

They ignore my sarcasm, yet again. I'm weary, heavy, like an old, black, crushing weight is descending.

"Are you familiar with Groudle Glen on the Isle of Man?"

Groudle Glen! OMG Groudle Glen!

"I am yes, we lived not far away. It was somewhere my mother was fond of. She felt it had *spiritual qualities.*"

"Spiritual qualities?"

Aah! Don't ask me to explain my mother, please.

"Yes. Maybe you'd call her a Druidess of sorts. She claimed a spiritual journey using nature to promote healing. She thought there was a portal to the underworld at Groudle Glen. She said she felt *the energy*. She went back there at the end of her life, became an Ovate, a kind of nature-based prophet."

This sounds mad. Loony tunes. I'm not helping Adam at all. I'm making our family sound like a mad, screwed up cult.

"Excuse me, I don't mean to be disrespectful, but this is a million miles from Adam. He had very little to do with our mother at the end of her life. Distanced himself from all that. We took her in and nursed her for the last year of her life. Adam saw her briefly maybe once or twice."

I've never talked about the past with Adam. Or mum. Or the fairies and underworld and nature, her healing, prophecies, divination and teaching. Was that a mistake? We both conveniently shut it away and screwed the lid shut. Just a normal family. There are millions of us. Borderline Normal. We're all Borderline Normal. Life is an exercise in Borderline Normality.

"I'm making it more dramatic than it sounds. For the most part, mum was a maths teacher and a mother. That's it."

I remember that was the source of some of Adam's childhood nightmares. A fairy story too far, courtesy of our mother. He became convinced he was a changeling. A fairy boy planted to replace the real Adam. He used to burn himself to prove he could feel. That he was real.

"Your father, Mr Waters."

The officer doing all the speaking, the thin, mean one, consults his notes again. I am coming to realise that it's not a good thing. They have more information about our family than I'm comfortable with.

"He died in a Psychiatric Hospital, yes?"

Are they trying to make us out to be guilty through insanity? This is preposterous. They clearly have nothing on Adam, or whatever they're trying to pin on him. They're chasing ghosts.

"The psychiatric unit of the local care home." I correct them, I'm not having them blow this out of proportion. He's been dead for ten plus years and was barely in our lives when he was alive.

"What was the reason for admission?"

Intrusive bastards. None of your business. Take your insinuation and pop psychology elsewhere.

"He was having difficulty looking after himself. My father was a magpie towards the end of his life, officer. He spent his days collecting things. To the point where no-one could get into the house. His main crime was hoarding junk. Hardly a dangerous man."

I'd often wondered if that's why Adam had latched onto Amy, or Amy onto Adam. Adam's biggest fear was turning into our father. Someone who spent his days disconnected from anybody and anything, and collected junk. Eventually being forcibly removed when his flat became a health and safety hazard and the neighbours complained to the council about the vermin and the smell. Amy sorted everything out and more. She controlled every aspect of his life, and more. Forever, redecorating, rearranging, tidying and cleaning. They had a cleaner for a bit. Lovely big woman from Nigeria. Amy would tidy up for her coming then still managed to have a fight with her every visit. Eventually she refused to have anything to do with 'the lady of the house' and resigned. Maybe Adam got solace from the fact that his house would never become a health and safety hazard. It was scrubbed, organised and reorganised to within an inch of its life. He never had to make a decision about anything.

The last time I visited, we aimed to drink beer and get pissed. Escape the wife, kids and responsibility. Fun for old time's sake. Men in their 50's can still do that, we thought. Amy had cooked dinner. I was happy with a kebab. She insisted. It wasn't dinner. It was a medieval banquet. The nutter had cooked three different types of roast meat, just for the two of us. Then screamed at us for not eating them and taking the piss out of her. The woman terrifies me. I have no idea what Adam sees in her. That's why I haven't visited since. Now I feel awful.

Actually, I do know what Adam sees in her. Adam doesn't do being on his own. Not unless it's on his terms and he can pick her up again when he needs her. He's always been a little ambivalent around commitment. I kind of admired him for getting away with it.

"And what was he like?" Thoughts rudely interrupted. I look vacantly at thin-meano, trying to orient myself.

"Your father, what was he like?"

Again with the pointless questions, what fecking relevance does my dad have? He was a womanising, abusive bastard who didn't give a shit about us, didn't give a shit about anyone bar himself. He destroyed my mother. She spent the rest of her life desperate for love and finding a string of abusive twats. She ricocheted between forgetting us, being annoyed by the nuisances we were, dancing with fairy people that only existed in her reality, and swamping us with love.

"He wasn't a big part of our life. My mother would send us off on the bus to visit. We'd be lucky if he remembered to meet us. Eventually we stopped going."

We outgrew the need to have an aggressive, abusive, neglectful asshole in our lives. An aggressive, abusive, neglectful asshole who was also a charming, award-winning wordsmith. Published poet and local treasure. The contradiction reminded me of Adam. He's more like our father than either of us would want to admit. Maybe I would have been too, if it hadn't been for meeting Paula, getting married and having kids.

"And he died just after your mother died?"

"Yes. It was a weird time. Three deaths in three years. First my mum, she had dementia and was living with me, Paula and the kids. Then my dad. Then Jo, Adam's girlfriend. Heart failure, they think, triggered by a bad bout of pneumonia. She was only 42. Adam got through it. He's more resilient than either of our parents. I mean, he needs to have the nature of a saint to deal with Amy. He's a good person."

I say the last bit almost defiantly. Good people don't do bad things. He's my little brother. I'll not let them set him up. I wish I'd braved the Amy-madness and made more of an effort to see him. Families stick together. I'm all he's got. I'm a shit brother. If I could have taken his pain, I would have done. Willingly. Four years makes a big difference when your four and eight.

When we're through this madness, on the other side, I'll make a real effort. We'll go away, just the two of us. Boy's adventure. Beer, bikes, open roads, tents and campfires. If you can't rely on family, who can you rely on? He must know I love him. I am utterly exhausted. I want Paula. I want to curl up in bed with her, I also want to get on my bike and cycle furiously, a thousand miles from here. Into the hills. The wind behind my back. I want to be back on the North Coast 500, with Adam. Ass burning miles of iconic cycling followed by cool beer with the boys. Adam pontificating about all sorts of nonsense. A self-proclaimed expert in most things on the outside. My wounded, vulnerable 4-year-old little brother on the inside. I want to go back to the Isle of Man and rescue little Adam. That's what big brothers do. That's what my two boys will do for each other. Having your own kids puts the drive and need to protect them into sharp focus. Everyone should have someone who has their back, no matter what.

"I'm exhausted, gentlemen. It's been a long day. Are we almost done? I'm not sure I can add anything more to your enquiries. Can you tell me exactly what it is you think that my brother had done? Deliberately, I'm only being given snippets."

And losing my never-ending patience.

"We're almost there, Mr Waters. Thank you for your patience."

My never-ending patience is finally wearing thin.

"Can you please tell me exactly what it is you think Adam has done?"

They look at each other. I think I see one nod, almost imperceptibly to the other.

"Does the name Sarah Emmerson mean anything to you?"

Sarah Emmerson. Nope. Nothing. I shake my head. Rack my brains even.

"Nothing at all. Who is she?"

"Sarah Emmerson was a business contact of Adam's. She was murdered on the day she was due to meet him, a frenzied knife attack at Groudle Glen, before being tossed into the sea. At the moment, we're following up various lines of enquiry."

Sweet Holy Fuck. That's a brutal coincidence. Was she having an affair with him? Surely not.

"What motive could my brother possibly have had?" I am incredulous. This was far worse than anything I could have imagined.

"Sarah transferred almost a million pounds from her company's accounts before disappearing. Whilst she was missing, they thought it was embezzlement. Given the state of her body, things look more sinister."

They love their drama. 'Things look more sinister?' Fuck's sake. The idea that Adam could kill anyone is ridiculous. What would he do with dirty money to the tune of a cool million? The law really is an absolute ass. Groudle Glen. That's spooky. Too much of a coincidence. My mother has come back to haunt both of us. The wheel, the waterfall, the little house, the polar bear enclosure, mother in her druid's robes chanting about the underworld. An icy hand touches my soul. I need to see Adam. I can't lose another family member. Most of all I long for the comfort, stability and normality of my wife. I thought I'd left this world behind a long time ago. Even she doesn't know a quarter of what went on there.

31 ADAM: The Last Dance

"You're a fool, Adam. A stupid, waste of space who amounted to nothing. You ruin everything you touch. Now you're going to rot in prison 'til the end of days. You thought you were better? You're not. You're worse than your father. I should have killed you at birth."

I bang my head off the wall. I wish she'd leave me alone. Please leave me alone. I walk in the bathroom to take a piss. Please don't come in here. Open the door. Fuck's sake. Sarah Emmerson, bloodied, monster-like, dissolving in front of me, all over the bathroom tiles. Her eyes stare at me as she dissolves.

She mouths: "Why? I had babies too, you know."

She moans as her mouth disconnects and a putrid jaw falls to the floor and bounces towards my foot, with a blood curdling yowl. I close the bathroom door again and piss into a vase on the hall table. I can't go in there.

My precious stash lies on the kitchen table. At least I still have contacts. God bless my gangster youth. 30

tabs of 30mg Codeine, 30 tabs of 30mg Temazepam, and the piece de resistance, 50 Blue Scoobies. Oh yes. I finger the blue pile. I move the three separate piles around the table like a game of Chase the Lady. Where's the Queen? Which one of the three piles will finish us off? Which should we take first? I circle and slide them round each other like a magician. Was it Rachel that said three is a magic number? A three-course pharmacological delicacy. It's a sign. Too much of a coincidence. Three is the pass to the underworld.

Full circle would have been taking Amy and the baby to Groudle Glen. Not practical. She'll have to make do with Greater Manchester. My mother's here. So is Sarah. The portal must work. Three tells me it works. Today is my day.

I should take two-thirds of everything, Amy takes one third. It works on body weight, doesn't it? She's tiny. Even pregnant, she's tiny. No one can survive 17 Scoobies, 10 Temazepam, 10 Codeine. Maybe I'll give her a bit more than one third. 20, 13, 13. That's better. Don't want the baby to suffer.

A full bottle of Grey Goose vodka. My final ritual is an unopened bottle of craft gin, from the Isle of Man. Magic. Full circle. Phynodderree, a word from ancient Manx folklore, the north of the island where the last juniper tree grew. It's all so right. Everything leads to this point. My brother gets the house. Sarah's money dies with us. I raise the bottle to my mother. She'd have appreciated the irony. Is it irony or is it magic? Full circle. I open the seal on the bottle of gin, with it's proudly displayed sticker declaring it to be Craft Gin of The Year 2021. I take a large swig, neat from the bottle.

"Cheers, mum. Who's Sorry Now?"

I take another swig and put both bottles beside the tabs. You need to do these things in style. Going out with anything but the best is wrong. Isle of Man gin is classy. Like Sarah. She would have approved. Make her life meaningful. Something to tell the kids. If your putrid jaw hadn't just fallen off.

"Why aren't you more like Cal? Cal made something of himself. Cal's not a monster. Evil Adam. Evil Adam Waters. That's what they'll remember you as."

What? She can't even appreciate the beauty of the situation? Isle of Man gin, a beautiful, intelligent sacrifice for the Groudle Glen Fae? An adoring girlfriend and a new baby, all willing to give their life up for me? I must be pretty powerful, no? You don't give your life up for a useless fucker, do you? You don't travel thousands of miles to meet a useless fucker, then give yourself up to him, do you? I was something. I am something. I pulled it off. Genius.

"Shut the fuck up, mum."

I throw a bottle of Peach Schnapps hard in the direction of the voice. It smashes against the wall and sprays into a zillion fragments, sending globs of sticky, sweet, sickly liquor into the air as well as down the wall. Peach Schnapps, the only drink that even a desperate man won't drink. It was Amy's. Not something I would buy. I should have kept it for her.

Might have slipped down easier. No, she'll appreciate the ceremony of Isle of Man gin and Grey Goose.

I look at the phone charging on the table. It's a cheap 'pay-as-you-go' phone. My old 'friends' brought it along with the tabs. Apparently, it's what all the 'entrepreneurs' use now (aka minor 'gangsters'). Simple, untraceable, disposable. I've drowned my old phone in the bath. They'll have trackers, tracers, even cameras on it by now. Water kills everything electrical. The bath is full. It's got my phone, my mac, my pc, the TV and the kettle in it. It's a big TV. When I put it in, the bath overflows. I can't be bothered to mop it up. Besides, Sarah Emmerson has a bad habit of turning up, looking gruesome in all the bathrooms and toilets. I'm not sure why. Maybe it's the water. Maybe it's linked to the Irish Sea.

I make sure all the doors are locked. I open the door of the bathroom enough to just throw the keys into the filled bath from the crack in the door. Sarah's in there. I can hear her. Maybe she'll settle and pass over when me, Amy and the baby go. Mum too. They'll not want to stay when I'm gone. It's a family house. It would be nice to think of a family here, in place of where baby Blue should have been. We all deserve to be at peace. I make sure all the window locks are on and close all the curtains.

I get a beer from the fridge, crack it open and head upstairs. A wank and a doze whilst the phone charges and I phone Amy. I lie on the bed. Even that's not working and that always works. I'm too agitated to wank. I don't want beer. Fuck's sake. Maybe I shouldn't ignore all those calls from Dr Walker. No point in ruminating now, I've drowned the phone. He'll not be able to get me. Maybe he was the one who put the camera in. Psychiatrists like to do that shit, don't they?

"Useless little cunt. Cal was always the bright one, the good one, the successful one."

My mum's in the room again.

"Juniper. Juniper has the strength of fire, the warmth of the sun, masculine energy, freedom. It frees anger. It gives courage, Adam. Take the tabs now. Don't wait on Amy. You're a free spirit. Take the tabs. Drink the gin. Juniper heals everything. It will help you pass. Take the tabs. Drink the gin." She sounds like she's giving a lecture.

Now I'm confused. My mum doesn't want Amy and the baby to pass with me? That's what she said she wanted earlier. It made sense earlier.

"No, mum. I'm waiting on Amy. We all pass. I can't leave her alone. She'll never cope. She won't manage the baby without me."

I close my eyes. Try and doze. It just makes the voices stronger. Sarah's in here too now. I can hear her gurgling and moaning. Are her kids in here too? Fuck's sake. I can hear them calling to her. I don't want to open my eyes. I don't want to know what's there. I'm scared. Really, really scared. I haven't been this scared for a long time. Years. 4-year-old years. I screw my eyes tight shut. I wish Cal was here. Mum would listen to Cal. Cal would make everything ok. Maybe I should phone him. I drowned the phone, I don't have his number. I need another piss. I have to open my eyes.

I can feel Sarah on top of me. She's straddling me, grinding on my groin. Nothing's happening love. I've never felt less like sex. Her hair is brushing my face as she does her best to get a response. Nothing. She sits deeper, tries that whole 'figure of eight' grind thing. Nothing's happening. I'm scared. I've had this before. It's a gruesome metamorphic demon. I have to open my eyes. I know that. I see.......

The chest of drawers, the chair, the rug, the desk my PC would normally sit on, the drawn curtains. Nothing else. I stand up. I'm desperate for a piss. I don't want to go to the bathroom. There's a pint glass on the bedside table. That'll do. The relief is overwhelming, cathartically normal. At least my body functions still work. I must remember and piss before we take the tabs. The final indignity is pissing yourself as you pass over. No-one wants to deal with that. I check the phone. It's mostly charged. I've written Amy's number down in case I forgot it. The slip of paper lies by the phone. I punch her number in.

"Hello?" a tentative voice answers. Of course, she doesn't recognise the new number.

"Hi Amy. How are you?"

"ADAM?!! I can't talk to you. I have to go." I can feel panic rising. I need her to come here.

"NO!" Please Amy. I need you. I can't survive without you. Don't abandon me. Please. Just a minute or two."

"I can't Adam. The police told me we can't talk."

"Amy, I can't breathe. It's like the last time. This time I'm going to die. I love you. I don't want to die without seeing your face, holding you, telling you I love you. Please. Don't abandon me. My heart, I can't breathe. It's going to end. Help me."

I'm crying. Sobbing. The release of everything. I want her more than anything. I am having difficulty breathing. Gasping. The pent-up emotion of the past few days is hitting me. The walls are closing in. I'm going to be squashed to a pulp.

"Adam, are you ok? Are you actually having another attack? Have you phoned an ambulance?" She sounds concerned. Good.

"I won't get through the night, if you don't come over. I don't want to die without you. Please Amy."

I hear the hesitation in her breathing. She's stressed and upset. It touches something deep and I crack. I'm howling like an animal about to die.

"I can't say goodbye like this Amy."

She cracks too. I can hear her crying. "Shall I call an ambulance, Adam?"

"I don't think the doctors can sort this one, Amy. I need you. I just need to see you, hear you, touch you. If you come, I'll be ok."

Her resolve goes. "Ok, I'm on my way."

"Quickly Amy. Please."

"Ok."

"Come to the back door. I've got the house locked up. I can't face anyone."

With that, she's on her way. It should only take her about twenty minutes. I hope she has the sense to park away from the house so people don't see the car. We can't take any risks that this fails. The doors are all locked up. What did I do with the keys?

I search the kitchen, the dining room, the living room before remembering that I'd thrown them in the bath with all the electrical equipment. I'll need to retrieve them. I've not been in there since I saw gruesome Sarah. The phone call with Amy must have been enough to silence her. The bathroom is empty. The floor's wet. I pad through it. I can't see them, even moving stuff about. I have to take everything out, soaking myself. Got them. I put everything back in again. Can't risk anyone being able to get through or connect with us.

Still wet, I put the key in the lock of the back door, but keep it locked, waiting on Amy arriving. That's wasted fifteen-minutes, just five to go. The three piles of tablets and two bottles of alcohol are still sitting on the dining room table. I should move those. Too soon for Amy to walk in, see them, turn on her heels and walk back out again. I need to time the telling of the plan to her.

I empty the 'spoons, ladles, utensils and tin opener drawer' into the cutlery drawer and place the three piles of tabs in the empty drawer. I put the bottles on the worktop, beside the microwave where they don't look out of place. That's better.

Right on cue, I hear a tap on the window of the back door. I turn the key and open it just wide enough to let Amy squeeze through. I lock the door, take the key out and slip it in my pocket. I need to get that back up to the bath. I draw the curtains tight across the door. She looks white faced and so thin. Is it my imagination or can I see the beginnings of a bump in her belly? The sight of her opens a dam and I wrap myself around her. For the first time in forever, I let myself go. I cling on to her, wrap myself around her and sob. She lets me. She just holds me. Doesn't say a word. Just holds me. We just stand there. Eventually the sobs subside. Amy's presence quietens my mother down. Amy pulls back slightly and looks me in the eye.

"Hey you," she says simply and gently.

The gesture makes me fill up again.

"Shhhh…." She wraps me up in her arms again. "You're in a state, shall we sit down?"

She takes me by the hand and leads me to the sofa in the darkened living room. She goes to put the light on.

"No," I shake my head, "no light. I need darkness."

"Ok," she says simply and pulls me to the sofa, where we lie wrapped in each other in silence. Eventually she asks the question.

"Did you do it, Adam?"

Pee in a vase? Breakdown? Wet the bed? Have an affair? I shake my head.

"I'm not a bad guy, Amy. I did not. I couldn't hurt anybody."

And that's it. That's all she asks.

"I love you," I say and bury my head in her soft chest as she holds me. "I want to be a good father."

"I know."

We lie for ages, not speaking. Eventually she speaks.

"Where's the TV?" She's noticed it's missing.

"In the bath."

"In the bath? Why?"

I mean, isn't it obvious?

"I don't want anyone watching or listening to us. We need to leave it there. We're safe if the TV, laptop, PC and phone are drowned."

She doesn't enquire any further. I don't tell her that gruesome Sarah Emmerson has been inhabiting the bathroom. I figure it might freak her out. It freaks me out. My mother appears to be banished temporarily. She'll be back before the night's out. She'll not be able to resist a sacrifice to the Fae of Groudle Glen, even if it does take place in Greater Manchester.

"I brought you this," says Amy suddenly, and feels under her to get to her pocket. She brings out a dark brown tube with a rollerball on the end. "It's a pulse point stress reliever. You put spots on your pulse points. The smell reminds you of good times and calms you down." She puts a hand out. "Give me your wrists." I oblige. She takes them in her hand and rolls a spot of oil onto each wrist. "Lavender and Sandalwood."

"It smells like you." I say, sniffing at them.

She laughs. "I use it too. Anytime you're stressed, have a sniff and imagine we're lying here, relaxed and happy, on the sofa. The three of us."

"I like it," I say, sniffing again. "I have something for you too."

I get off her and go to the kitchen, leaving her in the living room. I collect the three piles of tablets from the drawer and put them on a wooden chopping board, neatly arranged in their three mounds. Starter, main and pièce de résistance. I tuck the bottle of vodka under one arm, gin under the other. I'm balanced. I manage to get the chopping board, three piles and both bottles through to the living room without mishap. I lay them down on the coffee table with a flourish. I should have got a sprig of mint or some grapes or something just to finish the visuals. I see her looking at them. I scrutinise her face, I enjoy seeing her take the scene in. I knew she'd understand as soon as she saw it. I watch the changing emotions like a TV show. I feel the beginnings of euphoria. She'll feel it too.

"I love you, Amy Hawes. The thought of living without you is more than I can take. More than we can all take. The three of us. This is the right ending."

She licks a tongue slowly along her lip. I see her closing her eyes and breathing deeply. She gently mouths numbers.

I watch. 5……. 4…… 3…… 2…… 1…… 4…….. 3……. 2…… 1….. 3…… 2.

It's incredibly sexy. I feel myself harden. She looks beautiful. The scene is beautiful, more beautiful than I imagined.

"Well done, Adam. You did it. She gets it. You're a good boy. Mummy's perfect boy. She looks beautiful."

My mother is back in the room with us. Weirdly, it doesn't feel intrusive. It feels right. The voice activated speaker that I use for radio and music. I didn't put it in the bath. That's risky. Must do that. It collects data on you, everyone knows that. Damn, should have thought of that. One last song. Then I'll drown it. One last song isn't too much of a risk. We have to, for my mother.

"Play Connie Francis, Who's Sorry Now," I say to the rotund pod on the bookcase.

I hold my hand out to Amy, ready to pull her off the sofa and into my arms. She's still got her eyes closed, so I gently take her hand and kiss it. She jumps and snaps open her eyes. The familiar soulful introduction has started. It's a beautiful song, mum. You danced with me, now I dance with Amy, Amy dances with our baby. The cycle of life and death. I understand your philosophy. I'm sorry it took me so long.

"Dance with me sweetheart." I help Amy off the sofa and pull her into me.

We dance around the room wrapped in each other. Amy has her eyes closed again. She's enjoying this. This moment, right here, this time, this place, this pin-prick of life in the universe. This is pure love. Amy morphs into my mother as we dance, then back to Amy again. I press myself into her, smell her hair and allow my hands to roam over her belly as we dance. Life I created. Life I extinguish. I close my eyes and savour our last moments of life. We have a forever of death to look forward to. The music begins to fade.

"Want more?" I whisper in her ear, "shall I replay? You're so beautiful tonight."

She shakes her head, almost imperceptibly. "I think that's enough. I'd like to sit down."

"Ok, darling." Whatever you want tonight, you got. "I'll silence the device."

Reluctantly I let her go. I unplug the speaker. I run upstairs with it, feeling for keys in my pocket at the same time. I can hear, Gruesome-Sarah, Guardian of the Bathroom, moaning in there. I don't mind now. She seems quite happy to stay there. As long as she doesn't come into the living room. She doesn't belong there. I don't want her upsetting Amy. I think she knows that. I throw the speaker and the keys into the filled-up bath from the doorway. Sarah watches from holes where her eyes used to be. It's fine. I can pee downstairs.

"Goodbye Sarah. I hope you find peace now." I close the door on her.

I pee into the vase in the hall again. I've had enough of bathrooms. When I go back into the living room, Amy is examining the three piles of tabs on the wooden chopping board. She's spread them out. My mother is sitting on a chair opposite, keeping an eye on her. She can't escape anyway, mum. I've locked all the doors. I'm not stupid.

"What are they?" Amy asks as she pokes them.

"Round white ones are codeine. White oblong ones are temazepam. Cool blue ones are Scoobies. Street Valium. The good stuff."

I see her closing her eyes and counting again. I imagine popping a pill in every time she opens her mouth to mouth a number. I haven't finished explaining the delicacies.

"Award winning Isle of Man gin. Phynodderree is an ancient Manx word. Manx druids. Legend says the Phynodderree is a huge, hairy beast with fiery eyes that comes alive at night. Stronger than any man."

I see my mother nodding her approval in the background. I'm going back to her druid roots. It's appropriate that a Phynodderree takes us to the underworld. We'll be looked after there. Mum will make it so.

"Oh, and some Grey Goose for good measure. You can never go wrong with that."

She is still poking at the tablets. I begin separating each pile of three into two piles. I give slightly more to myself. Amy looks at me. Her face looks a little stricken. She's rubbing her belly.

"What about Blue, Adam?"

"This stuff is good Amy. I've got enough to sink an army of elephants. It's going to be peaceful, happy beautiful for all three of us. We go holding hands. Together for the forever. It's perfect. We're meant to be together. You won't survive without me. You know that. You need me."

She nods. It's true. Amy can't survive without me. She could never cope with being a single mother. What kind of life would Blue have? I'm glad she sees it too.

"Shall we start?" Three piles have become six. I move Amy's three towards her.

"I need to pee first. Whilst I'm still able to. Please Adam, I couldn't cope with the indignity of not being able to make it to the toilet. Let me empty my bladder before we start?"

"Of course, sweetheart." See, she gets it. She gets how perfect it is. She wants it to be perfect too. "Use the downstairs one. Upstairs isn't working." I don't want her bumping into Gruesome Sarah upstairs. That's bound to freak her out. "Do we want glasses for the gin, or will we just slug from the bottle."

"Bottle's fine, Adam. You stay right here. I'll be back in a moment."

"Downstairs Amy, yes?"

"Downstairs. Got it."

She disappears out the room in the direction of the downstairs toilet.

"You've done well Adam. You've grown into the

man I always wanted you to be. You've stepped up and taken control. I'm proud of you."

I love those words. I feel the flush. I take a swig of gin from the bottle.

"Thanks mum."

I go to check that Amy's not gone upstairs.

I catch her coming out of the downstairs toilet. Good.

"Everything ok?" I know this is difficult for her. She's handling everything so well. She gets the plan. She smiles at me.

"Everything's fine."

I kiss her. "Come taste the gin. It's not like anything you've tasted before." A thought occurs to me. Risk management. We can't take risks. "Actually Amy, before we start, do you have your phone on you?"

"What?" She looks panicked.

"Your phone, did you bring it with you. Give it to me." I hold my hand out, wiggling my fingers. I need to get her phone off her.

She obliges, pulling it out of her back pocket and handing it over.

"You never know who's watching us, or listening in. We need to drown it.

I dash upstairs and fling it into the bath from the doorway. I don't even notice Sarah. Job done. Safety restored. Well remembered, Adam. As I walk back into the living room, my mother nods and smiles her approval from her chair opposite. Wow, Amy has started on her tablets. She's taken from all three of her piles.

"You started without me?"

"You know how bad I am at getting tablets down. Sometimes they make me gag. I get self-conscious. I thought I'd make a start. They slip down surprisingly easily. Try them." She shoves my piles towards me.

"What did you start with?" I look at her piles trying to work out how many she's taken.

"I did four Scoobies in a oner," she tells me proudly. Awesome. "That went down, so I did four codeines and four jellies."

"I am so proud of you, darling. Wash down with gin, go on try it." I take the top of the gin bottle and hand it to her. "It's really nice gin."

She sniffs it reluctantly. "I'm not sure I want to slug neat gin, Adam. I'm scared I'm sick."

"Do it. Go on. It's fine. Make me proud of you, go on. You're the best, sweetheart. I love you. Do it for me."

It makes me feel proud to see her take a swig of the bottle. She fights to get it over without gagging, but she manages. She closes her eyes to feel the burn.

"Good girl. Well done. Four scoobies, eh? Impressive."

I count four Scoobies and pop them, taking a swig of gin to wash them down. Easy. Four codeines next. And four jellies. Now we're even. I'm on a roll, I repeat the four, four, four manoeuvre. Four Scoobies, four codeine, four jellies. A massive swig. Half the bottle of gin has gone. I look expectantly at Amy. Four, four, four. It's her turn.

"I'm worried about being sick Adam. Please. I don't want them to discover me covered in vomit. Will you bring me a bowl and some kitchen roll? Just in case, please. I'd feel so much better."

"Your wish is my command beautiful."

By the time I get back, she's popped another four, four, four and the gin bottle has gone down. Good girl. That's the spirit. I don't hang about. I can feel wooziness setting in. Quickly I pop a four, four, four combo. Another slug to wash it over. Turns out this is easier than I anticipated. I pop another four, four, four for good measure. The piles are going down fast. I turn to Amy. Her shoulders are shaking. She's crying, but silently. Tears are streaming down her face. Her t-shirt is all wet. She's breaking her heart. I wrap her in my arms. I kiss her forehead, smooth her hair, hold her tight.

"Hey, hey, hey. My beautiful girl. What's up?"

I am feeling so woozy now, tinged with euphoria, but also desolation for Amy's sadness. It's all muddled. I'm not even sure the words came out. Things are hazy.

"Just hold me, Adam. Please. Just let me lie in your arms here and feel you. Hold me. More pills in a bit for now, just hold me."

"One more round of tabs. Just one more, then we can rest."

I need to make sure that if we doze off, we've both taken enough to do the job. Nightmare if we're found and they manage to bring us round. One more round I reckon will finish the job for sure. I scoop 4,4 and 4 from Amy's piles.

"Open-up, last one." I get her to open her mouth and pop the first four in, handing her the other 8 whilst I reach for the gin. I watch as she swallows. Good job done. No gagging or anything. Good girl. I turn my attention to my 4,4,4 last round. I see my mother nodding approval as I leave Amy with the gin for her remaining tabs and I open the vodka. I manage to get them all over in two big mouthfuls.

"I'm feeling woozy, Adam. So sleepy. Can we just cuddle. Things are slowing down. I want to sleep."

Amy seems quite chilled. Benefits of overdosing on street Valium, I guess. Not a bad way to go. I feel euphorically chilled. Amy makes me lie back on the sofa and positions herself between my legs, her head on my chest. I wrap my arms around her and we lie there. It's nice. It's lovely. I love this woman. We're both sinking into the warm comfort of the sofa. Things are beginning to dim. I'm drifting off. I don't know where my mother went. I don't think she's here anymore. Finally, she's at peace. I love you, Amy. I don't even know if I said that out loud. I think she's sleeping. She's breathing deeply and not moving. Good girl. I kiss the top of her head, or I think I do. Maybe it's in my head. I don't know anymore. Everyone is at peace. It's nice. It's how it should be. I close my eyes too and surrender to the darkness.

32 RACHEL: Call for Help

Just in from work, bag flung in corner, I reach behind and unhook my bra. There is something so nice about liberating your chest from its confines after a long, hard, day. It's like kicking your shoes off. A simple, quick, free indulgence that says 'oh yes, you're home, time to unwind.' I don't know if I can be bothered cooking tonight. I might just do soup and some crackers.

Is that my phone? My bag is buzzing. I rummage it out. Text message from Amy. Wow!

AMY: 19:24 *URGENT* HELP ME RACHEL. I'm at Adam's. He killed Sarah Emmerson. I'm locked in. He's hidden the keys. Suicide Pact. 50 Street Valium, 30 Temazepam, 30 Codeine. Vodka. Gin. He wants to kill us both, SEND HELP NOW. AMBULANCE AND POLICE. I'm in the toilet. I CAN'T CALL. I WON'T BE ABLE TO MESSAGE AGAIN. Please help me. I don't want to die. I'm pregnant.

Holy Fuck. Clever girl, giving me the drug names

and the fact she's pregnant. They'll need Naloxone. The benzos are harder to deal with. I don't hesitate and immediately punch out emergency services.

"Which Service Please"

"Police" I say. They'll contact the ambulance service.

As quickly and efficiently as I can I relay the information.

"You need to send an ambulance now. It's life threatening. They could both be dead already. 50 Street Valium, 30 Temazepam, 30 Codeine. Vodka and Gin. No, I don't know if it's all been taken or whether they are unconscious or still breathing."

"They're on their way Dr Donaldson."

"The doors are locked and he's hidden the keys. You'll need to break the doors down. He's trying to kill both of them. She's pregnant. She says he killed Sarah Emmerson."

"Police are on their way alongside. Try not to worry."

How the Hell do I not worry. This is worse than anything I could have imagined.

"No, I don't know how pregnant she is." I read the whole text out to them again. They note it and the time it was sent. It's taken eight minutes to get this far. "The phone's off now. She says she can't phone or text. He may have found it on her."

Professional head. Try and stay calm. Panicking won't help. Oh my God, poor Amy. It's horrendous. I knew something was up. He killed Sarah Emmerson. Oh my God. He's a killer. I slept with him. I loved him. I wanted to spend the rest of my life with him. He brutally murdered a young mother and threw her body into the sea. He's killing another at this precise moment.

"We've got your details, Dr Donaldson. As soon as we have any news, we'll let you know."

"Just hurry up, please. That amount of drugs will kill anyone. She's a slender, pregnant young woman. He's manipulative. She's terrified. He'll kill her and the baby."

"We've got armed units on the way, as well as an ambulance, a negotiator and a specialty medic. Things will happen quickly now. I know it's hard, but please try not to worry. You can't do anything else."

Stop telling me not to worry. I'm terrified too.

"As soon as we know anything, we'll let you know. We have your mobile number."

And I'm alone, 300-miles away and helpless. I need to do something. I'm going to Manchester. It'll all be done by the time I get there, whatever the outcome, but at least I feel like I'm doing something.

I need to do something. I can't just sit here. I put my shoes back on and grab my bag. I'm on my way Amy. Hold on. For fuck's sake hold on. I'm sorry for everything. I realise I'm crying. I call Guy from the car and explain what's happening. I'm sobbing.

"I'm on my way Rach."

"What?"

"I'll set off for Manchester from Edinburgh. I'll meet you there."

"Guy, you don't need to. I don't know what I'm going to find. I don't know if they're dead or alive. They're treating it as a hostage situation. They've sent armed police. One way or the other, it'll all be over by the time I get there. I just need to do something. I can't sit at home. Even if it's a drive for nothing and I can't get close to anything."

"Neither can I. Sit at home, I mean. I'm coming down to support you. Even if we both end up doing nothing, as least we're doing it together. I'll meet you there."

"Honestly Guy you don't need to," but oh my goodness, I so, so want you to, you wonderful man. I have never been so scared of anything. I'm terrified of what I'm driving into.

"Rachel, that could have been you in his house, holding you hostage, trying to kill you. That terrifies me. The thought of someone hurting you makes me mad. You are not dealing with this alone. I'm on my way. No silly driving though. Promise me. We both drive sensibly and within speed limits and we meet there. You don't do anything until I get there, right?"

"Ok, got it. Thank you, Guy."

"Keep your phone on, we'll stay in touch. I am literally getting into the car now. Sat nav says Manchester in three hours and twenty minutes. How about you?"

"Same. Three and a bit hours."

"Good. You do nothing until we find each other. We can hook up at a service station and leave a car."

"See you soon." The relief in my voice is palpable. This is a nightmare I don't want to face alone.

Thirty minutes since Amy's text. I hope emergency services make it on time. Armed police, a hostage situation? Fuck's sake. We're all terrified to think about how this ends. And yes, the thought that it could have been me crossed my mind too. I wish it had been. I'd have ripped his testicles off. I'm more of a match in a hostage situation. She's so vulnerable. Ironic that it's a suicide that brings the three of us back together again. Bookends of a story that start and finish with a damaged man and suicides. It's hard not to speed. I need Guy. I don't want him. I need him. Sign of a stressed woman, I realise I hadn't even remembered to put my bra back on.

33 AMY: Rescue

The penny drops. I realise Adam killed Sarah Emmerson. Maybe I always knew, I just couldn't admit it. I can pinpoint the exact moment I open the part of my brain I'm scared of. I don't admit it when I'm driving to his house, thinking he's dying and that he needs me to save his life. I don't admit it when I park three streets away and run to his locked back door because I've been forbidden to see him for my own safety by people who know better than me. I don't admit it in the horrible police interview room when they're dealing with me breaking down. I still believe I know him better than anyone else and they've all got it wrong.

I loved him. Correction, I love him. I'll always love him. I can't turn love off like a tap. I can't save him. There's a difference. I never could. That's something I have to live with. The best way is to surround his child with unconditional love, kindness and protection. I finally allow myself to see what he's done moments after squeezing through the back door and having him wrap himself around me in his kitchen. I feel it. Icy claws around my heart. He killed her. This is his Armageddon. For him, it ends here, now. The pain, the unresolved distress and damage, the inability to accept that he's always been the most vulnerable of us and needs help.

I need strength I've never been able to muster before in order to protect my baby from her father. This isn't about me or Adam or Sarah anymore. I can't save him. I need to outsmart him. He can't know that I know.

I'm not surprised by the wooden chopping board of drugs. I know Adam has connections. I make a mental note of what they all are and how many there are of each. That might be important later. My mind gallops at a million miles an hour about how best to play the game. Even one or two of those tablets could harm the baby. Alcohol too. Ugh. The doors are locked, the keys are gone, the curtains all drawn. We're not both getting out this house again, are we? Then Adam says it. There's a gleam in his eyes. He sounds almost excited. The same way he sounded when we were buying the campervan.

"I love you, Amy Hawes. The thought of living without you is more than I can take. More than we can all take. The three of us. This is the right ending."

I feel sick. I feel panic rising. I want to scream, bang on the windows, throw myself through the glass to escape. I want to gouge my fingers into his eyes. Escape. A primal need to flee danger. Threat to life. I can't die. I have a baby to protect. I have an overwhelming urge to cradle my belly, but I know I can't give the game away.

I count. 5 places I'm going to take Blue when she's born, 4 foods she's going to love, 3 bedtime story books I know, 2 nursery rhymes, 1 special teddy bear.

Oh my God, he's playing music through the voice activated speaker thing. Creepy, or what. It's some old song. I recognise it. Some song from the 50's that his mother loved.

He pulls me to my feet. He pulls me into him. We're dancing. I feel like a helpless rag doll, a puppet. He's pulling my arms and feet around. He's pressed against me. It's like a horror film. If it wasn't for the piles of tablets on the table, I'd expect to feel a knife slide into my back. Like poor Sarah Emmerson. Maybe he could get the knife through all of us, skewer the three of us together forever. Dance Amy. Go with it. Let him ragdoll you round. Despite the exercise and closeness to him, I feel ice cold.

After an eternity, he asks if I want it again. My heart speeds up. I want to scream, but I manage to just shake my head and somehow, I smile as I sick up some bile into my mouth. He unplugs the speaker and disappears. Presumably it's following the same fate as the TV.

Quick, I've only got a minute. Window's locked, there's no-one on the street. Front door is locked. There are no keys anywhere. Not a soul around. Shit, I can hear him coming back. Back to the sofa, sit down, examine the tablets. Look interested.

He says the words I've been dreading. "Shall we start?"

I tell him I need to pee first. That I can't do anything undignified. That it has to be perfect. I can't believe he takes it at face value. I am close to tears in the downstairs toilet. I have to be quiet. No crying. I have to be quick. I'm all fingers and thumbs. I keep mis-typing. My head is fuzzy. Concentrate, concentrate, concentrate. Rachel Donaldson from contacts. Type. Quick type. It has to make sense. What were the three drugs again? Remember. I need to remember. I feel like I'm deleting every word and retyping it, then mis-spelling it. I have big, numb, sausage fingers.

AMY: 19:24 *URGENT* HELP ME RACHEL. I'm at Adam's. He killed Sarah Emmerson. I'm locked in. He's hidden the keys. Suicide Pact. 50 Street Valium, 30 Temazepam, 30 Codeine. Vodka. Gin. He wants to kill us both, SEND HELP NOW. AMBULANCE AND POLICE. I'm in the toilet. I CAN'T CALL. I WON'T BE ABLE TO MESSAGE AGAIN. Please help me. I don't want to die. I'm pregnant.

Send. Send. SEND. I've been ages, he's going to come looking for me. I flush the toilet and run the tap in the wash hand basin. Make it look convincing. He's prowling around in the hall when I come out. Please Rachel, look at it. Please do something. It's in the lap of one God now. The Rachel God.

He's taken my phone. That's it. My only hope is Rachel. Please Rachel, come good. Please Rachel. I take 4 of the scary blue tablets. I'm sure they're super-strength jellies. I thrust them down the back of a chair. 4 of the second pile, Temazepam? I thrust them down the back of the other chair. Codeine down the back of the sofa. I pour some of the gin on the floor behind the sofa. Look Adam, I take your tablets, I want to get started. I'm a good girl. My heart is racing. I can't believe he buys it. It'll never work a second time. I watch him take his tablets. A piece of my heart cracks. I know it's the only way I'm getting out of here. With lightning speed, I manage the same routine when I send him for a sick bowl and kitchen roll. Look. 4,4,4. I'm a good girl. He's pleased with me. It's almost like old times. I want to please. I get a thrill when I please him. Only this time, I'm faking it.

4 down the chair, 4 down the other chair, 4 down the sofa. Gin pool behind the sofa. He's taking more. The piles are halved. He slips them over like sweets. I can smell gin. He seems oblivious. My senses are all heightened. How can he not smell it?

Shit, he's opening my mouth so he can pop tablets it. Blue jellies. The bad ones. Holy fuck. My heart races. He pops them in, hands me the gin.

I must have been a magician in my previous life. I still don't know how I do it. As I go to take a swig of the gin, I put my hand up with the bottle. I have to drink the gin, but with sleight of hand, I manage to hook the four blue tablets out my mouth, hide them in the palm of my hand and clench it. I do the same with the second four, and crikey with the third four. They're wet. I feel them dissolving into the palm of my hand. Can you absorb benzos through your skin? The mouthful of gin hits my stomach and wants to come straight back up again.

I keep those hands clenched. It feels like things are dissolving to paste in there. Ugh. Adam has done another round for himself. He's starting to get vacant, slurry, sleepy. I need to get him to doze off. No more tablet rounds. Please, no more tablet rounds. No looking in my hand.

Lie him back on the sofa, ask him to hold me. Settle myself, pressed on top of him, so he can't move. He can't get to the tablets. Ask him to hold me again. Play the game. The tablets are hitting him. It feels like they're hitting me too. I'm not sure how. Most have been fed to the sofa and chairs. The rest are turning slimy in my hand. Lie still. Don't move. Like a rock. Close eyes. Pretend to sleep. Adam seems confused. He's jerking a bit. His breathing has become raspy. I lie still. Eyes closed. I breathe deeply.

5 songs Adam and I used to listen to. 4 films we've watched together. 3 things I've cooked him. 2 of his favourite after-shave smells. Remember what they smell like. Imagine the smell. Breathe in. Breathe out. 1 is the last time we made love.

Adam has stopped twitching. The raspy breathing has stopped too. I lie still. He feels cold, despite my body heat. 5 friends that we both know. 4 restaurants that we've been to. 3 pubs we like. 2 holidays we've been on. 1 wedding we've been to together. I don't dare open my eyes. Time has gone all bendy and wobbly again. Like a panic attack, but I'm calm. I think I hear a noise outside. I think I can see lights outside the curtains.

"Adam?" it's a tentative, scared whisper. It barely comes out. There's no response. I'm not even sure he's breathing. I can't feel his chest moving. "Adam?" I call louder, I shake him as I call. There's no response. "Adam?" This time, it's almost a shout and a vigorous shake. Nothing.

I slip off him and go to the window. I shake the paste and tablet fragments off my hand, wiping it on a throw which has been slung over the back of a chair. Ugh, it's a mess. Adam is motionless. An arm has fallen to the floor and trails limply. His head has rolled backwards into an awkward, unnatural position. I still don't see his chest moving. I don't hear anything. Even that awful rasping would be a comfort, but I hear nothing.

Someone is at the window. I jump. I pull the curtain back so they can see the scene and point at Adam. He nods. It's a man. He points to the door, almost as a question. He wants me to go there. I nod and make my way to the front door. I can hear him through the door now.

"Amy Hawes, is that you?"

"Yes." He can't hear me. I can barely hear me. It was just a breath that came out. "Yes, it's Amy Hawes."

"Amy, thank goodness. Are you ok? Are you hurt?"

"No. I'm not hurt. I think I'm ok. I've only had a mouthful of gin and I've been holding a pile of tablets in my hand until they turned to mush. I don't know if they go through the skin."

"Is that Adam on the sofa?"

"Yes."

"Is he conscious?"

"No, I don't think so. I couldn't wake him. Even shouting and shaking."

"Amy, is there anyone else in the house?"

"No."

"You're sure?"

"Yes."

"Can you open the door, Amy?"

"No. It's locked. He's hidden the keys. All the doors are locked. Windows too. I've tried them."

"Ok, listen to me carefully Amy. You're safe. We're here now. We're going to get you out of there. We need to break the door to get in. You need to stand right back. At least 4 metres. It's safer if you go into the next room. Do you understand? Can you do that Amy? Can you go into the first room?"

"The living room?"

"Yes. Go into the living room. You'll hear a loud bang. Then we're coming in to get you. Ok? Go now, go into the living room. Someone will be at the window, making sure you're safe. Ok? Go? My colleague will tell me when you're there. Then we know you're safe."

I do as he asks, and there is another man at the window who smiles and uses his hand to motion that

I stand beside the window. The bang of them breaking the door down is like the shot of a gun. I can't help screaming. Suddenly people are flooding in.

I'm shaking. I hear someone call my name. It sounds like the man who was talking to me through the door. He appears in the doorway. Relief and tears and exhaustion, I don't know what else, everything overwhelms me. He's holding me. I'm sobbing uncontrollably and clinging on to him. Paramedics stream past me. They're on Adam. They've got him on the floor. They inject him with something. They put wires on him. My rescuer just holds me as my knees give way. He says the thing I need to hear, gently.

"You're safe now. Everything's going to be ok."

I know Adam's dead. I don't need to look. They've not found any electrical activity. No pulse. No heartbeat. No breathing. Naloxone doesn't work on dead people. He's gone.

"Can you walk?" my rescuer asks me.

I nod. Actually, I'm not sure I can. Nothing works. My body is broken. My brain too. He puts his arm around my waist and keeps me upright.

"Let's get you and the baby checked over. It's been quite a night. You've done well. I don't know how you did it, but well done on getting a message out. It was brave. It saved your life. You are one strong lady."

Rachel saved my life. She got the text.

"Has Adam gone?" I ask him. I don't know if he knows the answer. I'd heard them say, there was no activity. I think that means he's dead. I'm sure it does, but I'm not thinking straight.

"I'm afraid so."

I shake my head. "It's what he wanted. He wanted peace. I couldn't fix him. I tried. He killed Sarah Emmerson."

My rescuer nods. "Yes."

"I didn't know. Not until now. I believed him. I shouldn't have come. I didn't know. I'm sorry. I didn't know. It's not my fault." The words come through sobs. I know I'm not making sense. He has to believe me. I didn't want this. I'm breaking down all over again. He thinks I'm a mess.

"It's not your fault. All that matters is that you're safe and that the baby is safe. We're going to look after you. You can trust me. Everything's going to be ok."

He's so gentle. And normal. He takes charge. I have to trust him. There are two ambulances and lots of cars. I've never seen so many cars in Adam's street. Cars and lights and people. Adam's street? There isn't any Adam anymore. It can't be his street. He killed a woman. Now he's dead. It's what he wanted. He was happy when he thought he was dying. Someone wraps a foil blanket around me. One mouthful of gin can't harm her, can it? I need to scrub my hands. I wipe them on my jeans. I need to really scrub them. He told me I'm safe and that everything will be ok. The nice man did. The one who sorts everything. It will now, won't it? Be ok, I mean. I run my hands over my tummy and my legs give way. My body embraces relief and safety. Someone is lifting me into the ambulance. It's the nice man. As long as she's ok. I have to be a good mother. I will be a good mother. She deserves the best start after all this. I'll make it right. I never want to see that house again.

34 Epilogue RACHEL: New Beginnings

I turn the platinum, diamond engagement ring around my finger. Delicate, modest, perfect. Feeling it on my finger makes me think of the constancy of Guy. The constancy of his presence ever since we met all those years ago. I can't remember a time before him. I'm not into rings at all, I've never really wanted them or worn them. But this one is so pretty. I adore it. Which seems strange for a someone who claims to place such little store in 'things.'

Guy and I have lived happily and minimally for the past four years. South America is a minimal, happy kinda place. Here it's all about the senses and the experience. Simple pleasures, simple life. We are adventure junkies. I don't miss luxuries. Possibly with the exception of whole-nut chocolate. Amy's been known to rescue me periodically with a box of whole-nut chocolate.

My engagement ring is my indulgence. My wedding ring will be too. The thought of it makes me flutter. Wedding ring. Honestly? I can't wait to get married. I want to be Mrs Guy, the Wife. The doctor his mother always wanted her son to marry.

I do like Guy the guy dressed for a wedding. Few

men look bad in a kilt. Guy looks phenomenal in a kilt. A beautiful mid-green Henderson tartan. He's breathtakingly handsome. Scottish, but tall, tanned, toned and outdoorsy adventurer.

Four years in South America has suited us both. We're both fit, more tanned, more laid back and happier than we've ever been. We'll come back to the UK at some point, but neither of us are in any hurry. I'm ready to experience it as a married woman, with my husband. I love that word. Husband. I can't wait to have a Guy-Husband.

We went out for a six-month vacation. Four years later, we've only come back because of the wedding. I appreciate that getting married in South America is not for everyone. Guy's mum said we had to get married in Scotland, or she wasn't coming! Up until then, I'd quite fancied a South American affair. All colour and joy. Guy proposed at 'the place.' Of course he did. Iguazu Falls. One knee. Ring at the bottom of a protein smoothie. Romantic, eh?! Right after we decided six-months here wasn't long enough and that we could both pick up work. We don't want the adventure to end.

We plan to stick around for a fortnight after the wedding, catching up with relatives and friends. Then we're heading back again. I know Guy's hankering to build a little place of our own. It's a special place. Anyway, tomorrow the wedding, tonight is catching up with old friends who are also checking-in the night before the big day.

I haven't seen Amy in ages. The trip back home is worth it for that alone. I'm so excited. I miss her.

"You ready to go down?" Guy appears from the

bathroom, smelling and looking gorgeous. I love this man more and more, each week, month, year that passes. I beam back at him.

"You're excited, aren't you?" He laughs, "you're positively beaming. Marrying me or seeing Amy?"

Right now? Seeing Amy. I'm bursting to see her. Texts and phone calls aren't the same. As we enter the bar, a small boy comes zooming up to us, squealing. I catch him round the waist and whirl him in a aerobatic circle around me. He shrieks with delight, shouting my name over and over.

"RACHY, RACHY, RACHY, RACHY, RACHY, RACHY."

Of course, it's Amy's boy. The little curly, blonde, delightful cherub that he is. I love this boy almost as much as if he belonged to Guy and I. He's got so big. He grows every time I get an update. He's not a toddler anymore. He's a boy.

"Alexander Hawes," I set him down. "You are getting sooooooo big! Almost too heavy for twirlies. How old are you now?"

"You know how old I am Rachy," he scolds me, "you sent me books and a big teddy for my four birthday. I'm four. School next year."

"Of course you are!" Aunt Rachy is a silly doughnut, yes? I've got another present for you. All the way from Argentina. But first, where's your mum?"

He drags me across the bar area and I hear another squeal. There she is! Amy never changes. As beautiful, blonde, slim and fragile-looking as ever. She's like an ethereal angel you could snap if you touched her the wrong way. She looks exactly like she did when we had our first coffee-shop, post Adam-threesome meet-up. This time no candles or cakes, sadness or recriminations. This time a joyous wedding, true love and a genuine forever fairy tale. I feel a rush of affection.

Our lives are forever entwined, ever since that first fateful social media message. That seems like another lifetime ago. Several lifetimes ago. As if it happened to other people. She rushes over and throws her arms around me.

"Oh my God, it's been too long, Rach. I've missed you soooo much. You look AMAZING. You both do! South America suits you guys more and more. We need to get out to see you again. We must. Soon. I can't believe it takes a wedding to get us all together."

"Is he here?" I look around.

"He sure is. He's at the bar. I've warned him we're on strict rations tonight. Two drinks max. I can't do a wedding hungover."

A tall, handsome fair-haired man comes over with a tray of drinks. He sets the tray down and kisses Amy on the cheek. She slips a hand around his waist. They look so natural together.

"Paul, this is Rachel, Guy. Rachel, Guy, this is Paul."

At that moment, Alexander flies up to Paul and leaps on him.

"Daddy, daddy, daddy, daddy, did you get my juice?"

"I did get your juice, super-hero-Zander-Boy. Swap you. Juice for a cuddle. It's been at least half an hour since my last one. Page boys need to cuddle the groom, it's part of the deal. Sons need to cuddle daddies too. Otherwise, we get older faster. Quick!"

The small boy does a flying leap into Paul's arms and buries himself in his neck.

"Mummy too," he clings onto Paul's neck with one arm and stretches the other one towards Amy for her to join in the threesome. Amy laughs and they embrace, kiss and tickle, whilst Alexander snorts with joy. Eventually they set him down. Alexander turns to me with a serious face as he says something important.

"You know my mummy and daddy are getting married tomorrow?"

"I know, pumpkin. That's exactly why we're here. We've come all the way over from Argentina specially to see your mummy and daddy get married."

"You know my name's gonna change? We're all going to have the same name."

I beam at them all. It's such a happy family scene. These guys are adorable. Amy looks so happy. So does Alexander. A perfect family. Paul Perfect - boyfriend, husband, dad, confidante and healer. Gentle, trustworthy, solid and lovely. Perhaps everything you might expect from the policeman he is. One of the few human beings able to lay the spectre of Adam Waters to rest. He'd wrapped Amy and Alexander in a blanket of love and slowly she began to accept that she deserved the future and the happiness he wanted to give her.

"Can't believe you beat us to the wedding though." I grin at them both. "But I have at least got the engagement ring." I hold up my hand for Amy to inspect. "No plans yet though." I slip my hand around Guy's waist, "we'll get round to it at some point."

"So you should," Paul chides Guy good naturedly. "I'm certainly not letting this pair get away." He hands drinks out to his fiancée and to their son. "It's not often you meet an incredible duo with so much love to give, who have been through so much, yet stay open to so much more. If I can make them happy, make them realise how much they deserve it, I'll be a happy man. They make me a happy man. The best day of my life when this wee guy looked at me and said it, said 'daddy'. My heart is theirs." Alexander climbs up onto his lap and cosies in. "He's the best present anyone has ever given me." He takes Amy's hand.

I look at the love emanating from the trio and know that Amy has found her match. The perfect piece of the jigsaw to both heal and complete them. No-one deserves peace, love and a happy-ever-after as much as Amy and Alexander Hawes soon to be Boardman. They're going to be safe. They're going to be ok. Everything is going to be ok. He promised that to them both that awful night as he put his arm around her middle, absorbed her sobs, her stress, saved her life. He led Amy Hawes out of Adam Water's life and into his own.

There couldn't be a more perfect end.

About the author

Borderline Normality is my third book, but my first foray into Psychological Suspense. It's been a rollercoaster. A testimony to the magic of storytelling.

Chapter 1: **Amy – Borderline Normality** was originally written as a standalone short story. Intended as a first-person account of living with Borderline Personality Disorder, it was shortlisted for the Scottish Mental Health Arts Festival literary award. At that point the tale had barely begun. Once created, the characters couldn't leave until their story was told….

A bit more about me?

By day, I work in adult mental health. I have a particular interest in how psychological and psychiatric factors, including stress and trauma, affects our physical health and have spent the last twenty plus years working across oncology, palliative care and chronic pain.

I grew up and trained in Edinburgh, but defected to Glasgow, then North Ayrshire where I now live with a gaggle of geese, a cute, but very greedy Labrador and three 'not so small' children, all at various stages of leaving the nest to embark on exciting adventures of their own.

I find that cake is the answer to most things. Closely followed by the antiquated UK-centric chocolate, Revels, best consumed alone (save for a Labrador) on a windswept beach.

Finally…..

If you like my writing, please make contact with me and leave your email address, so that I can update you on forthcoming work and new stories.

www.lauren-lloyd.com

Also by Lauren Lloyd

A TRIP TO THE MOON

Life can just be so……. unexpected. Sometimes it presents you with a choice. Seize the moment and have an adventure? Or go home fantasising about what might have happened if you'd been a little bit braver.

Lyndsey Forbes, a 28-year-old doctor specialising in palliative medicine, crammed her belongings into a white Volkswagen golf and set off for a new life in Glasgow. En route she had an adventure which changed things. A Trip to the Moon follows the lives of three Glasgow doctors dedicated to making life better for people who are coming to the end of their lives.

Life, death, love, sex, humanity, and being inadvertently imperfect. Life is short. Life is precious. When we grow old, wrinkles are our memories of a life-lived.

'Wherever the art of medicine is loved, there is also a love of humanity.' *Hippocrates.*

Printed in Great Britain
by Amazon